Flame of Deception

The Wielders of Power

Matt Trevizo

D1519249

Flame of Deception

The Wielders Of Power Book One

www.trevizobooks.com

Published by Matt Trevizo

This book is wholeheartedly dedicated to my wife, Lycia. You have been my guiding light, a constant source of inspiration, and the driving force that has pushed me to become a better writer. Without your unwavering love and support, I could never have accomplished what I have, and for that, I am deeply grateful.

I also dedicate this book to my father, Ray Trevizo. Your steadfast encouragement and belief in me have been the pillars that allowed me to turn this dream into a reality. From the depths of my heart, I thank you for your unyielding faith in me, and for teaching me to believe in myself.

Contents

Chapter One

An Unforeseen Attack

As Ron woke up to the smell of smoke in the air, he heard the faint screams of the villagers in the distance. While his ears adjusted to the sound, he hurriedly threw his blankets from his bed and sat up, grabbing his boots and jacket to head downstairs. He met up with the rest of his family as they collected in the living room, discussing the commotion.

"What's going on?" Ron asked in a panicked voice, throwing his arms through his jacket. "It looks like someone is attacking the other end of the village," Ron's older brother Nathill said as he peeked out the window. Ron rushed to where Nathill was standing and caught a glimpse of the fires rising from the buildings at the northern end of the village, the thick black smoke billowing upward into the sky. Their mother and father were busy grabbing items they could carry quickly and without burden, so their escape from the village could be swift.

"Boys, go grab what you can—quickly, we need to get out of here!" William shouted as he was helping Evelyn pack. Ron continued to look through the window and saw soldiers approach from around the corner of a house, gathering in the streets, readying their arrows, and pointing them in the direction of his home.

Ron yelled, "Get down!" He and Nathill ducked below the windowsill as arrows started to crash into the house, breaking through the windows, shattering the glass. Ron brushed away the shards and looked out the bottom of the window past the fragments remaining in place. Men clad in black armor with a deep-blue border were approaching. Ron didn't see any markings or emblems on their armor. They were an unknown force, not matching any of the kingdoms Ron had learned about as a child. As he and his brother stood up, they turned to make their way into the living room behind them.

They looked on in horror at both of their parents lying on the ground in a massive pool of blood. Arrows had pierced William and Evelyn, causing fatal wounds. Nathill suddenly grabbed Ron by the arm, and they made their way through the living room, disregarding anything that would be a hindrance, then continued running through the kitchen and out the back of the house.

The sky was dark with a red glow given off by the fires. Embers rose into the night, followed by thick trails of smoke; it couldn't have been later than four in the morning. The brothers ran out the back of the house, stopping at the corner of the west end to peek around and see where the enemy was. The soldiers were raiding and setting fire to the nearby houses. Finally, Nathill said, "We have to get out of here. We could take the road southwest and make for the forest—hopefully, we can lose them."

"What about everyone else? We can't just leave them?"

Ron had a point, but his brother said, "We don't even know where anyone is. They could be dead for all we know, or they were smart and ran like we should."

"I know, but—" As he tried to finish what he was saying, a soldier spotted them from the east corner of the house.

"They're here!" the man shouted to his comrades. He charged toward Ron with a sword in hand, but Ron quickly kicked over a wheelbarrow that was leaning against the back wall of the house, causing the soldier to trip and land on his stomach. The sword fell to the ground, and Ron picked it up, feeling it shake in his hand. "What are you going to do with that?" the soldier mocked, looking up from the ground. Ron didn't really know; he had never killed a person before, just animals when he went hunting with his brother.

Gathering his wits and resolve only took a moment—he was prepared to protect himself and Nathill at any cost. Before he could get ready to strike, though, his brother grabbed the sword from his hand and stabbed the soldier through his back, giving the blade a quick turn through the heart.

"You got to be faster than that, little brother. I don't want you to die—I need you around."

They started to run, but three more soldiers came from around the house. Seeing that one of their own had been killed, they rushed toward the brothers. Nathill blocked the first strike and slashed a soldier across the chest, splitting his armor and slicing deep through his skin. He grabbed another sword out of the dying soldier's hand with a quick turn and threw it to Ron.

Ron caught the weapon and started to fight. Wide-eyed with fear, he felt the adrenaline course through his body, his heart pounding as he defended himself. Ron blocked and parried like he had done countless times when sparring with his brother. The soldier swung wide in an attempt to kill Ron, but he jumped back just in time. He didn't get eviscerated right then and there, but he wasn't quite fast enough. The tip of the soldier's blade drew some blood from Ron's stomach. Swinging rapidly in response, Ron cut off the soldier's right hand, which was holding the sword. The man fell to his knees, screaming in pain, clutching the newly made stump. Then Ron stabbed him through his chest, silencing the screams.

He looked up at Nathill, who had just killed the third soldier. "Okay," said Ron, "it's time to go."

"Agreed."

Soldiers filled the streets; panicked citizens ran among them, pleading for their lives once they were caught. Yet the soldiers mercilessly struck down anyone who struggled against them, relishing in their defeat. Ron saw mothers carrying their children, fathers slaughtered as they tried to give their loved ones extra time to get away. Seeing the horrified faces of the people Ron knew, the people he grew up with, made him rethink his decision to leave them to the brutal fate that was descending upon the village. The thought crossed his mind only for a fleeting moment, though, before more soldiers came from around the street corner.

The men who were not resisting the soldiers tried desperately to smother the fires in their homes before the flames had a chance to build, only for the passing soldiers to throw more torches around the bases of the houses, through windows, and along the shingles lining the rooftops. They rolled into the rain gutters, igniting the leaves that had yet to be collected from the fall season into quick bursts of fire, setting the eves ablaze.

Ron and his brother ran, occasionally hunkering down behind recently collected hay bales and around the outside of the surrounding houses to avoid detection from the soldiers moving between each home, continuing their raids. To make it to the forest, Ron and his brother had to make it through a clearing that spanned from the last house to the trees, no more than fifty yards away, but cutting through the clearing with the ample light from the fires would leave them open and exposed.

"That's a long way to run," Ron said, catching his breath while he leaned on the backside of a house, looking at the trees. Glancing down at his torn shirt, Ron saw the bright red blood soaking into the white fabric. Pressing with his hand, it felt like nothing more than a scratch.

"I know, but we have to make it—we have to try," Nathill said. Ron saw that his brother had fared as well as he had, with light bleeding from numerous minor wounds.

The soldiers were scouring the nearby houses, kicking in doors and smashing windows, looking for anyone they could find. Finally, Nathill peeked around the corner. "Here is our chance. We need to run. Are you ready?" He was eyeing the soldiers, waiting for them to pass by before making a move.

"I'm ready when you are," Ron replied. Then, with as much energy as they could muster, the brothers sprinted for the trees. Partway there, the light from the fires died out and the darkness of the night took over. Ron's heart pounded hard, but he knew they could make it.

They were almost in the clear, and then a rush of arrows flew past them. "Hurry!" cried Ron.

Before they could make the tree line, Ron felt a burning pain in his lower left calf. He stumbled, scrambling on the ground until he could stand up again, pushing through the pain from the arrow that had struck him. Looking for his brother, Ron saw that he was lying on the ground. An arrow had found its way into Nathill's back. Ron bent down to pick him up. "Come on, get up. We can make it—let's go!"

"I can't, it's . . . it's hard to breathe." Nathill gasped for air, and Ron could hear that the arrow must have punctured a lung. There was no time to try and pull it out. So instead, Ron decided to drag his brother away to the forest as more arrows flew past them.

"Ron, they are getting closer—you need to go. Now!" Nathill yelled.

"I can't just leave you here. Come on, you have to try." As Ron was pulling him away, the soldiers grew closer and drew their swords. They were gaining ground, closing in; soon they would be right on top of the brothers. Another burning sensation raced through Ron as he felt a pain in his left shoulder. He stumbled, falling to the ground beside his kin.

"Go, Ron. I'll be fine, don't worry."

"How will you be fine? They'll kill us both. This can't be happening—why are they even attacking us?" cried Ron.

"I don't know, but you have to go now!" his brother wheezed.

"No, I won't leave you. Come on." Ron tried to lift Nathill once more, feeling the pain of the arrowhead move in his flesh. He pulled, trying to make his way to the tree line, but another arrow hit him in the stomach.

"Ron, Ron!" He could hear his brother yelling his name, but he didn't understand why his head felt fuzzy. Looking down at his stomach, Ron saw the arrow sticking out, blood slowly oozing over his hands as he placed them around the arrow.

Ron felt tired; he couldn't keep his eyes open. When he opened them again, he saw he was being dragged away from Nathill, toward the tree line.

He heard the voices of the people dragging him.

"We got you, Ron."

"Let's go, they're here."

Others emerged from the dark trees, firing arrows at the soldiers to aid the people who had Ron. With what strength he had left, he yelled, "Wait, my brother—he's still over there! We need to get him."

"We can't. There's no time," the voices said. Ron could see Nathill's hand reaching for him, so Ron stretched his out as if to try and grab it. As he was starting to lose consciousness, Ron saw the soldiers standing over his brother, and then he saw the quick thrust of a sword.

Ron yelled with all he had. Then a dim blue flame began to engulf his hand and fade away.

Chapter Two

Eight Years Later

R on woke from sleep with a light sweat upon his brow. It almost felt like he hadn't slept at all.

It had been eight years to the day since he'd lost his family in the attack from the unknown force, back when he was only fifteen. Standing up, Ron scratched his shaggy brown hair and proceeded with his morning stretches. Standing at six feet, he was not uncommonly tall, but he was not short by any means either.

He heard a knock on his door. "Hey, Ron, you awake?"

"I am. Come on in," he said. As Ron sat on the edge of his bed, he looked down and noticed he hadn't taken off his clothes from the night before. He reached for his boots. Grabbing them, he was just beginning to lace them when Grant entered the room.

"Are you almost ready—we're going to be late for training. Last time we were late, we had to stay till the sun went down. I don't feel like training all day." Pausing, Grant saw Ron wipe the sweat from his brow. "You feeling alright?"

"Just had a bad dream, that's all," Ron said, standing up.

"Another one, huh?"

Grant had been Ron's training partner since they started in the Arena six years ago. Ron disregarded his partner's question.

"Maybe being late is better—we're still a lot better than the others. Well, I am. I don't know about you, though." Ron let out a laugh.

Grant, feeling amused, said, "Very funny—we will see who's laughing later."

They left the room and made their way down the hallway, passing numerous other rooms. Regardless of the day, Ron or Grant would venture over to each other's room even though they lived in separate dormitories. Due to how extensive the training was, spanning multiple years, this dormitory housed more than twenty other students.

The pair passed the kitchen on their way out, and Ron grabbed two apples out of a bowl sitting on a counter left out by the kitchen staff. He tossed one to Grant as they exited the dormitory. They turned and passed by two other dorms and a stable on the way to the training grounds. The dormitories were split up, housing students by training class. There was separate lodging for students who chose swords, daggers, staffs, long-range weapons, and hand-to-hand combat.

Greyland was a larger town than Ron was accustomed to, even though he had lived here for eight years now, but he didn't mind since the people were kind and treated everyone respectfully—even the local drunk who most nights found himself waking up in the horse stables.

Shops lined the streets on either side of the road, resting on the freshly trimmed grass with the owners waiting to open the doors. Others were getting their carts ready for the daily market. Ron and Grant walked by the road that led to the residential district on the way to the training grounds. Houses lined the east side of Greyland, and each had its own distinctive look depending on who built it.

When the doors to the training grounds came into view, Ron saw other students running to get in.

"I guess we should hurry to the Arena, so we're not late," he said to Grant, and they started to run. After entering through the doors, they descended the stairs separating the rows of benches sculpted from the hard rock surface. Then they got into formation before the instructor, whom they simply called Cap, came and closed the doors behind them.

The Arena was circular, and the floor at the bottom was formed from hard, compact dirt. Spectators could watch competitions by sitting in the stands around the perimeter.

Cap walked to the front, then stood before the formation of students. "Alright, looks like everyone is here and on time. I'm shocked." He looked directly at Ron and Grant. "Today, we will be going over sword, dagger, and staff styles of combat, while another instructor will work on ranged and hand-to-hand combat on the opposite side of the Arena. For you new people, you will break off and begin your novice practice with Instructor Paller." He motioned the students to look to their left, where they saw a middle-aged man, thick around the belly, waving. "For those who are about to graduate, I want you all to pass the exams that are coming up these next couple of days." Cap was a tall, dark man in his mid-forties. He was intimidating in stature, standing six-foot-two with a bald head. Since he was the instructor, he was fitter than most people in Greyland, except for some of the students.

Ron and the other students did not know a whole lot about their instructor. They only knew what he had told them when they first started their training, the same as he told all new students who got accepted. Cap told them of his time spent in Altara, working his way up through the ranks, becoming captain of the Altaran Guards. He told his students he was forced to retire due to an injury he suffered while on patrol outside the walls of the kingdom. He never went into detail or specified what exactly happened to cause such an injury. All he said was that once he decided to hang up his sword, he relocated to Greyland to instruct new recruits in the Arena.

"Pair up with your partner and begin training. When you have gone through the sets of your respective weapon, find another group and spar with them. I want you to rotate until every group has fought every other."

The day of training wore on; in the midafternoon, Ron and Grant were doing well, as expected. They beat the other groups with ease. Being late so often had its odd advantages. As punishment, they'd been forced to come in on days off, and over time had racked up more hours as a result.

Cap was watching when he overheard Grant boasting about his skill.

"Oh man, I hope you guys have more in you. I could do this with my eyes closed," said Grant in a condescending tone to the students that were taking a break from sparring. Ron let out a small laugh, but it did not go unnoticed.

Their instructor shouted, "All groups, I want you to take a seat in the stands." The students made their way to the seats, but then he called again, "Everyone except Ron and Grant." The pair's eyes went wide, and they found their way to meet the instructor's gaze, which was already fixed on them. Ron looked confused as to why his name had been called, but the instructor cleared it up rather quickly. "You two think this is so easy, huh, laughing and joking at the expense of your fellow students? Well, how about you two fight me? Both of you at the same time."

"Wouldn't that be unfair, Cap?" Grant asked.

"Only for you two—I won't be holding back," the man said with a smile that put an ounce of fear into the two friends. "Begin."

Ron and Grant rushed at Cap, swinging wildly with their practice swords to confuse him, but it did not work. Cap planned on the lack of teamwork, and he was right—they were uncoordinated. The instructor was able to dodge and parry their attacks without the slightest hesitation.

Ron noticed that trying to overwhelm Cap with attacks from all angles was not working, so he called to Grant, "The sun is already so high." Grant nodded, understanding what he meant—it was a tactic they'd used against the other students. Cap, on the other hand, was confused.

"What are you two talking about? But of course it's high. It's the middle of the day."

Ron suddenly went to attack the instructor's upper half while Grant dipped down and attacked the legs. Still, neither could land a single blow. It didn't take more than a moment for Cap to see through their thinly veiled ruse.

As the attacks continued, Cap saw the potential Ron and Grant had. He also saw flaws that would ultimately lead to their downfall if they were not fixed. The instructor decided to finish the sparring match after figuring out their plan to try to trick him. He parried Ron's oncoming frontal attack and hit him in the face with the hilt of his wooden sword. Ron dropped to his knees, holding his bleeding nose; Grant tried to stab the instructor in the stomach, but Cap parried his sword down toward the ground and sidestepped. He then landed two blows to Grant's back, knocking him to the ground.

Cap turned to the rest of the students in the stands, pointing his sword at the crowd. "This—this is how you lose. You get overconfident in your abilities, just as these two have. There will always be someone better than you are out there, and if you want to have any chance of winning, never underestimate them. Never think every fight will be the same. It doesn't matter if you fight one battle or hundreds, all it takes is just one moment, one shred of complacency, and your life could be over."

As Ron and Grant stood up together, Cap came over to Ron and said in a quiet voice, "Ron, you asked me to train you when you first got here—you wanted to learn more, so that what happened to you would never happen again. Am I wrong?"

"No," Ron said, looking down in shame.

"Then do not let your pride get the better of you. Think with your head. Don't rely on tricks to get you through a fight. I've seen what you can do. You're one of the best students I've had in a long time, and I want to believe it's because you have a reason, a purpose to put your training toward. One day you may find yourself in a similar situation to the one you have just faced. Don't be a fool—think about every move, every possible outcome. Trust in your abilities."

Turning away from Ron, knowing his words held weight, Cap focused on Grant. "Grant, you're good, but don't be thinking you're the best fighter in the world. You will be disappointed or killed. You have the talent to be great, but if you always follow and rely on others to lead you, you will not be happy with the outcome of your choices. I saw multiple chances for advancement during our session, but for some reason, you held yourself back, waiting for Ron to make the first move."

He continued, "There will come a time when you have to act first. You will have to make the choice for yourself. I just hope when the time comes, you can take it seriously. If you did that and stopped with the jokes and overconfidence, people would see the talent you have. Got it?"

"Yes, Cap," said Grant, embarrassed.

"Alright, everyone, we are done for the day. Go home and get some rest. I'll see you all tomorrow. Come prepared."

Ron put his sword back on the rack and walked out the doors of the Arena with Grant chasing behind him.

"Hey, wait up," said Grant. "What did Cap mean, 'happen again'?" Ron was caught off guard, thinking Grant hadn't been close enough to hear what Cap had said to him.

"Nothing, don't worry about it," Ron said, deep in thought, reliving the events of eight years ago. The day was shifting into night, the sun beginning its slow decline in the sky. All the students were headed to the local pub, House for Ale—their usual meeting place after training.

"Ron, are you going to come to House for Ale with me? We could get some drinks, maybe some food," Grant suggested excitedly.

"No, not today. I'm not quite in the mood for it." But as Ron walked north toward his building, Grant kept following him.

"Is it because of what Cap was talking about?" Grant asked.

Ron wished he would stop asking. "Yes, it is. But it's not something I feel like sharing right now."

"Okay, no problem, I'll let it go," Grant said. Feeling relieved, Ron kept walking. His friend continued, "You know, why don't we go? I bet Nora will be there. Maybe she could get your mind off whatever it is you're brooding about."

Finally, after a long pause, Ron said, "Okay, Grant, you win. I'll go, but you're buying."

When they arrived at the pub, they quickly found some seats before the rush of students came. Grant ordered two ales and some food while Ron looked around to see if Nora was there. He didn't find her.

The drinks arrived shortly. Ron and Grant grabbed their mugs, and Grant made a toast. "To getting our asses handed to us in front of everyone."

They clinked the mugs and each took a drink. "You know, I don't think I entirely deserved that. You were the one spouting off at the mouth. I was an unfortunate bystander," Ron said.

Grant smiled. "True, but I didn't think Cap was able to hear me. He has ears like a hawk." Ron went back to the bar to order another round of ale. Then he noticed Nora walk in. She didn't see him right away, not until Grant saw her too and made a scene, standing tall and waving his arms around.

"Hey Nora, Ron and I are sitting over here—come sit with us!" he shouted from across the room, pointing. Surprisingly enough, Nora grinned and made her way over. Ron headed back to his seat once he placed his order.

"Wow, Ron, what happened to your face? It looks like your nose is broken," Nora said.

"Well, Grant over here thought it would be a good idea to have a sparring match with Cap in training today. Unfortunately, he got hit in the back, but I got lucky with getting a new face," Ron said sarcastically.

"I see. Well, maybe next time you should duck and not get hit in the face. I hear ducking works pretty well," Nora said, letting out a laugh.

"I'll definitely take that into consideration next time." Ron smiled.

Ron could feel his shame from earlier in the day fade away as he continued to talk to Nora. He looked over to Grant, seeing a broad grin on his friend's face. He had been right about Ron's mood improving once he saw her.

Grant knew very well how Ron felt about the girl, but he didn't understand why they never got together. There had been so many occasions that would have been perfect had Ron just made a move, but when Grant tried to ask about it, Ron would just make up an excuse or change the subject. Finally, he told Ron he would keep asking until Ron gave him a reason. Until then, he had no intentions of stopping.

They drank and ate until House for Ale closed. Seeing an opportunity, Grant decided to walk home with a handful of other students, giving Ron and Nora more alone time. They sang as they went on their way, repeating the tunes drunkenly sung in House for Ale. Grant did not have a good voice by any stretch of the imagination, but he was always the most enthusiastic, belting out the words whether they were the correct pitch or not; he enjoyed being the life of the party.

Meanwhile, Ron walked with Nora to her house, making small talk along the way, stealing glances every now and again as the glow of the moon reflected off of her light brown skin. When they arrived at Nora's house, he said, "Well, goodnight Nora." He spoke rather hurriedly, as if he had somewhere else to be.

As Ron moved to turn away, Nora caught his arm.

"Hey, let me take a look at that nose. I think I can set it for you, so you can look halfway handsome again." Immediately, before he had time to react, Nora grabbed his face with a loud pop.

"My god, that hurt, but I can breathe," Ron said, laughing and wincing at the same time as he felt the natural curvature of his nose return.

"You're welcome." Nora smiled.

"How did you know how to do that?"

"I do know a thing or two about medicine. Before my parents left, they taught me some basic skills, and I have tons of books on my bookshelf that I read from time to time."

Ron knew her parents had worked in the ward of healers, but he didn't think she was teaching herself. His relationship with Nora was complicated. Ever since they'd met, every time she would begin to ask him anything personal that related to his life before coming to Greyland, Ron would refrain from talking about it. However, she was always very patient with him, as she knew that it was traumatic. She only knew that much by volunteering at the healers' ward when she was younger. Before she and Ron ever got to know each other, she saw him in a bed in the ward.

"Would you like to come inside? I can show you some of the books I'm currently reading." Biting her lip, she continued talking while taking his hands in hers. "Perhaps you could tell me what your parents were like or where you grew up?"

Ron wanted nothing more than to go inside with Nora, but he wasn't ready to relive the past out loud. He also felt that if he divulged what had happened, it would taint the current mood with sadness. Ron had always waited for the right time when it came to Nora. However, the timing for them was never right.

As much as Ron felt for her, he didn't know if she felt as strongly as he did. So they never voiced how they felt, only giving subtle hints or going off the mood when they were together. Ron didn't want to risk losing her as a friend if he tried too hard, so he kept his feelings aloof, only giving in on occasion. He didn't want to tell her more about his previous life; she might think he was too broken of a person to be with. Deep down, Ron knew the only thing stopping him was himself, but he wasn't ready to deal with it yet.

"That's a long story for a different night. It's not something I enjoy talking about, so maybe one day I will tell you about it, but, uh . . . I had a great night, and we should do this again. Maybe next time it could be just the two of us?" said Ron, trying desperately to change the subject.

Nora blushed. "I would like that. Don't make me wait too long this time."

She smiled as Ron said goodnight; he gave her hands a gentle squeeze while he leaned in, giving her a kiss on the cheek. Then he walked back to his dormitory, quietly entering the building so as not to wake anybody. He opened the door to his room, kicked his boots off, and lay down in his bed. He was glad the day was over, and closing his eyes, he fell asleep thinking about Nora.

Chapter Three

The Message

Ron felt the sun's morning rays coming through his window, warming the small bedroom. He could hear the birds chirping, the people outside walking and talking amongst each other. *Today's the day,* Ron thought to himself as he opened his eyes.

Exam day. Where he and Grant would have to use every ounce of skill to pass their weapons combat test. Ron was ready, though. He knew he had the talent and felt reenergized after Cap had spoken with him the other day. The instructor's words had refocused Ron and put a drive back in him to be better, to remember why he started this process so long ago.

Sitting up in his bed, Ron threw his feet over the side, reaching to grab his white, short-sleeved shirt and brown pants from the chair. He stood up, got dressed, and put his boots on. His pants had seen better days, with some holes getting larger in the knees with each training day. Ron fastened three leather straps around his midthigh, belonging to a worn leather pouch that he used for storing odds and ends.

To his surprise, when he went to open the door, Grant was there, just about to knock as Ron pulled it open.

"Early for once. That's new," his friend joked.

"We can't afford to be late today. Cap is not going to go easy on us, especially after the other day."

Grant nodded. Standing in the door frame, he waited for Ron, to make sure he was ready. "How do you think the exam is going to go? I've heard several stories from graduated students. They all said the exams are never the same."

Ron double-checked his pockets and pouch, then headed toward the door. "I don't know, but whatever happens, we are more than capable of handling it. Cap trained us well."

"Yes, he did," Grant agreed.

The two young men walked down the hallway and through the kitchen, grabbing a pair of apples like they did on every other morning. As they continued to make their way toward the Arena, Ron spotted Nora heading in through the doors; she must have gotten up early to start her exam with the staff. Ron didn't think twice about if she would pass or not. He knew she could handle anything thrown at her.

"You ready for the exam, Grant?" asked Ron.

"Of course I am. Cap's little reminder the other day was a nice way of telling me I got this in the bag." They both laughed and headed into the Arena.

When they got into formation, the doors closed behind them. Cap came out and began speaking. "I want all students using blades over here on the right, and all students using hand-to-hand to proceed to the instructor on the left. Today's exam will consist of three challenges. First, you will go against one another, paired up randomly one-on-one. As you advance and a winner emerges, there will be a chance to rest while the next match begins.

"The goal here is simple—be successful in more than three matches. A win consists of your opponent submitting in defeat or if they are knocked unconscious. If you can achieve that, then there will be no penalty for any losses obtained afterward. On the other hand, if you lose more than three matches, you will be disqualified. Once disqualified, you will no longer be eligible to attend the completion ceremony. You will be retained for another two months until you can retake this exam.

"The second part is contingent upon you and your training partner both winning three or more matches. Once you and your partner do so, you will face off against each other. They will know your every move. When you come up against a better-trained opponent, and they are more well versed in combative tactics, you will have to think on your feet or die. Am I clear?" Cap asked the students.

With a resounding "Yes, sir" from the group, it seemed as if everyone was ready to win. Ron and Grant looked at each other. They already knew who the better fighter was, but they decided they would put on a show anyway.

"The third part of your exam will be challenging and the most difficult by far, but for those that pass, you will be perceived as the top-ranking students during the ceremony. In addition, you will also be receiving a personalized award from myself and the other instructors." Whispers began to hum through the formation of students about what the award might be, but Ron stood silent, thinking neither of the prestige of being named top of the class nor what the award would entail. Instead, his thoughts were focused on what he had to do for the third part of the exam.

Cap held his hand up, silencing the formation of students. "There is a catch to the third part of the exam. It will only be available to those that meet the requirements of winning three or more rounds and besting their training partner. If both terms are met, then the winner will be allowed to choose the instructor of their choice in one-on-one combat."

Again, no whispers came from the formation. It seemed the students' resolve had been fortified—each one wanted the recognition of being top of the class and the award. However, Ron's resolve was different; he wanted something else. He wanted to show Cap that the last six years had not been a waste of time. He wanted to not only prove to Cap that he was ready to complete his training, but also to himself that if he ever needed to fight in defense of his life or his loved ones, he would be ready.

One voice in the formation asked Cap a question that showed not everybody would be cut out for the third part of the exam. "How can we win against an instructor if we are too tired from the other matches?"

Cap had known this question was coming. There was always one who asked.

"This exam has been made to simulate the hardships you will face on the battlefield. Its purpose is to test the limits of all who enter—to push you beyond the boundaries of exhaustion, just like what could happen in a real situation. Out in the world, it won't matter how tired you are or how much pain you are in. All that will matter is who has enough strength and will to keep living. Only those who give all they have will be granted a chance to rise above the other students and know that they have earned their title."

Sitting on the carved benches, Ron and Grant watched as names were called. Students were chosen at random and began to fight, using different variations of wooden swords, ranging from short sword to long swords, broad two-handed swords, and even one sword in each hand. Ron preferred using a short sword since he liked the amount of control it offered.

Grant, on the other hand, was much more accustomed to the dual wielding of daggers. As much as he never took anything as seriously as he should have, he knew his way around a pair of daggers. In addition, they allowed quick movements. During sparring sessions, if Ron wasn't careful, Grant would be able to land more than one consecutive blow, ending the match.

The matches went on, with some lasting only a matter of minutes while others seemed to drag for hours. Since the students all needed to pass with three or more wins, they had to employ different tactics throughout. Finally, Ron's name was called, and he made his way down the steps, picking up a short wooden sword from the weapons rack.

Ron's opponent was a bigger student, one he had seen fight before—this guy's strength was incredible. He selected a two-handed wooden sword and stood across from Ron on the compact dirt. Once Cap shouted, "Begin!" the larger student charged for Ron, bringing the sword overhead. He swung down hard, burying the blade in the dirt. If Ron had tried to block that attack, he would have been knocked to the ground.

Instead, he'd rolled to the right to avoid the falling stroke. Ron prepared to attack, only to drop quickly to his stomach to dodge the large sword as the student lifted it and swung it sideways. Ron got to his feet while the other man regained his footing from the heavy attempt. There was no chance of beating this guy by going head-to-head with him. So Ron dodged and rolled away from more attacks, making no attempt to strike back. Finally, he got to his feet and saw the hulking student prepare for another strike, and that was when Ron saw how he was going to win the match. As Ron moved out of the way, his opponent breathed heavily, staggering as he tried to regain balance. Sweat poured down his face as he yelled at Ron.

"Stop running around and fight me!" The large student wiped the sweat from his face between breaths and came for Ron once again. Repeating the same process, Ron sidestepped and saw an opening for a counterattack. He raised his sword and swung, striking behind the left knee, bringing the large student to the ground. Anger radiated from the other man, but he was tired, and slow, and Ron was already in the middle of his next swing. It connected with the left side of the large student's ribs. The dust settled around him holding his side, trying to get his breath back. He raised his hand, forfeiting the match.

Back in the stands a few minutes later, Grant asked Ron, "How did you know he would get tired so quickly?"

"He was putting a lot of effort into trying to hit me. However, I noticed him slow down after each attack, so it made sense that his biggest strength was his size and aggression, which happen to be his weakness as well. Cap reminded me to use my head in a fight after we sparred with him, and after fighting the big guy, I intend to use it in every match." Ron leaned back.

Then Grant heard his name called; he stood and walked to the center of the Arena, but not before saying to Ron, "Using your head is good, but I'll take my skill with a little luck for now." Ron shook his head, knowing his friend wasn't taking this exam seriously.

Grant's match began. He took to the ground, daggers clutched in each hand, jumping up and down, loosening his muscles while maintaining a smirk. Ron knew he was treating the exam as a game, taking more risks than he needed to when fighting, but he couldn't deny that Grant was talented. His opponent had mimicked Grant's weapon style, but instead of daggers, he'd chosen two short swords.

The instructor shouted for the match to begin, and Grant rushed his opponent, stopping short, smiling as he watched the other boy go into a defensive stance. Again Ron shook his head in the stands. To some, it would look like

Grant was fooling around, and no one would be wrong in thinking that, but really, he was testing his opponent's reactions.

He continued to get close, then back away, only to approach again, keeping the same spring in his step as when he started. By the time his opponent went to strike, Grant had already planned a countermove. He deflected the sword, spun, and planted an elbow into his opponent's back. Grant used his speed, and the other student panicked as his back became exposed.

His opponent turned quickly, raising his swords to defend the upper portion of his body. It seemed like a reasonable defensive move, and it would have been against anyone else. However, early on, Grant had been scoping out his opponents' reaction time and ability to switch between defenses.

So when the young man raised both swords to defend his upper body, Grant knew he was close enough to strike low before his opponent could switch. Grant made it look as though he would strike high and have his daggers clash with the swords, but then he slid on the dirt, kicking the other man's feet out from under him. He used his own momentum in the slide to propel himself upright, listening to the thud of the student as his face made contact with the ground. Grant walked over to land a finishing blow, but the young man didn't move.

An instructor motioned for Grant to stand back. He rolled the student over and gave him a couple taps to his cheeks before he came to. Grant was announced the winner of the match.

He returned and sat next to Ron, watching the other students continue their matches, as they waited for their own names to be called once more.

"Did you enjoy yourself out there?" Ron asked sarcastically.

"I did." Grant chuckled, but not loud enough for Ron to hear. "I assumed the first match would be easy. As they continue, the next people we are up against will be more difficult. Just have to wait for the better students to weed out the weaker ones."

Ron watched the potential opponents intently, studying their form, looking for weaknesses he could exploit to gain an advantage. He had no doubt the others were doing the same thing. Each time Ron and Grant heard their names called, they went to start their match. Ron didn't know if the students truly posed more of a challenge as he advanced or if he was becoming tired. Probably both.

After the fourth match, Ron returned to the bench, breathing heavily, as more effort was needed with each one. He ran his fingers through his hair, feeling the lightest breeze cool the sweat on his head. It didn't take long until Grant rejoined him. Grant's match had ended, but the outcome was not what he had expected.

"What happened out there?" Ron asked.

Grant was clearly upset at losing his fourth match, more frustrated with himself than his opponent. "I thought I had him. I really did. He must have watched my other fights and lured me in. So stupid—I can't believe I fell for that." Grant had lost the match by forfeit, thinking it was better to fail than be knocked out. Even though he'd won three matches, he didn't want to risk the time it would take to recover from being unconscious.

"Looks like you're going to have to try something else for the last match," Ron said, observing the fighters on the other side of the Arena.

Ron heard Grant reply with a simple, "I guess so," but his attention was elsewhere. He'd spotted Nora in the middle of her latest match, noticing how impressive her footwork was and how she made her staff seem to glide through the air with ease. Her precise yet smooth movements reminded him of the times he had seen her dance, and on fewer occasions, the times he'd danced with her. The grace in each step and action captivated him.

Upon receiving a nudge from Grant, Ron heard his name called for his last match.

It resulted in his fifth win, but he barely came out the victor. It was more luck than skill; he was not the only one who was feeling tired and sluggish. Ron took advantage of his opponent's mistake. While blocking an attack, he and the other student locked swords in a battle of attrition, but his opponent tried to shift his weight onto his back leg for more leverage. In doing so, he eased the pressure that pushed against Ron's sword, giving Ron the chance to deflect the blade and strike it from his opponent's hand. Tired, weaponless, and with Ron's wooden sword point at his throat, the other boy signaled for the match to end.

Afterward, Ron lay on the bench, trying to let his body rest, but soon a shadow blocked the sun from his face. Grant sat with him, having won his own match. He was on the ground, leaning his back against the bench. Speaking between rapid breaths, Grant said, "Glad that's over."

"Me too, but for how long?"

Neither wanted an answer; they just had to enjoy the time for rest.

When the last match between the students had ended, Cap stood before everyone.

"This concludes the first phase of the exam. To those of you who passed, congratulations. To those who didn't, you will be allowed to retake the exam in two months. Use that time wisely, and train hard. All those who did not pass, please exit the Arena." More students stood and left than Ron had expected. By his estimated count, a little less than half the students had failed to win three matches.

Cap got the remaining students' attention before continuing. "The second part of the exam will begin shortly. Rest and drink some water. This will be the only break you get for the remainder of the exam."

Ron and Grant stood across from each other, waiting for the instructor to begin the match. They squared off against one another just like every other time they had sparred, but this was different. Ron had never looked at Grant as a true obstacle before. Now, his friend was the last person that stood between him and the validation he wanted from Cap, but most importantly, the assurance he needed from himself.

Once the instructor shouted, they began fighting. They gave all the energy they had into swinging their weapons, dodging attacks, and quick movements to make the other stumble. Ron and Grant both performed an overhead swing, locking swords with daggers.

"So, this is going well," Ron said, catching his breath.

"It is, isn't it?" Grant smirked.

"Do you want to bring it up a notch?" Ron asked.

"Might as well—just remember, I know how you fight. This won't be easy."

"I wasn't counting on it, but don't try any of those tricks of yours. You will only be disappointed," Ron said with a push, breaking away from Grant's daggers. After he jumped back, Ron took a few steps and closed his eyes. Then, without thinking, he moved his hand around the hilt, turning the sword so the blade faced the rear along his forearm and the bottom of the hilt was pointed up.

When Ron opened his eyes, Grant looked at him with confusion written on his face. He had never seen Ron hold a sword like that. Ron noticed the look on his friend's face and smiled. He charged at Grant, feigning an upward swinging strike, but then slid on his left knee, spinning to the left and using the sword to take out Grant's feet.

Falling forward, Grant hit the ground hard. Ron broke out of the spin, stood up, and tried to hit his friend in the center of his back with a quick slash. Grant rolled quickly, redirecting the path of the sword with his daggers, pushing it to the side.

Rising to his feet, Grant laughed. "I see what you did there." He began to pace. "Using my own move against me—clever."

"Thought I'd give it a shot. It was worth a try," Ron said, rushing at Grant, trying to keep him on the defensive long enough to find a weak point, but Grant's speed was getting the better of him. The young man blocked the sword with his right-handed dagger, sending it toward the ground. Before Ron could counter, his friend's left fist landed on his jaw.

Ron fell but quickly got up. He rubbed his face, cursing under his breath. He should have seen that coming, but he hadn't. It seemed Grant was taking this match seriously. He outclassed Ron when it came to speed, but his strength was lacking. There was only one way Ron would be able to win this.

The wood of the practice weapons dented and chipped with each blocking strike, threatening to crack and splinter. Ron let Grant think he was getting the upper hand by staying on the defensive, avoiding each attack. Finally, blocking a downward strike, he let himself fall to one knee.

Grant raised both daggers, rapidly thrusting the blades down. Ron turned his own sword so that he was holding the hilt with one hand, then placed his free hand on the flat side of the blade near the tip. It caught Grant's wrists, stopping his attack. Ron stood, using his momentum to push Grant's arms away. Moving his free hand, Ron grabbed Grant by the throat. Then, he straightened his knees and lifted Grant off the ground before slamming him into the hard, compact dirt.

Both daggers flew out of Grant's hands as soon as his body hit the ground. The force from the impact took the air out of his lungs. Gasping, Grant rolled to his side. Seeing one of the wooden daggers lying in the dirt, he crawled to reach it. His efforts abruptly ended once he felt Ron's arm wrap tightly around his neck. Ron rolled him onto his back, trapping Grant's legs with his own, applying pressure to bar any chance at breaking free.

He saw Grant's hand raise, forfeiting the match, and let him go. Grant rolled to the side, coughing with what air he was able to retain. Ron extended a hand, helping the boy to his feet. Cap looked at Ron and motioned for him to make his way to the stands.

"What the hell was that?" Grant asked. "You never told me you knew other techniques. I've never seen you learn that."

"The thought just came to me. You were too fast for me to keep up, so I had to bring you in close. I learned that when I would wrestle with my bro—" Ron caught himself. "Some days I practice on my own. It was quite a surprise, wasn't it? A break from what we normally do."

"Surprise? That's what you call a surprise? More like a nightmare if you ask me."

The two boys walked to the stands, laughing. Ron sat down while Grant kept walking to the other section on the left, separated by stairs. Ron was joined by a handful of other students who had passed the second exam. He patiently waited for the remainder to finish their matches. While waiting, he turned his attention inward, thinking of the best strategy and style to take down Cap. He could not come up with anything that would work. After all, Cap had taught him pretty much everything he knew about sword fighting.

Ron's thoughts drifted once more to the only other person he had learned to use swords with. He and his brother had used to spar quite often. However,

Nathill had always used a technique that wasn't conventional. After using it on Grant, Ron thought utilizing the technique for a final exam would probably not be the best time to try it out again. Against Cap, there would be no element of surprise.

Nonetheless, the idea was in the back of his mind as Cap called Ron down from the stands. He walked down the stairs, looking back toward his friend. Grant gave Ron a thumbs up and leaned back to watch the match. Ron reached the bottom of the stairs and grabbed a sword from the rack, one that didn't have chips missing from the wood.

"This is it. Once you pass this, you are done. There is no more training I can give you. Show me that you are no longer the boy that came here weak and afraid. Show me the person you want to become. Are you ready?" Cap asked.

Ron was focused and determined. "I'm ready."

Ron rolled up his sleeves, took his stance, and prepared himself to fight despite the exhaustion that rampaged through his muscles. Six years of training, and the culmination was upon him. Ron knew he could not lose this fight; if he lost, he would not only be disappointed in himself, but Cap would be disappointed in him as well. Ron was the one who'd sought out Cap in the first place, so for him to lose now would be a massive waste of time. Cap looked at Ron, and as the boy lifted his head, he gave the instructor a look that showed his determination.

With a nod, the fight began.

Cap was even faster than Ron had expected. Ron used all the tricks he had to fight; he would never beat the man with the basics. He tried upward slashes, and from left and right. He even tried to disarm Cap by using his hands as he had with Grant. Unfortunately, nothing was working, and soon Ron was the one on the defensive.

Cap hit hard and fast; Ron could block the incoming attacks, but he was losing ground, and his footwork was getting sloppy. At this point, Ron knew this was all or nothing. However, once he was able to put some distance between himself and Cap, Ron took a new stance. Ron spread his feet shoulder-width apart and grabbed the hilt of the sword upside down in his hand.

This was the way his brother had used the sword against him while they sparred. His brother's words crept into his mind: *switching between more than one technique is better than focusing on a single one.* It made sense; that was how Ron could win. Cap only knew what he had taught, but if Ron were to use his other training, switching between techniques, Cap might not be able to predict his attacks.

Ron bent his knees and held the sword level with his chest, the blade running along his forearm. Then he ran at Cap, using the sword as if it were an extension of his arm. Ron blocked the heavy blows that the instructor delivered while the sword was against his forearm, offering him more stopping power. When Cap came with a quick strike, Ron turned the blade using his free hand against the flat side to counter the attacks. Putting some ground between them, Ron took a breath as he felt a sharp chill course through his body.

It lasted no longer than a second, so he shook it off and began his attack. Now the boy was able to do more than just slashes and stabs. He was able to twist and turn the sword in any way he deemed necessary. Cap had not expected this; he had no idea what form Ron was using. With the added mobility, Ron was able to get back onto the offensive. He went to slash at Cap's right side. The instructor blocked the blow, but Ron knew that would leave his left open for an attack. Ron spun around and placed his foot into Cap's ribs. He heard a crack, and the man fell to one knee.

Ron then held the sword to Cap's throat. Cap looked up at him, managing to stand using his own sword to balance himself while holding his left side. "That was unexpected, Ron. What do you call that—the way you hold the sword, that is?"

"I really don't know. I saw it when I was younger, and it just came into my head."

"Well, congratulations. You beat me and passed the third part of the exam. I was worried for you at the start, but you came through—good job. I guess this is payback for breaking your nose." As Cap shook Ron's hand, he noticed dark bruising on the boy's right forearm. "I guess that's the drawback of using a sword that way. Just be careful when using a real sword—it will do more than bruise."

Ron looked at his forearm and saw dark red and purple. While he was defending himself, the sword had dug into his arm with each blow.

"I guess I didn't feel it during the exam," Ron said. "Thank you for everything, Cap. It means a lot that you would take your time to teach me over these last years."

"Just put what I taught you to good use. Stay out of trouble, and keep Grant in check. We know he can do just fine, but he is a little wild," Cap said.

"I will, sir," Ron said, and they laughed together.

He went to sit with the other four students who had beaten the instructors of their choice. Cap took his place in front of the group. "You all have done well in your exam. I have full confidence in your capabilities, but make no mistake, these are perishable skills. Maintain your training, and always strive to be a better version of who you are. I am proud of each of you. Before you leave, remember that the completion ceremony will be held a week from today. Show up on time, dress accordingly, and behave yourselves. The five students who successfully passed the third exam will be awarded at the ceremony. I will see you all there. For the last time, you are dismissed."

Ron went to the stairs to get Grant so they could head back to the dormitory. The exams had taken almost all day, and by the time they walked out of the Arena doors, the sun was beginning to set.

"I'm glad that's over with. Now we don't have to get up early for training. I, for one, plan on sleeping in until midafternoon." Grant laughed.

"It has been a while since we got to relax without having to worry about training, but don't worry, I'll still get you up before noon. Can't have you waste the whole day," Ron said with a grin.

The two boys were walking back when Ron heard someone call his name. He turned around and saw Nora waving at him. "Hey, Nora."

"Hey, how did you guys do on your exams?"

"I did exceptionally well, beat everyone that challenged me. Ron over here struggled quite a bit," said Grant in his smuggest voice possible, stretching the truth.

"I'm sure that's what happened," she said with a smile. "But really, how did it go?"

"We both passed, and Cap was a lot tougher than I imagined. But I won, and I may have broken his ribs," Ron said.

"What? Broke his ribs? You went pretty hard in there, didn't you?" Nora said playfully.

"I wasn't about to lose and fail, so yeah, I did." They began to laugh, and Nora walked the rest of the way to the dormitory with them, explaining how excited she was to be among the few staff users to complete all three parts of the exam.

Once they got there, Nora said goodbye and continued walking east to her house. Ron and Grant parted ways, with Ron telling Grant he would see him in the morning. When he finally got to his room, he took a much-needed soak in a tub, removing the caked-on dust that had stuck to his skin and his sweat-stained shirt. He put on some gray cotton pants and an overly large shirt. Lying down in bed, he was finally able to let his body fully relax; the tension in his muscles ceased, and he let the exhaustion take over. Pleased with how the day had turned out, Ron closed his eyes and fell asleep.

The following morning, he woke up feeling more rested than usual, except for the bruises and soreness. The sun was creeping in through his window while the birds sang for the new morning. He thought to himself that it might be because it was the first time in a long time he had woken up without having to go to training. He was so used to Grant waking him that he couldn't remember the last time he woke naturally.

Ron got up, got dressed, and went across the way to Grant's dormitory. He could hear the snoring coming from the room halfway down the hall. The other boy must have really been out.

When Ron knocked, he got no answer. So he did it again, louder this time. Ron could hear the snoring stop, but Grant still did not come to the door. Ron checked to see if the door was unlocked; jiggling the handle, he slowly turned the knob, cracking the door slightly ajar, just enough to be able to peer inside. He tiptoed in slowly and saw Grant sleeping on his bed. He was stretched out with his feet hanging off the sides, blankets strewn about like a whirlwind had dispersed them.

Ron decided it would be fun to play a little joke on him. He started shouting and pounding on the open door.

"Grant, wake up! We're going to be late for training. Hurry up, get dressed." The boy's eyes opened wide, and he jumped up out of bed and began to grab his clothes. He had his boots on and made it halfway out the door with his shirt draped over his shoulder and one pant leg pulled up before he realized what was happening. He stopped and turned around to see Ron trying to hold in his laughter. The young man was unable to do so, and started chuckling uncontrollably. "You look ridiculous, all half-dressed and whatnot," Ron said through gasps.

Grant pulled up his pants the rest of the way and put his shirt on. "So, you think that's funny, do you?' he asked. He threw his boots at Ron and charged straight at him. With a bounding leap and arms spread wide, Grant tackled him to the floor. The two wrestled there, neither gaining any advantage over the other. Ron attempted to break free of Grant's hold, but his friend grabbed another leg or arm to restrain Ron the second he tried.

After a minute or two, they heard laughter.

Looking up, they saw Nora standing in the doorway, watching their foolish play. "I see you guys wanted a little exercise this morning," she said sarcastically. "Why don't we go get something to eat before you destroy this room?"

"I like the sound of that," Grant said, letting go of Ron's right leg. They stood up and brushed themselves off, and Grant finished getting ready.

They walked past the kitchen and past a bowl full of apples, but Ron decided not to grab one since they were going to eat. Once outside, they continued down the road. They overheard some people talking on the way to grab breakfast, gossiping about seeing a strange man on horseback near the town. Thinking nothing of it, as it could just be a traveler from some other town or city, the trio found somewhere to eat.

"I wouldn't mind visiting another town or city even. I haven't ventured very far outside of these walls, only a mile or two. I've really just stayed here all this time. I think it would be fun," Grant said.

"I don't know. It's nice here. I may not have grown up here, but these last eight years have been some of the best of my life," Ron replied.

"You would be saying otherwise if you were stuck here your whole life," Grant said with a snicker in his voice.

"I agree. I would like to see some of the world someday," Nora said.

"So, where exactly are you from, Ron? You never really told us that," Grant said.

"I, uh—I'm . . ." Ron paused, turning his ear to a sound. "Did you hear that?"

"Hear what?" Grant questioned.

"There it is again—someone screamed. It sounds like it came from the west gate." Ron started to run in that direction.

"Ron, wait, what are you doing? Let the guards handle it!" Grant shouted, but he was already down the street. The other two chased after him to see what was going on.

When Ron arrived at the town's front gate, he found a crowd, and a man on an old, dust-ridden brown horse sitting in the archway. A thin metal rod fixed a transparent, solid glass lantern to the horse's saddle, with a small blue flame suspended in its center. The man was wearing a black cloak, but underneath, Ron saw a shade of deep blue on the borders of his shirt. The man on the horse looked up; his face was old, not with age but with wear. His skin was shades of black and blue with a hint of yellow, from bruises new and old. Blood had dried around his eyes, nose, and mouth.

The guards of Greyland had surrounded the man and his horse, their swords drawn.

One guard said, "I'm only going to ask you one more time. What is your business here?"

"I am looking for someone. A young man who should be about six feet in height by now. Brown hair—mid-twenties, I believe," the man replied in a raspy voice, pausing to scan the crowd, looking intensely at everyone. "Him, right there." The man lifted a trembling finger and pointed. Ron turned to see if he was pointing to someone behind him, but then turned back, looking at the man. The finger was aimed directly at him, and Ron was unsure what to think.

"Me? Why would you be looking for me? I don't even know you," Ron said, trying to make out the details of the man's face, but with the hood drawn, the bruising, and the blood, he couldn't clearly see any discerning features. The man then raised his hands and proceeded to remove his hood and cloak, revealing his full face and black clothing with a deep-blue trim around the edges.

Ron's suspicions were confirmed. He immediately recognized the color pattern of the man's clothing. While it was not armor, it bore the same look as the soldiers who'd burned his town and killed his family.

He twisted his face in anger and yelled, "What the hell do you want?" Then he started pushing his way through the crowd, making his way to the man on the horse.

Grant had caught up with Nora in tow, and they grabbed Ron from behind, holding him back. Grant was shocked; he had never seen his friend act this way before, with such anger and hostility. He had seen Ron lose his temper, but nothing this volatile. Grant was having some trouble holding him as he thrashed his arms about.

"I have a message for you," the man on the horse said. Ron stopped struggling and looked closer at the man's face.

"Wait, do I know you? You sound and—and your face. It looks familiar," said Ron.

"I used to be a blacksmith before this life consumed me," the man on the horse said.

Ron studied him. Grant slowly let go since he'd stopped struggling, and now free, Ron moved closer to the man. With each step, he was able to see his face more clearly.

"You lived in the same village as I did. I remember running past your smithy as a child. I thought everyone died. What happened? How many are still alive? Who caused all of this?"

"Stay where you are; come no closer. If you want answers, you must return to where all was lost. It is time to return, time to reconcile for past grievances. Then, the path will be made clear. That is the message—that is all I can say. I am sorry, but I must take my leave now." The man started to turn the horse away.

"No! No, that's not good enough. You knew my parents. You have to tell me more!" Ron shouted, unable to control his voice.

The man on the horse turned to look at him, and Ron saw tears welling up in his eyes. "You do not truly understand, not yet. In time, you will learn what happened. I'm sorry—the one who did this, the one who caused all this pain, this suffering, is . . ." The man paused. He looked panicked, as if something were about to happen. His eyes widened as he heard the glass from the lantern crack; jerking his head toward it, he started talking to himself. "No, you've come too close. I thought this was enough space. No!"

The man wasn't making any sense.

"What are you talking about?" Ron asked. Then the glass of the lantern shattered, and the blue flame exploded. The man started to scream in agony as it engulfed his body, burning him and his horse where they stood. Their screams were joined by those of multiple guards who'd been standing too close when the lantern exploded. The sounds echoed throughout Greyland.

In a matter of seconds, the man and horse were reduced to ash, along with the guards. Ron stood there speechless and in shock. The townspeople began to scream as well, and run; they ran to their homes or the nearest shops to escape the carnage. The remaining guards quickly closed the gates, sounding the bells to alert the town. Then they turned their swords to Ron.

Nora and Grant were still standing there in disbelief. The guards circled Ron, anger painted on each face as they yelled at him, demanding he drop to his knees. Before Ron could process what was happening, a guard kicked the back of his knee, forcing him to the ground. Once his hands were restrained, he was escorted away toward the holding cells. Nora and Grant tried to follow only to be held at sword point.

"He's coming with us. I would stay put if I were you, unless you want to be thrown in a cell with him."

Ron heard the guard threaten Nora and Grant; he also saw the look on their faces.

"Do as he says. I'll be fine!" Ron shouted, hoping that they would listen. But as he was being hauled off, he tried to turn his head, only catching a glimpse of Nora and Grant walking away. Then, the force of the guard's hand on the back of Ron's neck tightened, bringing his head forward.

Chapter Four

Departure

R on was shoved into an old wooden chair that creaked with the slightest movement. Chains restrained his wrists, securing his arms to each side of the chair and running beneath the seat to attach to his ankles. The guards began yelling, questioning him all at once; there was no order to the madness and no way to answer anyone. The guard's voices all melded together to create noise, noise that didn't subside for what felt like hours. During that time, they began lashing out in frustration, punching Ron in the stomach, backhanding him across the face. Each guard was careful enough not to draw blood but forceful enough to hurt.

When it seemed like they were getting tired of yelling, they left the room. Ron savored the quiet moments he was given. Unfortunately, when they stormed back in, the process repeated itself. At that point, Ron lost track of time.

Finally, the door to the holding cells burst open, and the commander of the guard walked through the door.

"Alright, alright. Enough with the yelling. I hope you didn't rough him up too bad, or else the mayor will have my hide. Now get back to work," said the commander. The guards grew silent and began to back away from Ron, mumbling under their breath. Some went to sit at their desks, shuffling stacks of paperwork around, pretending to work while hoping to listen in on the conversation. Others went outside to return to their posts at the gate.

"So, you want to tell me about the incident at the gate, boy?" asked the commander as he pulled up a chair in front of Ron and sat down.

The commander was a large man, not so tall but wide around the middle. He had years of experience, as told by his gray hair and short, bushy mustache with matching beard.

"I'm not sure what happened. That man . . . I barely knew the man he used to be. I was a child, but that was years ago," Ron said, trying to remember the face.

"Where does he come from? Are there more like him? Why was he looking for you?" the commander asked, his voice growing in intensity with each question.

"He is from a village that isn't around anymore. I don't know if there are more like him or why he was looking for me," Ron answered.

"What do you mean you don't know?" shouted the commander. "He was looking for you. He pointed you out in a large crowd, and then he burst into flames, taking my men with him. It all seems a little suspect, and I think you know something. I'll arrest you if you don't start talking, boy."

Ron had had his fill of being yelled at and beaten and not having any answers.

"Arrest me? Arrest me for what? Knowing someone from a decade ago, someone that just showed up out of nowhere? You can't arrest me for that. And what is it I'm supposed to tell you? I don't have any answers for you. I can't tell you what I don't know."

Ron had called his bluff. The commander's frustration was evident—he knew full well he could not arrest Ron.

"Fine. You might not know, but don't think this is over. I'll have more questions for you, so you stick around." The commander stood up and walked past Ron, bending to unlock the chains. "Get out of here before I make up a reason to arrest you." Ron got up and walked out faster than he came in. He was tired and sore, and needed a break from people and questions. He wanted to be alone, and he knew just the place that would give him some solitude.

Ron managed to make his way home after spending most of the day in a chair being interrogated by the guards, as well as the commander. Once they accepted that Ron was not involved and had no idea what had caused the lantern to explode, they reluctantly let him go.

He went straight to his dormitory and up to his room, closing the door behind him. There, he tossed and turned in his bed, trying to find a position that didn't apply pressure to his new welts courtesy of the guards. Finally, he was able to get comfortable.

Internally, he recounted the events of earlier in the day as he drifted off. Why had the blacksmith come now? How had he known Ron was here? Who had sent him?

Then he slipped into an uneasy sleep.

When Ron woke up, Grant was in his room, staring from the end of the bed. Ron rubbed his forehead, realizing he had forgotten to lock his door.

"So, are you going to explain what happened yesterday and tell me what caused that explosion? I mean, lanterns do not just break and explode into flames, do they? Honestly, I've never seen anything like that in my life, and now the whole town is talking about it."

Ron sat up in bed. "Can I at least get up and dressed first before you start asking me a thousand questions?" Without waiting for a reply, he rose and grabbed a white shirt from his dresser drawer. "I'm not even fully sure of what happened, Grant. It all happened so fast. I—I knew that man once, though he knew more about me since he saw me grow up as a child . . ."

"Why was he all beaten and bloody?" Grant asked.

Ron looked around the room for his boots so he could walk out and grab his morning apple when he was ready. He found them lying on the floor next to the door.

"I don't know, Grant. Can you go in my closet and grab my pack, please?" Ron asked, pointing to the closet.

"Sure."

Grant went into the closet and looked for the pack, but then he heard a door close behind him.

"Sorry, Grant," Ron said, grabbing his desk chair, tilting it on its back legs, and sticking it under the door handle. Ron knew Grant would be able to get

out of the closet shortly, but he needed to think. So he left his room, hearing
Grant's voice fade away.

"Come on, this isn't funny. Open the door, Ron," his friend shouted thinly.

But Ron didn't feel like answering any more questions, not after yesterday.
There was a lot to think about, and he needed time to sort it out. With Grant
around, he knew he would never get the chance to think peacefully.

When Ron walked past the kitchen, he grabbed his morning apple even
though he did not feel hungry, and he began to walk. Once he was alone, he
thought back to the questions he'd asked himself last night and took a bite.

Walking hadn't helped him find the answers to any of the questions he asked,
but it was giving him time to process and digest the events. Before long, he found
himself tracing a familiar road in the residential district. Finally, he managed to
reach Nora's house. Ron was so caught up in his thoughts that he didn't even
remember walking past the shops or other houses to get there. He definitely
didn't notice the number of people who had stopped to stare at him as he was
walking by. Ron was about to turn around and head toward the Arena for some
solo training to clear his head before he heard his name being called.

"Hey, Ron!" Nora shouted.

Ron turned around and saw her leaning out her second-story window.

"Hey Nora," Ron said with a wave of his hand.

"Are you doing okay?" she asked, looking him over.

"I am—as much as anyone can be after what happened yesterday," he said,
meeting her gaze. Ron turned slightly to walk away, but then changed his mind
and looked back. "Can I come in? I need to talk to you."

"Of course." Ron walked to the front door while she pulled herself back
inside and came downstairs to unlock it. There, he gave her a tight hug. "Ron,
are you okay?" Nora asked, holding him tight with a look of worry.

"Remember all the times you asked me to tell you about myself over the
years?"

Nora nodded.

"Well, as you now know, that rider was someone from the village that I grew
up in. I don't remember everything; I only have vague memories of him."

"I know it must be hard for you to talk about," Nora assured him. "That's why I never pushed the subject any further than asking about it every now and again. I figured when you were ready, you would eventually tell me," Nora said, searching Ron's eyes.

"I think that time has come whether I'm ready for it or not," he said.

"If you want to tell, then I am here to listen."

Before Ron started to explain, Nora took his hand and led him inside, closing the door. She brought him into her living room, where they proceeded to sit on the oversized lounge chair. Looking around the room, Ron noticed that Nora had quite the collection of books, everything ranging from basic and advanced weapons and tactics to healing minor cuts and abrasions, as well as a guide to setting and splinting bones.

Paintings of her mother and father hung in frames on the walls. The only other reminder she had left of her parents since they passed away were the flowers placed in a vase on a small table next to the lounge chair. Once they sat down, Ron told Nora of the events that had happened eight years ago. How his village was attacked for no reason known to him. How his parents and brother were murdered in front of his eyes. He recounted that the soldiers were wearing armor of the same color that the rider had worn. Ron told Nora of his escape, dragged away by some of the surviving villagers. He decided to leave out the fact that before he lost consciousness, he saw a blue flame emitting from his own hand.

Nora looked at Ron in shock after hearing the full account. She'd known something had happened to him when they first met, but had never imagined it was something so traumatic and that he had held on to it for so long. She quickly wrapped her arms around him. "Ron, I'm sorry that happened. Have you told anyone else about this?"

"No, I haven't. I mean, I kind of told Cap a short version, but other than him, I didn't want anyone else to know." Ron paused for a moment. "I don't know why it happened or who was behind it, but I've been thinking, and I've decided that I need to leave."

Nora let Ron go. "Leave? what do you mean?"

"The message from the rider said if I want to find answers, I need to go to where all was lost. I think he means go back to my village," Ron said.

"Why would you want to go back? That man died yesterday, and you want to go back?"

"He told me that for a reason. I don't know what path he was talking about or what grievances need to be reconciled. But honestly, Nora, I'm really tired of not having any answers. I have to know what happened."

Ron looked at her, and a long pause lingered until Nora said, "Well, then I'm coming with you. I told you I want to see the world, and even though this is a different way to see it, I feel I need to go with you."

"You can't. What about the completion ceremony? I don't want you to miss that. You worked too hard to not be there," Ron protested. "Also, what if it's dangerous? We don't know who or what is out there. I don't want to put you in that position."

"You are not putting me in any position. I am choosing to go with you. Besides, I can take care of myself, so I'll be okay. As for the ceremony, I knew I would pass all the exams, so missing it wouldn't be a big deal. I care more about you than some award or recognition from my peers. I want to do this."

Ron felt the argument slip out of his favor. He knew she could handle anything, and once her mind was made up, it stayed that way. "Alright," he said.

Out of nowhere, they heard a voice call out, "Don't think you can leave me behind!" Grant came down the stairs, taking both Ron and Nora by surprise.

Nora jumped up, shouting, "When did you—where did you . . . How did you get in my house?"

"I followed Ron after he tried to lose me by locking me in his closet. Amateur move—it took me all of a couple minutes to get out. Oh, and by the way, you may need to replace the hinges on the door. I don't know what happened, but they broke. As for getting in, I climbed up to the open window. You know, you should really close your windows, Nora. It's not safe to leave them open. Anyone could have just climbed on in."

Ron shook his head, and Nora threw the closest object within reach at Grant's head. Luckily for him, it happened to be a pillow.

"Hey, easy now," Grant yelled with a smirk on his face. "I only followed because I was worried Ron would do something dumb like try to leave on his own. You're kind of predictable."

"You haven't told him," Nora said, surprised.

"No, he started asking me questions the second I woke up. I needed to clear my head, and then I ended up here." Ron sighed. "By now, all of Greyland knows that something strange is going on, and I'm in the middle of it."

"So, what are you going to do now?" Nora asked.

"I'm going to leave within the next day or so. I don't need much for the trip, but I'm not entirely sure how to get there."

Nora and Grant looked at him. "How do you plan to get there if you don't know where it is?" Grant asked.

"I know it's somewhere to the west—but only because the rider came through the west gate."

"Well, okay then, we have a very vague plan on how to get to . . . where did you grow up? You still haven't told us.".

"It was called Regis," Ron said.

"Alright, we should be packed and ready to go by tomorrow morning," Nora said.

"Okay, I'm going to go and make sure I have everything I need."

As Ron stood up to go, Nora gave him another hug, this time a little tighter and a little longer than the last. Ron didn't mind; he always enjoyed Nora's company. Every time he was with her, he felt comfortable and safe, but Ron didn't feel entirely okay bringing his friends with him. He let go of Nora and walked out the door.

As he walked, he thought to himself, *Maybe I should tell them everything. No, I don't want them to worry or think it was my fault the lantern exploded with the blue flame. I haven't even tried to use the flame since that day.*

Stuck in these thoughts, he wandered back to his dormitory. He went through the entrance and up the stairs to his room, opening the door and locking it behind him.

Chapter Five

Through the Wild

After taking a few minutes to breathe, Ron walked to his closet, inspecting the damage Grant had inflicted upon the hinges. Even though the door was broken, Ron saw that his friend had actually retrieved his pack from the closet. He must have thrown it on the bed before following. The bag itself was a simple, brown, travel-size bag that Ron had acquired when he first came to Greyland. It was well worn at this point, with a long strap Ron could sling across his shoulder. He walked to his dresser and grabbed a couple pairs of clothes for a few days. Since he did not know where his old village was, he didn't know how long it would take to travel there.

Ron put a few white shirts, a couple pairs of pants, and a handful of socks in his bag. He grabbed one pair of the warmest socks he owned, just in case it got cold at night. Next, he piled some blankets on the bed to pack for later. Finally, Ron took to one knee and looked under his bed for a small tent he'd purchased a few years back when he would go camping with Grant. Ron also grabbed his bedroll from behind the tent. After ensuring all his clothes fit, he checked the straps securing the tent and bedroll to the pack.

He double-checked everything, making sure he was ready to leave. Then he went to the back of his closet and grabbed a sword that had been tucked away in the corner, collecting dust. He was surprised the people at the ward of healers had let him keep it. The most Ron could remember was holding onto it as tightly as he could whenever he thought someone was trying to take it from him. He just didn't remember why it was so important to him at the time. Ron pulled the sword from the sheath, looking at the blade.

It was the same blade he had used to defend himself eight years ago. It was an ordinary blade like most others, but there was an insignia with the letters "FB" engraved on the hilt. To this day, he did not understand their meaning.

Ron put the sword back in its sheath and tightened the leather baldric around his waist on the left side to get a feel of it before he took it off, leaning it against his pack. Ron sat on the edge of his bed and, with a sigh, let his body fall back. *I can't believe I'm going back. It's going to be hard enough to relive those memories, even harder to see it all again.* His body still felt heavy with aches and pains from the last two days. It would have been back to normal by now after completing the exam, but after his run-in with the guards, he knew he needed more rest. Trying to keep his mind clear, he closed his eyes and drifted into sleep.

Ron slept longer than intended and was woken up to the sound of banging on his door. "What the hell?" he said aloud, startled by the sound. "What time is it?" He stood up and moved toward the door. From the other side of the door, he heard shouting.

"Hey, open the door! We're packed and ready to go." Grant wasn't much for being subtle. Ron opened the door and rubbed his eyes.

"Did we wake you up?" Nora asked.

"You did. Sorry, I must have overslept."

The pair were standing in the hallway with their packs and weapons ready to go. Nora carried her staff, which attached to a small clasp. It had a quick release when pulled with enough force. Grant had two small blades on either side of his belt loops.

"So, are you all set, Ron?" Grant asked.

"Yes, I'm ready. Are you sure you two still want to come? Is there no way I can make you stay?" Ron asked halfheartedly. He knew they would come anyway.

"You can't get rid of us. Plus, I just spent all morning making sure I had enough food to bring for this adventure," Grant said.

"Alright." Ron swung his pack across his shoulder before he picked up his sword, fastening the baldric around his waist. Grant noticed instantly, as Ron had never owned a sword in the time he had known him.

"Wow, where did that come from?" Grant asked, moving toward Ron to get a closer look.

Nora stayed by the door—she knew the answer already. When Ron had first been brought in, Nora was still volunteering, helping her parents in the ward of healers. That was the first time she had seen Ron, covered in blood, clutching the sword to his chest. Now that she knew the whole story, she was able to piece the rest together.

"I hid this in the far back corner of my closet. I got it on the night of the attack; it belonged to one of the soldiers," Ron told Grant.

The other man eyed the silver shine on the metal sheath, moving his eyes upward. Leather lined the top opening where the hilt rested. "What does 'FB' mean? It must mean something important. Why else would someone take the time to engrave it?" Grant asked.

"I don't know—I've asked myself the same thing for eight years now, and I can't think of anything."

"Oh well, let's get going," Grant said, his interest dissipating.

All three headed down the hallway, and as they passed the kitchen, Ron took one apple for the road. He didn't see the point in passing it up since he didn't know when he would be back. When they walked out the door, Ron noticed it was mid-afternoon already. "Oh, I must have slept for a long time. I went to sleep around this time yesterday."

"You did? We thought we would have seen you around town this morning, getting some last-minute supplies. Who would have thought you'd still be sleeping?" Grant said sarcastically, and laughed.

They made their way to the western gate. The old gatekeeper said in a kind voice, "Where are you three headed off to today?"

"We're just heading out, going to see the sights. Then we might make our way toward the forest for some camping," Ron said, not wanting to give any information away about where they were really going.

"Well, be careful out there. I may only maintain the gate every other day, but I hear what goes on outside the walls. Travelers have reported hearing strange noises coming from around the forest areas and whatnot. Even the animals have made themselves scarce, I hear."

"We will take our chances," Ron said.

"Okay, but don't say I didn't warn you. It's been a long time since I've heard talk of similar noises."

Not heeding the old man's advice, Ron, Nora, and Grant passed through the gate. The gatekeeper watched the three as they left, shaking his head as he scratched his long, gray beard.

The trio headed down the only road that led west from Greyland. The dirt road was surrounded by stretches of grass all the way to the tree lines, miles off.

After walking along the path for a couple of hours, they came to a fork in the road. With no map and no posted signs to guide the way, Grant looked up at the sun, which had started its descent.

"Well, this shouldn't be too hard; the sun is setting in the west, so we should take the most northwest path on the right. If we go south, I believe the only thing we will find is water or mountains. Sound good?" Grant asked.

"Sure, sounds fine to me," Ron said.

Nora had no complaints either. As they continued to walk, Ron noticed an eerie lack of sound. There were no birds chirping, nor distant cries from animals. The surrounding area should have had some life about it. The green trees in the distance and the tall, lush grass seemed like they would be welcoming to small animals or birds. Instead, there was no humming of flies or buzzing of bees; crickets were absent as well. Even occasional families of deer bounding through the grass or trees were missing. Ron saw and heard nothing. He assumed the others were picking up on how strange and lifeless the countryside was as well.

Nora walked up beside Ron. "Do you feel like you are being watched?" she asked.

"Not watched, but I definitely feel uneasy. We may be a few hours outside of Greyland, but something doesn't feel right."

"I feel like there are eyes everywhere, just watching and waiting. What noises do you think the gatekeeper was talking about? I mean, of course, travelers hear strange things, but why did he say noises like that haven't been heard for a long time?" Nora asked.

"I'm not sure. I have no clue what he was talking about," Ron said.

"We should at least stay on guard then."

As the sun began setting, the group decided it was time to make camp. All of them were hungry, and Grant's stomach could be heard growling from ten feet away. Ron and Nora set up the tent as Grant gathered sticks and dried brush to start a fire. They placed the tent off the path, about twenty feet away into the tree line, which had grown much closer here. Ron and Nora set it up between two trees and covered the top with leaves and grass, so it would blend in during the night. Ron saw that Grant, along with starting a fire, had gathered a random assortment of logs just big enough for them to sit on comfortably. They each went into their packs and grabbed some food to eat as they sat around the fire. Ron went for the dried fruits and walnuts, while Nora ate dried, salted pork.

Grant, on the other hand, only ate a loaf of bread he'd gotten from a local baker the morning before leaving town. He claimed it to be the best bread in Greyland, but that was debatable. Grant had a palate that could be easily satisfied by most foods he encountered.

"I think we should go to sleep in shifts tonight. I still feel as though there are eyes all around us. I know it doesn't make sense, but the feeling just won't go away," Nora said, uneasy.

"Okay, Grant can take the first watch," Ron said, then smiled, as Grant had clearly been about to suggest that Ron do the same thing.

"That's fine with me, I don't mind. I like to stay up late anyway. Besides, I'll just call and wake you two up if anything happens. Ron, you have the next watch, though, so don't get too comfy in there," Grant said with a snicker. Ron understood what his friend was implying and shook his head.

Grant remained outside the tent, huddling by the fire as Ron and Nora went inside. The tent was big enough to fit four people, but squeezed tight. The bedrolls overlapped each other as Ron and Nora laid them down, placing their blankets on top.

"We should make some good headway tomorrow," Ron said, lying down next to Nora, "Hopefully, we make it to Regis sooner rather than later." Nora didn't reply. "Is everything okay?"

"All I want is for this feeling to go away. Call me paranoid, but I don't like it. So, the quicker we get there works for me. What are you going to do when we get to Regis?" Nora turned to face him.

"I think I'll visit my old home. It seems like the best place to start. I haven't been there in eight years, though. The house might not even be there anymore. Who knows how much got burned down."

"I hope you can find what you're looking for," Nora said reassuringly.

"As do I, Nora. As do I."

As the conversation went on, they both started speaking less, and eventually fell asleep.

Ron awoke from sleep suddenly when he heard the sharp snap of a twig from outside the tent. He paid little attention, assuming it was just Grant walking back and forth to stay awake. Looking over, he saw that Nora was fast asleep. He smiled to himself and thought how beautiful and peaceful she looked. Ron's head suddenly turned when he heard another twig snap. He sat up, pulled on his boots, and went outside the tent to see what was happening. It was still dark out, and the fire had turned to glowing embers as Ron looked around for Grant.

The other young man had fallen asleep on the log he had been sitting on, on the opposite side of the fire. Ron turned his head around in circles to see where the sound had come from. A bead of sweat rolled down his face. Ron was a well-rounded fighter, and skilled with a sword, but this night he was afraid. He felt it. He felt eyes watching him, eyes that he could not see. Ron turned to the left of the tent, and in the glow of the embers, Ron could see a figure standing not ten feet away from him. Ron tried to bend his knees and reach for his sword, but he was paralyzed with fear. He had never faced someone who was not an instructor or student, not since the night he was forced to fight for his life. He could not make out the entirety of the figure, but by the shape, he could tell it was a person's outline.

Ron had to think quick—he needed to move. With all the strength he could muster, he kicked at the embers. They erupted into a small flame for a brief moment. Ron was able to see that the figure was clad in black armor with dark blue borders that accentuated an insignia on the upper left of the breastplate. Ron's eyes quickly took in the image of a dark upside-down triangle with "FB" on the inside before shifting his gaze, trying to make out the figure's face, but he was unable to.

The figure wore a white mask that engulfed most of its head. Ron saw that two black lines on the left half of the mask were finger-thick. One line stretched above the eye and one line below, almost reaching the back of the mask. Feeling as though he was regaining control of his body, Ron bent down and reached for his sword inside the tent without taking his eyes off the figure. While he reached for his sword, he saw the figure raise its hand, and a blue flame started to emerge from it. The flame snuffed out what fire remained in the smoldering embers, then disappeared itself, making the campsite pitch black.

In the darkness, the figure rushed at Ron, grabbing him by his jaw and lifting him off the ground. It raised its other hand to Ron's face, shining the blue flame upon him. Ron struggled to break free, feeling the powerful grip on his jaw, but he couldn't move. The fear came back, and he froze.

"It is you. I'm surprised," said the figure. "I had my suspicions, but now I know without a doubt it's really you. You are a lot weaker than I thought you would be. With how much time has gone by, I thought you would have embraced the flame by now. Pitiful. No matter, just make sure to stay alive. We will make certain you become a wielder. It is only a matter of time."

And just like that, the figure let go of Ron and disappeared into the dark.

He fell to the ground, dropping his sword. The clang of the weapon on the ground woke up Grant.

"Who's there? What's going on?" Grant said as he slowly grabbed his daggers and stood up. "Is it time to switch already?" he added with a stretch and a yawn.

Grant saw that the fire had died, but he could still feel the radiant heat, so he put some small wood chippings and dried leaves on the embers.

With the fire restarted, Ron stood to his feet, fists clenched. "You fell asleep, Grant. You fell asleep, and I saw someone out there watching us!"

He decided not to say anything about what had happened with the figure other than that he was there. Ron didn't know if this was because he was ashamed of himself for not doing anything or because he was afraid. Either way, he was becoming more and more upset by the second.

He didn't like the idea that he'd been frozen with fear. With all his training and the time he'd spent practicing, it felt like a huge step backward to freeze.

"Are they still here?" Grant asked.

"No, they left, but something bad could have happened. We could have been killed or captured for all we know. I told you and Nora this would be dangerous. I don't know what I would do if she got hurt, let alone killed. I would lose my mind. And all because you fell asleep."

At that moment, Nora poked her head out of the tent. "What's with all the yelling?" she asked.

"It's nothing. Grant fell asleep when he was supposed to be on watch. I'll tell you the rest in the morning. I'm taking over for the rest of the night. Grant, go to sleep!" Ron said, the anger still in his voice.

Grant knew his friend was furious, and rightfully so. "I'm sorry, Ron, I didn't mean to."

"Just do better next time," Ron said, staring into the fire.

The other man went into the tent, and Nora went back to sleep. It didn't take long before Ron heard Grant snoring. It seemed to him that his friend did not take falling asleep too seriously. Ron knew if he told Grant and Nora what had really happened, they would understand the gravity of it. A couple hours went by as he sat outside the tent, watching and waiting.

Finally, he saw that dawn was coming as the stars faded in the light of the rising sun. Ron sat there, thinking of anything he might have seen or heard that could connect to what the man in the mask was talking about. *What's a wielder? Embrace the flame. How do I do that? Who was that?*

Ron could not come up with any answers, but the more he thought, the more he couldn't shake the memory of when he froze. His anger grew. *I'm not weak, but I couldn't do anything. What was everything for if I can't defend myself?* Ron clenched his fists. *Never again. I can't be weak. Not now.* Ron looked up and saw the sun peeking over the horizon. It was time to wake up his friends.

Before he went to the tent, he grabbed Grant's pack from by the fire and rummaged through it, looking for food he could make for breakfast. Ron found a small pot and some dried oats; he threw twigs on the burning embers and started the flames, then poured some water into the pot and began to boil the oats.

Once breakfast was ready, he woke the others. Ron grabbed a couple small bowls from the pack, and everyone ate a quick breakfast.

"What happened last night, Ron?" Nora asked.

He told them about the figure watching them and how the person could create a blue flame in his hand out of nothing. "You were right, Nora—we were being watched. Whoever this person is, they were wearing the armor of the people that attacked my home, but this one had a mask as well. It doesn't make sense. I don't know what they want. First the rider, and now this guy." Ron rubbed his face and sighed.

"There might be answers at Regis. We just have to get there," Nora said.

"That's right," Grant added, "and this time I won't fall asleep on watch. Last night really got me thinking. I could have been killed without anyone even knowing about it. That's a scary thought. But I promise I won't make the same mistake twice."

"Good, it should scare you." Ron was still angry at his friend, but he knew no good would come of staying mad.

As they cleaned their bowls, they put out the fire and packed their belongings, making sure to cover their tracks as they left.

They continued on the path for a few more hours. Finally, it stopped traveling straight and started curving, going up and down with a slight incline in the rising hills. The fog was still trapped in the low valleys they came across, but it was nothing they couldn't see through. While walking on the path, Grant spotted something in the middle of the road. It was brown, and no bigger than a fawn. From a distance, it looked like a deer. As they got closer, they could see the white spots on its fur, and its white tail. It was the first deer in almost two days. The animal was not moving, just lying on the ground, barely alive when they approached it. It looked as though the creature had bite marks on its neck and hind legs.

"This poor thing, it looks like it's in so much pain. I . . . I don't think we can help. It's lost a lot of blood," Nora said, pointing to a trail of red left behind by the deer.

"We should put it out of its misery," Ron suggested.

"That would be the kind thing to do," Grant agreed.

Ron pulled out a knife from his pack and prepared to stab the deer in the heart. The animal looked at him with eyes that longed for the release of death. Ron lifted his hands, holding the knife, staring back at the deer with a look of understanding as to what he was about to do, but before he could plunge it into the deer, he heard a deep growl. Two wolves jumped out onto the path in front of them.

Ron, Nora, and Grant leaped back, caught by surprise. The wolves looked each of them in the eyes, then jumped on the deer, tearing it apart. The helpless, wounded animal cried in agony until one of the wolves bit down on the deer's throat. Now covered in blood, the wolves turned their gaze back toward the trio.

Ron noticed there was something different about these wolves. They did not seem interested in the deer as food as they circled around it toward the group. Instead, they'd wounded it, letting it suffer, then brutally killed it as if for sport. Wolves didn't intentionally cause suffering, but these ones looked rabid, blood dripping from their gray muzzles, matting their fur, their stained fangs exposed. Their eyes were piercing, with a hint of orange behind them as if they had found their next victims. With a lunge, one wolf sprang toward Nora. She side-stepped, and with her staff delivered a swift blow to the animal's head.

The wolf only stumbled, as if dazed by the loud crack that should have put down an even larger animal. Then the other wolf began to run at Ron. He drew his sword but was not fast enough as it jumped right on top of him, forcing him to the ground. Ron was able to get his blade up in time to prevent it from biting his face. Holding his sword sideways, he kept the handle in his right hand and the flat side of the blade resting against his left. The wolf was unfazed by the sword and kept trying to bite at Ron. It bit down on the blade, cutting its own mouth to mangled shreds but never stopping the attack.

Nora kept her eyes on the staggering wolf, the one that she'd hit. It swiftly turned toward her and Grant and began its second assault. This time, Grant was ready. As the wolf moved closer, Nora used the staff to sweep at its legs. The wolf jumped in the air to avoid the staff, only to meet Grant's daggers. The young man stabbed the wolf in the chest; then, turning quickly, he used the giant creature's momentum from its jump to slam its body to the ground. The wolf tried to get up and attack again, but as blood dripped from the open wounds in its chest, Grant came down with a heavy stroke and cut open its throat, deep enough to expose the spinal cord as blood rushed forth. Nora and Grant started to run over to Ron, who was still fending off the attacks of the other wolf. Before they could reach him, an arrow flew into the animal, piercing its left eye, sinking halfway into the skull to the middle of the shaft. The wolf dropped right on top of Ron, dead.

Ron used almost all his strength to push the heavy body off of him. He was covered in its blood when he stood up. As he looked at the wolf's body, he asked, "Where did that arrow come from?" The others didn't reply, but they maintained their guard. Finally, after a minute of them looking around, an old man came out from the tree line. He carried a long, wooden, hand-crafted bow and had a quiver of arrows slung over the right shoulder of his forest-green cloak. "Who are you? What do you want?" Ron shouted as they raising their weapons, preparing to fight.

"I want you to stay alive, boy," the old man said as he continued to walk toward them.

"Wait, I know you. You're the gatekeeper, aren't you?" Nora said.

The old man's features became more prominent the closer he got. "Yes, I may be an old gatekeeper, but at least I can take on a couple of wolves. Even though these ones are a little different."

"Different? How do you mean?" Ron questioned.

"These wolves," said the old man as he bent down and grasped one dead face, looking into its dilated eyes, "they are unlike the others. Normally, wolves are not this aggressive. They take their kill—they don't let them suffer in torment. But, if I'm not mistaken, this also looked like a trap. Regular wolves are not smart enough to lay bait. These ones may have come from the forge, but that hasn't happened for centuries." The old man said the last bit in a hushed whisper, letting go of the wolf's head to rub his chin.

"Hold on, what the hell is the forge?" Ron asked.

As the man was about to say more, loud howls rang out in the air from the trees. Everyone knew what a wolf's howl sounded like, but these echoed differently.

"We have no time. I will tell you more later; we have to go," the old man said.

"How can we trust you?" Ron asked.

"You can trust me now and not fight an entire wolf pack, or you can stay here. The choice is yours."

Ron looked at Nora and Grant. They silently agreed, and all began trailing behind the gatekeeper. Without looking back, they ran, cutting through the trees, uphill and downhill across varied slopes within the forest for what seemed like most of the afternoon. Then the old man stopped abruptly in the middle of the path. The howls tapered off in the distance. He looked around as if searching for something, then raised his hand and pointed into the tree line to the left of the path. He started walking deeper into the trees as the trio followed.

Ron grew worried as they got farther from the path. He knew they were traveling west, but in the forest, he couldn't get his bearings. Finally, Ron noticed a slight shift in the ground. It felt like he was going downhill, and he knew at that point he was traveling southwest. It seemed to get dark much faster than Ron expected; with more than a few hours left before sundown, the light stopped coming through the trees. He hadn't been paying attention, so he wasn't able to tell when exactly the light started to fade away. All he knew was that the farther they went, the darker it became. Finally, the old man stopped.

"We are here."

Ron looked around to see what he was talking about. "What do you mean? There's nothing but more forest."

Nora tapped Ron on the shoulder. "Look up into the trees."

Ron and Grant looked up, staring into the dark canopy. First, they heard the slight rustling of leaves, and then they saw it. Thick ropes descended down, six in total—four empty ropes, and the last two with men on them.

The men were holding on to the ropes with one hand, one foot stuck in a loop at the bottom of each rope. They were clad in dark green armor. Ron noticed it was the same shade as the gatekeeper's cloak. The old man took a step toward the new arrivals, extending a hand.

"It's good to see you, Solis—and you, Versal. I brought Ron here. I know it wasn't planned, but we need a place to hide out for a bit. I can think of no safer place than this. I will tell you the rest later."

Solis and Versal looked at each other. "You brought Ron. How long has it been? Seven, eight years?" Solis remarked.

"Well, then bring him and his friends up. Arnet will have much to discuss," said Versal. The pair looked at Ron with worry as he was still covered in blood.

"Don't worry, it's not my blood," Ron said, trying to wave off their concern. They both shrugged.

"Grab a rope, you three, and hold on tight," the old man said. They put their feet through the loops and grabbed the ropes.

"Here we go," Solis said as he gave his rope two sharp tugs.

Then they rose up into the canopy. It looked as though they were going to hit the tree branches on the way up, but as they rose, their ascending path was clear. The canopy had been structured over the years to impede someone's natural line of sight, keeping it concealed. The branches overlapped each other, intertwining and creating a complex maze. The trees grew tall and thick so that even on the brightest day, the sun's rays could not break through the top of the canopy to shine light on the bottom.

The higher they went, the more they saw. The ground disappeared as the branches got thicker from below. They saw homes built around the trees and across the thick branches. Rope bridges spanned the gaps between the trees; the houses were formed around the trees in a circle formation with a rigid base built on top of the thick branches, penetrating deep into the massive trunks.

There must have been over a dozen houses that Ron could see. He looked up to see that the ropes they were holding were being operated by a pulley system attached to a hand-cranked wheel that required two men to operate.

They arrived at a wooden platform and stopped. The gatekeeper got off first, followed by Nora, Ron, and Grant. "Go tell Arnet we are here," the old man said to Solis and Versal. Then he motioned to Ron, Nora, and Grant to follow him, and they moved along the wooden platform to a connecting bridge.

"Is this safe?" Grant asked. "I've never seen anything like this in trees before."

"Yes, it's quite safe. My home is just across the bridge." They crossed the bridge, and while walking across, Ron was amazed at how he could not see the ground.

"How is this possible?" he asked.

"I'll answer all your questions soon. Let's get inside first."

Ron couldn't believe what he saw. The craftsmanship alone was impressive. After each step he took, he was able to feel how solid the platform was. Not even the wood-laid floors in Greyland had such strength and stability. The bridge itself had little to no sway or bounce despite four people walking across.

The old man's home was visible from the bridge, and bigger than Ron had initially thought, but at this point, he decided it would be foolish to assume anything. He could see that it was connected by three trees. Each round portion of the house had a walkway connecting it to the others. Thick wooden beams sank into the trunk, wrapping around, providing full support to each section of the house. To compensate for the extra weight of the walkways, beams were constructed in cross-sections to share the load, distributing weight to either side. The old man opened the round door of his home, inviting them all inside.

Chapter Six

The Gatekeeper

The gatekeeper shut the door behind him as they entered his home. He took off his cloak and set it on the back of a chair next to a small brick fireplace. The first circular portion of the home was small but accommodating, seemingly intended as a space to entertain a few guests while enjoying the comforting warmth provided by the fire. A small table rested a few feet away from the fireplace with four chairs around it.

"First things first, please have a seat, make yourselves comfortable. It has been a long day, and I'm sure you all would like to sit and rest for a little while. Also, I believe some introductions are in order. My name is Shaw, and as you can see, I was charged with maintaining the west gate of Greyland. Now, before we go any further, Ron, go get cleaned up and put on some clean clothes. I don't think you want to be covered in blood all night. You can wash up and change in that room over there. There should be plenty of stored water, but it will be cold." Shaw pointed to a door across the room.

Ron nodded, grabbed his pack, and went to the other room.

Nora looked at the man. "How did you find us?" she asked.

"Well, you three were not the hardest to keep track of. Throughout my years, I have acquired many skills, and tracking is certainly one of them. The only time you covered your tracks was when you camped the first night. After I found what you tried to cover, it was simply a matter of time before I found the rest of the tracks."

Ron came back from changing his clothes, His face was freshly rinsed, and his hair looked messy as he'd used a hand towel to dry himself.

"You followed us from the gate. You made sure to stay far enough away but close enough to pick up our trail, didn't you?" Ron asked, continuing to rub the small hand towel over his hair.

"I did, yes. I've been watching over you for years now. As hard as it has been to stay distant, I wanted you to grow and not have to deal with any other burdens relating to what we have been through. I have no secrets to keep from any of you."

Ron looked surprised; he never would have thought the gatekeeper had paid any attention to what he did throughout the years. "You may not remember much of who I am," the man continued, "but I knew your mother, Evelyn, quite well. She was a lovely woman. She loved you and your brother very much. Then that dreadful night happened. William kept to himself, so I never got to know him like I should have. He was a kind man, but reserved."

Ron's look of surprise turned to a look of grief.

"I see you remember that night as well. It would be hard to forget. Do you recall being dragged away after getting injured?" Shaw asked.

"Of course I do, but some things are kind of hazy after that," Ron said.

Shaw looked at him as if he knew Ron was holding back. "Well, in any case, when you were unable to walk, I was one of the people that protected the ones who dragged you to safety. The people within these trees are what's left of Regis. There are not many of us here, but the handful that are made quite a new life for ourselves. Believe me, it was not easy getting this place up and running.

"It took time, almost two years, to get the first full homes established. We did lose some people along the way, but we are here now. After we got you to safety, there was little else we could do. At the time, we did not have the medicine or capabilities to heal your wounds. Our healers were some of the first to be killed that night."

"Sorry, I don't mean to interrupt, but why were you watching Ron all these years without saying anything?" Nora interrupted.

Shaw looked at her. "You see, there is a burden Ron must carry, and I figured the longer he didn't know about it, the better off he would be. He would have a normal life in Greyland, grow up, and mold himself into the person he wanted to be without the weight of such a burden. But once I heard about the rider, I knew something was not right. I know you all saw it. Ron, you must have told these two about that night."

"I did," Ron said, keeping his gaze away from Nora and Grant, hoping Shaw wouldn't reveal any more.

"So you told them?" The man made it sound as if what he said was a question, and given Ron's hesitant demeanor, he knew he was right to keep pushing. "You haven't told them everything, have you? Did you tell them about the blue flame?"

"Ron, what is he talking about? You said you didn't know anything about the lantern exploding or the blue fire inside it," Grant said.

"That's because I don't. I mean, not really," Ron said as quickly as he could.

"Ron, I think it's time you tell them all of what happened that night," the gatekeeper said.

Ron recounted the events of that night. First, he told them of how he was shot with arrows and how his brother was lying on the ground while being pulled to safety. Then Ron had to watch Nathill get stabbed by a soldier in black and dark blue armor. Finally, Ron described how when he saw his brother get stabbed and dragged away, he reached out for Nathill, and a blue flame surrounded both their hands.

Nora and Grant looked surprised.

"How could you not tell us that, after what happened with the rider? Don't you think it would have been helpful? Why would you keep it from us?" she asked.

"I didn't want to scare you or have you think it was my fault just because I am connected to it somehow. I didn't want you to think I played a part in getting that rider killed. I don't even understand how I had the flame in my hand in the first place. Telling you would just lead to more questions that I don't have the answers to," Ron replied.

"Are you going to tell them about what happened last night?" Shaw asked.

"There's more? What else happened?"

Before Ron answered Nora, he looked at Shaw. "Wait, you saw what happened? Why didn't you do anything?" He was starting to get angry, wondering how Shaw could watch what happened and choose to do nothing.

"If I had chosen to act right at that moment, it's possible that night could have turned out very differently. Sometimes the best option is to do nothing, and for that night, it was the right choice."

Ron didn't like the man's reasoning, but he understood. Turning his attention back to Nora, he went into detail about the man with the mask and the two black lines above and below the left eye and how he used the flame. "That's why I was so angry at you, Grant. That man was watching us for . . . I don't know how long. Then he was able to lift me up by my face with one hand. He talked about being a wielder or something and embracing the flame. We all could have died. I may have been a little rough, and I'm sorry. I was also mad at myself, and I took it out on you."

"It's okay. I made a mistake that could have cost us all our lives, and we'd just barely left Greyland," Grant said, understanding what his actions could have resulted in.

"Do you know who it was?" Nora asked, breaking the silence.

"No, I don't have the slightest idea. I've only seen the flame used by myself and my brother that night, and he's dead." Ron looked back to Shaw. "Do you know who that man was?"

"No, I don't," said the gatekeeper, "but I can help you find the answers. Based on what I was told, the rider gave you a message. So I'm assuming since you left Greyland in the direction you did, you're going back to Regis. I know the way back, and I will take you there. We will have to travel fast, though. If these wolves were any indication of what's out there, then I feel there are worse creatures."

"You said you hadn't seen these animals or heard reports of creatures in a long time when we were leaving the gate at Greyland. Has this happened before?" Nora asked, wondering what else could be out there.

"It has happened multiple times within the last millennia if the stories are true. When the first War of the Wielders started, these creatures emerged. Some said they came from the forge, but no one has ever been able to prove that. The only evidence is the unnaturalness of the creatures. That was almost seven hundred years ago. The last time they roamed around was when the sky broke open at the Battle of the Storming Mountains. After the battle had ended, an army was dispatched to find and finish off the last of the creatures. Only a few soldiers came back, but they left shortly afterward. No one has seen or heard of them since. Everyone just assumes they left to find peace due to what they witnessed, or they ended up dying of old age. Some believe they looked into the forge and saw the horrors within; others say the army saw the Essenti trying to escape. No one can know for sure," Shaw explained.

"You mentioned that earlier. What is the Essenti?" Ron asked.

"It is neither man nor beast. It is eternal. Something that has been on this earth for far longer than any person. You could refer to it as the essence of life or the essence of creation, as others have. It's mostly folk stories, stories parents tell their children when they misbehave, and songs that, while still sung, are no more than fairytales. No one believes anymore.

"Some books can still be found throughout the kingdoms that attempt to detail what happened initially. While words have been changed or lost during the translation process, from what I've read, most accounts are similar. It was said that there were five Eternals birthed among the stars. Somehow, they journeyed to this world through the forge, creating it however they deemed fit. After a time, when people began to populate, the Eternals left, leaving behind all they created to the new inhabitants. All but one.

"One remained. For one reason or another, it was fascinated by people, always watching but never interfering with the rise and fall of man. For ages, it watched, until one day it wanted more. The books described the Essenti as a living fire with no physical or tangible form, but other books detail it as a person on fire.

"Like I said, these books can have different meanings. Anyway, the people of that time worshipped the essence or living fire as a god, giving it the name Essenti. The only problem was that when the Essenti spoke, there was no way to understand it. Many attempts were made to communicate, to little avail. When it seemed as though the possibility to talk to their god would never come, someone found a way. The Essenti was among its followers when it came across a child drawing pictures in the dirt. The Essenti saw the images of men fighting each other. Thus it was made known that the Essenti wanted the people to fight and find a champion among them.

"The Essenti's need for a champion reached people far and wide, culminating in hundreds of thousands seeking the opportunity to be champion. Finally, one emerged to stand next to the Essenti. It was then that the first awakening was performed. The Essenti gifted the power of the flame to the champion, rivaling its own power, and with that power it instilled the language of the Essenti. People learned the language, and throughout the years, the Essenti performed the awakening to all loyal followers, imbuing them with the gift of the flame. The Essenti, in turn, asked for nothing more than for the people to worship it.

"In time, the people had begun naming themselves wielders and testing the limits of their gifted power. As a result, they stopped worshipping the Essenti altogether, choosing to instead give their devotion to the champion, whom they now proclaimed as the champion of the wielders. Finally, angered by the selfishness and betrayal of the people, the Essenti tried to rise up and destroy every last person that no longer remained devoted. That was when its chosen champion defied it for the first time, for he was the people's champion, the champion of the wielders.

"The Essenti and its champion battled, using a power that destroyed the surrounding areas. Their clash blew craters deep into the ground, shattered mountains, and decimated cities. Finally, with their power evenly matched, their battle became a standstill. That is, until the other wielders joined their champion. They overpowered the Essenti and its followers, banishing it and its people back to the forge. Many years later, it was discovered that people were born with the flame's power after the awakening. Its power passed along through the generations. That is, until the War of the Wielders happened."

Shaw told these stories as if looking back on past events, spinning a bracelet on his left wrist all the while. Before the man could continue, there was a knock on the door. "Ah, they're here," he said, getting up from his chair and walking to the door. He opened it to see Solis, Versal, and Arnet.

Arnet walked through the door first, and Shaw greeted him with a handshake. Arnet was a tall man, well kept, and carried himself with a sense of purpose. He had long, brown hair and a clean, shaved face. However, his youthfulness did little to dissuade others from following his lead. The other two followed.

"Let's move into the next room—there is much more space there for everyone," Shaw said. Ron, Nora and Grant got up and followed him through a side door, passing through an archway connecting the larger of the three houses by a wood-covered platform. The room had an arrangement of pillows laid out on the floor, forming a circle as if a meeting had taken place or was about to happen. Ron sat next to Grant and Nora while Shaw sat next to the three newcomers.

"It's good to see you, Ron. Welcome to the Canopy, our humble village here within the trees," Arnet said with a friendly smile. "It has been a while—I don't think you remember me. We didn't spend much time together, but I saw you walk around the village a lot. My name is Arnet. I was the blacksmith's son."

Ron, Nora, and Grant were taken aback by this. Ron started to say something, but Shaw interrupted.

"Arnet, there is something you should know before we begin. It partially pertains to the reason we're here," the gatekeeper said with a heavy tone. Then he told Arnet of the rider who'd showed up at the west gate of Greyland. "Arnet, your father was alive. He was wearing a cloak in the same fashion as those soldiers that came to Regis eight years ago. My guess is that they took your father captive. When he arrived at Greyland, he gave Ron a message—that's why we have come this way."

Arnet's brow deepened at the news of his father. "You said *was* alive. Is he not anymore?" he asked solemnly.

"No, he's not," Ron said, jumping into the conversation. "He was killed when a lantern carrying a blue flame exploded."

Arnet looked angry and sad at the same time, but an odd calm fell over him. "I thought my father had been dead since the attack. From what I saw, those soldiers did not take prisoners. I guess I was wrong. As much as it pains me to know he was alive all this time and possibly suffered a fate worse than death for so many years, he is gone now to what I believe is a better place. Hopefully, wherever he is, he can finally have the peace he deserves."

Arnet let out a sigh and took in a deep breath. "Nothing has changed. Please do not mistake my demeanor as crude. I loved my father, and I will remember him until it is our time to meet again. Thank you for telling me about him." He looked around the group, a small smile of relief coming across his face.

"Ron," Arnet continued, as the news of his father did not deter him from his train of thought, "do you remember that night?"

"I remember most of it, but I don't know what happened after I passed out. I remember waking up in Greyland in the ward of the healers," Ron said.

Arnet scratched his chin, contemplating. "When I said the men who attacked didn't take prisoners, I must not have seen it happen. But, on the other hand, if they did, then that makes more sense."

Ron looked at Arnet. "What makes more sense?"

"I saw them take your brother's body. I don't know why, but it may have something to do with that flame you both could conjure."

Ron looked confused. "Why would they have killed him then? How would they have even known to come to our village? That was the first time I had ever seen an army that size. It doesn't make sense."

"That's exactly why we are going there," Nora said. "I don't know what we will find, but there might be something there, something left behind. Thankfully, Shaw brought us here after we were attacked."

Arnet nodded, agreeing with her; it was worth checking out even if it was a fool's errand.

"I see," he said. "Now, tell me about these wolves that attacked you. What happened?" He turned his attention to Nora as she told him about the wolves, the trap they set, their eyes, and the strangeness of the howls.

"That is odd," he said when she finished, and tapped his fingers on his knee. "Even up here, we have heard a difference. That explains the wolves, but not the other sounds."

"There is one more thing," Ron said. "Besides the wolves on our way here, I encountered a person in black-and-blue armor with a white mask. They were able to summon the flame. Have you seen or heard of anyone around here like that?"

Arnet squinted his eyes and looked at Solis and Versal. "No, we haven't, but that is very concerning news. We hadn't heard of anything involving the flame since that night eight years ago. Solis, Versal, go tell the guards they need to pull extra duty. And from now on, once the sun goes down, there are to be no lights." The two stood up and walked out in a hurry. Arnet stood as well. "It's getting late. We can talk more in the morning, but for now, I'll take my leave so you can get some rest. I'm sure Shaw will let you stay here, and he will entertain you with a story or two. Whenever you decide to head out, we will give you some supplies."

"Thank you," Grant said. "I don't suppose any of you would like to come with us?"

"No. Since the day of the attack, we have vowed never to go back there. We are safe here, and we want it to stay that way. Also, I don't think a lot of us could face going back. It would be too much," Arnet admitted.

"We thank you for your hospitality," Nora said.

"You are most welcome. Now get some rest." He walked toward the door. Shaw got up as well to see him out. Ron could hear the two having a low conversation but could not make out the words. Soon, Shaw closed the door after Arnet and turned back toward them.

"I have no further information for you tonight. I think we covered a good portion of what needs to be discussed. I do, however, have a map I could give you. In the event we somehow manage to get separated, you will be able to find your way. I will show you where we are on the map, but do not mark our location," he said with caution in his voice.

"We won't. You have my word," Ron said.

"I will go fetch some pillows and blankets for you three. I'll be back in a minute." Shaw turned to walk into the other room.

Ron looked at Nora and Grant. "Are you sure you still want to come? Arnet seemed worried once I mentioned the person in the mask." He wondered if either of them had changed their mind.

"Of course we're still coming," Grant said. "Why would we come this far and turn around now?"

"We can't leave you now. We need to see this through." Nora added, putting her hand on top of Ron's.

Ron looked at her hand on his, and he got that feeling of warmth and comfort again. He smiled at her, then turned to Grant. "Thank you."

Shaw returned with blankets and pillows and laid them on the ground. "Now, I know it's not what you are used to, but the floor is better than nothing."

"We appreciate it," Ron said, taking a pillow.

Nora and Grant lay down, and Ron decided to lie next to Nora. He still had that feeling, and as Shaw went to his room, he capped all the candles before opening the door leading to the last and smallest connected home. Ron felt safe and comfortable next Nora, and with that sensation, he fell asleep.

Chapter Seven

To Regis

R on woke up feeling well-rested from the night's sleep. He lay on the ground, enjoying the pillow's comfort as it cradled his head, the warmth of the blanket he slept under, and the quiet of a morning that was just beginning. He went to stretch but felt pressure on his right arm.

Opening his eyes, he noticed that Nora had rolled onto his arm during the night. Ron didn't mind; it made him happy to see that she'd slept peacefully through the night as well. Ron continued to look at her dark brown hair, watching the light from the sun brighten her soft skin—until he saw Grant out of the corner of his eye. His friend was staring at him from a chair resting alongside the closest wall, his hand under his chin and a giant grin on his face.

"What in the world are you doing, Grant?" Ron asked in a hushed whisper.

"Nothing. I was up early. I think I slept on my back wrong, so I couldn't lie down anymore. Both of you looked so comfortable, so I didn't wake you. I was just watching you two lovebirds until you woke up. I saw the way you were looking at her. Why don't you just tell her?"

"Shut up. She could wake up and hear you. I'll tell her when the time is right. I don't want to tell her now and find out she doesn't feel the same. That would just make things really awkward. With everything going on and what we have to do, it just seems like a lot right now. It's not the right time," Ron said, stressing the point.

Grant still had the grin on his face. "To me, it sounds like it's never the right time. You've been saying it's not the right time for years now, and I have a strong feeling that she cares for you, Ron. Maybe it's not about the timing. Have you ever considered that maybe you should make it the right time instead of waiting?" Grant asked as Nora rolled over, beginning to wake up.

"Oh, good morning, boys," she said. Then, noticing she'd trapped Ron's arm, she added, "Sorry, I hope I didn't put your arm to sleep." She sat up, let out a yawn, and raised her arms high for a stretch.

"It's okay, I don't mind," Ron said as Nora let out a smile.

"See, I told you," Grant said pointedly.

"Told you what?" Nora asked.

"Nothing," Ron quickly replied. "He was just wondering if my arm was asleep right before you woke up." He paused, thinking about Grant's words. "You know, I think you're right."

Grant laughed. He'd seen Nora's smile.

Shaw walked into the room wearing a lighter shade of the forest-green cloak, with similar-colored pants and a brown shirt. "Good morning everyone, I trust you all slept well. So, what is the plan for today?"

Ron rubbed the sleep from his eyes. "Is there anywhere that has supplies?"

"Of course, it's right across the way. I was going to stop by before we left anyway."

"Alright. Oh, I also wanted to thank you for the other day. That shot you made with your bow—it was impressive," Ron said.

"Well, I have been using a bow since I was a boy." The gatekeeper shrugged. "My father taught me at a young age, even if his teaching methods were a little unconventional. He would take me hunting, and to help me get better, he told me that if I wanted to eat dinner, I would have to catch it myself. So there were more than a few nights we didn't eat. He and my mother shared in the success or failure of each hunt, prompting me to get better. Speaking of food, how about I make a quick breakfast while you all gather your things?"

"Sounds good to me," Nora said, ready to have something in her stomach.

Ron and the others all put on some fresh clothes and got their packs situated with their gear. Shaw made them a breakfast that seemed like a feast compared to what they'd had to eat for the last couple of days.

Once they were done eating and cleaning up, they walked out into the new morning sunlight. During the night, when they'd arrived at the Canopy, the homes and walkways had looked dark, the few candles allowing them just enough light to follow Shaw. During the day, the Canopy seemed utterly different. Ron now understood why it had seemed so dim before, beyond just the sun being down. The homes had been painted dark brown and green, blending into the surrounding trees they inhabited, making it more difficult to spot from the ground. The walkways and bridges held the natural color of the wood used in their creation.

Shaw led the way, taking them to another hut a couple of bridges over. It looked the same as most others, with a dark brown exterior, built around a tree in a circle. How did anyone keep track of where their homes were?

As they came to the entrance, Ron noticed a sign above the door. It read "General Shop." Shaw opened the door, and they all walked in. The shop had a wide assortment of odds and ends, ranging from nuts and dried berries to healing oils and common home cleaning supplies. Nora walked over to the oils to see what she could find, as she was the only one of the trio that knew a thing or two about how to use medical supplies. Grant made a dash to see what other food the shop had to offer so he could restock his bag.

Ron and Shaw went up to the shopkeeper, and she introduced herself.

"Hello Shaw—and oh, you must be Ron. I'm Loa. I heard from Arnet earlier this morning that you will be heading back to Regis. Well, whatever you need, feel free to take it. Arnet has already covered the expenses. It won't be easy going back after all these years, after what happened, so I'm happy to help any way I can."

"Wow, I wasn't expecting that. I'll have to thank Arnet when I see him," Ron said, his shock evident in his voice.

Nora and Grant came up to the counter with their arms full. Nora was holding a collection of colored oils, three green and three brown. The green oils were for helping to heal common wounds, from minor cuts to lacerations. The brown oils helped with sickness by reducing fevers, chills, and aches. Nora wanted to be prepared for the rest of the way to Regis since they'd already been attacked once. Grant, on the other hand, had his arms full of food. He'd managed to find packs of dried meats, jams made from an assortment of berries, and dried bread to accompany them.

Ron looked at Loa. "I am very grateful for the help, but please allow me to pay for something. I don't know how much Arnet covered, but it wouldn't feel right if I didn't pay for anything." He reached with his hand into the pouch he kept strapped to his thigh and pulled out a handful of silver coins he'd taken from his room in Greyland. "I think there are about fifteen coins here. They are all yours," he said.

"Thank you. Although that's unnecessary, I appreciate it. Good luck out there, and do be careful. So much was lost in Regis. I just hope that forsaken village doesn't claim anything else," Loa said, shaking off the memories.

Ron could hear the pain in her voice; he shared it as well. He chose not to say anything, but gave her an empathetic smile. As he turned away, Nora and Grant started to put their items in their packs. Ron looked around the shop for other things they might need but didn't see anything he thought would be helpful.

When they headed outside, Arnet was walking across the bridge in their direction.

"Ah, are you ready to make your way to Regis?" he asked.

"We are," Ron said.

"In that case here, I have one for each of you." Arnet reached out his hand, giving Ron three dark green cloaks matching the one Shaw had worn the night before. "It will help you blend in when you're going through a tree-laden area or tall grass." He looked at the gatekeeper and raised an eyebrow. "Are you going with them as well?"

"I've watched over Ron this long. I might as well see it through. Also, I need to make sure these three don't do anything foolish." Shaw gave a small laugh as the last few words came out.

"I wish you safety in your travels, and I hope you find what you are looking for," Arnet said as he went to shake everyone's hands. "Oh, and I almost forgot, if you ever find your way back here, you are more than welcome to stay." Arnet dug in his pocket, searching for something, then pulled his hand out to reveal a silver whistle. "This will help you if you decide to come back. This whistle mimics the call of the wren. It's a small bird, but loud. Blow the whistle three times and wait. After you hear three calls in return, continue to use it until you find the origin of the call. We have multiple guarded areas that are listening and standing by to lower the ropes for our people."

Ron and Grant both reached for the whistle, but Arnet saw that Nora patiently waited. He retracted his fingers, pulling it away from the two young men, then handed the whistle to Nora. "I hope to see you all again. Be safe."

"We will, thank you," Nora said as she reached around to the side of her pack, tucking the whistle away.

Shaw led Ron and the others across a couple more bridges back to the hand cranks, pullies, and ropes where they'd first arrived. Everyone put a foot into the loops of the ropes, and the guards operated the pulley system, lowering them down. The Canopy faded, and they were thrust back into the dark of the forest, with only traces of usable light.

The second they touched the ground, Shaw got into a low, squatting stance. Ron, Nora, and Grant followed suit. "We need to be careful now. There are more than wolves as we go deeper into the forest. Who knows what has come through the forge, and I hope we don't find it. Have your weapons at the ready." He told everyone to keep their head on a swivel and look for anything out of the ordinary. Even the smallest detail could be vital. "I know this forest well, but since things are not like they used to be, we must move with haste."

"Sounds like a plan," Ron said.

He unsheathed his sword while Grant pulled out his daggers. Nora took out her staff from behind her back where it was latched and used it as a walking stick. Ron and Shaw started walking in the front, with Nora and Grant pulling up the rear. "How long do you think it will take for us to get to Regis from here?" Ron asked, still not sure of the distance.

"If we don't have any issues, then it should only take a day, maybe a day and a half at most if we keep a steady pace," Shaw said.

The tree line became thicker and more filled in; they could no longer see farther than ten trees or so. The sunlight was broken and fragmented, with pieces finding their way in through the top of the canopy. The path that Shaw led them on was starting to thin. They had to start walking single file. Not a sound could be heard from animals that usually scurried up trees or rustled in bushes. The path was thin, resembling an old deer trail, but no deer had been spotted for days, not since the encounter with the wolves.

Shaw navigated the unused trail for hours, and the others followed, pushing tree branches aside and clearing the broken cobwebs that drifted through the air onto their faces after the old man initially broke them. The grass on the surrounding ground started to give way to hard, compact dirt. With no grass to cover them, the roots from the trees protruded from the ground.

Ron noticed how everything was becoming more lifeless as they went farther into the forest. Something about this area was not right. He could see that the others had sensed it as well. Nora, Grant, and Shaw had their weapons ready, walking cautiously, scanning the area. It was hard to determine what time of day it was; they had been walking through the dark since the morning. The only indication of time was when Ron caught a small glimpse of the orange sun, ready to set. Small, varied rays of light penetrated through the canopy as the party walked between the increasingly barren trees.

Shaw suddenly stopped and turned around. "I think we should make camp. We have walked long enough. We should get some rest, and by high noon tomorrow, we should reach Regis once we get out of these accursed trees."

Nora and Grant pulled out the tent and the bedrolls, and started to set up camp while Ron and Shaw pulled guard duty.

"Why does the forest feel so empty?" Ron asked.

"I'm not sure. It could be from years ago after the attack. Those soldiers continued to pursue us while we tried to make our escape. We didn't look back once we started running, but we heard the sounds of fire and screaming. They tried to burn us out, but they only got this far before ending their search.

As you can see, there are scorch marks on multiple trees, and the dirt is . . . well the ground itself is useless, and by the looks of it, most areas are." Shaw breathed a heavy sigh. "After all these years, I thought—I hoped that some of the damage done that night would have been fixed, but I was wrong. Everything they touched died."

Ron sat quietly, trying to remember that night in its entirety, but nothing came to him from after his hand had emitted that flame. Ron hoped that tomorrow he would find answers, answers to what happened or why. He just wanted to understand. He reasoned that whoever had given the message to the rider thought it was time for him to know the truth. He couldn't see any other logic behind it.

Ron wanted to know; he had asked himself why it happened, time and time again. He was ready for the answers, or at least he thought he was. Then another thought came into his mind. Who would have given the rider the message in the first place, and why they would have waited eight years to do so?

Nora came up to Ron as he was lost in thought. She grabbed his arm, startling him. He stood up, and she pulled him aside. "I need to talk to you." They walked a little ways away from the camp, just far enough to have privacy.

"Okay, is everything alright?" Ron was concerned, as Nora sounded worried.

"Yes, the camp is set, and we are okay, but that feeling is back. It's the same one that I felt a couple nights ago. I feel like there's something out there watching us. I don't see how, though. There's no place to hide. Everything is so bare and empty."

"Are you talking about the night the person in the mask came to the camp?" Ron asked.

"Yes, exactly. It's the same feeling."

"Okay, I'll tell Shaw, and we will stay on guard all night."

"Are you sure?" asked Nora. "We can take turns; I'll be able to keep Grant awake. You need to rest. I just don't want to be the one to cry wolf if what I'm feeling turns out to be nothing."

"Hey, I would rather be safe than sorry, and you were right last time. If there was ever a time to trust yourself or your instincts, it would be now. I know I do. I never doubted you."

He looked at her, then took a chance. With his hand, he gently brushed Nora's hair out of her eyes, tucking it behind her ear. Ron took a moment to take in her beauty as he gazed into her eyes. "I think we will be okay."

Nora put her hand on top of his by her ear and looked at him. "I believe you," she said as a blush and smile broke out across her face. At that moment, Ron wasn't worried about returning to Regis or concerned about being watched. It was this that he wanted to hold on to. It felt safe, comfortable. It was everything he wanted.

"Hey, we got a small fire going. Come sit with us. You two can continue your intimate moment later," Grant said as he popped out from behind a tree with that same annoying grin on his face. Ron was no longer in the moment as Nora let go of his hand and headed back to the campsite, and all of his worries came flooding back. What would they find at Regis? Who, if anyone, was out in the forest watching them? Could Ron keep everyone safe?

He made his way back to camp and sat down by the fire next to Grant. "So, you and Shaw have the first shift, huh?" Grant asked as he nudged Ron, who was staring into the fire.

"What? Oh, we do. You and Nora have the next one, and you better not fall asleep this time," Ron warned.

"I won't, and if I do, I feel Nora won't let me live to regret it," Grant said, standing up to go to the tent. After making small talk about Greyland, Nora decided it was time to retire to the tent as well. Shaw and Ron sat staring into the fire.

"What do you think we will find when we get to Regis?" Ron asked.

"Honestly, I'm not sure. I haven't given it much thought in the last couple of years. I honestly never thought I would return." Shaw poked the fire with a stick. Both men just sat idly watching the fire, the elder spinning the bracelet on his left wrist and periodically looking around, scanning the forest for any sign of movement.

"If you had to guess, where do you think those soldiers came from?" Ron asked.

"You know, I've asked myself that same question, and to this day, I'm still not sure. I've done my fair share of traveling, visiting most of the kingdoms and outlying towns, but in the years since, I have never come across anyone wearing that armor." Shaw continued to poke at the fire.

"What else do you know about these wielders?"

"I know a fair amount. What do you want to know?"

"Why did the people and the champion turn against the Essenti? It doesn't make sense to betray something like that."

"This is the way I see it," said the gatekeeper. "It didn't go into too much detail in the books I read, but it seemed as though the Essenti, besides gifting the power of the flame, did not involve itself in the politics and disputes among its people. It wanted the peoples' devotion; anything other than that did not concern the Essenti. Like with any leader, people want to rally around one with similar views as themselves. So the people brought their issues to the champion since the Essenti refused to hear them out. Over time, the champion became a beloved ruler among the people, and I believe that is when people stopped their worship of the Essenti."

Ron ran his fingers through his hair. "How is all that real? It's hard to believe. I don't understand how something like that could have existed."

"You can't be expected to believe nowadays, so much has happened since. But, as with most stories, people tend to embellish, mixing facts with their own opinions or beliefs."

Ron paused before responding. "So here is something I don't understand. If I have this flame, which I didn't know I had at the time, why was Regis attacked? No one else could have possibly known my brother or I had it."

Another sigh came from Shaw. "I wish I knew what to tell you. But, hopefully, tomorrow will tell us something."

Lost in thought with only the task of keeping the fire lit, Ron felt the hours pass. Finally, he heard some rustling in the tent. It had to be time to switch. Nora came out first, looking sleepy. She sat next to Ron and fed a few sticks to the fire.

"You guys go get some sleep; Grant is up, so you can go to bed," she said.

Ron and Shaw got up and went into the tent.

The sun rose in the morning with no more than a dozen rays of light finding their way to the ground beneath the thick canopy. The rays faintly brightened the darkness underneath the canopy, allowing a farther line of sight than on previous days. Nora put out the fire and covered their tracks as Grant woke Ron and Shaw. Nora and Grant had nothing to report from the night, even though Nora still had a bad feeling.

After breaking down the tent and packing the bedrolls, they continued their walk to Regis. On the way, they caught the smell of burnt wood drifting through the air. Shaw stopped the group as he went to look at a small wisp of smoke coming from the north side of a tree. Shaw was puzzled as he looked at the burn on the tree, and motioned for Ron to come over and take a look.

Ron saw that there was a handprint burnt into the trunk. Nora and Grant came to look as well.

"How did that get there?" Grant asked.

Shaw shook his head, and Nora said, "I have no idea."

Ron just kept staring at it. "I think it's from that masked man. He must still be out there somewhere watching us." He scanned the area.

"What do you think that means?" Shaw asked.

"I'm not sure," Ron said as he moved to touch the marking.

Shaw reached out, grabbing his arm. "If it's still smoking, it could burn you!"

"I don't think so," Ron said, moving closer.

"What do you mean you don't think so? If it's hot, it's hot." Unfortunately, Shaw's words were lost to Ron.

He reached out again and traced the handprint with his finger. Ron's right hand fit the size and shape of the print perfectly. He felt drawn in. Sounds became soft and dull; he focused more intently on the marking, to the point where he could not see out of his peripheral vision. Shaw and Grant tried calling out his name, but nothing shook him out of his fixation. Ron could feel his hand tingle with a sensation he had not felt before. It began to feel like a thousand small needles were piercing his skin all at the same time. His hand felt as if it were burning on the inside, the pain growing by the second, becoming more intense. Then a sudden lack of sensation came; Ron could not feel his hand. As abruptly as it became numb, a flash of bright blue fire emerged from it, passing into the tree, igniting the mark with a blue glow.

Nora yelled for Ron, swiftly pulling him away and into her arms. The flame went out, and Ron could feel his hand again, but he also felt weak. His legs felt heavy, his body sluggish. He held on to Nora, holding her tight so he would not fall. Finally, Ron's hearing and vision returned to normal.

"Ron, what the hell was that?" Nora asked, slowly letting go.

"I don't know. I'm not sure how I did that. That was strange, but it felt . . . good." Ron said.

"It definitely wasn't normal," Grant said, looking confused and a little scared. "Nora, I think that feeling you had was right. Someone was out here, and they put that handprint on the tree, so I have no doubt we were being watched."

Ron's eyes scanned the forest.

"Why would someone do that? What's the point?" asked Grant.

"I'm not sure, but I think—I think it may have been a test of some sort." Ron paced back and forth, trying to put his thoughts in order.

"How could that have been a test?" Grant was asking questions too fast for Ron to think of a clear response, but Shaw spoke for him.

"The only ones that saw Ron wield the flame before were the soldiers eight years ago, and from what Ron has told us of his encounter with the masked man, they intentionally drew him away from Greyland. Now, eight years is a long time, and if I had to guess, I would say that this handprint can only be activated by someone who can wield the flame. In doing this, Ron has confirmed two things." Shaw squinted his eyes, searching the surrounding area. Slowly, he unshouldered his bow, drawing an arrow, readying it to fire. "First, Ron proved that he is who they think he is, a wielder; and second, whoever set the handprint is still somewhere nearby, close enough to see Ron activate it. They are out there somewhere."

They slowly drew their weapons, and then Shaw saw a dark blur moving from the corner of his eye. He turned and fired an arrow that struck the trunk of a tree as the blur ran behind it. He readied another, waiting for his target to move.

Once he saw movement, he fired. The arrow tore through the trees with deadly accuracy, intent on hitting its target, only to disintegrate as it passed through a wall of blue flame raised mere inches away. They all looked at the rippling wall, shielding the one behind it.

It was a good way off, so how Shaw had seen movement was beyond any of them. As quickly as the flames appeared, they were gone just as fast, and the masked man was standing in the distance with one hand engulfed in blue fire. Shaw went for another arrow, but before it cleared its quiver, the masked man's hand lost the flame, allowing him to slip away into the dark.

"We need to go after him!" Ron slid his sword back into its scabbard, readying to give chase.

"We can't," Nora argued.

"Why not? He's right there."

"Because it could be a trap. What if he's planning on that?"

"I agree with Nora," said Shaw. "It could be a trap. He has all the proof he needs to know that you are the one he wants. We should keep on the path that I know. He could have an army out there waiting for all of us."

Nora took Ron by both shoulders. "We need to be smart—we can't just run off chasing someone in the dark. We have a plan, and we should stick to it. Take a deep breath and clear your head."

Ron did as Nora said. After a deep breath, he came to his senses, realizing he'd been about to make not only a rash decision, but also one that could have gotten everyone hurt or killed.

"You're right. I wasn't thinking clearly. We'll stick to the plan."

Once they set out again, Nora explained to Ron that she didn't have the feeling of being watched anymore. She told him it went away when the masked man ran off. It made Ron happy to hear that, but he didn't let his guard down.

After a couple hours of walking, Ron noticed the trees beginning to thin out. The canopy was not as thick, and the first true rays of sunlight could break through the top and reach the ground. Ron was relieved to see the light; he was tired of walking through a dark, desolate forest for hours at a time.

"Not much farther to go," Shaw said. Everyone's ears perked up; they were all ready to be rid of the forest.

Another hour went by, and finally the trees had sunlight breaking through the canopy like a summer rain piercing the clouds. Based on the sun and the shadows, it was later than they expected. It must have been past the afternoon, working well into the evening.

Ron and Shaw were the first to approach the tree line before going out into the open field. Crouching by the base of a trunk, Ron and Shaw looked ahead to see if anyone was waiting for them to exit the forest. The masked man could not have been far off, but Ron and Shaw saw no one. Just an empty stretch of grass leading up to what looked like some burned-out buildings in the distance. Nora came to Ron's side.

"Is that your village?" she asked.

"Yes, that's it," Ron replied.

"We don't know what's there, so stay on guard while we search, okay? We don't need any surprises," Shaw said.

They moved out of the tree line, walking slowly, scanning the open field to make sure no one was around. As they got closer, the buildings became more visible, showing what was left of Regis. Finally, Ron recognized where he was.

"There used to be farms out here," he said, pointing toward the large, empty fields neighboring Regis. "People would grow crops and trade them at the market. I used to get some and bring them home for my parents. Now it's nothing but land marked by death."

The village wasn't small by any means, but not anywhere near the size of Greyland. Home to only a few hundred people, this farm village had been far removed from the politics and concerns of city life. It was a peaceful place, which had made the attack all the more shocking.

They entered the village on the west side. Slowly moving eastward, Ron saw half-burnt homes and stores with shattered windows and splintered doors. Some houses were half collapsed on themselves from the night of the attack and the following years of rot and decay, roofs caved in from fire burning through the wooden support beams that once held strong. Scorch marks could be seen on other houses where the fires had been lit but shortly extinguished by the inhabitants that died protecting them.

Walking down the dirt path, Ron could remember coming through here as a child. Running around the village, playing with friends throughout the day, or going to the shops with his brother after their mother sent them on errands for items she needed. Once Ron and Nathill were old enough, they mostly went to the markets to get food for dinner or new thread and sewing needles for their mother so she could mend the tears in their clothes.

They kept walking, and soon came upon the old schoolhouse. What once had been a grand building meant to house dozens of children, ranging in age, was now nothing more than wood, brick, and mortar. The foundation was all that was left, but through some of the rubble, Ron saw pieces of torn clothing trapped between charred beams. Bones were visibly sticking out of the destruction, contorted and broken, some separated from the bodies they once belonged to. Ron looked on in horror as he realized what had taken place within the schoolhouse that night. He must have pushed it from his memory after it happened, but now, seeing it again, all the memories came back.

Shaw came up to Ron and put a hand on his shoulder.

"This is where most of the screams came from that night, isn't it?" Ron asked.

Shaw looked at the rubble. "Yes, people came here for safety when the attack began, thinking that no one would be cruel enough to harm a school. It was thought to be a sanctuary. The soldiers barred the doors and lit the school on fire. Women, children, and men were all inside. There was no way for them to get out." His voice was heavy.

"Who would do that?" Nora asked as her eyes began to water.

Ron turned away from the school; he couldn't bear to look at it. All those lives lost, and for what? He didn't know. He also knew there was nothing he could have done to help. Even if he had convinced Nathill to try and save as many people as they could, they'd still been outnumbered ten to one.

The village was in utter ruin. Whatever was not consumed by the fire had been ransacked and broken into. Ron passed the blacksmith's shop on the right after going by more collapsed houses. The forge was still intact, but nothing else was. Not a single hammer or tool was left behind. Ron could remember as if it were yesterday running by the blacksmith, catching a glimpse of him working on custom-crafted swords or decorative pieces for the people who paid a high sum for the excellent craftsmanship put into each one. The blacksmith would work on anything, whether fixing a furnace or pounding a training weapon for those who wanted to leave one day and join the city guard.

Now, the only image of the blacksmith Ron could picture was the bloodied and bruised man who had arrived in Greyland. The screams echoed in Ron's ears as he recalled the explosion. He continued rounding the corner, passing the blacksmiths, and then stopped in his tracks.

Ron could see his home at the end of the row on the left. He'd known he would see it, but actually having it in front of him affected him more than he was prepared for. The memories of his parents, his brother, growing up in that house all came flooding back to him.

Seeing Ron standing still, Grant went up to him and put his hand on his shoulder. "Are you ready for this?" he asked.

Looking at his friend, Ron let out a deep sigh. "No. But I'm as ready as I'll ever be."

Grant gave him a slap on the back, and Ron started walking toward his home. It looked the same from the outside except the windows were broken, the door ripped off its hinges and splintered on the ground. Ron could remember the arrows that flew through as he looked at the front side of the windowsill he'd once hid behind. Ron walked up to where the door would have been. "I guess they searched the house when they came back," Ron said, stepping over the doorway. Ron walked into the living room where the fireplace was. The furniture was flipped upside down and shredded apart, the chairs were thrown around the room, and the center table was split in two.

In front of the fireplace, Ron saw the remains of his parents. Their bones and clothing were slumped over each other, with pieces of wood and glass scattered on and around them. Ron didn't see any arrows lying around. He walked into the kitchen to the right and went through one of the only remaining drawers still in the dresser pressed up against the wall. He came back with a white tablecloth. Ron shook the cloth, unfolding it, and dragged it over his parent's remains.

"Those bastards couldn't have the decency to cover their bodies, but they came back and ripped the arrows from them. What kind of animals . . ." he said through clenched teeth.

Ron turned to the mantle above the fireplace and beat a hole into the wall with his fist. This was the first time Nora and Grant had seen him behave in this manner. They had both seen him upset before, but this was different. This was more than being upset; this was only a taste of the rage Ron felt at having to relive that night. Shaw stood back and watched as the young man continued to hit the wall, until Nora rushed over and grabbed his arm.

"Ron, stop. I know you're upset, but stop," she said.

He looked at Nora, then at the bloodied mess he'd made of his right hand and the large hole in the wall smeared with red. Ron turned around, looking at Grant and Shaw, then walked out the front door to the outside. Everyone watched and followed as Ron walked here and there. He moved around to the back of the house, where he and Nathill had fought the soldiers. Their decayed bodies were still there. The black armor with the deep blue lining covered the skeletal remains.

"They attacked us here once we got out of the house," Ron said in a low tone. "This one right here"—Ron pointed—"this was the first man I ever killed. They were relentless. My brother Nathill and I had to kill them." He kept walking. "We started to run for the trees over there." Raising a finger, Ron pointed to the tree line. "We didn't make it too far before we got hit with arrows. Nathill told me to run. He said one of us must live. I wanted to stay, but he said run, so I did."

Then he stopped in place. "This is where they killed him; they stabbed him as he lay on the ground, right here. That's the last time I saw him before I was pulled to safety." Ron knelt down, touching the ground where Nathill's body should have been, had the soldiers not taken it.

Ron felt the sharp needle sensation in his hand. "That's strange," he said, looking at it.

"What's strange?" Nora asked, crouching down beside him.

"My hand. It feels like it did at the marked tree in the forest, but it's not as intense this time," Ron said, standing up.

"Maybe because it's bleeding. Here, let me see it."

Nora took Ron's right hand and reached into her pack. She cleaned it with a small hand towel. After pouring some water over it, she applied pressure and stopped the bleeding. Then she pulled out the green healing oil.

"I didn't intend to use this so soon, so I'll have to be sparing. This might sting a little." Nora said as she put the oil on Ron's hand. He could feel the skin on the more minor cuts sting as the oil seeped into the damaged tissue. After a couple of minutes and a few more drops of oil, Ron's hand felt better. The oil covered the wound, sealing it from the outside air and allowing the skin to slowly repair itself.

"Thank you, Nora, that actually feels a lot better." With the pain from the cuts all but gone in his hand, Ron could still feel the sharp needles from when he touched the ground. He looked from his hand up to the house. "When Nathill and I were little, he would teach me how to fight. At first, I didn't want to. I thought it was a waste of time. Back then, I would have rather run around the town with my friends. Without him, though, I would probably be dead right now."

Nora put a comforting hand on his shoulder. "Let's go finish looking at the house," Ron said as he started making his way back.

He took a deep breath before reentering the house. He went past the fireplace, rounding the corner to the stairs, and made his way up. At the top of the stairs, he took a left turn and opened the door to his room. Everything was turned over—his clothes were thrown about the room, his bed was torn to pieces, and his dresser was smashed, missing all the drawers. Even the books he read as a child were torn apart.

"I guess I shouldn't be surprised," Ron said. The others were silent. They just exchanged glances as he picked up the pieces of his old life. Every item he lifted, he put back down; it was strange to him, but nothing seemed like it had been his since the day he left. Finally, Ron picked up the pieces of a yellow handmade vase. "I remember making this for my mother." Shuffling the pieces around in his hands, he continued, "I made it for her birthday. It took so long for me to make the sides thick enough so they wouldn't fall inward. When I finished it, I picked some flowers for her and put them in. She was so happy when I gave it to her." Setting the broken pieces on the ground, Ron walked out of his old room to check the other rooms in the house. He kept left as he made his way down the hall to his parents' room.

It looked just like his. Nothing had been left untouched. Ron closed the door; he didn't need to look any further in there. Retracing his steps down the hall, passing the stairs to the right, he stopped at the foot of Nathill's door.

Ron slowly opened it. Again, his brother's room was trashed, but something was different. All the other rooms in the house were torn apart, but Nathill's wasn't nearly as bad. Ron looked around, picking up little things, from old toys to the practice swords they used to spar with. Finally, Ron became frustrated. "Why would the blacksmith give me a message to come here if there's nothing to find?"

"Is there anywhere else to look?" Grant asked.

"No, this is where I lost everything. It was taken from me that night." Ron began pacing back and forth. The others didn't know what to say. They wanted to comfort him, but they didn't know how. Saying they were sorry or that they felt terrible would just be a waste of words.

"Maybe we should go," Shaw said.

"What was the point of all this? The rider, the person in the mask, the marking on the tree. Everything that happened to get to this place. What the hell is the point?" Ron yelled, picking up a ceramic mug that had been knocked over on a desk and throwing it against the adjacent wall. However, the cup did not break on impact. Instead, it went through the wall. "What the . . ." Ron said, walking toward the hole in the wall. "That's not a wall."

He put his hand in the hole and tore away some of the thin, plaster-like material. "There's something back here. Come help me," Ron said to the others as he tore more and more wall away. Nora, Grant, and Shaw came over and started to pull at the wall. In moments, there was an opening big enough for Ron to walk through.

The room on the other side spanned the length of Nathill's room, but it was only a few feet deep. Though it was dark, Ron could see a desk on the right side with the light coming through. "We need some more light."

Grant put his pack down and grabbed a small torch, wrapping the top of it tightly with a lightly oiled piece of cloth. He quickly struck some flint together and lit the torch.

With the room now illuminated, Ron could not believe what he saw. The desk was pushed up against the wall and had papers strewn about the top in no organized manner. Ron looked around the room; notes and hand-drawn pictures were seemingly linked together using a string nailed to the wall. Next, he looked at the papers on the desk. Some of them were unreadable, in a language he did not recognize. Finally, he saw letters that were addressed to Nathill. He picked up one and blew a layer of dust off of it.

Nathill,

Today is the day. Everything is in place for what will occur tonight. I know you have been patient, I know you have been tested, but tonight all that hard work will come to fruition. The power of Taroth will be yours, and together no one will stop our achievements. We have two out of three, and when the third is converted, the fires will be brought forth, and the merging of the two worlds will commence.

Ron looked at the signature to see who'd sent the letter, but there was no signature. There was only a red wax seal with the letters "FB" imprinted in the center. Ron's fingers traced the FB on the hilt of the sword that hung at his waist. "Who is FB? Why do you have one of their letters? What does two out of three mean? What worlds?" Ron asked out loud, not really expecting an answer. The papers in a different language interested him, so he took them and put them in his pack. Then he moved over to the wall that had the string connecting the pictures to each other. Ron saw an image of his parents there, and his father had a circle drawn around him. Ron followed the string connecting the picture to a piece of paper with one word, "wielder," circled with a question mark on it.

He was even more confused now than before finding the room.

"Ron?" Nora called from the other side of the room. "Is this you and your brother?"

Ron walked over to where she was standing to look at the picture. He saw that it was a picture of him and Nathill when they were younger.

"Yes, that's Nathill and me. I was twelve, and he was sixteen around that time. We just got done sparring. He definitely was better than me back then. I don't know why he would draw all of these pictures." A slight smirk crept to the corner of his mouth, remembering the day the drawing had captured. Ron returned to the wall and looked at the pictures again, tracing the string once more. It bounced from pictures of his brother to his mother and father and to him. Finally, there was a drawing on the far left of the wall, of a man in a black-and-blue cloak. His face was obscured, so Ron could not make out who it was—not like he would know who it was anyway. He grabbed it nonetheless; it was the only link he had to the person in the forest.

"What does all this mean, Ron?" Grant asked.

"I don't know. I'm not even sure what half these papers say, but it looks like Nathill was talking to someone about wielders. It still doesn't make sense. The initials on the letter are the same as the initials on this sword," Ron said. "What if someone found out Nathill could wield this flame and came after him? He might have been in trouble the whole time, and I missed it." Ron's mind was racing with thoughts of everything he could have done differently if only he had known.

"Alright, let's calm down. I have an idea." Shaw's relaxed demeanor helped calm Ron. "Before we get ahead of ourselves with all this speculation, why don't we figure out what these other papers have to say?"

"You can read these?" Ron asked.

"Me? No, no, but I do know someone who can," Shaw said.

Everyone looked at him. "I have an old friend. Well, friend might be too strong; he was a fellow scholar, educator. It has been a while, but he lives around the kingdom of Oroze, somewhere on the outskirts."

"We should go see him, then," Ron said.

"It's a long journey. It will take at least a week and a half to get there by horse, and seeing as we don't have any of those, it will be longer."

"Then we should start walking."

Ron collected the rest of the pages he could not read. More than twenty were scattered around the desk and on the wall. He walked out of the room and into the hallway before stopping at the top of the stairs.

"What's wrong?" Nora asked, stopping at his side.

Without answering, Ron turned around and headed back into Nathill's room, grabbing a picture of his family that his brother had drawn. "I just wanted something to remember them by."

They all went downstairs and walked out the front door. Grant moved to put the torch out in the dirt, but Ron stopped him. He took the torch from his friend's hand and stared at the house with a look of longing in his eyes, longing for what used to be. It grew in his heart, the desire to be with his family again. To see his mother and father, to see Nathill, to share one more hug with them since he never had that chance.

Ron knew what he felt was a fleeting moment, so he threw the torch into the house.

"Ron, what are you doing?" Nora asked, looking at him with confusion.

"As much as it hurts, I think it's time to put this behind me. I've thought of what happened here every day for the last eight years and how it changed everything in my life, but it's not my life anymore. You guys are my life—my time in Greyland is my life. This is nothing now, just a memory, and while I still need to find the truth about what happened, I can finally let this piece go," Ron said, taking one last look before they all turned away as the house caught fire. Flames started pouring out of the broken windows and doors, and a column of smoke escaped the chimney.

As the house burned to the ground, Ron walked away without looking back.

Chapter Eight

To the Linguist

A s the days progressed and they headed north, Shaw stayed on the lookout for any inconspicuous places to camp. Finally, after a couple hours and a long stretch of miles, the old man saw a spot at the base of the Storming Mountains.

"This should be a good place to rest."

"What makes this better than any of the other places we passed along the way?" Nora asked as she laid her pack on the ground and sat on it.

"These are the Storming Mountains. Not many people come this way. Some time ago, during the Battle of the Storming Mountains, the last two remaining wielders clashed so violently that they broke open the sky, causing storms to constantly erupt above these mountains. The wielders and their armies battled in the mountains for weeks, using their power to try and kill one another. That was when the sky broke open and made way for the storms. Then, one day, the fighting stopped, and after that, no one knows what became of the two wielders or the rest of their armies. No one knows who prevailed—light or dark, good or evil. Everything just stopped.

Shaw sighed. "Another army was sent to track down the creatures that managed to escape from the forge. But that is just the story, even though the storms continue."

Ron was looking over the papers and pictures he had taken. Without glancing up, he asked, "What else do you know about the wielders from back then? And why is my father circled in this picture?" He wished for an answer, but he didn't trust his belief in hope.

"The wielders from that time are just a myth to some," said Shaw. "They are supposedly the ones who shaped the world to what it is today after the Essenti was exiled to the forge. The wielders of old possessed a power, as you know, granted to them by the Essenti, but when the wielders were destroyed, and the Essenti long since banished, the power of the flame left as well. It seemed like it was tied to them somehow. They, too, were able to control a blue flame, same as you. It's been beyond a century or two since the wielders have been around. They're barely even mentioned nowadays. There is no one to teach or carry on the teachings of the flame. As to your father, I have no idea why he would be circled or even remotely connected to them."

"Who is your friend that can read these letters?" Ron started putting the papers back in his bag.

"He is an old acquaintance. I haven't seen him in quite a few years, but he was a scholar and a linguist. He was always learning new things. He's a little bit of a hermit, always liked staying to himself."

"Where can we find him? You said he lived near Oroze. Where exactly?"

"Somewhere to the east of the Storming Mountains as my memory serves me, but it will take some time to get there. So let's get some rest and start fresh in the morning?"

Grant liked this idea, so he jumped up and started unpacking the tent while Shaw got a fire started. The sun had retreated once more, and the moon was rising.

Shaw and Grant took first watch, so Nora and Ron could get some rest. Ron lay down on his bedroll, Nora to his left. She rolled onto her side, looking at him.

"Are you doing okay?"

Ron could hear the concern in her voice. "I guess so. I just don't know what to think of all this. Why would my brother have all those papers and letters in a secret room, signed 'FB' no less? Not to mention my dad—what is his connection to all of this? It's . . . It's just a lot to take in." Ron was lying on his back, but when Nora reached over and put her hand on his chest, he rolled to his side. She held the back of Ron's head and ran her fingers through his hair.

"Whatever happens, you know we are all here for you. I am here for you," she said.

Looking deep into her eyes, Ron put a hand on her cheek, then pulled her in, kissing her lips gently. "Thank you, Nora. I need to stop looking at the past and focus on now, on everything, everyone I have, and you most importantly. With everything that's happened in my life, through all the pain and loss, there is one thing I know. If none of that had ever happened, I would never have met you. You are the light in my path. You have been the one to pull me back and keep me grounded. Just thinking of you or hearing your voice, whether it's out loud or in my head, having you with me is something I would never want to give up."

"Do you know how long I have been waiting for you to say that?" Nora's cheeks felt warm with a slight red blush. "I was hoping you would have said something that night you walked me home before all of this started, but I understand why you didn't. I'm just glad you did now. Being with you is what I have wanted. Every moment I get with you feels too short, and every time you leave, I have to wait until I see you again. I've wanted to be more than your friend for such a long time. Now, knowing everything, I understand why you were distant at times."

Ron smiled. "I feel the happiest when I'm with you, and I'm sorry it took so long for me to tell you. I was just scared you wouldn't feel the same. I shouldn't have been so hesitant to tell you about Regis. I guess I was worried that you would think I'm too broken. I know that sounds ridiculous, but now I'm glad that you know me. I mean, all of who I am."

"You can rest assured that no matter how broken you think you are, it would never change the way I feel about you. All those times we would look at the stars under the giant oak and talk about our lives, this is the moment I was waiting for. I wanted to know the person I was falling for, and now I know I chose the right person." Nora ran her fingers through his thick brown hair again, and this time brought his lips to hers.

Her hands held Ron tightly while he pulled her body closer, embracing her affectionately, feeling the warmth pressed against his and the softness of her lips each time they joined together against his own. With each kiss, their passion and longing intensified, and they lost themselves in their shared, wanting embrace. Their hands held tightly, begging with each moment to explore and caress one another as years of suppressed feelings rose to the surface, threatening to be liberated, to consume them in their affection for one another.

Then the sharp sound of Grant coughing and clearing his throat brought them back from the moment. Nora let out a giggle. "I guess we shouldn't get too carried away."

"I suppose not." Smiling, Ron leaned in, kissing Nora once more before pulling her close and then rolling onto his back. Nora lay on Ron's chest as he held her in his arms. Ron had that feeling of being safe and comfortable as they both fell asleep.

After a few hours of being on watch, Grant decided to look into the tent and wake up Nora and Ron. "Hey Shaw, I'm going to go wake them up for watch,"

"Alright, I'm tired," Shaw said with a stretch of his arms.

Grant made his way over to the tent and opened the front flap. He saw Ron holding Nora as they slept. Looking at the two of them, he felt a small smile run across his face as he muttered under his breath, "Finally. Took you long enough." Grant closed the flap, turning to walk back to the fire. "I think I'll let them sleep for a while. You can take a nap, Shaw. I'll stay on watch and wake you in a bit."

"That sounds good. Don't let me sleep too long. You need some rest eventually as well." The old gatekeeper lay on the ground by the fire, using the log he was sitting on as a headrest.

As the sun rose in the east, Ron woke up and looked down to see Nora was still asleep, lying on his chest. He lay there smiling; for a moment, he forgot about his anger, sadness, and worry. It felt to him for the first time like none of that mattered. Ron was happy.

Then Grant poked his head in the tent. "Hey, it's time to get up. We're heading out soon." And just like that, all the worries, sadness, and anger came flooding back to Ron.

At least he'd been able to enjoy the moment. Ron nudged Nora. "It's time to wake up," he said softly.

"Is it that time again already?" Nora said as she sat up, rubbing her eyes.

When they exited the tent, everything was already packed up and ready to go. The only thing left was the tent itself. Once they had that packed, they looked at Shaw. "Okay, which way do we go from here?" Ron asked.

"We need to head northeast toward Oroze. We will follow the mountains for a little while, then cut east toward the Red Band River," Shaw said, pointing.

"Sounds good. Let's get going."

They walked a few miles, then heard a loud crack from the sky. Thunder was crashing down on them, but the rain had not found them yet. The darkening clouds above definitely invited the rain, but the group was lucky they did not have to endure it. They made their way north along the mountain roads until it was time to cut over. The roads climbed in elevation; as they made their way up, they could see the mountain peaks, jagged and rough, with what looked like giant pieces missing from the sides and tops of the surrounding summits. The way down was going to be tricky.

Nora noticed what looked like a path. "It looks like there used to be steps here."

"The steps must have deteriorated and washed away over the years," Shaw reasoned. The area was sloped, but not nearly as steep as the rest of the mountain.

"I think we can make it down this side if we can anchor a rope to something," said Nora.

Grant looked around for an anchor point and saw a decayed, broken stump of a tree on the other side of the path. "We can use that stump over there. Hopefully the roots are deep." He pointed. "All we have to do is tie another rope to the end of this one, and we can make it down." Grant took two ropes from his pack and looped them together, knotting them tight, then slipped them over the tree stump.

As they began to descend down the side of the mountain, Ron thought of something. "How are we going to get this rope back?"

"Well, you know—" Grant scratched his head. "Getting the rope off the stump didn't really cross my mind."

They all began to laugh, and continued one by one down the mountainside. When they finally got to the bottom of the mountain, they stood in thick green grass up to their knees. "Hey Grant, can you light a torch for me?" Ron asked.

"Sure, what do you need it for?" his friend asked as he went into his pack, pulling out the torch and some flint.

"I'm going to light the rope on fire, so no one can follow it down in the event someone was watching us," Ron explained. He walked over to the rope and held the torch under the tail end until it caught fire. "Alright, let's keep going."

The land at the bottom of the mountain was stark in contrast to the Storming Mountains and the wet, saturated dirt covering the roads. The ground was moist and soft, almost as if the rain had come not too long before they all arrived. The rainwater created natural runoffs flowing down the mountainside, keeping the ground below well fed and nurtured. As a result, the trees had more life than the forest they'd walked through on their way to Regis.

"Be on your guard. It is much easier for creatures to hide in this forest than the last," Shaw said warily. As they walked, they could all see that there was no clear path. With the forest being supplied with such a large amount of water, the grass had been able to grow tall, covering any trail that might once have been seen.

"Shaw, which way do we go?" Nora asked.

"We are going to need to use the sun to find our way. Just stay close to me, and if I need assistance, I'll ask Grant for his input. I saw that you guided them in the right direction after you left the west gate from Greyland," Shaw said, looking at Grant.

"I did. I learned a little bit of traveling skills on my own time, in between training and other activities," the young man said with a smile.

While they walked, they kept their hands on their weapons. Ron had his hand on the hilt of his sword, ready to unsheathe it at a moment's notice, touching the engraved letters. He wasn't going to let something get the jump on him like the wolf had. He would be ready this time. Nora was using her staff as a walking stick, taking the pressure off her back to alleviate a slight throbbing that was slowly gaining traction, and Grant had his two daggers tucked against his forearms. Shaw left his bow slung on his back. He knew he was quick and good with his hands, so he focused on leading the way.

A couple hours went by. The sun was in the south, slowly making its way to the west. Shaw was leading the group when suddenly he made a fist and threw it up in the air. At the same instant, Nora felt the throbbing pressure in her back pulse along her spine, causing her to shout. Everyone stopped without a word, and Ron went to Nora's side. She indicated she was okay with a silent head nod, but whispered in his ear, "Something is here."

Shaw turned his head back and forth, looking through the trees. Ron heard twigs breaking and a rustling sound coming from behind them. "We are being followed," Shaw said, taking his bow off his shoulder and notching an arrow.

"More like we are being hunted," Nora whispered.

"What's out there?" Grant asked.

"I'm not sure, but whatever it is, it can't be good," said the old man.

They heard footsteps not too far off, then a deep, low growl. Ron pulled his sword from its sheath—they were all ready to fight. He saw a bulky figure out of the corner of his eye run in and out behind the trees. Shaw noticed too, and let loose an arrow in the direction of the figure. A loud, deep roar emerged from the trees.

"What the hell is that?" Nora asked, taking a few steps back, holding her staff ready.

With wide eyes, Shaw said, "That's not possible. That should not be here!" His voice was full of fear.

"What do you mean it shouldn't be here?" Ron asked.

"That thing is not of this world. It's called a Ybarra. Now there is no denying, the forge has somehow been opened."

The Ybarra stepped out from behind a tree, exposing itself as gasps echoed from person to person. The creature was tall, nearly seven feet; its arms rivaled Ron's body in length when stretched out to each side. The hands had sharp, cracked nails it could use for claws. The Ybarra had short, thin black hair covering most of its body. It stood on two feet and walked with a hunch. Its face was a cruel, malformed mixture of bear and wolf. It was unnatural. The head was large and round, with pointed lupine ears on top. The snout was short, bearing sharp teeth. The strangest thing that Ron noticed about the Ybarra, though, besides its entire existence, was its eyes. They had a dull, orange glow to them. Despite the Ybarra looking like an amalgam of different animals, the eyes proved the creature did not belong to this world but that of the forge.

The Ybarra roared and charged at Shaw with drool dripping from its coated mouth. It looked rabid as it got closer and swung its long-clawed arm. Shaw ducked, rolling to the right as the Ybarra swung with its left. The old man recovered and shot an arrow, hitting it in the right shoulder. The Ybarra looked at the arrow sticking out of its shoulder and pulled it out with ease, treating it more like an annoyance than a wound.

Nora came up from behind, swinging her staff at its feet. The Ybarra fell to its back and Grant rushed to stab the creature while it was down, but the Ybarra used its long arm to swat the young man to the side. The strength of the blow sent Grant through the air into a tree, where he crumpled to the ground. Grant heaved and coughed as he crawled on the ground to pick up his daggers. His entire left side was pounding with pain from the impact. The Ybarra stood up and made its way over.

Grant raised his hands in a futile attempt to block the thinly haired claws from cutting him into pieces. Then Ron jumped in front of him, deflecting the Ybarra's swipe with his sword.

"Quick, grab your daggers, hurry!" Ron shouted.

He began to attack the Ybarra. He slashed right, left, up, down, just trying to find an opening, but the creature was fast and had unbelievable strength. It used its claws to block the sword strokes. Ron had to make sure not to lose his footing from the Ybarra's force as it drove the sword away.

Shaw saw this as an opportunity to fire a few more arrows around the creature's head. The Ybarra kept snapping the arrows out of its own body with little concern until one lucky shot hit it in the eye, taking its vision away on the right. The Ybarra screamed, grabbing in agitation at the protruding arrow. Backing away from Ron's attacks, it reached up with one hand, grasping the arrow shaft and pulling in one swift motion. The eye came out of the Ybarra's head still impaled on the tip of arrow. Blood ran down its face as rage deformed its features. Grant stood up and moved next to Ron.

"What do you think? How should we stop this thing?" he asked with a panting breath.

"I have an idea. You attack the knees on the right, and I will attack the top half," Ron panted back. He looked at Nora, motioning for her to distract the Ybarra, then turned to Shaw. "Fire arrows around its head. We need to overwhelm it."

The old man fired, while Nora ran at the Ybarra and swung her staff again. This time, the creature grabbed it mid-swing. She held it tight, trying to pull it free, but the Ybarra was much stronger and picked up the staff with Nora still on the end of it. "Now, Grant!" Ron yelled. Grant rushed around toward the back of the Ybarra, sinking his daggers into the soft skin that covered both knee joints of its hind legs.

The Ybarra dropped the staff, along with Nora, and fell to its knees, roaring in pain. Ron ran up toward the Ybarra as Shaw's arrow found its target, plunging into the creature's last good eye. Ron jumped into the air, and with a strong swing, he struck the Ybarra's neck, severing its head from the body. The head fell to the ground, rolling to a stop. The body started to contort and bend as if possessed. Its powerful hands were reaching for where its head used to be as it stumbled around wildly. Everyone was watching, waiting for the beast to die. Instead, it started swinging its arms in an uncontrolled manner. "Give it some room," Shaw cautioned. They all took several steps back, still watching warily. Finally, the Ybarra slowed down, falling to its knees again and then keeling over dead.

"How could it move without a head?" Grant asked.

"The body had to die. It takes a minute for the body to realize that the head is no longer attached, so it goes into a frenzy as the nerve endings go out of control," Shaw explained, taking a deep breath.

"That's crazy," Ron said as he turned to look at his friends. "Are you two okay?"

"I'm alright," Nora said. "Nothing I can't handle."

"I'll be fine, just some bruising. That tree is not as soft as it looks," Grant said sarcastically.

Ron and Shaw let out a laugh. "Shaw, where did that come from?" Ron asked.

"It came from the forge, but I'm not sure how. The forge has been closed since the Battle of the Storming Mountains. These creatures live longer than they should, but seeing as many as we have in such a short time is not a good sign. Nothing is normal in the forge. Everything there is off. Abominations come from there, as you can see. We will be able to get more answers when we get to my acquaintance. Perhaps he will know how these creatures are here." Shaw shook his head. "Okay, we need to go now. If that thing is out there, who knows what else is?"

Ron and Grant cleaned off the weapons as the gatekeeper grabbed the arrows he could salvage from the ground and the dead Ybarra. Ron took one last look at the body as they started walking away. He had never seen anything like that before. Ron kept thinking about the color of its eyes. Thinking how something like the forge could exist and be so different.

The sun was beginning to sink in the west, and Ron noticed Shaw had picked up the pace.

"Shaw, what's going on? Why are we going faster?" Ron asked.

"I want to cross the Red Band River before nightfall and get out of this forest. We have about another two hours of sunlight, and I swore I heard the sound of more Ybarras on the wind. I can't be sure, but I don't want to take the chance of running into more of those."

Ron relayed the message to Nora and Grant, and they began to run at a bearable pace. Soon the trees started to thin, and they could hear the sound of running water.

"There it is—once we cross the bridge, we can set up camp and rest for the night," Shaw said.

Finally, the bridge came into view. It was big and sturdy, made out of wood tightly compacted to look like one solid piece. Both sides had handrails as well. They walked across, looking over the railing at the water below. The river was broader and deeper than Ron had thought. He was not accustomed to seeing such massive amounts of water all at once.

Once they made it across, they were surprised to see there were no more trees. The land was mostly flat, with rolling hills intermittently spaced across the open valley. The short grass changed color from green to a wheat brown, spreading far and wide, waving as a light breeze pushed across the Valley of Oroze.

"Let's go a little farther north and follow the river upstream. We should arrive in a couple days. See the mountains way off in the distance? That is where we need to go," Shaw said.

They walked along the riverbank, taking in the beauty of the river and valley. The light of the sunset reflected off the water, casting its natural warmth upon the valley. With what little light they had left, they set up camp. Ron and Grant had first watch, so Shaw and Nora went to sleep. Grant grabbed wood for a fire while Ron made a rock circle to contain it.

"Ron, that thing we fought earlier, the Ybarra, did you notice its eyes? Those won't be leaving my mind anytime soon, that's for sure."

"Yeah, I saw that. Hopefully, Shaw's friend will have more answers on what the forge is and how creatures can come through it. That thing was massive. I never would have thought something like that was real. But at least it's dead now, and you and Nora are okay." He poked the fire with a stick. "How's your side? Your body hit the tree pretty hard."

Grant lifted his shirt. "It looks worse than it feels. I don't think anything's broken, but it's going to be sore for a while."

The fire reflected off of his skin, showing the dark bruises covering the entirety of his left side before he let his shirt fall. "Can you believe this?" Grant asked, staring into the fire.

"Believe what?"

"Any of it. I mean, I didn't believe all of this was actually real. Growing up, I would hear the stories from my friends that they heard from their parents.

Stories of these great wars, creatures being slain by heroes, and people having extraordinary gifts. I don't know. It's just—" Grant rubbed his face. "It's hard to believe that less than two weeks ago, none of this was real, and now we have seen it. We killed creatures that only used to be in stories for children." He shook his head in disbelief, laughing only to himself. "Do you think anyone will believe us back home?"

"I don't know," Ron said. "They might be more open to the idea since half of Greyland saw the blue flame for themselves. On the other hand, it's still hard for me to wrap my head around as well. Honestly, I don't know what to do half the time. We're constantly figuring things out as we go, and it scares me."

Having known one another for close to ten years, there wasn't much Ron and Grant hadn't talked about before. They had established a trust between them that allowed them to really talk to each other about whatever they needed to express.

"You don't need to be afraid. You have all of us here with you, plus you know how to use a sword better than anyone I know. That should be some comfort, at least. You know, after that night with the masked man, I was too scared to fall asleep. I think we are all scared, and maybe that's a good thing. Who's to say being scared won't help us? Remember what Cap said to me about being overconfident? What if he meant being overconfident could get us killed, but being scared could make us cautious?" Grant asked.

Ron smiled. "I'm surprised you remember one of Cap's lectures. Usually you tune them out, but you have a point. Although it's not the fighting that scares me. Don't get me wrong, seeing that Ybarra thing, that was horrifying. I think it's the fact we are going up against something we know nothing about. It feels like we are playing against a stacked deck of cards; someone is always one step ahead. I don't know how to win against that. Either way, I'm just glad you, Nora, and even Shaw are with me. I don't think I could do this alone."

They made small talk for a little longer, then just listened to the wood crackle in the fire.

After a few days of walking, camping, and more walking, Ron and Grant got up early and had everything packed so everyone could continue along the river while rubbing the sleep out of their eyes. Ron could see the mountain range in the distance. It would not take long to make it the rest of the way.

"So, Shaw, what is this guy like?" Grant asked as they continued along the riverbank.

"He mostly stays to himself. His name is Collins. We grew up together before we went our separate ways as we got older. He was always reading old books and looking up historical research in the libraries. That's what interested him the most. I was interested for a time, but I wanted to move to a quiet area, and Regis seemed like that perfect place for me. Collins, last I heard, retired from his profession of teaching in Oroze. He was an instructor of language and history," Shaw explained.

"So, he really is the best person to ask about all these creatures, letters, papers, all of it?" Ron asked.

"He might be, yes, but don't get your hopes up too high. It's easier to keep expectations low so as to not be disappointed by a different outcome than expected."

"Any answer is better than nothing. At least we would have something," Ron said, keeping in mind what Shaw said about expectations.

A small house came into view as they reached a minor summit atop a rolling hill. "There it is." Shaw pointed to a small house pinned against the mountain range. It looked like it was just a single room. The roof was covered in light brown moss to match the grass that grew around it. The house was made out of weather-worn wood. Two windows occupied space on either side of the door. Gray smoke rose from the brick-laid chimney, a sign of life. Ron could see a vague silhouette move from one of the windows, and wondered if Shaw's friend could see them as they approached the house.

When they came up to the door, Shaw told them, "Let me do the talking. Collins can be a little timid with groups of strangers. He can also be a little rough around the edges." Shaw walked up to the door and knocked three times. As soon as the third knock hit the door, a man pulled it open swiftly, staring at the group as if sizing them up to see if they were dangerous.

Collins was an older man with an aged face that was beginning to droop down. He had long, brown hair with ample gray mixed into it. His beard was as long as his hair and covered most of his face, revealing only his eyes and nose. Collins wore long, white robes with an old, red cloak pulled over them. "Ah, Shaw, haven't seen you in quite some time. What brings you to around these parts and with these miscreants?"

"It's good to see you to Collins," the gatekeeper said. "These are my companions—Ron, Nora, and Grant." He pointed to each one. "We are here to see if you could help us out with some papers that need explaining and deciphering."

"Deciphering?" Collins scratched at the chin hidden behind his long beard. "What do you have?"

"We have a few letters and papers in a language we cannot read. We were hoping you could help."

"Well, come on in and I will have a look, but don't touch anything." Collins looked directly at Grant as he said it.

They all walked into the small home. It was bigger inside than it had appeared. Ron looked around and saw random stacks of papers scribbled with writings scattered everywhere. Piles of books littered the tables and bookshelves. All the books were worn and covered in dust, and the papers had marks and notes written on them, seemingly at random. "Please make yourselves at home. You can put your things there, by the door," Collins said, pointing to a spot on the floor. Ron discerned from his tone that he only said it to be polite.

The house was dark, with only natural light coming in from the front two windows. The dust had settled on magnifying glasses positioned on the corner of a table; particles hung in the air, reflecting the dim light from the windows.

"So, what is it you would like me to look at?" Collins asked.

Ron grabbed some papers out of his pack and handed them to the man. Collins grabbed a pair of reading glasses from the table. "This is an old language. I haven't seen this in a long time. Where did you find these pages?"

"Someone I knew had them, and I just wanted to know what they said."

"Why are you here if the person these belong to could read it for you?" Collins asked.

"The owner isn't alive anymore," Ron explained.

Collins waved it off. "My apologies."

Ron looked at the man with distrust. There was something Ron did not like about him. It might have been his demeanor, or just the way he was, but something wasn't right.

"Do you know what they say?" Nora asked.

Collins lowered the pages from his face. "Yes. Let me see the other pages." Ron handed a stack over. The man took them and sat at his table. "Where did you say you got these?" Collins grumbled.

Before anyone else could answer, Ron said, "We found them in an abandoned house that belonged to my late grandparents." He knew the man wouldn't believe such a poor lie, but he held firm anyway.

"Did you now?" Collins lifted an eyebrow. "It looks to me that whatever is written here was written in the language of the Essenti. Yes, I do believe. Back in the days of champions and wielders, people used a different dialect. After a time, the language changed and adapted, eventually dying off altogether. This here looks to be the oldest dialect, the original language of the Essenti. I can't say the reasons for writing this now, but I did my fair share of studying the old tongues. Although, this will take some time—it's not easy to interpret the exact meaning of the words, as some words have multiple implications. You can sit and wait; just don't touch anything." He looked directly at Grant as he said it again, as the young man was perusing some of the books on the shelf.

Ron paced back and forth as the others sat quietly, waiting for Collins to read the pages. Finally, after a couple hours, Collins put down the last page. "That was quite some reading."

"What does it say?" Ron asked.

"Won't even let me collect my thoughts, will you?" Collins said sarcastically. "If you must know, this is the recounted history of Taroth and Thalom. It documents the events of their early years very accurately. It seems the only reason for this story is to sharpen one's understanding of its written language. Perhaps the purpose of this is academic in nature, or its use is to learn enough to communicate."

Ron looked at the others in confusion. They looked back at him with the same expressions on their faces. All except for Shaw—he knew a little of the lore of Taroth and Thalom, but not enough to tell a tale like Collins. "Communicate? Communicate with who? The language is dead," Shaw said, rubbing his chin.

"I don't know what the reasoning is. Those are just my thoughts. I can see by the look on your faces, though, that you have no idea who or what I am talking about."

They all shook their heads. "No, we don't," Nora said.

"Okay, if I am going to tell this story, then I need to throw a log or two on the fire and get a cup of wine." Collins got up and grabbed a log from a wooden box that housed at least a dozen others. When he threw the log in the fire, there was a flash of red. "A little mood lighting to set the tone," he said as he moved toward the farthest window on the left. Collins had what looked like no shortage of wine; he pulled a glass bottle from a case stacked on six other crates. Once he had poured a glass of red, he went back to his chair by the fire and motioned for the others to take a seat.

Ron grabbed the papers, but Collins said, "You can leave those on the table. Now that I have read them, I can tell the history in its entirety. I did teach quite a bit of history in the days of my youth, so I am well versed in this subject. Taroth and Thalom's history used to be taught until it was decreed banned."

"Why would people not want to learn about them?" Nora asked.

"Well, it happened many centuries ago, but how about I get on with telling this history first? Then, if there is time, I can tell you why," Collins said. Shaw had been right to tell the others that this man was rough around the edges. Ron shot Collins a look of anger anyway, as he did not like how he'd spoken to Nora.

"Alright, let's begin then," Collins said, meeting Ron's gaze.

Chapter Nine

Taroth and Thalom

*S*oon after the War of the Wielders ended, a new power began to surface. It did not form overnight but grew quietly for years. When the war ended and Ermon slew Kallot on the battlefield, it was thought that the wielders of the flame would go back to living normal lives of peace and tranquility now that the tyrant wielder Kallot had been defeated. So, when Ermon decided to track down and kill all the remaining wielders who could use the flame, he thought he was doing the right thing. His battle with Kallot only strengthened his justification for slaughtering thousands of people. He believed his reasoning was sound, for it was too dangerous to leave such power to those who would seek to abuse it. Once his decision was made, his act would be known as the cleansing of power.

Little did he know that Kallot had a wife, Vivian, who was carrying his son. Although, when the child was born, Vivian did not see him as her own son. She had named him Taroth; she had also blamed him for being the reason Kallot died in battle. If it were not for the child growing inside her, she would have been there in the fight alongside him. Instead, she was left alone, abandoned in their home, deemed incapable of fighting for fear of losing the child. Bitter hatred and resentment grew for the unborn child, a feeling that Vivian would hold against the boy as long as he drew breath.

Taroth's mother showed no compassion for him. It was something she made abundantly clear—she made sure to make him feel as she had when Kallot died. She wanted him to feel empty, weak, and unwanted. All the feelings she'd endured *since the death of Kallot, his father's death, and the pain of it all—that was what she tried to project onto Taroth.*

Over the years, Taroth was fed scraps of food after his mother ate. She did not let him sit with her at the dining table, but made him sit on the floor and eat his scraps like a beast. For even the slightest disobediences, she would lock him in a small chest only big enough for a five-year-old. She would leave him in the chest for hours as punishment, tucked away under her bed.

As Taroth got older, Vivian's temperament grew colder. When Taroth turned eight, he tried to stand up for himself after suffering years of abuse and malnourishment. He refused to be locked away in the cramped, suffocating chest after taking food from the dinner table, which he was not permitted to eat from.

Little did he know that his mother was a wielder.

When Taroth openly defied her commands, taking the food and eating as fast as he could, she walked up to him, anger written all over her face. She grabbed him by his shirt, throwing him against the dining room table. Then she picked him up by the collar of his ripped shirt, throwing him once more. Taroth slid across the table, displacing the plates of food, some shattering on the floor, others barely hanging over the edge of the table. His body crashed to the floor.

Vivian kicked him in the stomach and cursed him for being disobedient. Taroth pleaded for her to stop, but she kept kicking and yelling. She hit him until he had trouble breathing, until his vision went blurry, until the words coming from his mouth were incomprehensible, joined only by the sobs and blood gathering in his mouth. It was then that his mother picked up Taroth by his face and, with her right hand, lit a flame, taking her finger and burning a line in his skin above and below his left eye, pulling her finger along the side of his head. According to tales, the line above represented failure, and the line below represented uselessness, as the rituals of ancient wielders dictated the branding of weaker wielders being marked as such in days long forgotten.

Taroth screamed as his mother let him go, dropping him onto the floor. The boy curled into a ball and started to cry, holding the left side of his face next to his knees as smoke drifted into the air from his burnt face. He could smell the singed flesh.

Vivian looked down on him like a wounded animal, then turned around, but not before Taroth caught her smiling as though what she had done satisfied her.

That night, while Vivian slept, Taroth was in the washroom looking at his face in the mirror to see what his mother had done to him. It looked as though she'd melted the skin on the left side of his face. He went to touch the lines, but the slightest touch caused immense pain. Taroth had had his fill of being weak and beaten, and as he looked in the mirror, tears welled up in his eyes. Then, Taroth began to feel an intense sensation of needles inside both his hands. It grew in an instant, coursing through his whole body. He almost started screaming as the pain became too much; his body went numb moments later.

Taroth knew what he wanted to do. As his mother slept, he opened the door to her room. He walked in silently, tip-toeing his way closer toward the edge of her bed. He watched as she slept peacefully, wrapped in warm blankets, her head nestled in the center of two fluffed pillows. He wondered how she could sleep so well after all the hell that she'd made of his life. With tears in his eyes and his rage building, he stood at the side of the bed where Vivian slept unencumbered of any guilt or remorse. The anger raging within Taroth caused him to bring forth the flame. It came instantly, almost as natural as breathing. His anger grew as he recounted all the years of suffering that his mother had caused him. With the flame engulfing his hands, he grabbed her by the throat, squeezing tightly.

Vivian woke up in fear, her eyes wide with panic, darting in the dark to find her son's face staring at her. She opened her mouth to speak, but Taroth pushed his hand down on her neck, severing her head from her body. He watched the life drain from his mother's limp body, and Taroth felt a sense of calm wash over him, a feeling of peace that he had never felt before—he was free.

With a smile, Taroth turned from his mother's bedside and walked out of the room. He stretched out his arms, pushing the flame from his hands to the walls. A steady stream of blue fire burned everything it touched in the room.

Taroth felt good; he enjoyed the feeling of power, of freedom. He now knew he was able to be strong, and he never wanted to let that feeling go. The fire spread quickly throughout the house, moving from the walls to the ceiling, reaching into the empty rooms and igniting the furniture. Rolling, dark smoke filled the house, sinking lower and lower toward the floor. The roaring flames broke into the walls, blazing their way up to the roof. Taroth stepped outside, watching the flames consume the house, admiring his greatest achievement, freeing himself from his prison, his tormentor; he watched as it all burned down.

He took no items with him, since he had no possessions that held any meaning. Taroth walked throughout the countryside for weeks, finding food where he could, making small traps to catch animals that might happen wonder into one. He looked for berries to eat, and when chance gave way, he would steal what fruits or vegetables he could from farms he would come across along the countryside. Taroth tried to conjure the flame during his weeks of solitude but to no avail. Try as he might, he didn't understand why he could not do it. The more he tried, the more frustrated he became. Finally, during the night, when Taroth was walking among the tall grass, trying to find some shelter and a place to sleep, he saw flashes of light coming from a house not so far off in the distance. Trees were scattered around the house and the surrounding land, leaving areas for Taroth to hide.

Choosing to hide behind the closest tree to the house, Taroth then inched toward the nearest window. Candlelight reflected on his face when he peeked into the house from the windowpane's bottom corner. He saw a tall man wielding the flame with ease, and thought to himself that he should be able to use his gift in the same fashion.

Then Taroth saw the man pick up a child who looked to be around his age. The boy held up his hand and generated a small flame in the middle of his palm. Taroth now understood that the power of the flame could be taught.

It was then that Taroth decided to devise a plan to make sure he would be able to stay with these strangers. He moved from behind the tree closer to the front of the house. Then he grabbed a handful of dirt from the ground, rubbing it in on his face and clothes, making them appear dirtier, more worn out and ragged than they were. Taroth lay on the grass twenty feet or so away from the house so it would appear as if he was lost, cold, afraid, and too weak of a child to take care of himself in the morning. In truth, Taroth was tired of walking, and the grass was as good a place as any to rest for the night. His plan would come to fruition in the morning, and with that thought, Taroth slipped into a calm sleep.

When morning came, Taroth was woken up by the concerned yelling of a woman calling for her husband. Taroth knew he could play the victim quite well since he had been one for all his life, so he continued along with his plan. When the woman called her husband over to the front of the house, he came running. He scooped Taroth into his large, strong arms and carried him inside. There, they laid him on the floor next to the stone fireplace. Taroth enjoyed the warmth of the fireplace as it replaced the cold that had gripped his body during the night.

The woman gently tried talking to him, asking Taroth what had happened and how he'd ended up in the grass outside their house. As they began to clean him up with a warm hand towel, Taroth mumbled and deliberately stuttered his way to answering their questions. He told them how a fire had broken out in his home one night, and his mother was trapped inside when it burned down. He said to them that there was no place for him to go, so he began to wander for weeks on end until he saw a calming light coming from this very home, but he had passed out before he could reach the door. The man and woman continued to clean Taroth, introducing themselves as they did.

"This is my wife, Shani, and my name is Ermon, and this—" The man called to his son, who was shyly poking his head around the door frame in the other room. "This is my son, Thalom," Ermon said. "Say hello, Thalom."

"Hello," echoed a small, nervous voice.

"What is your name, child?" Shani asked.

"My . . . my name is Taroth," he said weakly.

"Why don't we finish cleaning you up, and then we can talk more after we get you something to eat?" Shani said.

"That would be very nice."

Shani led Taroth to their bathroom down the hall away from the kitchen. She lit a fire to heat the water she had poured into a tub. Taroth was just about the same size as Thalom, so she grabbed some of Thalom's clothes for Taroth to wear. When the water was heated enough, she removed the coals from beneath the tub; she took Taroth's shirt as he handed it to her and let out a gasp. "Oh my . . . Taroth, what happened to you?" she said as she looked at the boy. His upper body was covered with scars along his back, shoulders, stomach, and chest.

Some of the chest scars were small and scattered, while others on his back were long and thick, where it appeared he had been cut quite severely. Taroth just stood there in the bathroom with a blank stare and didn't answer, even though in his head he revisited how he'd come to acquire the scars. "You know what, we don't have to talk about that," Shani said calmly. She took off Taroth's pants and had him get into the tub. "You can put these clothes on when you are done, okay? Take your time. I'll be back to check on you." Shani placed the clothes she'd taken from Thalom's room on a wooden chair next to the door. She walked out of the room, leaving the door slightly cracked open.

Taroth leaned back in the hot water when she left, letting the heat soak into his small, tired body. He closed his eyes, trying to push out the images of the brutal punishments his mother had given him as he relaxed, thinking of his next move. Everything was going according to his plan; he was playing his part perfectly. Shani walked into the kitchen where Ermon was cooking an assortment of breakfast foods, and Thalom was sitting in a chair at the dining room table playing with wood-sculpted toys his father had made for him.

Shani threw away Taroth's ragged clothes and looked at Ermon. "That poor boy, he has had some trouble. There are scars up and down his body. Not to mention his face. I think he should stay with us for a while, so he can feel safe. I wouldn't feel right sending him away with no place to go."

Ermon looked up at his wife. "Well, we can keep him here for a while until he has time to adjust. Then, when he is more comfortable, we will talk to him and see if he has any relatives or someone to go to. Plus, Thalom will have someone to play with. Does that sound good, Thalom?" Ermon asked.

The boy nodded. He was excited to have a new friend to play with. Shani went back to check on Taroth; when she tapped on the door to the bathroom, slowly pushing it open, she saw that the kid was already cleaned up and dressed. He was standing on a stool, looking in a mirror at his face. "Cleaned up, I see," Shani said. "Breakfast will be done soon. Why don't you come have a seat? You must be hungry." Taroth nodded his head and got off the stool, following the woman into the kitchen.

Breakfast was ready on the table when they walked in. Taroth could smell the butter melting on fresh-baked rolls. He walked over to a chair at the table and sat next to Thalom. "Well, Taroth, don't be shy; go ahead and eat what you like. There's plenty to go around," Ermon said, waving his hand over the table. At this, Taroth was actually surprised. He could not remember a time when he was able to eat a full meal, let alone a home-cooked meal instead of meat scraps that consisted of more fat than meat. The kindness of the family was something Taroth had never experienced, and for all his planning, there was still a part of him that sought affection as every child would. His eyes felt wet as a slight quiver appeared on his bottom lip.

He thought it would show his weakness if he cried, but he looked toward Shani, who just smiled at him. "It's okay. Help yourself to as much as you like." He filled his plate with a sample of everything that was on the table—the buttered rolls with rising steam, the crisp, savory bacon, and the potatoes cut up into little cubes that were perfectly browned on the outside while being soft on the inside. A smile came across his face, and for the first time, it felt genuine.

There was a time when Taroth had still wanted his mother's affection, never understanding why she treated him the way she did until he got older. He thought if he did everything right, she would show him the love he so desperately wanted. She knew he wanted to make her happy through his actions, but to her, that was just another way she was able to hurt him. She would pretend to be on the cusp of giving him praise or positive acknowledgment, but at the last second, she would break him down to nothing. Shani's compassion was most unexpected. Taroth had never known what it felt like to be cared for; he felt afraid, but he also knew this was different. This could be real.

After Taroth ate all the food he had amassed on his plate, he thought his stomach would burst. He had never eaten so much good food before. Ermon let his stomach settle before he spoke to him. "Taroth, Shani and I think it would be a good idea for you to stay with us for a little while. At least until we can see if you have any other family to live with. Perhaps an aunt or uncle?"

Taroth looked at Ermon. "I don't have any other family. My mother was the only family I had. She told me my father died before I was born and that there was no one left," he said, putting on a solemn face.

"In any case, we would still like for you to stay here. If you would like that as well?" Shani asked.

Taroth felt happy at the invitation to stay. His plan was working, and in all honesty, he had no place to go. "I would like that," he said with a smile.

As time went by, Taroth and Thalom became inseparable. They played together, learned together; they even managed to get into quite a bit of mischief. Taroth was living his childhood for the first time. In the first year, he got to experience what it was like to have people who cared for him. Thalom introduced Taroth to his friends whenever they went to the market for supplies. Taroth was happy, but he knew Ermon was teaching Thalom to use the flame and wanted to be a part of it. Every night, Thalom would go into his father's study and close the door behind him. Taroth could see the blue glow from beneath the door. Night after night, Ermon would teach Thalom.

One night, a year after Taroth had arrived, the two boys walked to their shared bedroom and were getting ready for the night. Taroth asked, "Thalom, what do you do in there all night?" The boy looked surprised, as he didn't think Taroth had noticed him going to the study.

"My dad gives me extra lessons. He wants me to be smart one day," Thalom said. Taroth knew it was a blatant lie, so he played along with it.

"Is there any way I can join you one of these nights?" Taroth asked.

Thalom raised his hands. "No, no, my dad says it's only supposed to stay in the family." "Can you tell me what you are learning at least?"

"I can't—it's a secret," Thalom said.

Taroth looked saddened but then looked up at the other boy. "If I tell you a secret, will you tell me one?"

"Only if it is a good secret."

"I can make fire."

"We all can make fire. We just need some sticks and dried grass. That's no secret, Taroth," Thalom said.

"I don't mean that kind of fire. I mean this kind." With all the strength and effort Taroth could gather, he closed his eyes. His mind went back to the night he'd killed his mother and burned his house to the ground. Taroth harnessed his feelings from that night and desperately tried to make the flame appear in his hand. If he was even to have a chance to learn how to use this power, he needed to show Thalom he could do it; he needed it more than anything. Finally, when he opened his eyes, he had a small blue flame in the center of his palm. Taroth couldn't believe that it had worked. He had not been able to conjure the flame since that night. After all his other attempts, he was finally able to do it. He smiled, feeling proud. Then he saw the shocked look painted on Thalom's face. He lost his concentration, and the flame went out.

"Taroth, I didn't know you could do that. How are you able to? My dad says there are no more people who can do that," Thalom said excitedly.

"I've only done it once before. I've tried tons of times, but I don't know how to make it happen when I want it to," Taroth admitted.

"That's what my dad has been teaching me." Thalom held his hand up and produced a flame in a matter of seconds. "It was hard at first; with his help, it got easier every time. We should tell my dad."

"No," Taroth blurted out. "This is a secret between us, remember."

"But my dad could teach you. He's really good. He knows everything about it."

"What if he doesn't teach me? I don't want to take the chance of asking just to be told no. Can't you teach me after your lessons with him?" Taroth asked.

"I'm not anywhere near as good as my dad, but I guess I could try and teach you," said Thalom. "It could be fun. Who knew both of us could make a flame?"

"Yeah, who knew," Taroth said as a smile edged its way across his face.

Every night for the next couple of years, Thalom taught Taroth how to use and harness the power of the flame, starting with the simple task of calling the flame to his hand and progressing to the more complex ways of wielding. By the time Taroth turned seventeen, he was able to wield the flame better than Thalom. Taroth and Thalom would walk to a secluded part of the forest that met with the edge of the river, far from their home, to practice using the flame in secret and grow their power. They would spar regularly, trying to learn more ways to control the flame.

Taroth would stand across from Thalom, and they would both call the flame into their hands. Once they did that, Taroth would send the fire at Thalom like a whip that would fly through the air. Thalom would use the flame to create a shield that would cover him from the ground to his head, canceling out the incoming fire that would have surely burned him on contact.

They both understood that the flame's power was only as strong as the one wielding it. So when they would spar for hours at a time, they never fought with all the power they could pull. Thalom stressed to Taroth the importance of that rule, just as his dad had told him. They would walk home talking about new ways to manipulate the flame and perfect their craft when they were done.

By now, Shani and Ermon were parents to Taroth; he had forgotten about using them to achieve his own goals. Instead, he was happy living where he was with Thalom, whom he viewed as his brother. He had the love of a family, and he had grown into a strong, capable, soon-to-be man.

But all it took was one night, and everything changed.

Before dinner, after Taroth and Thalom got back from an evening of sparring, they were getting cleaned up. Taroth was in the bathroom when he had an idea. He thought about what would happen if he tried to cover an object in the flame and wield it as a weapon. He finished getting cleaned up and saw he still had some time before dinner was ready, so he went out the back of the house to the old barn. The barn was next to the house on the right, mainly used to keep the firewood dry and extra tools organized.

Once he was inside, he looked around, moving Ermon's tools that lay on work-tables, benches, and stools the man had acquired over the years.

Taroth knew Ermon had a sword somewhere in the barn that he never used, and he was determined to find it. He'd overheard Ermon talking about the sword with Shani; the man had asked her if he should get rid of it or give it to Thalom when he was ready to leave the house. Taroth looked everywhere in the barn. He was about to give up searching for the sword, but as he walked to the door, he stepped on a floorboard that made a hollow sound. Taroth stopped and backed up. He knelt to one knee and tapped his knuckles on the board he had stepped on. Taroth conjured the flame, using it to burn the board to avoid wasting time finding the tools needed to pull up all the nails.

He looked into the space and saw the sword sitting there in its sheath.

The sword was covered in a thick layer of dust as if it hadn't been touched in years. Taroth reached in and took the blade; he blew the dust off the scabbard and unsheathed it. The light from the oil lamps flickered off the sword's steel. It was long and clean, with an indentation running down its middle. The sword had a gold handle with a blue marking on the hilt, just below the squared gold cross guard. The marking was in the shape of a flame on one side of the hilt. Taroth knew what this meant, as Thalom had explained it to him—the sword belonged to a wielder.

Taroth called the flame forth once more and held it in his hand. He then touched the blade from the base of the cross guard to the tip, spreading the flame over the sword. Then Taroth slowly took his hand away, letting go of the flame. The fire remained burning on the sword's steel blade. Taroth was surprised; he hadn't actually thought his idea would work. He used the sword, swinging it like he was fighting an invisible person. With every swing, the flame persistently stayed on the blade. While Taroth was swinging the sword, his back was turned to the barn door, and Ermon walked in. The man watched Taroth with shock written on his face. Words escaped him; he couldn't believe what was happening.

Taroth turned around as he swung the sword again, and stopped in his tracks when he saw Ermon standing there. They both looked at each other, not sure what to say. Ermon was the first to speak. "Put the sword down, Taroth." Taroth did, and as he let the blade fall to the ground, the flame dissipated. Ermon tried to think of something else to say, but he had not seen another wielder besides his son since the war. He was still trying to find the words. After a few moments of collecting his thoughts, Ermon said, "How is this possible? There are no other wielders alive. How long have you been hiding this from me?" He began to walk closer to Taroth.

"I've only been able to use the flame for a little while," Taroth said.

"Why lie to me, Taroth? Being able to imbue that sword is not something a beginner can do. I'll ask one more time. How long have you been able to wield the flame?" Ermon's voice became louder.

"For as long as I can remember. I used it once when I was little, but I didn't know how to control it," Taroth said.

"Who first taught you to wield? Who was it?" Taroth did not answer, looking away from Ermon. "Who was it! I am not going to ask again!" Ermon was inches from Taroth, his fists clenched in anger.

"Thalom! Thalom taught me. He has been teaching me for years," Taroth finally admitted.

"You are never to wield the flame again. Do you understand me? As long as you live here, you will not use it. It's a seductive power. Without proper training, you will fall to it." Ermon said, on the verge of shouting.

"Then teach me. I am already better than Thalom, and I can do more than he can, look." Taroth conjured the flame and was prepared to show Ermon how good he was at wielding, but as soon as he got the flame in his hand, Ermon raised his own hand, smacking Taroth across the face. Taroth let the flame go and grabbed his face as he backed away. Looking up, Taroth had tears in his eyes. Never had he thought that Ermon would hit him. It brought him back to when his mother used to beat and torture him.

"I'm sorry, Taroth, but I told you, you are never to wield the flame again. I want you to get your things and leave in the morning," Ermon said with a heavy heart.

"Why won't you teach me?" Taroth asked.

"Wielders are too dangerous. The power can be too much for some people. I'm not going to be responsible for another wielder losing control." Ermon pointed to the barn door. "Go get your things ready for tomorrow."

"This is my home. Where would I go?" Taroth asked.

"This is not your home anymore. We took you in. You are old enough now to make it on your own."

"So just like that, you are throwing me away. Just like trash. You are just like her," Taroth said as he clenched his fists and made a fire in both hands.

"What are you talking about? Like who?" Ermon asked, slowly backing away from Taroth.

"Like her. You two are the same, but you are worse. You took me in, showed me what a real family is. You showed me what it's like to feel love and have real

parents, and now you are taking it all away from me. I've had everything taken from me since the day I was born, so why should this be any different?" Taroth said through gritted teeth.

"Taroth, what are you talking about?" Ermon questioned.

"My mother may have beat me and tortured me since I was born, that's why I have all these scars, but at least she never showed me what love could feel like. She never gave me a false hope to believe in. With her, I knew what was going to happen, but with you and Shani, I started to believe I was your son. But I guess not, since you would teach Thalom to wield but not me."

"You are like a son to us, but you cannot wield here. Wait, you said you wielded when you were younger—how did the fire start when you were a child?" Ermon asked. He seemed to be putting the pieces together.

"She did unspeakable things to me," Taroth said with tears running down his face. "She did this to me, to my face. She wielded the flame and burned my face. That was the last time I would let her hurt me. The last time she would take from me. She deserved what she got. She—she looked so peaceful as she slept, but how could she? After all she did to me, how could she sleep so soundly! The look in her eyes that night looked like she was scared, almost like she knew how I felt every day of my life, but that night it was her turn. It was so easy, so easy."

"Taroth, what are you saying? Are you saying your mother was a wielder? Did you kill her? What was her name?" Ermon asked.

"Do monsters have names? I didn't kill my mother; I killed the monster that brought me into this world. You have no idea what it was like. She reminded me every day that it was my fault my father died in the war. She never let me forget that I'm the reason the great Kallot died. So she would beat me, feed me scraps every day. Do you know what it is to be so hungry that anything you eat is precious? To have nothing to eat for days except the breadcrumbs on the floor?"

Fear and what Taroth said paralyzed Ermon. "I had no idea, Taroth. We saw the scars, but we didn't want to ask."

"Why would you? She might have been a monster, but you, you won't even give me a chance, and now you want me to leave. This is all I have!" Taroth shouted

with his fists still clenched, the flame around his hands growing bigger. Then he saw something change in Ermon. "What is it? What aren't you telling me?"

"Nothing. Let's go talk about this inside, okay?" Ermon tried to keep his composure, but Taroth kept pressing the question.

"What changed?" Taroth sifted through what they'd just discussed, trying to see what had caused Ermon to act differently. Then it came to him. "You asked for my mother's name, but when I said my father's, you changed. Why?" Taroth stepped closer. "Tell me why that means something."

"Because I killed him," Ermon sighed. Taroth stood still, confused about what he heard, but Ermon kept talking calmly, trying to reason with the boy. "I killed him, Taroth. He waged war on innocent people—he had to be stopped. He was my friend, but he went down a dark path that he never came back from. If I knew he had a son—I'm sorry, Taroth. I truly am." Ermon walked closer to try and comfort the boy, but he backed away.

"So it was you. You are the one that made my mother what she was. It's because of you." Taroth's fists were tightening, and his body was shaking.

"Taroth, you need to calm down," Ermon said.

"Calm down. You want me to calm down. How? You are responsible for everything that happened to me as a child, and now you want me out of the house you raised me in. How am I supposed to be calm? How can I..."

When the words left his mouth, Taroth dropped to his knees, letting out a scream filled with his anger, his pain. He'd lost everything; he'd lost it all again. This time, it wasn't just getting free from a monster or having a family ripped from him, but to know the man he would have called his father caused his suffering. As he screamed, blue flames started to erupt from his mouth, and his eyes burned wildly. "No, I won't let you take anything else from me."

He stood up.

"Calm down, Taroth," Ermon said as he conjured the flame into his own hands. "Fight it, don't let it consume you."

"It's too late for that. This is your fault. You did this. This... This feels good. Just like the night I put my hand through my mother's neck. It felt like this. I feel—I

feel strong. I feel like I never have to be weak again. I will never be weak again!"
Taroth raised his hands and threw fire wildly at Ermon.

Ermon made a flame shield, protecting himself from the oncoming attack.
"Taroth, stop! This isn't you. You can control this!" he shouted.

"You don't understand. I am controlling this. I get it now. I always thought the
flame was a separate part of who I am, something I had to hide, something to be
used in secret. I'm done hiding this power—I've let it in completely. This is the only
thing that hasn't hurt me, the only thing that has protected me. This is the only
thing I can trust. This makes me happy. Why do you think I was on your lawn so
many years ago? I saw you teaching Thalom. That's the only reason I was there.
After you and Shani showed me what family was, I thought I could be happy, but
now I realize—this wielding, this power, this is what makes me happy." Taroth
said the last words menacingly as he bent down to pick up the sword.

"Taroth, we can talk about this." Ermon pleaded.

"No!" the boy said. "I've seen your truth. You don't want to teach me; you don't
want me. I'm not your son, and I never was. I shouldn't have made myself think
I was even remotely considered family. You destroyed my family before I was ever
born." Taroth took his hand and ran it across the blade, putting the flame to the
sword. He looked at Ermon with his eyes emanating the blue flame and stepped
toward him.

Ermon threw fire at Taroth, but every attempt to hit him failed. The boy used
the flaming sword to cut through. As he walked forward, Ermon kept backing up
until he was back against the barn wall. "All my life, I have never had strength,
never had power, but now, now I do. I will not let anyone take from me anymore."
Taroth said. He raised the sword in front of his face, admiring the blue glow
of flame surrounding the blade. Then, thrusting forward suddenly, he stabbed
Ermon through the stomach.

Shani opened the barn door. She'd gone out to see what was taking Ermon so
long to retrieve Taroth, but when she heard raised voices from the barn, she went to
see if they were okay. When she looked at Taroth standing in front of Ermon, with
his mouth and eyes smoldering in blue fire, holding the sunken blade as it pierced
through Ermon's stomach, she screamed. Taroth took the sword out of Ermon; his

body began to burn in the flame as he dropped to the floor, holding the gaping wound.

Taroth started walking toward Shani. "Was it your idea to throw me away as well? You were my family, and now I have nothing!" he yelled as he moved closer. Shani closed the door and ran back toward the house. Taroth used the flame, blowing the door off the hinges and chasing after her. "Why can't I be happy? Why can't I have anything in this life worthwhile!" he shouted as he continued walking.

"Thalom! Thalom!" Shani screamed as she ran toward the house. Taroth elevated his flame-covered hand and put a wall of fire between the woman and the house's porch. She stopped in her tracks, turning around with tears rolling down her cheeks.

"Taroth, why are you doing this? I love you," she said.

Taroth was done listening, done reasoning, done with all the lies. "No, you're just like Ermon. You don't want me. No one does."

"That's not true. I raised you since you were a boy. I took care of you when you were sick. I love you as my own," she said.

"So, why was Ermon so quick to throw me away? If he was my father's friend, why did he have to kill him? Why would he leave me to suffer at the hands of my mother?" Taroth paused. "Maybe they were trying to teach me something, teach me that I shouldn't put my faith in anyone. Maybe all I need is myself. That's all I've ever had anyway, that's all I have ever had."

"I love you, Taroth. I always will, just know that," Shani said as Taroth moved within inches, too consumed by the flames' power coursing through him to care for her words.

Thalom was on the porch, watching as Taroth pushed the flaming sword through her middle, killing his mother.

When Shani fell to the ground, Taroth let go of the flame and dropped the wall of fire, and the flame on the sword disappeared. The fire in his eyes and mouth left, returning his normal features. Thalom ran to his mother's body and held her in his arms, too distraught to think. "Why! Why would you do this? They loved you. You were our family. Why?" Thalom yelled, unable to hold back the free-flowing tears. Taroth just turned away without saying a word, "I'll never forgive you, Taroth, I'll never forgive you!" Thalom yelled.

"I don't expect you to. Now you know what it's like to lose everything, everything you held dear," Taroth said. Thalom got up and raised his hands; he brought the flame into his palms. Taroth turned around and looked the other boy dead in the eye. "You don't want to do that," he said. His gaze was piercing. "You know how it will end. You are my brother, and I love you, but I don't want to hurt you, so just stop."

Thalom let the flame fade from his hands. "You are not my brother. I hate you. I hate you with everything I am. One day, Taroth, I will come for you. I'll make you suffer for this. I don't care how long it takes—I will kill you," Thalom promised.

"Well, you had better be prepared then," Taroth said as he turned and walked into the dark of the night.

Chapter Ten

Betrayal

C ollins took a deep breath as he finished telling the tale of Taroth and Thalom that had been written on the pages, sipping his wine.

"What happened after Taroth left?" Ron asked. "That must have been years before the Battle of the Storming Mountains."

"It was. It was many years before that battle. But, unfortunately, we don't have time for the whole story, I'm afraid." Collins took another sip. "I will not be the one to finish telling you the tale's ending. If I am not mistaken, the First Born should be here in a matter of minutes, and they will be able to tell you the rest, I'm sure." The man stood up to get another glass of wine.

"The First Born? Who are you talking about?" Ron asked.

"Have you not heard? They are the ones that are looking for you," Collins said as he took a healthy pour.

"Ron, we need to leave—if these First Born are on their way, we won't be safe here. Collins, what did you do?" Shaw asked.

"Oh, you didn't think that red smoke from the log was for an atmospheric effect, did you? No, the First Born will be here shortly to take you. I was instructed to burn this log if a young man matching your description showed up," Collins said smugly.

"Why, Collins? We're friends. Why would you do this to me? I've known you for over thirty years. How could you betray me?"

"Don't be so dramatic. It's not about betrayal, Shaw. It's about picking the right side. I'm choosing the side of the First Born. They already have one city taken, and I don't see anything them from getting the other four with their power. To be honest, I had no idea you would be coming with them. All I was told was about this boy and his friends. It's an unfortunate circumstance, but there is little that I could do at this point for you anyway. All I could really do is offer my condolences." Collins's tone had grown increasingly patronizing.

"Who are the First Born?" Nora asked.

"I don't want to spoil any of the surprises for when they get here."

"We were friends, Collins—just tell me why!" Shaw yelled, his anger getting the better of him.

"Well, I suppose it doesn't matter if I do. I did this because I have been part of the First Born for almost a decade. I was the one who helped them claim the first city. I taught my students their practices, customs, and beliefs, and over the years, more people seemed to become accustomed to the thought of one king ruling over the five kingdoms. That way, peace and prosperity could be achieved, as long as the people followed the rule of the First Born. That's why the Lord of the First Born decried any histories that tell the tale of Taroth. He is building his own legacy."

Collins took a large sip of wine as he finished speaking. Ron traced the letters on the sword's hilt, now knowing the meaning behind the letters "FB."

"Ah, there are the banners now," Collins said as he looked out the window.

"We need to go!" Shaw shouted. Ron, Nora, and Grant stood up, rushing to follow the old man as he led them to the back door. Ron looked over his shoulder and could see the banners in plain view from the window, bearing a blue upside-down triangle with the letters centered inside. Shaw went to turn the nob on the door, but it was bolted from the other side. "Ron, give me a hand. We need to break the door down quickly."

Ron turned from the window and ran over to help the man; they bashed their shoulders into the door, trying to knock it down. After three attempts, Nora looked more closely. "The hinges—the door swings inward. We can break the hinges and take the door down that way. Grant, give me one of your daggers."

He did, and she wedged it in between the hinge of the door and the wall it was connected to. She lifted up on the handle of the dagger, pushing the hinge outward, forcing it until she was able to break the hinge from the wall. Then Nora bent down, utilizing the exact same technique on the bottom hinge, and in no time they were able to separate the door from the wall and escape.

Outside, they could hear Collins opening the door and telling the First Born soldiers they had gone out the back. There was no place to go. Their only options were running for the Red Band River or making a break for Oroze. Either way would take a lot of luck—the soldiers had horses, and both options were a ways off.

"We may have to try and fight our way out of here," Shaw said. Ron unsheathed his sword, bracing himself for the coming fight. They were all prepared as they moved in the direction of the Red Band River, hugging the mountainside that Collins's house resided next to.

In moments, the First Born soldiers saw them. Yet the soldiers did not take arms against them right away. Instead, they held their hands up as if to offer peace.

"We do not wish to fight," said the lead soldier, taking off his black helmet. "We only wish to talk for a moment and see if we could persuade you to come with us." More soldiers came from around the house, the clanging of their armor echoing. At least twenty now stood before them.

"That's a lot of men for just wanting to talk," Grant said under his breath.

"What is there to talk about?" Ron asked.

"You must be Ron. All we ask is that you come with us to meet with our lord. He has been waiting to talk to you for some time. Your friends can go on about their business, but he would prefer to have you come with us on your own accord. There is no need to fight. The lord did, however, give us orders to take you if you decide to not cooperate. He is giving you a choice."

"Why does he want to see me? What could I possibly offer him?" Ron asked.

"We do not know. It is not our place to ask when our lord gives us a command."

"Okay, I have one more question. Why the hell would I go anywhere with people dressed in the same armor as the people who destroyed my home!" Ron yelled.

"That is a question better suited to be answered by our lord."

Out of the corner of Ron's eye, he saw another man come out from around Collins's house. "Well, Ron," the man said as he walked closer with both hands behind his back, talking calmly, "it's up to you. If you come with us peacefully, we will not kill your friends and leave their bodies out here to rot in the sun." Ron saw that it was the same masked man who'd confronted him in the forest when they started their journey. The man stood in front of his soldiers, wearing a black robe and a white mask with two black lines above and below the left eye. "It's really up to you, Ron—come with us, and we will let your friends walk away. Resist, and we will kill them without a second thought. What do you say?"

Ron looked at Grant, Shaw, and then Nora.

"You can't just go with them," Nora said. "We don't know what they will do to you. So we will stay and fight with you."

"That's right, we aren't going anywhere," Grant added as he put a hand on Shaw's shoulder. Shaw nodded as Ron looked back at him.

Ron then turned to face the man in the mask. "We are just fine staying here. But, if you want me, come get me." He readied himself, preparing to fight.

"All right, have it your way. Just remember you chose this. Take Ron and kill everyone else." It almost sounded as if the man sighed with disappointment before he unleashed his soldiers.

The soldiers ran around the masked man, charging toward Ron, the sound of steel ringing in the air as they drew their weapons. Nora and Grant moved in front of Ron, bracing for the attack. The first soldier ran at Nora, swinging his sword, but she dodged and swung her staff, hitting him in the mouth. A loud crack reverberated from his head as his jaw broke, swaying side to side, unhinged from the rest of his face. The soldier went down, holding on to his face, shaking and screaming. While the soldier on the other side looked at his brother in arms, Grant rushed him and planted his daggers into his chest, puncturing his left lung and heart. The soldier stared into Grant's eyes as his body slid off the daggers, becoming encircled by dust as it hit the ground.

More soldiers came running, with Nora and Grant engaging them. Shaw was firing arrows at the incoming horde, picking them off one by one. Ron ran into the fray with Nora and Grant; he began to fight two soldiers closing in on Grant from behind him.

The soldiers switched their attack to Ron, swinging wildly. He was able to guard against the oncoming blows, and once he saw an opening, he went on the offensive. Ron could tell these soldiers were not as experienced as him; he saw the weaknesses in their techniques. Ron went for a strike on the right side of the closest soldier. Once the soldier blocked it with his sword, Ron stepped forward as he'd planned, giving the man a swift uppercut to the jaw. The soldier was dazed, so Ron made his next move. Pulling his blade back, he thrust it into the man's abdomen. Then, bending his knees, he used his momentum to lift the sword up, raising the soldier off the ground.

Ron pulled the sword out as he sank back to his knees. The soldier held his stomach, screaming, trying to pack his intestines back inside his body, hoping to stop the bleeding, but Ron kicked him in the chest. The man went down and didn't get up. The remaining soldiers looked at Ron, raised their swords, and with a cry ran toward him. Ron got ready to take on another soldier, but the first fell down dead before Ron's feet. He saw an arrow sticking out of his head and turned to look at Shaw, who was readying another arrow, preparing to fire again.

Ron looked around, found the man in the mask, and started walking toward him.

He knew that Nora and Grant could take care of the remaining soldiers, and as he moved past the fighting, he found himself within a few feet of the man. "It's foolish to think you can challenge me now. With what little you know about wielding, a sword will not be enough. Even if you were stronger and could wield on command, it would still not be enough. We could teach you, though," the masked man offered.

"We will see if it's enough. I want no part of what you think you can teach me. If you want me so bad, why didn't you capture me in the woods or when you left that handprint?" Ron asked.

"I had to know beyond a shadow of a doubt that it was you. Leaving Greyland after receiving the message was one thing, but I needed to see if you could still produce the flame. The rest played out as you see it now."

"You couldn't just leave me alone, could you?"

"No," said the man.

Ron walked closer, determined to fight, tightening his grip on the sword. The masked man looked over at his soldiers fighting and dying. "It seems like your friends know how to fight, but they will not be able to help you, Ron. They may kill all my soldiers, but they are nothing to me, just a means to an end. You are here now. It's time to go."

"I'm not going anywhere with you. I don't know who you are or what you want, but it ends here. I'm done running," Ron said as he raised his sword.

The masked man raised his right hand, looking directly at Ron. It became immersed in a blue flame. Ron stopped in his tracks but kept his sword at the ready, waiting for what was coming next. Without a word, the man made a fist, creating a wall of flame and cutting off Ron from the rest of the fighting.

Ron looked around, panicked; he didn't know what was going to happen. He looked through the flames to see Nora—she was still fighting alongside Grant and Shaw. The fighting was almost over, with only a handful of soldiers left.

Nora looked up and saw the wall of flame separating Ron from everyone else. She looked around for a way to get past the wall, but the man in the mask created more walls on either side, boxing the soldiers, Nora, Grant, and Shaw in against the mountainside.

Ron's attention turned back to the man. He walked closer, intending to kill him, and the man moved closer as well.

Ron swung his sword, but the masked man dodged it, striking Ron on the side of his head with his closed fist as the flame wavered from the quick motions. Ron stumbled but regained his composure, feeling the heat from the hit, then charged at the masked man again. This time he tried a combination of swings that would have worked on any soldier. The masked man didn't move but instead raised another wall of flame before him. Ron swung his sword, unable to break through. Looking at his blade after each strike, he could see small wisps of white smoke rising as it began to heat up. It felt as though the flame had a force of its own, pushing back when his sword struck. Not understanding how that could be possible, Ron stepped back, realizing he was in one of the moments Cap had lectured him about during his training. But Ron knew he couldn't back down now.

The masked man dropped the shield of flame. "Just come with me. It would be so much easier, and all of this will stop. I am not your enemy—if you just come with me, you would see that."

"I'm not going with you. Your army killed my family, destroyed my home, and ripped me away from the life I had. You are the enemy. You're also just a coward who hides behind a mask. Not even brave enough to show your face."

The man's tone changed, no longer calm, now a quiet and almost palpable anger. "I've had enough of this charade. I'm ending this. You had your chance. You were given a choice, and now you will bear the consequence of it. It's time to go."

Ron went to strike the masked man, but when the man dodged his sword stroke, the flame on his right hand grew, and he punched Ron in the side of the head again. This time Ron fell to his knees, dropping his sword. His vision grew blurry. How was he so fast?

Ron reached for his sword. His fingers wrapped the hilt and he buried the tip of the blade in the dirt, trying to prop himself up so he could stand. The moment he did, he lost his footing, stumbled, and fell back to his knees. His hearing was muffled, all noise drowned out by the droning in his head.

Nora looked through the wall of flame and saw Ron on his knees as the masked man approached him. "Ron, get up! Get up, Ron!" she yelled.

Grant finished off the last soldier who could fight and heard Nora pleading. He and Shaw looked on with her. The masked man stood beside Ron, watching him for a moment. Then, with another quick blow, he punched Ron in the face, and the others could only watch as their friend crumpled to the ground.

"Stop, don't touch him!" Grant shouted.

The masked man looked at the three through the wall of flame, not even given them a second thought when he turned away. He whistled for his horse with two fingers, and as it trotted over, he picked up Ron's body and laid him across the saddle.

Collins approached as the man was about to put his foot through the stirrup and mount his horse. "My lord, may I ask . . . may I ask for my payment. As you kindly offered to pay the person who led you to Ron's location."

"Ah yes, here you go." The masked man reached in the side saddlebag and threw a pouch of coins to Collins.

"My lord, what will you do with these miscreants?"

"For now, nothing. I have what I want, and for the time being, they are no concern of mine. The real question you should be asking is, what will they do with you?" The masked man jolted the reins and left with Ron while Nora, Grant, and Shaw looked on helplessly.

Collins stared off in bewilderment, watching the lord ride into the valley. When the masked man was almost out of sight, the walls of flame fell, leaving behind blackened scorch marks on the field. Grant wasted no time sprinting toward Collins as the old man tried to run. He grabbed Collins by the throat, forcing him back against the wood paneling of his home. "Where is he taking Ron, you son of bitch? Tell me!" Grant's grip got tighter around Collins's neck as he gasped for air. The color drained from the man's face as his hands frantically tried to pry at Grant's overpowering fingertips.

"Grant, let him go!" Nora shouted. "Let him go!"

The young man regained himself and slowly released his hold on Collins, peeling away one finger at a time. Collins fell to the ground, trying to catch his breath, still holding his throat. Grant backed away, asking Nora for one of the small brown vials from her pack, which she handed to him. He rubbed the oil onto the back of his neck. He must have pulled a muscle during the fighting—a warm, sharp pain still lingered.

Shaw marched up to Collins, picking him up, not affording him the luxury of sitting.

"Where is he taking Ron?" Shaw asked.

"I don't know. All I was supposed to do was alert them if he came around," Collins muttered.

"I don't believe you." Nora wanted answers. "You said you taught the teachings of the First Born. You know about their ways, their culture. How can you serve the First Born for almost ten years and not know anything? I think you know more than you're telling. Where do you think they are going?"

"He owns a lot of the land. He has spent years building his empire—he could literally be anywhere. He owns Oroze, but he has bordering villages under his control to the south and east. That's all I know—I was never one to ask too many questions. When I chose to ally myself with the First Born, I found it best to do what they requested of me. The side of power always wins, and they pay handsomely to those that are fully committed in their beliefs."

"So that's why you did it? That's all you wanted—you would trade a life for a few coins? What's wrong with you? Did you even care to think about what his life means to some people? You're the most pathetic kind of person, you poor excuse for a man. You deserve less than nothing," Nora said in disgust, then turned and walked up to Shaw. "We need to find Ron, but I don't know where to start. I guess we could start looking here."

As she finished talking, she walked past Grant, but then she saw him move from the corner of her eye. In the split second it took for Nora to realize what was happening, he had already removed a dagger and buried it deep into Collins's heart.

Grant looked into Collins's wide eyes, speaking softly. "This is what you deserve." Nora and Shaw stared in disbelief. They didn't know their friend was capable of outright killing a man. They understood; they felt the same, after all, but did not act on impulse. Collins's lifeless body slid from the dagger and fell to the ground. Grant turned around, looking at Nora and Shaw. "He deserved what happened. He would have done it again and again—he would have served the First Born or anyone for coin. It wouldn't be right if we let him live, knowing someone else could lose their life all because we didn't kill him. It's better this way. Now we can figure out where to start looking for Ron," Grant said, justifying his action.

"You're right. It just would have been less surprising if you let us know what you were going to do beforehand, but it was deserved. Who knows how many times he has done this while trying to find Ron?" Nora said.

The pain in Grant's neck was gone, but he felt more tired than usual. "What do we do now?" he asked, disregarding how he felt. He was focused on finding his friend.

"Well, before we head off blindly, going around to all these other places, why don't we see what we can find in Collins's house first. Maybe there will be some information as to where we may need to go," Shaw said.

Nora and Grant walked toward the house. The gatekeeper told them he would join them in a minute, lingering above Collins's deceased body. "How did you go so far? How could you trust this First Born? You knew more about them than anyone, and yet you still trusted them. I thought you were better than that," Shaw said with a disparaging look. Finally, he turned away from his former friend's body and walked toward the house.

Once all three were inside, they began looking at the papers strewn around on the tables, bookshelves, and end tables positioned around Collins's chair close to the fireplace. "What are we even searching for?" Grant asked.

"Look for anything that has mention of locations. If the First Born already controls Oroze, they may be housing prisoners in other places. Collins knew they have small villages and camps in their possession to the east. Look for any village that seems of note," Shaw said, scanning and moving papers around hastily.

After several hours of poring over letters and documents for any clue to where the man in the mask could have taken Ron, Nora began to vent her frustration. "There is nothing here. We have been looking for hours, and nothing we've found is getting us closer." She was visibly upset.

"Keep looking. We will find something. We have to," Shaw said, putting a reassuring hand on her shoulder. Nora continued to search, moving to the papers that lay on the end tables by the fire. She picked up a thick stack and shuffled through it. Soon, she noticed that the same name kept coming up throughout the writing. It couldn't be a coincidence, so she took the stack of papers from the end table and called over to Shaw. "Look at this—this same name keeps coming up. Is it a person or place? I've never heard this name before."

Shaw looked at the pages and came to the same conclusion. The name was used too much to mean nothing. "This is Noic, one of the smaller villages bordering Oroze. It's located somewhere between Oroze and Baddon, but I'm not entirely sure where exactly. I've never been that far east, but I do know that it's in that direction." Shaw pointed out the window as Grant walked over.

"So, is that where we're headed?" he asked.

"Yes, it looks that way. It may be nothing, but it's the best lead we have. We will have to be careful—others may not know what we look like, but I'm sure that masked man will inform whoever he works for that we intend to follow. We need to be cautious, and not draw too much attention to ourselves."

"How far is Noic from where we are?" Nora asked.

"Without a horse, it is quite a ways off, but since those soldiers came here on horses, we don't have to worry about that. Seems we got lucky this time," Shaw said. "Alright, let's take what we can use from this house. Collins will not be using anything anytime soon, but gather only what you might need."

Shaw continued searching and took a quick look through Collins's book collection. Nora and Grant started gathering what they could find, including food that had been well preserved and other essential items to help them throughout the following days.

"Alright, do we have everything we need?" Shaw asked after a few minutes.

"I believe so," Grant said.

"Okay, we need to leave now and use the night to help us get away from here unseen. I have no doubt that the First Born soldiers will be headed this way eventually." They all grabbed their packs and walked out the door. "We will need to walk the horses to avoid making noise."

Nora and Grant grabbed the reins of two horses that were standing outside the house. Nora brushed her horse's mane gently with her hand, talking to it to keep it calm. Grant took his by the reins and had some trouble calming it, but when he looked over at Nora, he followed what she was doing, and it worked.

Shaw saw a horse he liked and walked over to it. The horse eyed the old man as he approached, and backed away as if frightened. He put out his hand and moved slowly. "Shh, it's alright, girl. I'm not going to hurt you, shh. It's okay." As Shaw got closer, he put one hand on the horse's nose and softly patted its cheek with the other. "See, it's alright. You can trust me." He moved closer and ran his hand along the animal's face, between its ears to its mane. The horse stopped moving and started to relax its posture. Talking to it seemed to soothe it; Shaw figured the horse was scared of people and had not been treated well by its previous owner.

"How did you do that? Calm the horse, I mean?" Nora asked.

"I used to have one in my younger years. There was a time in my youth where I was like this horse here. I was afraid, out of control, and going from place to place. Doing whatever I pleased got me in a lot of trouble—until I met someone who could tame me, for lack of better words. Just like this horse here, sometimes all you need is a gentle hand, and animals can feel that." Shaw looked into the horse's eyes, thinking back on his younger years. As he grabbed the reins, the animal walked beside him.

"Follow me," he said to Nora and Grant.

Chapter Eleven

Searching

They continued walking, hearing the sounds of the horses' hooves crushing the grass, all the while looking in the dark, straining their eyes, trying to see if any of the First Born were lurking about.

After half an hour or so, Shaw held his hand in the air. Nora and Grant stopped moving as he turned around, putting a finger over his mouth. They could hear a faint gallop. "The First Born must be coming to check on the house to see if we are still there," Shaw said.

The gallops grew louder as they listened and waited. They were only a couple miles from Collins's house, but the dark made it feel farther. The light from the torches allowed Nora to make out a small group of soldiers riding toward the home. "There must be eight or so heading to the house," she said.

"Alright, we should keep moving. No doubt they're looking for us, and once they see that we have scattered all the horses, they may assume we took a few. So they may spread out," Shaw whispered as he started to pull the reins of the horse. "Let's go."

They kept a slow pace, making sure to not make any loud noises. Once the house was out of sight, Shaw motioned for Nora and Grant to get on their horses and ride slowly. Not long into their ride, a bright light rose from the ground, reaching into the sky behind them. Turning to see what was happening, they just watched. The flames rose into the sky, consuming Collins's house, shining like a beacon in the darkness.

While trotting along the mountain, they came upon a narrow pass, separating the mountains from Oroze, leading into the unknown northeast. "That is the outer wall of the Oroze," Shaw said. It didn't look like much, covered in the dark as it was, but with the help of the moon, they could make out the towering structure on the other side of the pass. "We should camp here on the mountainside; it will help us blend in a lot better, avoiding the eyes of the guards patrolling the wall. It won't be long before morning, and we need rest. I'll take the first watch, and don't bother setting up the tent. Just use your bedrolls in case we need to leave in a hurry. We won't want to leave anything behind."

Nora and Grant agreed, setting their packs aside for the night.

"I'm sorry things turned out the way they did with Collins. I can't imagine that was easy," Nora said, feeling sympathy for Shaw, though she couldn't bring herself to have any for Collins.

"Thank you, Nora. He wasn't always like that, you know."

"Why don't you tell us?" she asked, sitting on her bedroll.

"For starters, he was always somewhat of a grouch. Very opinionated, but smart. I met him in my early twenties. I couldn't have been much older than you are now. I was working toward being a scholar when Collins and I met. We had been partnered together and tasked with writing a critical analysis detailing the trades between kingdoms and the different histories of how they were established."

"That sounds like a riveting project," Grant sarcastically chimed in.

"It was—I was fascinated by the histories of the kingdoms. Collins and I worked day and night. We traveled all over, meeting so many different kinds of people. Collins had this way of wording questions so he could get the most information possible. We spent the next few years teaching the younger students, as we were both given a chance to become instructors. Collins took it without question, as I knew he would, but I didn't. I met this woman, and the way Collins saw it was that she was interfering with our chosen path. I suppose after I left, Collins held on to that resentment. Even now, when we first arrived at his home, I could see it in the way he looked at me."

"Why would he stay angry for so long?" Nora asked. "He should have known people change."

"He didn't have many friends that I knew of. He was either too busy reading, engrossed in other studies, or simply never took the time to socialize with anyone. The only way we became friends was not by a conscious decision but by the instructor that paired us together. I guess when I left, he closed himself off even more than he already had. Perhaps he became more bitter over the years until he became part of the First Born." Shaw paused to yawn. "However his life may have turned out, there is no excuse for his actions. He chose his path, but that's enough for now. You both should rest."

"Don't forget to wake us up for our shift. You need rest just as much as we do," Grant said.

Shaw nodded. Then Grant and Nora got in their bedrolls and fell into a light sleep. Later in the night, Shaw woke Grant up for his turn at watch, retired to his own bedroll, and slept.

Grant sat propped against a rock. He looked out at the stars shining over the valley, taking in the quiet of the night. While watching the night sky, he thought about what had happened at Collins's house. He didn't have any regrets about killing the man; he was just going over the moment in his head. He remembered how angry he felt, how much he wanted Collins to pay for what he did. Grant knew he would do it again if given the same opportunity, but he didn't understand why he felt so exhausted after killing Collins.

He knew he'd been tired from the fight with the soldiers but had felt drained only after he attacked Collins. Grant had never acted on impulse like that before, but he knew he was right for acting. The young man rubbed the back of his neck where he'd applied the brown ointment, thankful it was longer in pain. He didn't recall hurting his neck, but the pain had hastened his decision to stab Collins. He thought about that moment as he watched the moon drift through the sky until his watch was over.

Nora took over, and dawn was breaking by the time she stopped replaying the moment she saw Ron fall to the ground in her mind. She knew he was a strong fighter, but when she watched him fight the man in the mask, she had a sinking feeling that Ron was going to lose. She didn't want to believe it would happen, but as it unfolded in front of her, with no chance to stop it, she knew she was right. Nora didn't know how she knew, only that the same feeling pulsed through her spine. It was a feeling she'd had before, and it was becoming more frequent. She told herself that the next time she felt the sensation, she would pay more attention and understand what it meant. Nora stretched her tired arms before standing to wake up Grant and Shaw; she reported no activity during the night.

"Well, it's good no one came during the night. It must mean the First Born returned to where they came from," Shaw said with relief. He and Grant packed up their bedrolls and walked with their horses.

"How much farther do we have to go until we make it to Noic?" Nora asked, sounding rather impatient.

"It will be more than a couple hours before we can clear Oroze. It covers quite a few miles around. If the First Born control Oroze, they have to know that Ron had three companions with him. I'm sure they will be on the lookout for a group of three." Shaw looked like he was thinking of a plan.

"Can't we just cut through the valley? Wouldn't that be easier than being so close to the entrance?" Grant asked.

"You know, that sounds like our best option at this point. Based on our location, it's either go back and risk meeting up with the First Born if they stayed in the area by Collins's house, or go through the valley, where if we need to, we could make a break for the Red Band River."

Nora, Grant, and Shaw mounted their horses and rode back along the mountainside until they broke off, charging into the valley.

The valleys would give them cover as long as they stayed within the depressed segments of the rolling hills before the plain. They could see flags waving in the gentle breeze that presented itself upon the top of the gray stone of Oroze. The flags were definitely First Born flags, the distinctive solid black with blue borders. Nora and Grant's attention was pulled to the soldiers standing in the distance atop the large stone gate connecting to the city's outer walls, their prominent black armor made more noticeable among the gray stone. Sentries were placed at posts along the walls, watching to ensure no unexpected visitors could sneak their way to the gates. The walls themselves were not in the best condition, with scorch marks along the perimeter and holes from catapults that had struck true to their intended targets.

Nora thought, *The First Born must have recently acquired this place.*

The tall buildings behind the gate were made of the same stone as the walls themselves. It was a gray, seemingly lifeless city with no other banners flying except for those of the First Born. Small trails of smoke could be seen rising from above the walls and gates, proving there was still some life behind the walls. As the other side of Oroze became visible, they saw smaller homes bordering its walls until out in the distance, the neighboring villages came into view.

"It looks like we are getting closer. There, there is where we must ride to," Shaw said, holding up his hand and pointing to the village. Clusters of white and brown formed far off into the east without the watchful eyes of Oroze. "I'm not sure which one is Noic, but if we ask the right questions and don't draw attention to ourselves, we may be able to find it, then find Ron."

The villages were spread wide, with the ones in the east much farther as they approached the closest one. It seemed as though the first village was made in haste, with just enough room to barely hold its people. The tents were crammed together with little to no room to walk between. Shaw got off of his horse, walking it into the village; Nora and Grant followed suit.

They moved into the village cautiously, observing the inhabitants with wide eyes. It looked like the people living here were only getting by with the bare minimum of essentials needed to survive. Children ran in between tents wearing nothing but rags for clothing; rips and tears littered most of what they wore. Not a single child with shoes ran on the dust-covered roadway. The parents were no better off. Their clothes were covered in dirt, sweat-stained, with no formal way to wash themselves or their children save for taking the long trip to the Red Band River, a few hours' walk, to collect water. Villages were huddled around small fire pits, lined with stones by every other tent to maintain warmth when the night came. Nora saw a woman plucking feathers from an undersized chicken that was nowhere near big enough to feed a person, let alone a family of four.

As they walked up to the first set of tents, the villagers looked at them as if they were wealthy, from a land undiscovered—Shaw with his green cloak and well-kept white beard, Nora with her blue pants and form-fitted brown shirt. Even Grant, though the most disheveled of the group, with his scruffy blond hair, unshaven face, and faded clothes, looked as though he belonged living in a sprawling city with the leaders waiting for his commands rather than down among these inferior people. As they continued, their presence began to attract more eyes. Grant saw a small group of children huddled together; dry dirt clung to their faces, and he took to his knee next to them.

"Have you guys seen two men come through here recently?" The children looked down as if ashamed that someone like Grant would take time to talk to them. They shook their heads collectively, indicating that they had not seen anyone come through but were too afraid to use words. Grant, beginning to stand, said, "Thank you." He then reached into his pack, which was draped across his horse, and grabbed some dried meats he had been holding on to for Nora. Grant bent down again and looked at the children. "Here, take this," he said as he reached out his hand, giving the children what was left of the salted pork Nora had gotten from the Canopy. The children looked nervous at the invitation for free food. "Take it, it's alright," Grant insisted, offering once more with a kind smile. The children quickly snatched it from his hand and ran away. Grant stood up, smiling as he did. Nora walked up behind him, putting a hand on his left shoulder.

"I never pictured you for a bleeding heart, Grant. Looks like you made those kids pretty happy," she said.

"It felt like the right thing to do. I just don't understand how someone can let their people, their children, live like this, no matter how terrible they may be. It doesn't make sense to me." He sighed as the smile on his face washed away into a look of disdain.

They continued walking through the village until a man approached them, stopping abruptly in their path. "What business do you have here? Have you come to taunt us with your wealth and gifts as if we are merely peasants in need of rescue? Don't you think we have been ridiculed enough?" the man said with anger upon his face.

Shaw stepped forward. "No, we are simply looking for someone who was taken this way. Two men riding on a single horse. One was First Born; the other would have looked like one of us, only with shorter brown hair."

"Shh—we do not talk of them here. It is not appropriate. There could always be someone listening." The man's voice trailed to a whisper. "If what you say is true, then come with me." He motioned for Shaw, Grant, and Nora to follow, then took them down a row of tents and stopped. "Come inside, and we will talk." He grabbed the opening of the tent, pulling the flap out of the way and leading them inside.

The tent was bigger than the others, but not by much; it was wider than it was long, giving the impression that there was more room than there really was. "There are no chairs, but these pillows should suffice. Please, sit down," he said. Nora and Grant were the first two to sit. Shaw stood for a bit, taking in the surroundings, then sat along with the man.

"Why are you here looking for the First Born? Don't you know they occupy Oroze?" he asked.

"Yes, we are more than aware. We are looking for a man the First Born took as a prisoner. He rode on a horse and had a white mask covering his face," Nora said.

The man's eyes grew wide. Fear struck his face at the mention of the masked man. Nora caught this. "You know who we're talking about, don't you? What can you tell us about him?"

"I do. He is known around here as the masked wielder. I do not know his name, only that he commands the armies for the lord that now has control of Oroze."

"Do you have any idea where he would take a prisoner?" Grant asked with a fleeting bit of hope in his eyes.

"I may—I've seen the First Born take a procession of prisoners from Oroze farther east of here. I did not stay to watch for very long, seeing as how I didn't want to end up as a prisoner myself. So I have not gone that far, but that is where

I would look if I were you. No one has ventured that far east in fear of being taken. Ever since we were forced to leave our homes when they arrived, no one has wanted to get close to Oroze. The First Born said if we came back without pledging full fidelity to their lord, we would be killed, or worse made an example of."

"I'm sorry about what happened and all that you and your people have lost. Just know that we really do appreciate your help," Nora said.

"Thank you, but tell me this. Why would you care or give aid to those children? You don't know them or owe us anything. Why?" he asked, his eyes moving to Grant.

"It was the right thing to do. No one should be treated like this. It looks like these parents are trying to maintain a living while worrying about where their next meal will come from to feed their family. It shouldn't be like this," Grant said.

"Well, I am grateful you feel that way, but when you are stuck between Oroze and Baddon, and Baddon knows it's too risky to send supplies anymore due to the First Born capturing the wagons and sending the Baddonians back, there is not much choice in the matter. So it's not worth sending anything, regardless of who lives here. It has been a long time since anyone has tried to help us, almost a year by now." Sadness overtook the man's face. "But I will try to help you where I can." He placed a hand near his mouth, clearing his throat. "There are two other villages farther east of Oroze. This is the village of Meno. The others are Noic and Lalin."

Nora perked up. "Wait, Noic, that is the village we are looking for. How do we get there?" she asked, hope filling her voice.

"If you go directly east from here, you will find it. Lalin is the last village after passing Noic, but do be careful. If that's where the First Born takes prisoners, then they may have people working within the village. Not many people can be trusted. From what I have heard, Noic and Lalin get supplies sent to them for continued loyalty."

"So the other villages are full of First Born?" Grant asked.

"I'm not sure. When we left Oroze, we were branded as deserters, but we saw some friends and family go in the direction of Noic and Lalin."

Shaw rubbed his beard. "We will have to be careful. Like you said, it will be difficult not knowing who to trust."

"You trusted me well enough to tell me who you were looking for," the man said, raising an eyebrow.

"Sometimes, you have to take a chance." Shaw and the man stared at each other until they both broke into grins.

"Fair point."

Grant and Nora stood up. "Well, I think it is time we head back out," Grant suggested. Shaw got up as well and motioned toward the front of the tent. After exiting, they walked to their horses, noticing that some men and women had gathered around with their children to admire the fine animals.

Nora turned to the man. "What is your name?" she asked.

"Me?" he said, unaccustomed to being asked questions about himself. "I'm Alas."

"Well, Alas, it was a pleasure to meet you," Nora said before reaching into her saddlebag. Grant looked at her and caught on to what she was doing, and followed her lead. "I want you to have this." She handed the man half of the rations she had left. Grant gave his rations to Alas as well. "I want you to take this and feed who you can. It may not be a lot, but it will help. Also, take this." Nora turned to Shaw. Already up to speed on what was happening, he handed Nora more than half of the coin he carried with him after leaving the Canopy. "This should be enough to get supplies," Nora finished.

"I can't take this. It's too much." Alas said, his eyes beginning to water at seeing such generosity.

"I'm not asking you to take it; I am giving to you. You and all your people deserve this more than we do. These people need to be provided for, and now you can do that. Take it. Give these people some happiness they can hold on to," Nora said.

Alas took the rations and coin, then wrapped his arms around Nora, since words would not be enough. He gave her a hug she would never forget; clearly, this small gesture meant everything to this man. Alas let go of Nora, then also hugged Grant and Shaw. "Thank you. I will do my best with what you have given. If you need anything, come back, and we will be here for you," he said. His eyes were no longer watering, but tears of joy had begun to fall freely.

Nora, Grant, and Shaw mounted their horses and rode east as the villagers watched them leave for Noic.

Chapter Twelve

Alone

R on woke up to a small, dark room; the only light offered to him was shining through a small crack embedded in the top corner of the cell door, undoubtedly made by the many prisoners before him. Carved into the stone were old, browned blood tracks, left to dry from former prisoners' desperate attempts to escape, prisoners that he knew were long dead. Ron's head pounded as he sat upon the hardened cot. He was still somewhat unclear of the events that had led him to be in the room. Ron looked around, and to no surprise, there was nothing else to see except for a small steel cup of water and a bucket in the corner. He continued to investigate the room while his eyes adjusted to the dark, and he saw sporadic patches of mildew since the ventilation was close to nonexistent except for a crack in the wall.

The air was stale, warm, and thick. Ron stood up, and as he did, he felt his knees were not the most stable. So he took to sitting again to further compose himself, observing the situation he now found himself in. Ron patted his clothes, checking every pocket, to see what had been left on his person, hoping not everything had been taken from him. First, he noticed that his sword and baldric were gone. *Of course they would take that. Who would want a prisoner with weapons?* Then he checked his pockets; whatever coin he used to have was gone as well. *So, it's just me and my lonesome self. Alright, think Ron, think. How can I get out of here?*

As he was trying to visualize a way out, he heard footsteps moving outside his cell. Slowly standing up, Ron steadied himself to avoid losing his balance and made his way to the door. He put his hands to the door, feeling the cold, hard, heavy steel. It seemed impenetrable. There was, however, a slit toward the bottom where food could be passed back and forth.

Ron looked through the slit, peering left and right. He saw someone walking up and down a long hallway with dozens of similar-looking doors lit by oil lamps fixed to the walls. Ron fell back as the gravity of his situation came to a head—how would he get out, how would he contact anyone outside, and how would anyone find him here, in this dark, dank, godless prison?

A million questions raced through Ron's mind with no answers coming to him. Finally, he began to panic at the thought of never getting out or seeing his friends again. Then he thought of Nora, alone, out there searching for him. How long until she gave up looking, how long would she look for him until it became a lost cause? What of Grant and Shaw? Would they look for him as well? If the search ran cold, would they keep looking or give up?

Ron grabbed his head and tried to hold on to hope, even though hope felt like a faraway dream to him.

He was broken out of his thoughts by a loud pounding on the steel door. "Our lord would like to speak with you," said the man behind the door. "Don't try anything foolish, or it will become very uncomfortable for you. Do you understand me?"

Ron knew there was nothing he could do. "Yes, I understand you," he said as he stood up to meet whoever was on the other side.

The door was pulled open, making a scraping sound along the bottom as if the rusted door hinges were not holding properly. When the long, sharp scraping sound ended, a man Ron had not expected to see stood in the archway. He was not dressed in armor or the colors the First Born seemed mandated to wear. Instead, he was dressed in white robes, quite a stark contrast to Ron's surrounding area. He had his white hood pulled over his head and wore a brown belt fashioned with thinly braided rope. Ron stared at this man and didn't know what to think. "Who are you?" he asked.

"I am a servant to our lord. I am—"

Ron interrupted loudly, "Who is this lord that everyone is talking about?"

The man looked him in his eyes and said with an almost-sinister smile, "You will find out soon enough if you are deemed worthy." He motioned for Ron to follow him but not before having Ron hold out both hands so the man could put iron shackles around his wrists. "We can't be too careful. Who knows what trouble you could cause?"

Ron followed the man down the long, dark corridor. He couldn't help but wonder who else was behind all the other cell doors that lined the hallway.

Hollow screams echoed, but Ron could not tell precisely where they were coming from. They walked until they reached the end of the hall, turning right, continuing their way up two sets of stairs. Ron followed until they came upon a pair of large doors with intricate carvings, seared and polished to emphasize the detail in the wood. Ron squinted his eyes to make it out. It appeared to be a man standing on top of a mountain holding the flame within his hand. Ron looked closer and saw it wasn't just a man standing on a mountain; there was, in fact, no mountain at all.

The man in the carving was standing on top of people, people who could not wield. He stood above them, like a king reaching up to the gods. It looked like the man thought of himself as a god among the people.

The man leading Ron pushed the great doors open to yet another long hallway, but instead of being dark, damp, and godless, it had rows of First Born banners hanging off the walls. Big windows flooded the room with bright natural light. Ron kept walking, noticing the red carpet and tan-colored walls. The banners stood out, grabbing the attention of the room from the walls and floor. Ron couldn't stand the sight of them.

For eight years, the banners had plagued his memories, and now he was walking next to them. Ron could feel anger building inside of him as he moved through the hallway. Finally, the man in white robes stopped, turned to his left, and passed through another set of doors. Although these were smaller and not as grand as the hallway entrance, the same carving was engraved here. *This must be where the lord is.*

Ron noticed that the inside room was vastly different from the hallway he was presently standing in. When he walked in, he saw more of the same banners hung on the walls in the light pouring through the open door. There was no carpet to cover the ground, no windows to let in the light; it came through the room's roof. The walls were solid stone, exactly the same as the cells, but there was no mold or stale odor. The light from the ceiling focused on a singular point on the ground. Blood stained the illuminated spot. Ron could see different shades mixed together from what he assumed had been countless prisoners.

He didn't know if this was an execution chamber or if some unlucky soul had strung the wrong words together, leading to their untimely death. The robed man moved Ron to where the light and stone met, pushing him down to his knees, using more force than necessary. Ron looked up. He could see the outline of a throne and someone sitting in it. Unfortunately, he couldn't see any details of who it was

"Here he is, my lord." said the man in the robes.

"Thank you, Father. Those shackles won't be necessary."

"As you wish, my lord," the man said without question, taking a key from the small pocket in his robe and removing the shackles from Ron's wrist.

"Now, Father, do not interrupt," the figure said from the throne.

Ron looked at the man in robes with confusion. "Father?" he said.

Ron didn't think a place like this would have any sort of religion. The father turned from Ron without a word, walked toward the doors, and waited. Ron's breath was shaking and unsteady as he looked back at the man sitting on the throne. Even though Ron's hands were free, he still felt helpless; none of the skills he possessed would be of use to him. He had no control here.

The man on the throne stood up slowly, looking at Ron kneeling on the floor. "It didn't have to be like this, you know. You could have been in a nice room with a comfortable bed, warm sheets, and nice soft pillows. Meals could have been brought to you. Servants waiting on your beck and call."

He moved closer to Ron, walking with his hands behind his back. "I don't understand why you wouldn't just come when we asked you. We generously offered, and you still declined. If you just listened to reason, you wouldn't be treated like an animal. We could have had a pleasant conversation. That was all that was required, but you had to be so stubborn." As the man got close, Ron saw that he wore a mask. It was the same man he'd encountered in the forest and at Collins's house. The masked man walked behind Ron, placing his hands on his shoulders. "It would have been so much easier. Wouldn't you want to learn? I could teach you so much about this gift. All you have to say is yes. Even now, I still present you with a choice. You just have to be smart enough to make the right decision."

Ron sat quietly, giving no answer. Then he felt a burning sensation on his shoulders coming from the hands of the masked man. He pulled away quickly. "I see you have never felt the flame before—that is only a small sample."

"Who are you?" Ron asked.

"You will find out soon enough. Now stand up," the masked man said, walking in front of Ron. Ron stood and looked the man defiantly in his eyes. "You hate me, don't you. I can see it. All I want to do is teach you. I want you to learn to be a wielder. I can teach you. Just say yes, and all of this can stop."

"I do hate you. You have been following me from the start, taunting me and coming after my friends. I don't know you. I don't even know what you want. So why would I want to learn anything you have to teach? You keep talking about giving me a choice, but I have already made the right one," Ron said with anger in his voice.

"You have the right to be angry, I understand why, but don't you want to be strong? You possess something that has, for the most part, been stricken from this world, that only a select few can control. You can wield the flame. That is rare, and to not use this power would be the same as forfeiting your life." The masked man circled Ron as he spoke.

"My home was burned to the ground, everything was taken from me by you, and now you want to teach me? How does that make sense? You think I will just forgive and forget what you have done?" Ron shouted, clenching his fists.

"Your home was burned for a reason. I don't expect you to understand just yet, but in time you will," the masked man said. "To answer your other question as to who I am, that will come with time as well, but for now, you can address me as Regis. It is not my real name, as you must know. I also know that it may be hard for you to call me that, but I feel it's fitting."

Ron's anger hit a boiling point, and he felt his hands break into a million needles stabbing at the same time. In seconds they went numb, and the flame engulfed his fists. Ron rushed toward Regis, swinging furiously at his face. Regis ducked, avoiding Ron's punch, and stepped back. "Ron, this will not end well. You have no control, no power over the flame. With such recklessness, you will cause more harm than you realize. Just let me teach you."

"No, I want nothing from you!" Ron yelled, rushing at Regis once more in an attempt to hit him. Ron could feel his hands becoming hot. The man side-stepped Ron's punch again, and within seconds he had the flame in his own hand.

"You will say yes in time. Don't you worry about that," Regis said as he raised his flaming hand, punching Ron once more in the side of his head. The young man dropped to the floor. The hit was a lot harder than the last time he had been punched, and Ron stayed on the ground as the flame faded from his hands. His legs felt like jelly, and he was too weak to stand.

"Father, come here," Regis called, dropping the flame from his own hands. The father moved from the door to his side. "Bind his hands and take him way," Regis said, waving his hand at Ron. The father walked up to Ron, grabbing his limp hands, and put the shackles back on his wrists.

"Let's go back to your cell," the father said with a snap of his fingers. A large, hulking guard came in and picked Ron up off the floor.

"No, if he agreed, he would be allowed back to the cell, but I was informed if he refused, you must take him and string him up. Perhaps it will give him enough incentive to say yes. Those were the orders," Regis said, walking back to sit on his throne.

"Yes, my lord," said the father while the large guard carried Ron over his shoulder out of the room.

"You will say yes, Ron, mark my words. One way or another, you will say yes," Regis whispered, watching as the young man was carried away.

Ron woke up once more to his head pounding so loud he could hear it in his ears. He felt strange, but he didn't know why. Opening his eyes and slowly lifting his head, Ron looked to each extremity, held in place by worn, brown leather shackles that suspended him in the air. Chains were connected to the shackles, fashioned tightly around his wrists and ankles. Ron followed the chains and saw that the ones attached to his wrists ran through two large rings, with more running through the ceiling. The chains around his ankles connected directly into the floor below him. To his shock, when he looked down, he saw long, rusted spikes coming up from the ground below him.

The spikes were positioned to match where his shoulders, chest, and lower abdomen would fall if he were to somehow break free of his chains. They were thin, looking to be roughly three feet from the base to the rusted point, with a one-inch diameter at the top, gradually widening toward the base.

Ron's thoughts started racing; he did not know how he would get out of this situation. He tried everything, from pulling the chains with each of his hands and feet, to swinging left and right, hoping there would be some slack so he could get closer to either wall. He was looking for any form of leverage he could get over the other three chains connected to the wall. Sadly, all his efforts were in vain. In his panic, he failed to see that the tail end of the chains connecting to his wrists were locked in place on each opposing wall.

Sweat began to drip from Ron's face as he hung his head, trying to catch his breath after he had exerted energy his body did not have. Then, as he looked down at the spikes that loomed below, he saw a bead of sweat fall to the ground. When the bead hit the floor, Ron's eyes widened. The rust he'd thought covered the spikes was not rust at all, but streaks of dried blood that had rolled down them, collecting at the bases. Now, Ron understood why the chains were locked to the walls and why his upper body leaned farther over the spikes than his lower half. He understood what this room was. *No, no, no . . . I need to get out of here. Think Ron, think!* His eyes rapidly searched the room. Ron closed them and took a deep breath. He knew panicking at this point wouldn't help; it would only make him more exhausted.

The flame. He opened his eyes. *I could try to make one.* Ron shut his eyes again, opened his hand, and tried to make the flame come alive in the palm of his hand. He looked once more to see there was nothing, no flame to be seen. Not even the sensation of pain or numbness that would tear through his hand when the flame was being called.

Ron continued to try for what felt like hours on end, only growing more and more tired as time went on. He tried to tap into the anger that had helped him before, but it didn't work. Then he thought of Nora, Grant, and Shaw, hoping that maybe the thought of them would be helpful, but it wasn't.

He tried over and over to force the flame into his hand. Ron closed his hand and hung his head in defeat, unable to accomplish it. By now, he was covered in sweat and too tired to continue. The joints and muscles of his shoulders ached from holding the weight of his body over the spikes. Ron closed his eyes, finding it hard to keep them open even against the pain in his body, and once more, he let himself fade into sleep.

As Ron slept, he had dreams as vivid as life itself. He watched as he recounted his days in Greyland from when he first arrived. Waking up in a bed with pain radiating from his body, Ron looked around at his new surroundings. Startled to see that he was in the healer's ward, Ron quickly tried to stand up and walk to the nearest window to see where he was. When he stood up, pain soared through his left calf. He grimaced as he attempted to step forward, but the pain grew too great, and he fell to the ground.

Once Ron hit the floor, he cried out in pain. The stitches that were managing to keep his wounds closed tore open. Ron looked at the bandages covering his stomach, shoulder, and leg while blood began to stain through at a rapid rate. A girl with hair as dark as night came bursting through the door into the room once she heard the commotion from inside. Looking around frantically, she saw Ron on the floor and began yelling, "What do you think you are doing? You are supposed to be in bed getting rest, not walking around, or in your case, crawling on the floor."

Ron rolled over to see who was yelling at him. The instant he did, he revealed the blood-soaked bandages covering his wounds. The girl threw up her arms.

"You ripped all of your stitches! What were you thinking?" she yelled. "Let's get you back into bed so I can get the head healer for you." She moved over to Ron, grabbing under his arms to help pull him to his feet.

Ron groaned as the pain shot through his body. "I don't want to hear any complaining from you. If you just did what you were supposed to, you wouldn't be in this mess," she scolded. Ron slowly stood to his feet, reaching for the bed rail to add extra support.

"Well, I guess if I didn't get up, you would have nothing to do." He let out a small, sarcastic laugh followed by a wince from the pain. "I do appreciate the help, but who are you? Are you a healer? Where exactly am I?" Ron asked as he turned and sat on the bed. The girl helped him lie back down by lifting his legs and rotating his torso as he used his hands to push his upper body back.

"You are in Greyland, and no, I am not a healer. I just volunteer to help out when I have the chance, but that doesn't mean you get to make my job harder." The girl pulled the blankets from the bottom of the bed over Ron's legs, bringing them halfway up to his abdomen. "My name is Nora," she said.

Ron looked up. "It's nice to meet you, Nora. I'm Ron." He was amazed at the sight of her, the way her dark hair complimented her light brown skin, the scent of lavender and vanilla from her hair that remained on his cheek after she picked him off the floor. He couldn't think of a time when he'd met someone as enchanting as her.

The last thing he was able to recall was the sudden and complete decimation of his village. His disposition shifted. "Nora, I—" Ron began to say, but she cut him off.

"We will have plenty of time to answer your questions later, but for now, I need to go get the head healer, so he can replace your stitches and stop the bleeding. You need to keep still and get some rest," Nora instructed. Ron looked down at his hands, feeling slightly ashamed and a little bit foolish for trying to walk so soon, but he knew she was right. At that moment, Ron heard a high-pitched scream of horror. He turned his head to look up at Nora. He saw intense blue flames erupting from her eyes and mouth. She began to scream louder and louder, clawing at her face, trying to smother the flames.

Ron sat in disbelief. "No, what is this? This can't be happening!"

The fire consumed Nora as her screaming intensified; the whole room became engulfed in flame.

Ron's eyes shot open as he lifted his head. He looked around wide-eyed with sweat dripping off the tip of his nose, then let out a sigh of relief. "It was just a dream, just a dream. How did it feel so real?" He took a few deep breathes to compose himself. Seeing Nora consumed in the flame was a nightmare he never wanted to have again. Even knowing it was a dream, he couldn't get rid of how it made him feel. He could still feel the heat from the flame, smell the scent of burning hair and flesh. He knew it wasn't real, but it felt real.

Ron perked his head up when he heard the faint sound of shuffling feet echoing from outside the door of the room in which he was confined. The footsteps got louder, and Ron's heart began to beat hard in his chest. He was scared and apprehensive about who was going to come through the door. Once the footsteps stopped, he heard the turning of a key. The door opened with a creak that echoed down the hall. The father came through the door, still wearing his white robes, then closed the door behind him and turned to face Ron. "Seems you are doing well. I didn't think you wanted to hang around this long, but oh well," the man said, amusing himself,

Ron only felt more contempt for him. "What do you want from me?" he asked through gritted teeth.

"Me?" asked the father, looking around, pointing to himself with a confused look as if Ron were talking to another person in the room. "Nothing. I don't want anything from you, but my lord does. It's simple, really—he just wants you to say yes, that's all. Accept his offer to help train and guide you in the way of the flame. That's all he wants. In return for your cooperation, while you would be confined to the grounds, you would have meals, a bed, and clean clothes instead of these filthy rags. Also, you wouldn't be suspended in a dungeon."

Ron's contempt turned to hatred. He didn't have the tolerance for the father's joking manner. "The offer is compelling, but no! I will not accept. I have already told him that, and if he cannot understand that, he is too stupid to be a lord, or any kind of authority figure. How many times do I have to repeat the same thing to you people?"

The father's gentle face turned more threatening. He walked over to Ron and grabbed his face by the jaw, crushing his cheeks into his teeth.

"You will say yes! Why do you think I am here? Don't bother answering that, it's rhetorical." The father waved his hand. "I've gotten a lot more out of people than just one word. Oh! I almost forgot. Don't think I will forget about your insolent tongue. Oh no, I will enjoy this. You won't, but I will." He released his grasp on Ron's jaw, leaving behind red imprints where his hand had been. "Do you know why I am called Father? No? Well, let me tell you." He paced back and forth in front of Ron. "They call me Father because most times, when I am through getting what I want from people, they tend to beg to whatever god it is they believe in for death. That is where I come in. You see, I am the closest person between them and their god, so I am the peoples' deliverer, a savior if you will. I am the one that will grant their last and final wish. I am the one that will bring them to their god.

"Oh, by the way, do you see there?" The father pointed to the spikes gathered below Ron. Ron did not say anything, just looked at him with a glare that would have stopped most men dead in their tracks. "These are a little invention of mine. It's a simple design actually, very rudimentary." He circled Ron while he explained. "Simple design, yes, but through much trial and error, I have finally perfected the placement of the spikes below you. You see, the spikes won't kill you, but you will wish they had. It has taken time, but I have managed to place them to where if I lower you down, the spikes will pass through your body, missing every vital organ you have. So, in all actuality, you could live for quite some time with these spikes running through you. It sounds painful, I know, but it is effective. The ones before you did not last long before breaking. So, I'm going to ask you one more time. Will you accept the lord's offer or not?"

Ron did not break eye contact with the father. "No!"

"Well then," the father said, regaining the smile he'd worn when he walked in. He turned and walked to the door, tapping lightly on it twice. Two men entered the chamber, looking just about as content as the father did. The father closed the door, locking it behind the two men, who made their way to the walls on Ron's left and right side. Each man removed a key from their pocket to unlock the chains from the walls. Ron could feel his upper body sway ever so slightly as the men grabbed hold of the chains. The father placed his dry, nimble fingers under Ron's chin, lifting his head to meet his gaze. Then he smiled and said, "Shall we begin?"

Screaming passed through the door, down the hall, and along the corridor, carrying the echo as it reverberated against the encompassing walls. Ron continued screaming as the two men on either side lowered the chains slowly, letting the spikes pierce into the soft tissue of his body. Blood began to drip down the spikes, gradually at first, and as Ron watched, he saw the father's hand go up, signaling the men to stop lowering him.

Ron's breathing was heavy as sweat dripped from his brow. The father walked closer to him. "We can stop here if you like. It's up to you, after all. The spikes are barely going in. What do you say?"

Ron was shaking as he looked up. "No."

"Alright." The father shrugged, letting out a sigh before continuing. "Well, here is what I'm going to do. I'm going to leave you here, right here. Just long enough for your skin to start healing around these spikes, so when I get back, they will tear open all over again. It will almost feel like starting over." He patted Ron on the shoulder. "Lock those chains in place—we will be back in a little while," the father said to the two men holding the chains.

As the men went to lock the chains back onto the wall, the man on the left side put the lock lower than the man on the right. Once the men let go of the chains, Ron's left shoulder slid farther down the spike. He screamed, wincing in pain as the spike pushed farther in, clipping the bone and sending a massive amount of pain through his shoulder. "Do be careful—we need to take our time with him," the father said with no concern in his voice. He turned away from Ron and escorted the two men out of the room, locking the door behind them.

Ron hung his head, breathing heavily as he looked at the spikes penetrating his upper body. Turning his head, he saw two spikes entering through his shoulders just below his collarbone on each side. He looked at his abdomen as well and saw the remaining four spikes. Two were entering just above his right and left hip, and the last two were piercing just below his lungs. Ron tried to move his arms, but a surge of pain ran through his body, more and more with every attempt. He was completely immobilized. His breathing slowed as he started to calm himself. The less he resisted, the more the pain began to subside. Ron knew he had no options, no chances of escape, so he did the only thing he could: he tried to conjure the flame.

Ron tried for hours on end, and just like with every other attempt, he could not produce anything. Still, he continued his attempts to summon it. It wasn't until he picked his head up that he heard the faint sounds of footsteps at the other end of the hallway. Ron was running out of time to generate the flame before the others came back into the room. He pushed and strained, desperate, even though it caused immeasurable pain throughout his body.

As the footsteps grew louder, Ron's hand began to tingle; he felt the needle-like sensation take over his hand. He kept pushing and pushing until it went numb. Ron smiled. This was the first time he had made progress attempting to hold the flame on his own instead of just by being reactive. This was his first truly successful attempt.

Finally, the door to his chamber opened, and the two men in control of the chains walked in. Then the father entered and closed the door behind him. Ron immediately lost the sensation in his hand as his concentration was broken, and he refocused on the father. "I see the blood has ceased running," the man said as he bent down, inspecting the spikes that had entered Ron's body. "Yes, it looks to me like the blood has coagulated and begun to heal, perfect." A smile was firmly planted on the father's face as he rubbed his hands together. Ron's face held a look of disgust at witnessing this man's pleasure from the pain he caused.

The father paced around the room, seemingly admiring the early stages of his work. "Are you ready to cooperate, Ron?"

Ron knew the words that he was about to say would have consequences, but he spoke them nonetheless. "I'm not sure if you have terrible listening skills or if you are truly stupid, but I have already told you once—"

A sharp pain came across Ron's left cheek as the father's right hand returned to his side. Ron turned his head to face the man, and to his delight, the father's smile had been replaced with anger. Ron ventured to guess that the man did not like his self-proclaimed brilliance to be questioned.

"Your insolence will be rewarded. I hope it was worth it." The father motioned to the men on Ron's right and left side, and they unlocked the chains once more. Ron could feel his body shift on the spikes as the chains began to move, and he prepared himself for more pain.

The father didn't have to say a word. With a wave of his hand, the men lowered Ron further onto the spikes. Ron screamed as his entire body tensed. He could feel the tips of the spikes burrowing deeper, and each one continued to tear the skin wider as they went. Inch by inch, he felt the spikes push through the soft tissues of his body, making their way to the other side. The father waved his hand, and the two men held the chains in place just as the spikes were threatening to break through to Ron's back. The raised flesh stretched with the spikes inside. Then the father waved his hand again.

A sudden short drop was all it took for the spikes to make an exit through his body. Ron's voice hurt from screaming. He took a deep breath, hoping it was over, but the father was not finished. He motioned again, and the men lowered Ron once more.

Unlike the previous times, where it was a slow and controlled movement onto the widening spikes, this time the men would drop Ron's body a couple inches at a time. They would then jerk the chains with a sharp pull. Ron was dropped and lifted for hours until the spikes ran red and pools of blood gathered at the foundations. His screams grew hoarse as time went on. His mouth was dry, and his lungs hurt from trying to recapture air.

The father raised his hand, and the men stopped moving the chains. "Put the locks on. I think we are done for today. He looks like he may pass out if we keep going, and we do not want that. We want him to enjoy this." The men locked the chains in place and left the room; the father bent down to one knee, soaking his robe in Ron's blood that had collected on the ground. Ron's body was shaking. The pain was more than unbearable.

"I will be back, so we can continue, but again I want you to heal up a little bit. I can't have you bleed to death. No, the lord would not like that. Perhaps I'll be back in a day or so, who knows." The father stood up and walked toward the door. Then he turned back to Ron. "You could still make this easy on yourself and say yes. Your choice," he said before he walked out.

Ron gave a sigh of relief; he could feel his eyes getting heavy as he saw how much blood he'd lost, staring at the pool beneath him. He was not surprised that he felt like he would faint at any moment. Ron tried to pull himself together as best he could and control his breathing, so his heartbeat would slow down. Every blink became longer, sounds grew distant, his head hung low, and he let himself slip into sleep. Hopefully, his body would recover enough before the next time the father paid him a visit.

Ron woke up in what he knew to be a dream. He saw himself walking along a familiar dirt path lined with lively green grass, gently swaying in the light breeze on a sunny day with not a cloud in the sky. Ron was not walking by himself—Nora was beside him. Ron recognized this dream; it was not a dream but a fond memory he shared with Nora a year after arriving in Greyland. Since his time in the healers' ward, Nora visited his room each day she volunteered, ensuring he did what the healers ordered and didn't reopen his wounds. Finally, after a couple weeks, Ron's wounds had healed to the point he no longer needed to be watched. He had his stitches removed and was able to leave. However, from talking to Ron during her many daily visits, Nora knew he would have no place to go since he was brought in with little to no information about where he was from or what had happened to him.

Nora tried talking to him about it, but he was reluctant to go over those events so soon. Then she invited Ron to stay with her at her home while trying to figure out what he would do. Over the course of the following year, Ron decided to stay with Nora in Greyland; he later moved into the dormitory where others were housed while they awaited training or were currently training in the Arena. Ron and Nora would take walks together, talking about what they hoped to achieve within their lifetimes, the events of the day, and their training, which was soon to start. During these walks, Ron was beginning to rebuild his life in Greyland, and he had Nora to thank for that. Learning about her life and meeting the people who would become his friends made him feel like he belonged in Greyland; it made him feel like he could start over.

Ron liked this particular memory. It was one of the many moments he held dear, and it contributed to the feeling of love that would grow inside of him in the upcoming years. At the end of the dirt path, Ron and Nora would find themselves at the base of a giant oak tree. There, they would watch clouds go by and talk into the wee hours of the night. Watching clouds turned into stargazing. At times, the conversation would die out, and silence would engulf them. It didn't bother either of them—they were content to watch the stars.

Ron would glance over from time to time and get lost in Nora's beauty, catching the vanilla scent from her hair as the wind blew by. It was these moments at the giant oak tree where Ron began feeling safe and comfortable with her. A part of him wanted to tell her every secret he held about his past, yet every time he opened his mouth to speak, the words would get lost. So he just lay in the grass by the giant oak, watching the sky, knowing one day he would tell her, but for now, he was enjoying the way she made him feel.

Ron smiled to himself as he watched the memory play out, remembering the feelings he had that day, the feelings he still had. But his smile turned to fear as the giant oak tree caught fire at the base, igniting in blue fame.

"Get up! Get up! Come on, get up. Run!" He yelled as loud as he could, but his voice carried no sound. So instead, he watched as he and Nora remained under the tree until the flame consumed them both and continued to burn Ron's memory.

Ron woke up, jerking his body as a result of the dream. He let out a scream through his gritted teeth as he tore the skin that stuck to the metal. His wounds were healing around the spikes. Bright, new blood began rolling down the darkened streaks that coated the spikes, but Ron's attention was pulled from the pain as he heard a key turn over the bolt that locked the door to his cell. The door opened, and the footsteps entered the room. Ron didn't know how long he had been asleep, but he was still too tired to lift his head. As he listened to the steps, he heard their weight, a noticeable heaviness in each one. The father's steps were always light.

Ron strained to lift his head, and looked through squinted eyes to see a man dressed in black with a blue trim around the borders of his clothing. Dirt covered his boots and dotted the cuffs of his pant legs. Ron's eyes moved up, noticing the belt with a sword hanging off the right hip. His eyes opened wide as he looked at the sword; the hilt was worn, and the steel itself was dulled and scratched along the sheath, looking old and used, but that was not what caught Ron's attention.

Ron saw the marking upon the sword etched in the center of its golden hilt beneath the gold, squared cross guard. As weathered, faded, and worn as the handle was, he could still recognize the emblem. Ron saw the mark of the flame. The same mark that Collins had described when he told the story of Taroth and Thalom. *A wielder's sword*, Ron thought, looking up. His eyes stayed wide, and sweat began to gather on his brow.

Regis stood there looking down at him. Anger and terror began to fill Ron's heart as he held his gaze on the masked man.

Regis brought in the two men who had controlled Ron's descent on the spikes, and they went to their respective sides. The men grabbed the chains from the wall.

"This might hurt a little bit, but bear with me." Regis motioned to the men with his hands. "Go ahead, raise him up." The men pulled on the chains, causing Ron to bare his teeth, cursing under his muted breath.

Ron let out a long exhale as he felt the spikes leave his body. Blood began to pour from his injuries; Regis reached along the wall and pulled a small silver lever just to the right of the door, retracting the spikes into the floor until they were flush with the ground. The men then slowly fed the chains through the rings bolted to the ceiling, lowering Ron to the ground. Ron's palms touched the ground with no strength in this body, but he somehow managed to sit back on his knees. He tried to raise himself onto one knee, but the way the chains had kept a constant pull on both his legs for the last couple of days made it difficult.

"You two, leave us now."

Ron stopped trying to stand as blood oozed from the holes in his body, down his arms, chest, and abdomen, only stopping to stain his pants before finding the floor. Regis made his way over to Ron. "Let me give you a hand," he said as he put a hand on Ron's shoulder. As much as Ron knew it would hurt, he shrugged the man's grip off.

"Don't touch me!" Ron said as blood continued to flow onto the floor. Regis did not pay any mind to the words and helped him to his feet anyway. "What do you want?" Ron yelled as the sudden quick movement of his shoulder caused immense pain, along with the motion of his torso.

"Only to help stop the bleeding so you don't die. Looks like the father got a little carried away," Regis said.

Ron watched Regis raise his hand, bringing it closer to the hole in his shoulder, and noticed his hand was covered in scars leading up to his wrist. Ron looked into Regis's eyes as the man stared intently at his injuries.

"This is going to burn a lot, but hold still."

"No. No, don't touch me. Stop! Get your hands off me," Ron shouted, but it was too late. Regis's hands disappeared into blue flame, covering them to his wrists. He placed one hand on the opening and one hand on the exit of the wound in Ron's shoulder, then pushed the flame into his body. Ron felt his skin burn all the way through his shoulder as he screamed. He felt like he was being burned alive, but it was over after a few short seconds.

Ron breathed heavily. Sweat rolled down his face, and Regis withdrew his hands, putting out the flame. Ron looked at his left shoulder and saw a scar covering the hole where the spike had torn through his skin. "What did you do?" he asked.

Regis stepped back, looking at his work. "I healed you. The flame has many uses. Not all are for destruction or evil. It can also heal and nurture. There are many applications that the flame can be tailored to. You just have to learn."

Ron only felt more confused. "How? How can it heal? It's fire."

"With the proper training, you can accomplish this. The flame can speed up your body's natural healing process. Let me try to explain it this way. Your injuries are quite severe, so when I used the flame on both sides of your shoulder, it caused the blood to clot, essentially stopping the bleeding. Your body's next response would be to repair the damaged muscles and tendons or whatever tissues got damaged. The flame accelerates this, making your body create the necessary blood, tissue, and growth it requires. In the end, the flame helps your body create new skin that is then pulled inward from the edges of each opening, closing the wound. No injury will ever look the same as it did, however, since the flame causes the skin to grow back differently than what your body would have done on its own. The scars are permanent." Regis walked closer to Ron and brought the flame back to his hands. "I can teach you, Ron. Just say yes. Now hold still."

Regis began to heal the remaining holes in Ron's body, but Ron had trouble holding himself up as he got to the last one. He was getting weak in the knees, his vision becoming blurry, and he felt his legs buckle under him. Regis finished the last wound on the lower right side just as Ron's body fell to the ground, incapable of enduring the pain, the exhaustion, and the loss of blood.

The scent of dirt and sweat filled Ron's senses as he found himself standing in the Arena. An intermittent breezed kicked up patches of dust from the dry ground every so often. He turned around, looking out into the empty stands, knowing he was in another dream. The stands were empty, but upon the hard, compact dirt stood Cap.

Behind him, off a ways, Ron could see Grant sparring with another student. Nora was in the distance as well, training against another with her weapon of choice, her staff. The only difference with the Arena in the dream was where the oil lamps were placed along the outer perimeter. Ron looked back to Cap as the man spoke. "So you want to become a student in the Arena? I saw your application, and well, I'll be direct—there was nothing that made you stand out. We have a full class for the new year already, and the applicants are more promising than you."

Ron just looked blankly at Cap. He remembered this, but why was it different? The last two dreams were only of Nora. Why was it changing now?

"Well, answer me," Cap barked. "Why would I accept someone who has less to offer, fewer chances of being the best? I've never heard of you or your parents, let alone seen you around Greyland before. So what makes you think you deserve to be here?" Despite the fact he knew he was dreaming, the sting of Cap's words struck Ron just as hard as the first time he'd heard them.

Yet he answered Cap just as he had years ago: "You have never seen my parents because they are dead." Cap was taken aback, but Ron continued, "My family, all of them were murdered. I don't stand out because I'm not from here. I'm not looking to be the best. I just don't want to be as helpless as I was." Ron could feel the tears well in his eyes. Cap was the first person he'd ever told about what had happened to him. He had to pause and breathe so he wouldn't break down.

"What do you mean? What happened to you?" Cap asked, but when Ron looked at him, the man didn't have the expression he thought he would. He didn't look at Ron through the lens of pity, he didn't view him as an infant needing to be coddled—he saw who Ron was and who he could be.

"It may look like I have nothing to offer, but how many of these promising students have ever had to fight for their lives or the lives of others? I doubt a single one knows what it's like to watch your friends or your family die right in front of you. Not one of them knows what it feels like to kill someone, but I do." Ron continued to tell Cap what had happened in Regis, and the man simply listened. "You may not think I deserve to be here, but I at least deserve the chance to be trained, to be able to protect myself or the people I love. I want the chance to make sure that nothing like that ever happens again to me—or to anyone."

Ron wiped the tear rolling down his cheek, waiting for Cap to say something and beginning to wonder if he'd lost his chance at being accepted after everything he'd revealed.

"Alright."

Ron looked confused. "What do you mean, alright?"

"If you had said that when you applied, we wouldn't be having this conversation. Most students that come to the Arena have certain goals they want to achieve. I've seen most go off and join the king's guard for one of the kingdoms while they seek fame and prestige. I've seen others come unwillingly, as a means to stay sheltered within their family home, but those never last long. I rarely encounter a student with real purpose, real determination, a passion for bettering themselves—and not just for their sake, but for the sake of others."

"Does that mean you will train me?" Ron felt the hope rise in his chest.

"Yes, I will train you, but remember not to lose sight of why you want this. The training is long and difficult; it will test you mentally and physically. I have no tolerance for quitters, so if you leave, there is no coming back. But I don't think I'll have to worry about you."

Ron could only muster a thank you, knowing it wasn't enough for what Cap had done for him that day.

Then he turned as he heard his name being softly called. He looked behind him, but no one was there. Strange. Ron turned back toward Cap. His face frowned with concern as the instructor just stood still, on the hard dirt, staring off past Ron with a blank expression on his face.

"Cap? Cap?" Ron shook his shoulder, but the man didn't move; he just continued to stare. Ron heard his name called again. He was sure someone had to be behind him, but no one was there when he looked. Ron remembered Nora and Grant were sparring on the far north side of the Arena. He moved around Cap, watching to see if he would notice, but he didn't.

Taking a few strides, Ron stopped running toward Nora and Grant. They stood in the distance with their sparring partners, staring in the same direction as Cap, not moving. *What's happening? Okay, this is just a dream.* He closed his eyes. *It's just a dream. I can wake up, wake up.* Ron heard his name called louder than before, and he opened his eyes to see where it was coming from. He looked around and saw that Cap, Nora, and Grant had moved closer to him while his eyes were closed.

Fear was taking over. He couldn't wake up; he didn't know what was happening. Then the oil lamps he had paid no attention to all glowed blue inside. Ron had a feeling that he had seen these lamps before. They looked so familiar. Taking a few steps closer, he realized what they were—they were not oil lamps. All around the Arena were glass lanterns holding suspended flames just as the old blacksmith's had before Ron received the message. He backed away. "No, no, I have to wake up." A single crack of glass rang out in the Arena; Ron looked to Cap, Nora, and Grant as each lantern cracked, exploding into a consuming blue firestorm, annihilating everyone in its wake.

A loud hum began to buzz in Ron's ear. His head was pounding like a hammer beating a nail. Ron slowly opened his eyes and grabbed his head, hoping the pain would cease. Ron felt strange, oddly comfortable, which as it had for the past few days felt odd. Ron lifted his head from a cradling pillow, and he reached for his chest, pulling a hefty brown blanket off to make sure he hadn't dreamed up all the events that transpired.

To Ron's dismay, when he looked at his chest and shoulders, he saw the scars from the spikes. Ron looked around the room. It had the same stone walls, but a dim light from several small candles glowed; this room was different.

No chains hung from the walls, no spikes in the floor, and to his surprise, Ron found himself in a bed. Pictures of unusual-looking people, made to look flawed, hung on the walls, passing for art. A solitary, maple-stained desk with a simple wood chair sat in the corner of the room, adjacent to the bed. A red curtain hung above a darkened window, ready to postpone the light of the morning when the time came. He took a moment to breathe easy and soak in the fact that he was in a bed. Ron lay back down and relaxed as best he could, knowing someone might walk through the door at any moment. Ron could feel how tired he was throughout his body, so he took advantage of this comfort. He'd had no idea how much his body ached for the softness of a bed.

The pounding in Ron's head slowly came to an end, but soon after his head stopped aching, he heard a bolt slide from the door of his room. Ron sat up as quickly as he could to get ready for whoever came through the door, but the door only opened enough for someone to slide in a tray of food, then slammed shut again.

Ron could not remember the last time he'd had food. Just at the sight of the plate, he could feel his stomach turn, wanting to eat itself. He got to his feet and rushed over to the tray. It didn't have much on it, but he was happy to eat. First, Ron ate the loaf of bread. It was hard and had the consistency of sand in his mouth when it broke apart, but it was food. Next was the cheese, which had mold growing on the sides. Ron took a piece of hardened crust and scraped away most of the mold.

He washed it all down with stale water held in a small metal cup. While it wasn't much, it was more than Ron had had in quite some time. He stood up and walked back to the bed. This seemed like a good time to get more rest before anyone decided to bother him again. He needed to regain his strength if he wanted to conjure the flame again, but in his current state, he was still too weak from all the pain and blood loss. Ron lay down on the bed, placing his head back on the soft pillow. Then he pulled the warm wool blanket over himself and closed his eyes, hoping to be ready and rested when he woke up.

Chapter Thirteen

Problems Among the People

Nora reached down into her saddlebag, grabbing a piece of salted pork as she, Grant, and Shaw trotted along on their horses. She took a bite, looking around the valley, seeing smoke rising in the sky from the other camps that were a couple hours ahead in the other direction. She wondered what the other camps looked like, hoping they were not as lacking in basic necessities and that parents there were fortunate enough to clothe and care for their children. She tried to push the images out of her head as she knew she did not have enough gold or silver to help everyone. Not even with the combined efforts from Grant and Shaw could she have enough for everyone. So, she remained solely focused on the smoke rising in the east in Noic.

Grant, on the other hand, was smiling ear to ear. He was pleased that he could do some good for Alas and the people in Meno. Grant had never had to see or deal with these people's struggles due to constantly living in Greyland, never venturing farther than the bordering mountains that made up the backdrop. When they had first entered Meno, Grant had felt his heart break for the men, women, and children. However, once he put a smile or two on the thinned, wide-eyed faces of the children that looked to him, Grant felt his heart mend. He was able to do some good, even if it was only for a moment.

Shaw was happy with himself too, but through the years and during his travels, he had never seen people in such dire situations come out for the better. Concern washed over his face as it had Nora's, but they both knew there was little more they could do. The horses trotted at a steady pace, with each step bringing the smoke in the east closer and closer. Off in the distance, under the midafternoon sun, tents were coming into view.

"Hey Nora, look, I can see the tents—it shouldn't be long now. What do you think we'll find when we get there?" Grant asked, pulling his horse alongside hers.

Nora let out a sigh. "I'm not sure. I don't know what to expect, but we need to fight if it is a prisoner camp and Ron is there. No matter the consequences."

"We should at least have a plan," Shaw said as he pulled to Nora's right. "It would be well guarded, and from this point, it doesn't look like there is a fence or any movement to indicate guards patrolling the perimeter. I could be wrong, but we need to use caution."

The closer they got to Noic, the more they could see of the village. Shaw had been right; there were no guards to patrol the borders, and no fences or gates. Instead, they saw more white tents and the bustling of people, although this time, the atmosphere of the village was much different. Upon arriving in Noic, Nora was surprised at what she saw. The tents were the same as Meno in color, but their size and look were much more extravagant. The sheer magnitude was astounding; compared to the small one-family tents in Meno, these tents could easily fit four to five families comfortably.

The people were smiling, dressed in more than simple plain clothes or rags. They had colorful clothing that brought more life to the village. Almost all adults wore leather coats, belts, and accessories. The few children had shoes accompanied by clean, fitted clothes, and were actively playing with toys. There was not a somber face in the crowd; the trio heard laughter and cheer from the adults and children alike.

Shops were set up along the dirt roads leading into the village, everything from fruits and vegetables to butchers with hanging meats on display. Coins were being traded back and forth for goods that the people of Meno would give an arm to procure. No one batted an eye as Nora, Grant, and Shaw fastened their horses' reins to a hitching post that had a gathering of other well-groomed horses around it.

"This is not what I was expecting," Grant said as he finished tying a knot in his horse's reins.

"No, not at all. How can Meno have so little, but—but here, it seems everyone is happy. Why wouldn't the people from Meno come over here so they don't have to suffer?" Nora asked. She did not like how things were so different when these people had the means to help. They left the horses and walked through the tents, seeing just how grand this village was in comparison.

"While we're here, we should at least ask questions and see what we can find out." Shaw scratched his beard. "I think we should ask some of the merchants how often people come through on the regular and if there is any truth about prisoners being held here."

"I'm pretty sure we can't just ask those kinds of questions. We need to be at least a little tactful in how we go about doing this," Nora said.

"We could split up, talk to multiple people. How about we meet up in the center of the village in about an hour? Should be enough time to get some information." Grant liked the sound of his own idea.

Nora and Shaw agreed. It would be easier, and they could cover more ground. "Okay, I'll check the shops along the main road here," Nora said as she pointed out which shops she would be looking into.

"I think I'll meander around the other elderly people, as I have a tendency to blend in with the older crowd," Shaw said.

"I'm a little thirsty, so I'll see if they have a tavern anywhere. I can find an ale and get some drunk people to talk to," Grant said with a smirk.

"Of course. Just be careful, and don't act suspicious. We can't risk the wrong people finding out why we're really here," Nora reminded him.

"I think I can handle this one. I'm very endearing to drunk people." Grant let out a laugh and started off.

"I'm sure you are, Grant," Nora said under her breath.

Shaw nodded to her and began his stroll around the village to find people he could easily have a conversation with, and Nora began walking toward one of the first shops along the road.

Walking down the path, kicking up the delicate dust, Nora looked at each passerby and studied their faces—no dirt, no signs of unhappiness. It disgusted her to see these people living such comfortable lives while others were starving. Nora eyed each shop she passed, trying to discern which one was the oldest. "Alright, let's see. Which shop would have been set up when this place was first built?" Nora narrowed down a list in her head of shops to check first. The butcher's seemed the most appropriate, since people needed to eat. So Nora headed to her left.

Plucked chickens and ducks hung by their feet, dangling before the opening to the tent. Two thick posts were inserted into the ground, with a rope pulled tight to support the weight of the featherless fowl. As she made her way inside the shop, Nora saw several tables set up along the tent's walls; this tent was quite possibly the biggest within the whole village. Each table had a sign that read which meat was offered. Tabletops were covered with chicken, beef, and pork. The entirety of the animals were on display, with huge flanks quartered and presented, pigs' feet, racks of ribs, and what Nora could only guess were fine, select cuts of meat excised with precision from the animals. All parts were used, and nothing went to waste. The last table, which was actually four connected tables, had a horse, to Nora's surprise.

Eating a horse seemed barbaric to her at best. Maybe this tent wasn't the best place to ask questions. She turned around, walked out of the tent, and looked for a better choice. Soon, she saw a shop that had oils like the ones she'd procured at the Canopy, and since injuries and illness were common, this shop seemed as good a choice as any.

Nora made her way across the dirt road, passing a few smaller shops along the way. Seeing these shops and the people trying to sell their trinkets reminded her of the markets back home in Greyland. Finally, she reached the shop and entered the tent.

Looking around, Nora saw that this shop was much more established than she would have thought. Sturdy wooden shelves held all the wares being sold. There were more medicines on the shelves than she had seen at the Canopy, almost rivaling the supply of Greyland.

For these people to have this much stock of oils, herbs, and other medicinal products, they must be getting regular deliveries from one of the neighboring cities. Nora thought this would be a good place to try and gather some information. She inspected the items on the shelves, picking up one every so often, pretending to look as she really examined the shop owner in the back. She stood behind a wooden counter, waiting for customers to purchase the goods they sought. Nora observed her face. This woman looked no older than her mid-twenties, but she seemed rundown. Weariness enveloped her face. A yellow tint hung around her right eye and cheek, and her long, red hair was disheveled and in desperate need of a brush, but her undeniable beauty could still be seen underneath. Nora grabbed a few items off a shelf she didn't need just to retain the ruse, allowing her a reason to talk to this woman and not seem like she was just gathering information.

She approached the shopkeeper and placed the items down.

"Good afternoon. Will this be all for you?" the woman asked flatly.

"Yes, it is, thank you." Nora looked around while the woman priced the items. "This is a big place—you must get many customers."

"We do okay," the woman said.

Nora felt she might not get a lot out of her at this rate, so she asked, "What's your name?"

The woman looked up, surprised that Nora was taking an interest. She started to fumble over her words. "Me? Oh—um, I'm . . . my name is Abby."

Nora smiled and extended her hand, "Well, Abby, it's nice to meet you. I'm Nora." She saw a faint smile that faded quickly. "I have a question, Abby—I just came in today, and my friends said they would be arriving before I did, but I haven't seen them yet. Have you seen any groups of riders come through?"

"We haven't had any groups come through today. I only saw the First Born riders that came through a few days ago."

Nora felt a shock of anger when she heard the name, but she held it back from her face. "Oh," she said. "I sure hope they don't bring any dangerous people here. I was hoping to relax a little and not worry about seeing any criminals."

"They don't keep anyone like that here, oh no. They take them to the mountains by Oroze," Abby replied, lowering her voice. "From what I've heard, they have a cellar built into the actual mountain. I believe it's called the Ark of Redemption. We're not supposed to say anything, so—" Abby put a figure to her lips, implying silence.

"Sounds scary," Nora said quietly. Her eyes quickly shifted to the movement behind Abby; a man had come out from behind a closed curtain in the tent a couple feet behind the counter. Abby's expression change rapidly. No longer was she willing to talk or even look at Nora. She reverted back to grim distress as her eyes widened and a slight tremble ran over her.

The man walked over to the counter. "What have I told you about talking too much? Your job is to take their money and let them be on their way. I never said you could chit chat."

"I'm sorry, I didn't mean to, she just arrived and had a few questions, and I—"

Without warning, the man raised his left hand, backhanding Abby across the left side of her face.

"I didn't say you could talk, did I! I don't care for your apologies; next time, it will be worse than just one hit." Abby was sobbing quietly, holding her cheek as she slowly backed away from the man. "I do apologize. It's so hard to find help that will listen," the man said to Nora as he looked at the items she was purchasing.

Nora was beyond mortified. She looked over at Abby and asked if she was okay, but Abby did not reply. Instead, the man stepped in front of Abby and said, "There is no need to concern yourself with this one, she—"

Nora quickly interrupted the man. "I'm sorry, I wasn't talking to you." The man's face grew instantly red with anger, and as he was beginning to reply, Nora continued, "It takes a weak man to hit a woman. Are you trying to act tough? Does no one respect you, is that it? What does it take for a coward to hit a defenseless woman?" At this point, Nora knew what she was getting herself into. By the look on Abby's face, no one had ever talked to this man in such a manner.

The man looked at Abby and smacked her again. "She is my property, and you have no say in the matter. But I'll show you what a weak man can do!" Nora felt the anger burst inside her. The man placed his large hand on the counter and began to jump over, and Nora unhooked her staff from the clip on her back.

* * *

Grant slowly wandered along, looking for the nearest tavern; they were typically easy to spot, since visiting them was one of his favorite pastimes. He knew to look for the loudest or most rambunctious tent in the lot from personal experience with House for Ale in Greyland. Grant continued walking east down the dirt path, looking between tents for anyone that might be giving off the tell-tale signs of inebriation. Grant knew them well, of course, especially after participating in celebratory drinking soon after passing most of his exams while still training at the Arena.

He made his way to the center of Noic, where a sizable fountain spewed water out of four large orifices. The fountain's center formed a triangle as the waters crashed into one another, completing the cycle. Grant thought to himself as he stared at the fountain, *Well, that looks fancy.* His attention was pulled away from watching the water when he heard some obnoxiously shouting to his left. Grant turned to see men acting foolishly just down the road. *Ah, perfect. That's more of what I was expecting. Time for a drink.* Grant smiled and walked up the road toward the tavern.

The tavern looked like all the other tents—large, white, and unremarkable. The only differences were that both of the front flaps were rolled up and tied to the eves at the top. Men and women were talking, singing, and having a good time. Grant walked through the entrance, making his way to the bar at the back of the tent. Chairs and tables were set up on the right and left sides so the middle walkway could be clear for new patrons and customers who'd had their fill or indulged too much by chance. The bar was set up in a horseshoe shape, so the man attending to everyone's drink orders was able to serve them without having to walk back and forth, taking more time before people could get their drinks.

Stools sat around the bar and surrounding tables, leaving the middle walkway clear for Grant to make his way over.

"What could I get ya?" asked the barkeep without looking up as he finished polishing a brown ceramic mug.

"How's the house ale?"

"It's a good batch, made here fresh with a touch of orange from the market."

"Well, that sounds good to me. I'll take the biggest mug you got," Grant said.

The barkeep looked up at him and smiled. "All right, buddy." The man walked to the right side of the bar, where all the mugs, pints, and double pints were held. He reached for a double pint and filled it with a cloudy, light brown ale.

Grant took up a stool on the left side of the bar and surveyed the room while he swiveled around. "Here ya go." The barkeep handed Grant his double pint and turned to another customer.

Grant's eye grew wide. He had never had a mug with so much ale at once. In Greyland, they only served ale by the pint, so each person would have to order more drinks and pay more. Grant took a sip. The fragrant orange zest mingled with the hops, creating a flavor of splendor. A familiar, relaxing sensation rolled throughout his body as it commonly would back home after a long day. Being able to feel calm put a smile on his face as he thought of the last time he could embrace any form of comfort since leaving Greyland. Halfway through his ale, Grant leaned on the bar. "Barkeep?"

The man made his way over. "Yes? What'll it be?"

"I'll take another double if you don't mind." Grant slid one silver coin over to the man. "Also, what is there for a man to do around here? I see a lot of tents but not a lot of fun besides being in here."

The barkeep grabbed another mug and filled it. "Well, you could try the other village just up the road there. It would be about a four-hour ride by horse if you got one. Lalin is bigger, so it may have whatever it is you're looking for, or perhaps you could go to the kingdom of Baddon. Lots of goings-on there. A little too crowded for my taste, but whatever suits your fancy."

Grant finished his first ale and passed the empty mug to the barkeep. "Thank you, I will see about that." The barkeep nodded, and Grant grabbed the second glass. Observing the other people in the tent, Grant had no clue where to start; no one looked like they belonged to the First Born, and if they did, he would be smart enough to keep his head down.

They all looked ordinary, in plain clothes, with no distinct armor to speak of. After a moment, though, Grant overheard two men talking about what he believed to be the village of Meno. *Okay, that might be interesting. Now how do I get in that conversation?* he thought while he sipped his ale. *Ah, their drinks are almost empty; I'll buy them an ale and see where it goes.*

This was not Grant's greatest plan, but it was better than nothing. He ordered two more ales, but this time they were only pints. No need to spend more than necessary on strangers; Grant's pockets did not run very deep. He walked over to the men sitting at a small round table with four chairs placed around it. He set the drinks down and walked back to the bar, grabbing his own. When he returned, he set his drink down and slid the other pints to each man respectively.

"Gentlemen, I couldn't help but overhear your conversation, and being new to this area, I thought I would offer a drink and some company." The pair stared at Grant, not expecting this show of hospitality, but they accepted nonetheless. These men were fairly dressed, not the sharpest of lookers but comfortable in what they could afford to wear.

"What brings you here, stranger?" the man on the left asked, taking a sip of ale.

"Well, I'm from a small farming town, and before I settle down anywhere permanently, I wanted to do a little traveling, perhaps find somewhere that's more to my liking than the country. See the sights, if you will." Grant didn't mind lying to these people. He was only making conversation. He certainly wasn't going to tell them any form of truth.

"There's not much to see around here unless you go to the cities," the man replied.

"I wouldn't put much stock in this area. Around here are a bunch of deserters, elderly, or poor people. Might as well be a deserter if you're poor and can't contribute anyway," the man on the right said with a frown on his face, showing his disdain for people not like himself.

"If you can't contribute, what's the point then?" Grant added, not believing his own words.

"Here, here," the man on the left said, raising his glass.

"I passed through another village on my way here—it was small and pretty filthy, Meno, I believe it was called. Why is it so different from this village?" Grant asked before taking a swig of ale. The men looked at one other before continuing.

"Meno is full of those who do not follow our lord. Deserters who think our lord is corrupt, evil. What do they know? Should have killed them all before they left. Nothing but useless people living off the lord's land," the man on the left said, shaking his head.

"We will deal with them soon enough. Our lord has a plan," the other added, and both men began laughing.

Grant's heart sank as he listened to these men talk. Could they really be thinking of destroying everyone in Meno? "I'm only from a small farm, so I'm not too current with everything that happens so far north, but who is the lord?" Grant asked, trying to be coy about his questions. The men paused again, eyeing Grant suspiciously; they couldn't tell if he was an ignorant farm boy or just stupid.

"The Lord of the First Born. He's the one that's given us all of this." The man on the left pointed around the room. "Without him, we would still be living under Lord Ire. He was always trying to make peace with everyone else, all the other kingdoms. But what about us, the ones actually living in his city? We work hard, but no matter how much we work, we would never be allowed to rise to the top. Our new lord sees things a little differently. The more we do for him, the more rewarded we will be. We don't need to have substantial wealth or be a form of royalty for him to see what we're worth. That's the kind of lord to follow."

Grant took a long drag from his double-pint mug. *These are First Born supporters; I need to tread lightly.* With a splash of ale in his cup, Grant lifted to a toast. "To what we are given." He nearly finished his drink, but noticed the other men did not toast with him; they continued to stare. Grant reached in his pocket and pulled out a few silver coins, placing them on the table. "That should cover another round of ales for you gentlemen. It was nice talking to you both, but I must be off."

"Why the rush?" asked the man on the right. "You got somewhere to be?"

"It's a long journey back home, and if I am to see the cities, I should get an early start." Grant's heart started to beat faster.

The men continued staring. "Where was your town again?"

Grant stood, starting to move away. "Oh, it's that way," he said, pointing his fingers in the direction he thought was south.

"Why don't you stay and chat for a little longer? I'm curious to know which bridge you crossed to get here. Was it the Malen bridge or the Baddon bridge?"

Grant sipped what was left in his mug, trying to think of an answer, but he didn't know of either bridge; the only bridge he'd crossed was much farther west. "I believe it was the bridge crossing over from Baddon."

The men stood up, slamming their hands on the table. "There is no bridge crossing from Baddon. The only bridges are built in the city itself. So what are you really doing here, boy? Speak!"

"Well, you see, the funny thing is . . ." Grant backed away while both men moved around the table. Quickly, he grabbed the sides of the table, shoving it forward into their knees, causing them to stumble to the floor as the ale made them both unbalanced. Grant swiftly turned around and ran down the walkway of the tent. The men pushed the table off of them and chased after him. Grant started grabbing empty chairs, throwing them in front of the men. The men tried to jump over them, but wooden legs broke as the men came crashing down, along with a few tables they tried to grab for support. Grant ran out of the front of the tent and headed back toward the fountain.

* * *

Shaw walked along the path, making his way to the fountain, as he believed it to be the village's main attraction. Unsurprisingly, he was right. With the fountain's water flowing, children running around in circles, and plenty of birds to be seen, Shaw knew this was where most if not all of the elder people would converge. The fountain was the village's centerpiece, with pathways leading north, south, east, and west from it. Wooden benches had been placed around each bend where the tents met the curve of the road. As the day progressed and the sun rose higher, Shaw circled the fountain till he found a group of elders sitting and enjoying the day. "Good afternoon—do you mind if I join you?" Shaw asked in his most polite tone.

"Oh, not at all. Make yourself comfortable." An elder woman motioned for Shaw to have a seat.

"Thank you," he said, sitting down. "What a lovely day we have, isn't it?"

"Yes, it is," she replied.

"It's nice to see these parts again, but it's been so long since I've been back this way. It appears a lot has changed. I seem to be getting lost on my travels. These villages are new, that's for sure." Shaw wasn't looking at anyone in particular when he spoke; he made sure to put the comment out and see if anyone would follow up with anything.

"Yes, you would be right," an elderly man on an opposite bench replied. "We have been here for some time now, and the way things are going, this might be a permanent spot for us."

"What brought about all the tents in the first place? Last I remember, the fields of the valley were running through this region," Shaw said, stroking his beard.

"A couple months back, a self-proclaimed lord from somewhere got the idea he wanted to control Oroze. When we heard about an army coming to the gates, we couldn't believe it. That's when the fighting happened." The old man looked on with a blank stare.

"It was a hard day for all of us," a woman sitting close to Shaw said. "The fighting was terrible. We thought the walls and gates would keep us safe, but they broke through them. Once they got in, it was almost as if the fighting would never end. I can still remember the screams. I was in my home when it finally stopped. I went to have a look, and a man was standing just beyond the gate. The Orozian soldiers were all dead, lying on the ground, and then this man walked in with his hands glowing. Every soldier that raised a weapon was burned to death where they stood. It was the blue flame from the stories of old. The type of stories our mothers and fathers would tell us about. I didn't believe it to be real, not for my entire life, but now that I have seen it—" The woman paused, taking in a deep breath.

"I'm sorry to hear of such a tragedy," Shaw said solemnly.

"That man," the man on the other bench said, "after the kingdom had fallen, the man gave everyone a choice. He said we could join him and live out our days in prosperity and freedom, or if we opposed, we would be branded traitors and thrown out."

The woman looked up. "We do not support his kind of rule. Lord Ire was a fair and just king, and we would never betray him, but we are old and have a limited amount of time left. I just want my last few years to be in peace."

"What did this lord look like, if you don't mind my asking?" Shaw was curious if it was the same man that had been following them since the forest.

"The man was tall. He wore dark, plated armor that had a symbol on the chest. It was an upside-down triangle with the letters "FB" in the middle. His face was scarred. It looked like he was burned on the side of his face, with two lines to be exact." The elders collectively nodded, then let the conversation drift to other topics.

Shaw did not partake in much speaking unless directly spoken to. *She didn't mention a mask. How many of these wielders are out there? What are they trying to do?* While Shaw was thinking and caressing his beard, he swore he could hear his name being called, but he paid it no mind. Focusing back on his thoughts, he was interrupted again, but this time he heard his name very clearly, and it kept growing in volume. Shaw looked to where the sound was coming from, and he saw Grant running full speed toward the fountain, waving his arms like a madman.

"Shaw! Shaw! Come on, let's go!" Grant yelled as he rounded the corner, running west toward the horses.

Shaw got up and started to run as well so he could catch up to the young man. "Why are we running? What did you do?"

"I'll tell you once we find Nora and get out of here."

They ran down the dirt path. Out of nowhere, a man came barreling out of a tent, landing flat on his back. Grant and Shaw slid to a stop, taken by surprise. The man lay on the ground, unconscious, blood spilling out of his mouth, and his nose looked broken. Deep, red marks dug into the side of the man's head where an object must have struck him with brutal force. Grant and Shaw looked at the tent as the front flaps began to open. They saw Nora standing in the archway, putting her staff back on the latch behind her, and felt slightly confused but relieved.

"Nora, we have to go now," Grant said, still trying to catch his breath.

"Sounds good to me. Just give me one second." Nora went back into the tent, and just as she said, she was back within a matter of seconds. "This is Abby—she will be coming with us."

"Okay, great, but right now, we got to go," Grant said. Before they took off running, he and Shaw glanced at Abby's face. They looked back to the man on the ground and came to the same conclusion. With a shrug of their shoulders, they understood what had happened in the tent, so without a second thought, they ran.

"Hurry, untie the horses," Grant said as he unhitched his steed as fast as he could.

Nora helped Abby onto her horse, and once Nora got settled, they were all ready to ride. "Where are we going, Grant?" she shouted over the galloping hooves.

"Meno—we are going to Meno." Grant turned his head and saw the two men that had been chasing him watch as they rode away.

The horses galloped as fast as they could; running for over an hour was the hardest they'd ever pushed, but with the possibility of being chased by people that wanted to kill them, they did not have much choice in slowing down. Nora pulled her horse beside Grant's as she yelled over the sound of hooves smacking the ground. "Grant, what's going on? What happened?"

"I may have made some people suspicious while I was talking to them," Grant admitted, turning his head around, looking back toward Noic, hoping not to see anyone following them. He let out a sigh of relief and looked forward once he didn't see anyone in the distance.

They continued riding for another hour or so until the sun began to sink behind the western mountains. Grant eased back on the reins, slowing his horse down. The horses were panting and out of breath after running for most of the evening.

"We should reach Meno by morning if we don't stop to make camp. We will walk the horses for a bit so they can rest, but once dawn breaks, we'll need to push forward again," Shaw said as he and Grant got off their horses and walked alongside them. Nora and Abby stayed on hers; Abby was not as accustomed to riding a horse as everyone else. Shaw reached into his pack, grabbed some wilted carrots, and tossed one over to Grant so he could feed his horse. Shaw fed his own horse and Nora's.

"So, Grant, do you mind explaining what happened back there?" Shaw asked.

"Well, while I was having a drink and looking to find some information, I started talking to these two guys who looked rather suspect." Grant told of how he'd tried to trick these men into thinking he was just a traveler to learn about what was going on. In doing so, he drew more attention to himself than he wanted once they started questioning him. "When I tried to leave, they didn't want me to. That's when I made a run for it and found Shaw. The men told me how the people of Meno are traitors, deserters, and they said that the First Born are planning to kill them. I have a feeling they might speed up their plans now that we know their intentions."

"At least we have a head start toward Meno to warn them," Shaw replied.

Nora glanced over to the old man. "What were you able to find out?"

"The elders, they told me about how Oroze was attacked. One day everything was fine, and the next, the First Born had laid siege upon them. They said there was a man, a wielder nonetheless. The Lord of the First Born, perhaps. He's not the same man as the one who followed us earlier. This man did not wear a mask, but they said he had two scars on his face above and below his left eye, just like we saw on the mask." Shaw's attention was pulled to Abby. She was intently listening to what he had to say. "Who is your new friend, Nora?"

Abby didn't respond herself, just holding on more tightly to Nora, "This is Abby. She was working in one of the shops I wandered into." Nora looked back to the woman. "These are my friends—that's Grant, and that's Shaw."

Loosening her grip around Nora, Abby gave each man a respective nod. "What you say is the truth. We were attacked, and Oroze was taken by them."

"I'm sorry," Shaw said somberly. Nora glanced at him and saw the look upon his face, a fatherly expression she had not seen from him before. "I know this must be hard to talk about, for I have known loss myself a lifetime ago, but could you tell us what happened that day?" he asked.

Drawing a deep breath, Abby began. "It was just another day. I was at home tending to my son while my husband was preparing a meal when we heard the sounds. The ground was shaking, and people began screaming and running to their homes. I looked out the window and saw that a portion of the city wall had been blown out. Rocks and rubble were everywhere. soldiers littered the ground, dead or bleeding and screaming in pain. After the First Born broke through, they slaughtered anyone they could find until he came in. He walked in front of his men, leading them into the city square. The rest of our soldiers stood there looking at him, confused, like why would the leader just walk into an occupied city.

"That was when he spoke. He told us if we did not resist, we could live peacefully, but if we fought, he would kill everyone, every last man, woman, and child. So he gave those that did not want to fight an option to leave, and some people took it, but the soldiers fought. They began running toward the leader with their swords drawn, but the soldiers behind this man didn't move or pull out their swords. They just stood there. That's when it happened."

Abby's speech broke as she tried to collect herself to finish.

"It's alright. If it's too much, you don't have to keep going." The fatherly tone in Shaw's voice seemed to calm Abby down, so she was able to take some deep breaths before continuing.

"The man, he pulled up his sleeves, and his arms were covered in scars like someone had held his arms over a fire and let him burn. Then his hands themselves began to burn with a fire I had never seen before. It was blue, and it came out of nowhere. Somehow, he lifted his hand toward the soldiers running at him, and with one motion, he sent fire to the first row of men. They started burning and screaming, stopping right in their tracks. The other soldiers backed away, too afraid to fight. Their screams echoed throughout the city. That's when we knew the kingdom was taken. He then let his men loose, and they rushed into the city.

"I hid with my son in our home, but my husband, he—he went outside to try to help the others. I barred the door, but it didn't do any good. Some of the men broke the door down and came in; they grabbed my son and me. Since that day, I haven't seen my son, and the man who broke into my home took me. He said I was now his property. I tried to fight, but he was too strong. So he took me to Noic, and that's where I've been for almost a year now. I don't even know where my son is or—or if my husband is alive." Finally, Abby could not take any more; she began to cry, burying her face into Nora's back as she wept.

Shaw was at a loss for words. Even if he'd had something to say, now would not be the time. Nora heard something coming from Grant's direction, and looked over to see that tears had made their way down his face as what was left of the sun reflected off his damp cheek. Abby's sobs became less and less frequent as the horses walked on, and after some time, it became clear she had fallen asleep. Not another word was spoken.

After the sun had set and the moon and stars settled in the sky, Abby woke up. "How are you doing?" Nora asked, giving a brief look over her shoulder.

"Much better. I'm sorry about earlier—it's just hard to talk about."

"It's alright," Nora said.

"I wanted to thank you for helping me. I didn't think I would ever get away from that man. I owe you my life."

"You owe me nothing, Abby. No person should ever be subjected to being held captive." When the last word came out of Nora's mouth, she remembered Ron was still gone. Anger gripped her, and she squeezed the reins tight. Abby could sense that something in Nora had changed,

"What's the matter, Nora? Did I say something wrong?"

"No, Abby, you're fine. It's just, we went to Noic to find our friend Ron. He was captured by one of the First Born, the one that wears the mask. We were told Noic was where they took prisoners, but now we know different. So now we are also headed in the opposite direction of where we should be going." Nora could feel the emotion building in her chest, wondering if Ron thought they had abandoned him. There was silence for a moment. "Abby, you said something about a cellar where they keep people. What was it called? Do you know anything else about it?"

Grant and Shaw looked hopeful, eager for the woman to be the answer they were looking for. "I don't know much, just what I have heard in passing in the shop." The two men climbed up onto their horses and brought them toward Nora's horse in the middle. "There is talk of a place called the Ark of Redemption. I've heard that it's built into the mountainside of Oroze. I'm not sure where exactly it is, but it's there. It must have been built after the city was taken, but that is all I know. If anyone has prisoners, I would think they'd bring them there."

"That's where we need to go then," Grant said.

"We can't." Nora shot him a look that conveyed the hurt she was feeling at what she just said.

"Nora's right, Grant. We cannot head there now. If we do that, then what of the people in Meno? Should we just leave them to get slaughtered by the First Born if they intend to follow us? We have to help these people. We cannot abandon them," Shaw reasoned.

Grant was unable to keep the anger from his voice. "But what about Ron? We can't just leave him. Who knows what's happening to him!"

"I know, Grant—believe me, I know," Nora said.

"What do you mean you know? If it were any of us, Ron would be out looking for us. He would—"

Nora could no longer hold her temper. "I know he would! But what would you have me do? I get that we have to find Ron, but we also can't let these people be killed. Do you think this is easy for me? Do you think I don't want to find Ron as soon as possible? I don't know what to do, okay? Does that make it easier for you? Every day that goes by and he's not here breaks my heart. Day by day, it breaks. The last time I got to hold him in my arms was the first time he kissed me. If we can't find him, or if he is gone, I will have to live with the fact I never said . . . I never said how I truly felt about him." Nora stopped talking, and Abby held her tightly around her waist, resting her head on her shoulder. It was a comforting feeling for Nora, but the sadness had taken over.

"I don't think you have to worry about that part, Nora." Compassion gripped Grant's voice.

Nora wiped her face. "What do you mean?"

"I believe Ron knows and will always know how you feel about him. Even without words, he knows."

"Thank you, Grant."

Shaw pulled his horse closer to Nora. "We should start riding hard now if we're to reach Meno by daybreak. The sooner we can see these people to safety, the sooner we can get Ron back. I didn't watch over him his whole life just to lose him now." Shaw spurred his horse to a run, and the others followed, galloping as fast as the horses would carry them.

The sun began to rise, hitting their backs with its warm rays; smoke trails rose a few miles ahead of them. Meno was coming into view, the white tents with dust-covered sides, people doing chores while the children ran around playing games of hide and seek with one another. When they reached the first tent along the dirt road, everyone dismounted and walked beside the horses. Not wanting to waste any time with the First Born maybe less than a day away, they knew they had to find Alas.

They were walking down the dusty street when they heard a shriek. Turning to see where it came from, they saw an old, larger woman with sun-blond hair wearing an apron covered in flour. Her hands covered her mouth as her wide eyes looked directly at them. She dropped her arms as she started to run. "Abby, Abby, my dear Abby, is that you?"

Abby saw the woman, who for her age was faster than she looked, and began to run to her. The woman grabbed Abby with a hug that looked like it could have squeezed the life out of just about anyone. "I can't believe it's you. It's been so long. We have missed you terribly." Joyful tears were running down the old woman's face.

"Gretta, I'm so glad to see you." Breaking the hug, Abby brought Gretta over to the others. "Gretta, this is Nora, Grant, and Shaw. They saved me from Noic. They're the reason I'm here."

Gretta opened her arms wide, squishing them all together.

"Thank you, my dears. You have no idea how much this means to me. Thank you for rescuing our Abby from those dreadful people." Once Gretta had let them go, she turned back toward Abby, grabbing her hands with hers. "Now that you're here, there's someone more excited to see you than anyone else." Abby's eyes grew large and began to fill with tears as Gretta shouted, "Yulis!"

Abby turned toward the tent Gretta had been standing by and saw a young boy about seven years of age walk onto the street. Yulis turned toward Gretta and saw his mother. Without a second thought, the boy ran to her, and Abby to her son. She dropped to her knees and scooped up Yulis, holding him so tight as to never let him go.

"Now, that's a sight to see," Gretta said, wiping her eyes as she turned back toward the three. "I see you have a kind heart as well, young man."

Grant wiped his face as quickly as he could. "I've just never been part of something like this. Being able to help reunite a mother and son, it's—" Nora put a hand on Grant's shoulder; he smiled and collected himself.

A somber looked fell over Gretta's face. "It's the best news she will have today, unfortunately."

"Why is that?" Grant asked as Nora's hand fell from his shoulder.

"Well, her husband was brought to the village when we left Oroze, but the injuries he suffered proved to be fatal in the end. He passed on a few months back. It's going to break the poor girl's heart, but I'll wait for a more appropriate time to tell her." Sorrow had once again fallen across their faces, and the brief moment of joy had been stripped away.

Shaw turned toward Gretta. "We need to find Alas—it's rather important, and time is an issue. Do you know where he would be, by chance?"

"He should be around his tent. Just go up the road, and when you reach the first right, turn down it. His tent shouldn't be too far on the left side."

"Thank you, Gretta," Shaw said, giving her a nod.

Before they began walking to find Alas's tent, Abby held her son and turned toward them, making eye contact and smiling at each of them as if to say that she was more thankful than words could tell. Then her attention went back to Yulis, and Nora, Grant, and Shaw began to walk down the street, trailing dust as they went.

They looked into every open tent, trying to find Alas. Soon, the man walked out of his tent, holding a hammer in his hand and two wooden spokes in the other. Without noticing them, he bent down and hammered a few nails into a wooden wheel he was in the middle of repairing.

"Alas," Shaw shouted.

Alas turned around. "Ah, to what do I owe the pleasure?" he asked as he greeted everyone.

"I'm sorry to say, but this is not a visit we are happy about," Shaw said.

A look of confusion ran across the man's face. "I'm not sure I understand."

Grant took a couple steps forward. "Alas, we need to get you and your people out of here. We're not sure if we were followed, but the First Born are coming, and they plan on killing everyone."

Alas's confusion turned into a frown. "What do you mean? The First Born said anyone who leaves willingly can do so. So why would they come here now?"

"I talked to some men in Noic, and they seemed pretty intent on slaughtering all the 'traitors' to the First Born," Grant said with urgency.

"It's been almost a year since we left, so it doesn't make sense," Alas said, scratching his head.

Grant clutched his fist, getting upset with Alas. He didn't understand why the man was questioning everything he was saying. "I don't know why, but it's going to happen. Whether it be today or tomorrow. The point is, we need to get everyone out of here." Walking a few steps away from the opening of his tent, Alas put the hammer down in a box with a wide range of other tools.

"If what you say is true, then getting everyone out of here will not be as easy as you think." He paused to wipe his hands on a cloth. "We have a lot of women and children. We have men that have not fully healed from the attack on Oroze. How do you plan on telling everyone without starting a panic?" Alas asked.

Grant's patience was running thin. Even though Alas was finally entertaining the idea of leaving, Grant didn't have any answers to his questions. "I don't know, Alas! Aren't you the leader here? These are your people—we're just trying to help."

"Okay, Grant, just cool off." Nora motioned for him to take a step back and remove himself before he got more frustrated. Facing Alas, she asked, "Is there anywhere for you and your people to go? Or at least hide?"

The man scratched at his chin while he thought. "I'm not sure. I don't know who would take so many people."

Shaw said, "That's fine for now, but how about we focus on one thing at a time? First, we need to warn everyone in the village. Can you call everyone to the center?"

"Of course I can, but I don't know who will listen. There is no proof, no evidence. These are my people's homes—I don't think they will want to leave again," Alas said.

"For right now, it doesn't matter whether they want to leave or not. We need to tell everyone so that way we can all be on the same page. After that, we will go from there," Shaw said.

"Okay, I'll call everyone to the center. It may take some time to gather people."

"Thank you, Alas." Shaw let out of sigh of relief.

The man walked into his tent, shortly reemerging with a horn that looked fashioned from a bighorn sheep, the kind found around the hills of Oroze. Alas walked to the village center, but before he got there, he grabbed a crate from a neighboring tent and placed it on the ground in the center. He stood on top of the crate and raised the horn to his lips. Three loud blasts seemed to echo for miles. People turned their heads, looked out from their tents, and began to gather.

Grant was pacing back and forth by the crate as people slowly started to trickle in. This process was going to take time. Finally, after two hours of waiting, it looked as though everyone in the village had arrived. It had taken far longer than Grant had hoped, but Alas stood on top of the crate and held his hands up for the people to quiet down. "Thank you for coming. I apologize for the inconvenience, but my friends here have some news that I believe we all should hear." Alas got off the crate, motioning for Grant to climb atop as he took his place next to Shaw.

"Everyone, this news might be hard to hear, but please believe me when I tell you it's the truth. We were in Noic the other day, and to make a long story short, I heard men talking about coming here and destroying Meno." Whispers began erupting from the crowd into a dull roar. "I know this is difficult, but we need to get everyone out of here to safety."

A voice called out, "How do we know you're telling the truth? We don't even know who you are! You could be one of them. What if you are leading us to an ambush?" Rumblings grew louder within the crowd.

Grants anger was rising. He still didn't understand these people. Why wouldn't they believe him?

More voices shouted, "We can't just leave—this is our home. We can't leave without any proof."

Grant couldn't take it anymore. His anger was at a boiling point. "What is wrong with all of you? Why would anyone make this up? I'm trying to help you. Can't you see that?" His voice was shaking. "You want proof? Besides the fact that I talked to the people who plan to hurt you, I don't have any other proof. But you know what? Did you have any proof when the First Born attacked you the first time in Oroze? No, you didn't, but now you want proof before you believe someone that's trying to warn you? Or do you want to be killed?"

Grant took a deep breath and looked at the faces surrounding him. "If you don't want to believe me or any of us, then stay." Nora and Shaw couldn't believe what he was saying. "If you want to live full lives, if you want your children to grow and have kids themselves one day, then please listen."

Grant stepped off the crate and hung his head, not knowing if he'd reached any of the people. He turned his back and began walking away, feeling defeated for just trying to help. Then a woman pushed her way to the front of the crowd.

"Grant, wait." The young man turned around and saw Abby walking up to him with Yulis in her arms. A smile returned to his face. "I believe you." She took Grant's hand and handed Yulis to him. Abby then climbed on the crate to address the crowd. "I believe these people. I believe what they say is true. They rescued me when I thought the rest of my days would be spent being beaten, humiliated, treated as less than a human. They are trying to give us a chance. A chance we never had the first time. I intend to take that chance because, unlike you, I know what it's like to lose all hope. These people gave me that hope back when they saved me. Let them do the same for you. Let them help save you."

Abby continued to persuade the crowd into leaving while Shaw and Alas were trying to figure out where they could bring all these people.

"Alas, I have not been to these regions in a very long time. Do you know if the old treaties are still in place?" Shaw asked.

"I'm not entirely sure. No one knows how far the First Born have spread their armies. If the separate kingdoms are still intact and untouched, then I believe the treaties would still stand. I don't know if Oroze was the beginning of their assault."

"If the treaties are indeed intact, then I suggest we make for Malen," Shaw said.

"Malen is not an easy journey. It's four days by foot at least, and with all the people we have, what if we don't make it?" Alas said with worry.

"We have to at least try. If we stay here, your people have no chance, but we stand a better chance if we take whatever lead and push as hard as possible. Also, don't you have a carriage? I saw you fixing the wheel for one," Shaw said.

"We do, but it's old, and we don't have horses."

"Lucky for you, Alas, we have three."

Grant raised his hand to help Abby down from the crate as Alas walked over. "Well said, Abby. I hope they listened."

"Me too."

Alas got on the crate and looked around the crowd. "For those of you who are willing to come, we will be traveling to Malen." Voices started murmuring amongst the crowd. "I know it's far, and it will take time to get there, but if the First Born are indeed coming, I intend to be as far away from them as possible. I urge you all to come with me. We will be having the children, elderly, and wounded ride in the carriage. The men and women that are strong enough will walk with the rest of us. We will be leaving before the day comes to an end, so please, do not concern yourself with bringing unnecessary belongings. Take only what you can carry. Do not worry about the material things or your keepsakes. Your life is worth more than any object, because with life, you will have the memories of what is most dear to you. We leave before nightfall."

Chapter Fourteen

Old Treaties

"You get them into the carriage. They will ride upfront with me. Let's move the ones that can't fight to the front—we need all able bodies in the rear in case we are followed." Alas was directing his people as quickly as he could to get moving before sunset. As much as people were willing, some did not want to leave behind everything they had. The men that could fight did not have proper weapons, as such items were sparse. After fleeing Oroze, not many of these people were fighters to begin with, so they did not carry swords or any other useful weapons. Most were craftsmen or farmers, people who lived day to day not thinking about fighting for their lives. Weapons were provided, however, in the forms of pitchforks used for moving hay bales, and clubs were easily fashioned from table legs due to the tables not being needed anymore. Small knives were to be carried and concealed if anyone got close enough to attack as a last-ditch effort.

"Shaw, why are we going to Malen? Seems rather far for all these people." Nora was looking over the map Shaw had given them when they first arrived at the Canopy.

"It's not the closest, but it is the safest. It would be too risky to go to Baddon, since that would bring us closer to Noic and the First Born. Also, the small bordering towns there are too far southeast and do not have as much defense as a kingdom like Malen." Shaw pointed his finger at the map, showing Nora and Grant the path he proposed to take. "If we continue west, back toward the

Red Band river, and take the bridge before the river splits, we will have ample time to get to Malen safely, but we must reach that bridge before anything else."

The Red Band River was long and winding, with few bridges built along its banks. Due to the formation of the rock bed, some areas of the riverbed had been washed away, widening the river over time. Not all of it was deep; some spots could be waded, coming up no more than knee-high on an average-sized person. Other spots were impossible to cross as the river swept far below the tallest hills, creating a deadly drop from the cliffside.

"Do you think Malen will let all these people into the kingdom?" Nora asked. Not knowing of other cities and their customs made Grant and Nora apprehensive about how these kingdoms operated. Living in Greyland, they'd never been presented the opportunities to travel around and visit the kingdoms. Most people who grew up there dreamed of what it would be like to visit a kingdom and meet the kings and queens. Few did, and of those few, most went and joined the guard of Oroze after completing their respective training.

Oroze was one of the two most prominent cities within the five kingdoms, second only to Baddon. Though separate, the two kingdoms worked in tandem with one another for trade routes and mined materials. They were easily the wealthiest of the kingdoms, and young men and women would flock to either one hoping to live a grand life with endless possibilities that were not afforded within the towns where they grew up.

"It's my hope, Nora, that they do. For a long time, the kingdoms have had a lasting treaty with one another. When I was younger and more active in these parts, there was free trade among them. People could come and go as they pleased, visiting wherever they liked, but now, with the First Born inhabiting Oroz—and taking it by force, no less—I am not sure how the treaties are holding. Word must have spread by now to the other kingdoms of Oroze's downfall. With it almost being a year since its capture, many things could have changed." With a deep breath and a troubled look upon Shaw's brow, he said, "I can only hope Malen will help."

Alas walked over to where Nora, Grant, and Shaw were standing and placed his hands on his hips. "I think we will be ready to leave within the hour. I suspect not everyone will be joining us. I have told those who wish to go to gather on the western side of the village, and it looks as though we have a little more than half of our people."

Shaw looked around and saw the mass gathering in the west. Others were coming and going to their tents or continuing on with their everyday lives. Placing a hand on the back of his neck, Shaw said, "As much as it pains me to say, we can only help those who want it. It's their choice to make if they want to stay."

"I don't understand—we're giving these people a chance to live. Why won't they take it?" Grant was still visibly frustrated. Nothing he said or did could change these people's minds.

"It's their choice. We fled Oroze because we did not want to live under someone's direct rule. We chose to leave so we could be free. But, unfortunately, some people may hold on to that freedom of choice even if it's not in their best interest," Alas explained.

Grant heard what the man was saying, but to him, it didn't make sense. "Don't they see we are trying to save their lives? Can't we make them come with us? It would be better in the long run, even if they don't think so now."

"Grant, that's the whole point of their reasoning. It's their choice—they will not be forced to do what they do not want," Alas said.

"What good is a choice if you choose wrong?" Grant mumbled under his breath as he tried to find reason within the people who wished to stay. Alas shrugged, but knew it was time to move past the debate.

"Do you mind helping attach your horses to the carriage? Once we get that set, we are ready to leave. I'll go double-check with the rest of the people and make sure everyone is prepared." Alas turned and headed toward the crowd to make final preparations.

Nora, Shaw, and Grant headed to the post at the northern edge of the village by Alas's tent, where they hitched their horses. The horses were rested, fed, and given water by the villagers after they arrived. The horses looked refreshed and antsy to be unhitched, ready to stretch their legs. Grant untied his horse and began walking toward the carriage; Nora saw the bitter look on his face and went to grab his arm, but Shaw placed a hand on her shoulder.

"Let him cool off. He may need a minute to collect himself." Nora knew Shaw was right. She nodded and turned back to her horse and began to gently brush the massive beast. Shaw patted his horse's nose, placed his forehead on her long face, and talked to her. "How's my girl, huh? You have been great, but now I need you to help the others instead of me. How does that sound?" The horse made a slight whinny as Shaw scratched between her ears. "That's my girl." The old man pulled away and led his horse with Nora to the carriage. She watched Shaw while they walked and wondered what he'd been like when he was younger.

"Shaw, while we have been here, I have seen you act differently than before. There's a tenderness to you that is quite reassuring," Nora said.

"In my experience, there's a time and place for everything. By reading into the situation, I can be who I need to be to try to affect the outcome."

"When you were talking to Abby on our way here, you sounded almost like my father when he would talk to me when I was angry or upset."

Shaw smiled. "Oh, you caught that, did you. I did live a life before I left to live in Regis."

Nora recognized the hint of sadness behind his words. She thought it might be impolite to ask, but she did anyway. "You haven't told us much of that life. Do you have a family?" Nora knew that would be a complex question, and she didn't expect any form of response since she had never heard Shaw speak of one. She only asked because it seemed strange that someone could embody a father-type figure without being one. Shaw was silent for a moment, and noticing his hesitation, Nora said, "You don't have to answer that. I was a little forward."

"It's alright. I don't talk much of my younger years because while it happened so long ago, I can still feel the sting of pain every now and again when I search my memories. Even the happy memories can become bitter and painful the more I dwell on them."

"I'm sorry, you don't have to—" Nora was saying, but Shaw dismissed her words.

"I suppose it was only a matter of time until I had to open up about it. Since you expressed your feelings the other night, I will tell you mine." They took a few more steps before Shaw started, "When I talked to Abby on the ride here, she reminded me of my daughter. Of course, Abby is much older than my daughter, but that didn't change what I saw. When my daughter was upset, I would rock her in my arms until she fell asleep. No matter how much she cried or tried to wiggle away, I would hold her and tell her that her daddy was here, and everything would be alright. She would have been married with her own children by now." Shaw's voice began to tremble.

"What was her name?" Nora interjected to give Shaw a chance to calm his voice.

"We named her Allurin after her grandmother. What a lovely woman." Nora smiled, and Shaw continued. "Allurin would go with me everywhere. If I went, she went. She was quite the little adventurer—like her dad." Shaw let out a small laugh. "We went for a walk like we always did to see the countryside; we would hike up the mountains and look down upon the valley to catch the sunset together. It was always her favorite part, the sunsets. She would rest her head on my shoulder and tell me how she wanted to visit everywhere in the world, but I told her the world is a huge and dangerous place. She didn't care—she told me she would be safe because I would be with her every step of the way.

"We were walking back home down a hiking path when she saw a flower growing near the edge. It was a lady's thimble flower. It was shaped like a bell and was her favorite color, blue. She wanted to pick it for her mother because she thought it was beautiful like her. I told her that was a great idea and that I would get it for her since it was so close to the edge, but she ran ahead of me. A storm had just passed over the mountains a couple days prior, and I guess it made the edges of the trail brittle and washed out. Not long after she had plucked the flower, she turned around to show me how pretty it was. She smiled at me."

Nora could feel the tears falling down her face. He wasn't even trying to hide them. She looked at Shaw, and his cheeks were dripping as well.

"The edge of the trail gave way, and she fell. I didn't know what to do. One minute, she was there smiling, holding a flower as beautiful as she was, and the next, she was gone. I heard her scream when she fell, and then it was silent. I ran down the mountain as fast as I could, but it didn't matter if I had gotten down in one second or one hour. I found her at the bottom, lying there. I ran to her and held her in my arms. Even though I knew she was gone, I told her that her daddy was here and everything would be alright. I picked her up, and I saw that she still held the flower in her hand. She never let go. Even when she fell, she held on tight. She was eight years old when her mother and I had to bury her. I went back to that mountain every summer to pick as many lady's thimbles as I could find so I could bring them to her every year. I still have the first one she ever picked." Shaw reached inside his cloak to the inside pocket and pulled out a dried bluebell lady's thimble encased in hardened tree sap. "I carry this with me everywhere I go. I am taking Allurin with me, around the world."

Shaw tucked the flower back into his pocket. Nora didn't know what to say. Her voice was caught in her throat, and words had fled from her. Shaw turned to her and wiped the tears from her cheeks. "That's why when I saw Abby, I guess it was like I was looking at Allurin again. I just wanted her to know that no matter how hard things can get, everything will be okay. Even though I lost my daughter, I am still her father, and I always will be."

Nora cleared her throat. "What about your wife?"

"That can be a story for another time, but there is a reason I left and moved my life to Regis." Shaw used the sleeve of his cloak to clean off his face. "Even though the memories are painful, I would rather have all the moments than lose a single one."

Nora and Shaw met up with Grant, who had finished attaching his horse to the right side of the carriage. Grant was talking with Abby while Yulis ran around Grant's legs. The other two followed suit and hooked up the horses, and within a few minutes, the animals were ready to pull the carriage wherever it needed to go.

Shaw found his way to Alas. "Is everyone ready?"

"Yes, we can leave now. It has been a long time, but I still remember the way to Malen, so while I lead the way, could you three bring up the back just to be safe?" Alas asked.

"We will. Just make sure we move at a good pace. We have much ground to cover and not much time. We can only stop for small breaks, but no making camp, no slowing down. The faster we get to Malen, the safer we will be," Shaw stressed.

"Understood. Thank you for your help, all of you. I hope you understand how much this means to us, even if the others don't say it. You all have my thanks."

"You can thank us when we are inside the walls." Shaw extended his hand, and Alas gripped it firmly. Then he nodded his head and made his way to the carriage.

He climbed on top and made his announcement. "Everyone, the time has come. We are leaving. If you wish to stay, that's your right, but you are more than welcome to follow us if you change your mind. I wish you all the best."

Abby called Yulis to her and picked him up in her arms. "He seems to have taken a liking to you."

Grant blushed ever so slightly. "And I to him. He's a great kid."

Abby smiled. "I better get in the carriage before they take off without me. I'll see you in Malen, yes?"

Abby said it shyly, but to her surprise, he said, "Of course. Once we settle in and make sure everyone is safe, I will come to find you. You as well, little man." Grant ruffled Yulis's hair, and the boy laughed. Abby reached out and grabbed Grant's hand, giving him one more smile.

Then she set Yulis in the carriage, climbing in as Alas jumped down, taking his place in front of his people. He began walking west to Malen. Nora, Shaw, and Grant stood alongside while everyone moved along, waiting for the last people to pass them. "What was all that about, Grant?" Nora gave him a few jabs to the ribs with her elbow.

Grant smiled to himself. "She wanted to see if I was alright after talking to the crowd earlier. I told her how I was frustrated about it, and the conversation just kept going from there."

"Is she doing okay with everything that's happened today?" Nora only asked because she didn't know if Abby had been told about her husband passing away.

"She will be. Gretta told her about her husband. She told herself that he died when he left their home the day they were attacked, but finding out he was alive for a few more months after the attack was hard to take in. She hoped he didn't suffer in the end. They actually made a site to bury their people, so she went alone and said her final goodbyes."

"Poor girl. Life has not been kind to her. Let's hope the future will hold more promise than the past," Shaw said as he saw the last person pass by. He glanced back once more. It seemed a hundred or more people had stayed behind. Shaw looked at them one last time, hoping for the best. Finally, the trio turned their backs to Meno and trailed behind the crowd.

The grass-covered valley connecting to Baddon was not ideal for taking such a big group of people. Being out in the open and exposed made everyone on edge. They took a few short breaks, only an hour or less to rest their aching feet. Sleep did not come easy to anyone the first night. Most went without, and it showed the next morning in the dark circles under their eyes. Some collapsed from the sheer exhaustion and the heat beating down on them; luckily for them, some of the women and elder folk would switch places in the carriage so the ones struggling could get some rest.

Nothing about this journey was fast. These people were not accustomed to extended travel periods, whether riding in a carriage or walking. Most of them tended fields of crops or livestock; they were used to hard work but not the endless hours of walking. The hills throughout the valley didn't help matters. Moving forward almost felt like it came to a crawl for the ones bringing up the rear. Most of the hills were not steep, but they were numerous, causing strain as everyone moved along. Still, the looming fear and the possibility of being attacked kept the people pushing forward.

As the third day of the journey began, an appalling wind blew in from the east. An odor hung in the air. The first to catch the scent of the wind were the ones positioned in the back.

"Does anyone smell that?" Nora asked.

"Smell what?" Grant and Shaw looked at her.

"It smells foul, but I don't know what it is."

"I don't know. Shaw?" Grant asked, looking to Shaw.

"No, but now that you mention it, it smells familiar? It's aw—" Shaw paused mid-sentence and grabbed the other two as he recognized the stench in the air.

Turning swiftly around, he ushered Nora and Grant to run back to the top of the last hill they'd descended. At the crest of the golden-brown knoll, they could see smoke plumes rising from Meno. The smoke dissipated in the wind, but the aroma clung to the air. Nora's hands rose to her mouth..

Grant and Shaw knew what the smell was.

"They should have listened. We should have made them come with us. The fools." Grant balled up his fists as he watched the smoke rise and blow in their direction.

"We can't help them now. They made their choice. We can still help these people, though. We should hurry—we need to tell Alas what has happened. Who knows how quickly they may be able to catch up?" Shaw, Nora, and Grant ran back down the hill to catch up with the others, only this time, when they reached the crowd, they broke from their run.

"Why are we slowing down?" Grant panted.

"I don't want to alarm anyone yet, not until we can talk to Alas and form some kind of plan. It would be unnecessary to rile up these people." Shaw took some deep breaths as he set his pace at a fast walk, passing the villagers on his way to Alas.

The three could tell that Alas was pushing himself harder than he was really able to. Keeping a steady pace for three days with little rest, food, and water was taking its toll on him, and it was more than noticeable. Alas had refused to take anyone's spot in the carriage; he firmly believed that if a leader was going to lead, he should do it from the front. It was a noble gesture, but even the best leaders needed to know when to rest and regain their strength.

Shaw joined Alas at the front, tapping his shoulder.

"We need to talk," he said, pulling Alas ahead, out of earshot of the first row of people. Shaw spoke in a hushed tone. "Do you know what that smell in the air is coming from?"

"No, but it's terrible. It's been bothering me all morning." Alas had bags hanging under his tired red eyes.

"Before we discuss that, when was the last time you had some rest?" Shaw asked.

"Oh, I rested not too long ago. I'm fine," he said, brushing off the question. "What was it you asked me?"

Shaw noticed that Alas was walking a little off balance. "I think you should take a break; go sit down in the carriage."

"No, I'm fine. I need to lead my people. They are my responsibility—I can do this. I can . . ." Alas stumbled forward, falling as his legs gave out from under him. Nora and Grant caught him by each arm before he could land on his face. Then they turned to face the people walking behind them, some of whom were running to help Alas and see what was wrong.

Shaw held up his hand. "No need to worry. Alas is just tired." The men and women returned to the front row. "Do you two mind putting him in the carriage? We will let him rest for a while, then we can talk with him. I don't think he would be any good at this point." Nora and Grant nodded. They all but dragged Alas into the carriage, and he was soon asleep. Time was of the essence, and continuing on was the only option. Even with Meno and its remaining people destroyed, there was nothing else they could do—they had to continue forward.

Alas awoke a few hours later, not long into the afternoon, still feeling tired but more alert than he had previously. Abby handed him a thick slice of bread and some water. "Thank you, Abby, but why am I in the carriage?" The bite of the bread was the first thing Alas had eaten since he left Meno. He'd given the food he carried in his pack to his people when they approached him during the journey.

"You almost collapsed when you were talking with Shaw, so they put you here to rest," she said.

"Huh." Alas scratched his head in confusion. "I don't remember falling or anything. The last thing I remember is Shaw coming to me."

"That's okay. He said he wanted me to go get him when you woke up. There is something he needs to talk to you about." Abby began to stand, but Alas grabbed her hand.

"It's okay, you stay here. I feel well enough—I'll go look for him." Alas tried to rise, but his legs were slow. Aches and pains ran through his feet to his hip.

"I don't think so." Abby took her hand away and pushed down on his shoulders to make him sit. "You have done enough for us already. Let us help you for now, and get your strength back. Stay put. I'll be back in a second." Alas had no energy in his muscles or bones to resist, so he leaned back against the side railing. Abby told Yulis to stay with Gretta, and she hopped out of the carriage. Abby saw Shaw, Grant, and Nora at the front as they led the group while Alas rested.

"Shaw, Shaw!" she called out before she reached them. "Alas is awake now."

"Thank you, I'll go see him right away." Shaw made his way to the carriage, but Abby decided to stay with Grant and Nora for a while and stretch her legs while she had the chance.

"I never got the chance to properly thank you, Nora, for what you did back in Noic."

"It was the right thing to do, and I couldn't leave you after what I did, but you don't need to thank me. I'm just happy I was able to help," Nora said.

"You did more than that. You brought me back to my son. You saved my life. You brought me here, and now I have closure on questions that plagued my thoughts for almost a year." Nora knew what she was referring to but didn't have the heart to confirm it.

Grant broke the silence and said what they both were thinking. "We're sorry to hear about the loss of your husband, Abby."

A tear fell from the woman's eye. "Thank you. Gretta told me what happened, that Ari died months ago. She also told me that he helped many of these people get out of Oroze safely before he passed. He was also able to find our son and bring him to Meno. Gretta told me that when he found Yulis, one of the men that took him from our home still had him. They put chains on him, so my Ari went to get Yulis back. He fought those men, but during the fight, he was stabbed. He lost a lot of blood and died after he and Yulis made it to Meno. Ari was a hero—that's the way I will choose to remember him. Yulis will know his dad as the man who saved him, and as long as I have my son, I will always have a part of Ari." Abby smiled and wiped the tears away.

* * *

Shaw walked beside the carriage before jumping into the back with Alas. "How are you feeling?" he asked.

"Sore, tired, old. I probably should have done this when the others asked me to."

Shaw gave a smirk. "That would've been a good idea. Your heart is in the right place. Now, you just have to make sure your body is as well. You can't lead these people if your body doesn't work."

"I guess you have a point, my friend. Now, Abby said you have something you want to discuss with me?" Alas asked, raising an eyebrow.

Shaw's grin faded as his face became sullen. "Yes, earlier this morning, do you remember the smell in the air?"

"I do. What about it?"

"That's not just any smell that comes and goes. The First Born have attacked Meno. I'm sure it is all but gone at this point. Even the people."

Alas slammed his fist on the wood base of the carriage. "So they are coming for us."

"Yes, and by now, they are maybe a day or two behind us. I hope it's more, but they might have horses with them. We have a good lead on them, but in all honesty, I don't think we will make it to Malen without a fight."

Alas leaned in closer to Shaw and lowered his voice. "How are we going to tell everyone? These people are not fighters."

"I don't know, but I'm sure you will find a way. While you do that, I will find the men and women who are willing to fight. We will stay in the back and be prepared just in case."

Alas hung his head, exhaling. "I was hoping it wouldn't come to this."

"I believe we all were hoping for that, but when the time comes, if it comes, we will do our best to protect these people." Shaw stood up, jumped out of the carriage, and walked alongside it for a brief moment. "Take some time; we will stay upfront until you come back." Shaw broke away and made his way back to Nora and Grant.

Alas came to the front after a while and halted everyone. He had decided it would be best to address them all at once to avoid confusion spreading throughout the group. Explaining the situation to everybody was the easy part, but finding willing men and women to help fight if need be was another problem altogether. Some men raised their hands and volunteered, knowing full well they might die in the effort of protecting their people, but it was not many. Less than twenty people volunteered, and even with Nora, Grant, and Shaw to help, it was still not enough. But at least they would still have a chance if luck was on their side.

The next night was quiet, and the morning was uneventful; walking down another hill with a slight grade, they could see off in the distance that Malen had finally come into view. Smiles appeared on the peoples' faces, and joy filled their voices as they talked. The Red Band River was the only obstacle left for them to cross until they were within the kingdom's realm. The pace picked up as their excitement took over. Once they reached the bridge, they would be safe. The bridge wasn't far now, less than a mile as the eye could see.

Alas was leading the way when Grant grabbed his shoulder, clutching his chest as he tried to catch his breath. "Alas, you need to run—now!" he said between gasps. Grant pointed to the hilltop. Men on horses were perched upon the hill, gazing down at the moving crowd. The men in front carried a flag that flapped in the soft breeze. Black, with a blue border.

The First Born had arrived. Grant caught the crowd's attention and pointed. Within seconds of the people seeing the horses, panic set in. Men and women began to scream, making a run for the bridge. Chaos ensued as Alas tried to keep everyone together while they ran. Finally, the men on the hill spurred their horses and descended. Shaw and Nora yelled for everyone in the back to run as well.

Grant met up with them. "We need to get closer to the bridge. That's where we can make a stand," he shouted.

The people ran, but no matter how much effort they gave, the First Born were gaining ground on them, and fast. The riders would be on them within a matter of minutes.

Alas made it to the bridge but did not cross it himself. He motioned for the others, shouting, "Hurry, move it!"

Within a few minutes, barely half the people had crossed the bridge, and the First Born had almost reached them. "This is it. We must hold the bridge until everyone is through, then we will cross," Alas shouted. The men willing to fight turned to face the coming cavalry. Even though they were not soldiers, anger burned in their eyes. They were ready to fight this time; this time, they knew what to expect. They prepared themselves.

Shaw notched his arrows and began firing at the horses, trying to slow down the charge. Nora pulled out her staff, and Grant brandished his two daggers. With the twenty or so men behind them, they had a feeling of confidence. Hope was in their hearts, and a willingness to give everything for the others raged inside them. Alas came up behind Shaw, holding a sharpened wooden leg post. "Alright, Shaw, the carriage is set, just as we talked about."

"Perfect." Shaw notched another arrow. "We need to buy enough time to get everyone across, then we will make a run for it." He let loose another arrow; the First Born were seconds away. "We will run for the carriage, mount the horses, and drive them hard when everyone is safe. The carriage has been tied to the last two posts on the bridge, and we need to make it collapse. That is our goal. Once we do that, it will take whatever First Born remain days to go around. We must get to that bridge."

The men were so close Grant could see the malevolent expressions on their faces. He looked at the riders in front, then clenched his jaw and tightened the grip on the blades. "That's them," he snarled.

"Who?" Nora asked, trying to see.

"The men from the bar, they're in front. Those two are mine." Grant's face did not hide his intentions. He wanted them dead. He wanted them erased from this life, and all their hate washed away. Shaw let loose a final arrow and raised his hand. With a loud scream, the trio charged, leading an assault of their own.

The horses crashed into the surrounding men, stomping on the ones who were knocked down. Screams from both sides reverberated through the hills, the sound of men dying and killing echoing all at the same time.

Grant dove out of the way, narrowly missing the stampede. Once he rose to his feet, he focused his attention on the two men from the bar as they made their way onto the field and into the middle of the men from Meno. Grant was transfixed on the pair; he could feel his anger coming to a tipping point. The First Born soldiers jumped off their horses so as not to be bucked off when the men from Meno swung their makeshift weapons. Steel rang as the First Born soldiers withdrew their swords from their sheaths.

For the men of Meno, the real battle had begun.

The First Born outnumbered the men two to one, but that didn't stop Grant from making his way to the men he was set on killing. A First Born soldier ran at him, swinging his sword wildly, screaming for him to die, but Grant knew it would not be his end that was coming. Grant could see that this soldier had no proper form to his attacks. Maybe he thought brute force would do well enough, but Grant was ready. He raised his blades, deflecting the sword's swing with his left, then coming sharply across the soldier's neck with his right, severing both carotid arteries. Grant walked past while the soldier's hands clung to his throat, and he choked on his own blood as it spilled from his body.

Another soldier approached from Grant's flank, but Grant had already seen him coming. Turning both blades over in his hands, he crossed them together. When the soldier's sword met the daggers, Grant forced it down into the dirt. Then, flipping a blade back into his right, he shoved it into the right side of the soldier's chest only to tear the blade out through the front, slicing through his ribs.

Once the man was dispatched, Grant had a clear line of sight of the two from the bar. Men from Meno lay dead at their feet, and they were looking for more. The smiles on their faces only brought forth more anger within Grant. He was out for blood, and he was going to get it.

The men turned around to see him approaching.

"Hey, look who it is. Come to die with your friends, have you?" the man on the left laughed, pointing to the ground with his bloodstained sword. "Hopefully you put up a better fight than these ones. I'm not even tired. At this rate, we could have killed them all." Their laughter was the final straw Grant required. He was sure of his resolve, and knew what needed to be done.

Grant sprinted ahead, attacking the man on the right. He was smaller than both men, so he used his speed to his advantage. Steel clashed back and forth with Grant staying on the offensive while both men tried to attack and defend at the same time.

He remembered what Cap had said to him when he lost in the Arena during their sparring match. Never underestimate your opponent. The words rang out loud and clear in his mind. Taking in the men's movements as they continued to try and overpower him with hard strokes and force, Grant saw his opening. The men swung wide and hard, but using his speed, Grant ducked under a heavy swing, stabbing the top left thigh of the man on the right. A vibration rippled through Grant's blade; he'd struck bone. The man cried out and collapsed to a knee, still trying to attack.

The man on the left saw the blood from his friend's leg and screamed. Grant kept a calm head as the man began to attack. Grant dodged his blows, one after another, moving back ever so slightly to draw the attacker away from his downed friend. Once Grant had made enough space between them, he dodged a heavy stroke by rolling to the side as it came down. Grant jumped to his feet before the man could recover from his momentum. As he was getting visibly winded, Grant ran forward and kicked his left knee inward, breaking his leg. The man's knee bent in, and the total weight of his body drove him to the ground. Standing and walking to the man he'd stabbed in the thigh, Grant didn't hesitate. He came up behind him and embedded his blades into his back.

A scream briefly escaped the man's mouth before Grant's foot pushed against the center off his back, ripping the blades out and knocking the dying man to the ground, his lungs gasping for air with each shallow breath. Grant's attention returned to the last man left, who had fallen on his broken knee. The man turned and saw the gaze in Grant's eyes, and a smile widened on his pain-stricken face.

"What are you smiling about?" Grant asked as the anger seared through him.

"You don't get it yet, do you? It's happening. The lord knows. He will find you. He will find all of you. I can see it starting in you." Laughter erupted from his twisted face, and Grant raised his blades above his head and yelled.

* * *

Nora swung her staff, hitting the First Born soldier hard in the chest the second she sidestepped the charging horse, indenting his sternum. The soldier flew off, crashing to the ground and wheezing for air. Nora's staff came swiftly down, crushing the soldier's windpipe. More soldiers came hurling toward her on foot and on horse; she took her stance and danced with them in a game of life and death. Men were screaming and falling to the ground with broken bones and pouring blood. Nora was more than capable of handling the soldiers on foot, but the horses running back and forth proved challenging.

Nora was not familiar with the force the horses brought to the swing of each soldier's sword as they rounded and continued to fight. She was able to take down two soldiers from their mounts. Breathing hard while the dust settled around her, she stood up straight. When she took a deep breath, a certain feeling found its way back into her bones. She knew she had felt this before, but the last time, all she'd felt was the presence of being watched. This time was different. She had an urge to turn around, and it grew by the second. She was almost in a daze until she could no longer resist the urge to turn around. Quickly, she brought her staff up and spun. A sword cut Nora's staff clean in two, and the unsuspecting force from the horse running past her knocked her to the ground.

Shaw had just finished firing his last arrow into the back of the soldier on the horse that had surprised Nora when he saw her get to her feet. He ran over to her, and since the enemy's numbers had been thinned, Shaw called for all the other men to regroup around him and Nora. Taking a brief moment to see how his group had faired, Shaw was not surprised to find the remaining men numbered less than ten. Of course, with them being farmers and craftsmen, Shaw had expected some to die in the fight, but he had hoped for a better outcome.

Nora looked around and noticed Grant was missing. She started to call out his name but stopped short of completing it when her eyes found him. The falling dust mixed with the light of the sun held Grant's silhouette, and Nora saw him standing over a man on his knees. Then she saw him take both blades and ram them into the top of the man's head. Nora's eyes widened, it wasn't the fact that Grant had killed the man, as she'd killed people as well, but it was the brutality of how he did it.

Pulling the blades out of the dead man's head, Grant turned and locked eyes with Nora. He wiped the blood and brain matter that clung to the blades off on his pants and regrouped with everyone.

The First Born soldiers gathered their remaining men. One of the soldiers pulled a horn from a small sack on his belt, and more cavalry units gathered on top of the hill, just as before. Reinforcements had been waiting on the other side of the crest.

"We need to run—we have held them off as long as we could." Shaw slung his bow across his chest, and Nora and Grant put their weapons away and started to make for the bridge with the remaining men of Meno. It felt like the galloping of the horses was pounding in their ears, only for them to realize it was each of their heartbeats thumping in their chests. They were running faster than they'd thought their feet were capable of. Seeing the bridge get closer and closer gave a reassurance that they may have held out long enough as the rest of the people made it across. The First Born soldiers were right behind them, the horses advancing faster and faster.

The men of Meno reached the bridge and crossed to the other side. Nora and Shaw climbed atop their horses and spurred their sides, waiting for the posts to break and the bridge to collapse. Yet as much as the horses pulled, the posts did not give way, and the bridge did not break.

Grant stood with his daggers in hand, waiting for the soldiers on foot to reach him.

"You with the ax, come over here! Quickly!" Nora shouted to one of the men of Meno, he ran up to her. "You need to hit the post at the base so we can collapse the bridge."

"Yes, of course." The man took a few steps but froze when he saw the soldiers running to the bridge. Wide-eyed and afraid, the man felt a hand grip his shoulder.

"It will be alright. I will watch over you as you do what needs to be done." Alas gave the man an affirming nod and walked forward, joining Grant on the bridge. He held up a sword he had acquired from one of the fallen First Born. "I didn't think I would be standing here a couple weeks ago."

"Me neither," Grant said, looking at Alas.

"Thank you for your help in getting my people to safety. If we make it through this, I'll buy you a drink."

They both laughed.

"I'll hold you to it, Alas."

The First Born reached the bridge, charging headlong into Alas and Grant. Luckily for them, the bridge was narrow and could only fit four soldiers standing shoulder to shoulder, just big enough to get the carriage across but with little room otherwise. Swords struck each other, and screams of rage came from both sides. The best Grant and Alas could do was to be on the defensive. There were too many attacks coming from all angles to be able to press an assault of their own. They were being driven back step by step, just trying to buy more time for the man with the axe to complete his task. Grant blocked the sideways swing and spun to the left, driving a dagger into a soldier's ribcage.

"How are those posts coming over there?" Grant shouted.

"Only a little bit more." The next heavy swing struck the post, and Grant turned his attention back to the soldiers. Alas was doing well at holding his own; Grant hadn't taken him as a man who could fight, but he was glad he was wrong. Bodies began to pile up, falling over each other as they stepped back and countered more attacks. "Not much longer now," the man shouted.

Grant and Alas had been pushed back more than halfway on the bridge as the First Born continued to press. Blood stained their clothes and covered the First Born's armor. It seeped through the cracks in the bridge and ran into the water, giving the Red Band River a new meaning to its name.

The man with the axe finished his job and stood behind Alas and Grant. "It's done, let's—" His words were abruptly cut off from an arrow that found its mark right above his left eye. The man fell down dead.

Alas looked on in shock, witnessing the sudden death of the man he knew. And in the split second he gazed upon the body, a sword pierced through his chest. Alas turned to face his attacker and was greeted with a perverse smile of satisfaction. He fell to his knees, gripping the weapon.

Grant finished killing the soldier in front of him and looked past the residual First Born on the bridge to see that the horsemen had reached the beginning of the bridge. One of the men on horseback had fired the arrow. While Grant was too engaged in battle, he didn't realize Alas had taken his attention off the other First Born soldiers.

Then he looked at Alas and saw the sword in his chest.

His anger spiked and brought a rage forth that Grant was happy to feel again. The man looked up to Grant with the life fading from his eyes. "We will have to put a hold on that drink, my friend." Grant's eyes began to well up as the soldier ripped his sword out of Alas's chest. Grant could feel it now. He felt hot, almost as if he were standing too close to a wood stove that had just been fed a fresh log. His heart began to beat faster within his chest, and with a yell, he let himself fade into the consuming rage.

The First Born soldier who'd killed Alas was Grant's first target; he let his anger devour him, and his body moved without thinking. It moved like the wind, fast, strong, and swift. The soldier had no time to react. All he could do was let out a bloodcurdling scream as his hands fell to the ground, separated from his body.

Grant had already made his next move. He stood behind the man, and with one quick thrust, both daggers went into the spine where the neck met the shoulders, severing the spinal cord. He turned and faced the remaining men after he pulled his bloodied daggers from the body. The soldiers stood for a moment, trying to take in what their eyes saw, but they were not fast enough. Grant moved with a deadly purpose, the only thing on his mind this hunger for more blood from the First Born. And with that hunger, he struck.

One soldier's eyes grew wide as pain soared through his stomach; he looked down to see Grant's dagger plunged all the way into the hilt, only to be released from the pain when the other dagger tore through the front of his neck. Grant pulled both blades free while another soldier watched as his partner collapsed. The cowardly First Born tried to turn and run, but Grant was one step ahead. Before the soldier had time to make a complete turn, Grant was standing at his side, driving his right-handed dagger into the soldier's chest. Over and over, Grant struck; he held the back of the soldier's neck, not permitting him to fall but only to endure the savagery of each stab he delivered.

"Grant, come on, we have to go. Hurry!" Grant heard Nora's voice, and he let his anger go and returned to himself. A feeling of tiredness washed over him, almost as if he had been running for days on end. He saw the way the remaining soldiers looked at him, apprehensive, almost terrified. So he dropped the body and backed away while he still had the chance. He reached out and tried to drag Alas corpse to the other side of the bridge, but Grant could feel his energy fading. He didn't quite understand why he was so tired all of a sudden, but he had to keep up the appearance that he was still able to fight. A

After less than ten feet, Grant stumbled, falling backward. The First Born picked up on his exhaustion and advanced forward.

"You have to leave him! There's no time." Grant felt Nora's words hit his core, but still tried to pull Alas's body. Soon though, he knew that if he didn't let go, he would die.

"Damn it!" he yelled, letting go of Alas and turning to run to the end of the bridge.

The First Born charged, screaming wildly in their pursuit. Grant's legs felt heavy, like he was pulling them through the mud with every step, but he saw his goal. The end of the bridge was right there. Nora and Shaw were shouting for Grant to hurry, and when he was close enough, they spurred the sides of each horse.

With the force of the ties pulling on the beams, a loud crack echoed on the water. The bridge shook, and dust rose from the crevasses of each board, rope, and beam. Grant kept his footing in an effort not to fall over, running as hard as he could. The bridge began to give way as the horses continued to pull more and more. Grant jumped the short gap and felt a stinging pain on his right side above his hip as he leaped to shore. The bridge collapsed, and the First Born soldiers who were mere inches away from Grant fell into the river, becoming intertwined with the loose ropes and boards as they were rapidly swept away by the current.

Shaw cut the horses free from the ties that pulled what was left of the posts, and Nora went to aid Grant in getting to his feet. But even with Nora's help, he was slow to rise, and he winced as he moved. "Grant, you're hurt," she said.

"No, none of this is my blood." He reached to his right side. "I must have pulled something when I jumped."

Nora slung his arm over her shoulder, helping him get on the horse. As they pulled the reins, all three looked across the river at the remaining First Born. The next bridge was days away, and by that time, the people of Meno would be safe in Malen. Giving the soldiers no more thought, Nora and Shaw led the horses toward the rest of the people. They were not far off, only out of sight on a downward slope past the fallen bridge. Gasp rose at the sight of only the three returning, without Alas.

"Where is Alas?"

"What happened to him?"

Voices rang out from the crowd, wanting answers, and although Grant was tired, he looked upon the people.

"Alas is dead." He paused. "He gave his life so all of you may live. He fought till his last breath; he fought right beside me. He died as a friend." Grant felt he had been somewhat harsh initially, but there was no way to coat the truth of what happened. After he had finished speaking, Nora and Shaw walked the horses to the front and led the people along the stream to Malen.

The city's towers rose high behind its fortified gates. Along the back of the city, there were trees as far as the eye could see. They were thick and close together, making a natural barrier for the rear defenses. As the crowd looked ahead at the kingdom itself, the city shone almost blindingly in the sun; the towers and gate appeared to be made of polished white stonework, but as they got closer and fell under its arching shadow, the stone seemed to change color.

Within the shadow of Malen, the stone's overwhelming reflection receded, and it had a smooth, polished look to it, almost a glossy shine. The kingdom used the stones, lake, and sun to create a blinding effect, making it harder to see clearly. It used the sun's reflection off the water and stonework to almost cloak the city itself. The city was only visible in the early morning or once the sun had fallen behind the mountains as it set. No banners adorned the outer walls; the only mark to show that this was the city of Malen was the tree carved into the wooden gate. Iron bars ran the width of the gate in four sections to reinforce its strength.

"Shaw, why is there a tree on the gate?" Nora asked. The others were thinking the same thing.

"That's a sequoia tree. From what information I gathered during my travels, it represents strength for the people of Malen. A natural strength within the world. The tree on the door is a piece of the old world, before the War of the Wielders. That war changed this world—what you see around you now is a result of it. The lands were ravaged with conflict, and for the people fighting, there was nothing sacred.

"Whole cities and parts of this world are lost to history. Sequoias used to populate this region of Malen. The people took great pride in the trees, cultivating them for centuries. Ever since the war, the people of Malen adopted this symbol to represent their unwavering strength and dedication to their beliefs from before." As Shaw explained what history he knew of Malen, a silence fell over the people.

Sounds of running came from on top of the walls, and shouting from behind the gate. Moments later, archers had drawn their arrows back and waited for the order to rain them down on the people of Meno. Then, a loud voice rang out.

"Before I give a command to shoot, you have one chance to explain what you are doing here." A man, now visible in the shade, stood atop the wall. He had long, brown hair and a weathered face accompanied by a dulled breastplate with chainmail running the length of his arms encased by a yellow border. Strangely, he wore a single yellow plate of armor covering his left shoulder, one that no other soldier around him had. Shaw and Nora moved the horses a few paces in front of the crowd.

"We are here to seek refuge. We want no quarrel; we only ask for your help and protection for what is left of the people of Meno," Shaw replied.

"Why do these people need our protection.?"

Shaw cleared his throat. "Surely you have heard Oroze is now occupied by the Lord of the First Born and his army?" Shaw directed his hand back to the people. "These are the people that chose to leave their homes to live in peace, but now the First Born have launched another assault on them, trying to destroy all the people that opposed their lord's rule." A long silence took hold; only the rustling of grass from the soft breeze sounded until Shaw spoke again. "Does the old treaty not stand? The treaty for those seeking asylum. To be given quarter in times of need. Or is that a thing of the past?"

"You speak of things from a long time ago, old man. No one has talked about those treaties for decades," the man said skeptically.

"The last time I checked, the treaties still stood. We have men, women, and children that need aid."

The man turned, moving out of sight. Low murmurs started among the people of Meno. Shaw began to feel nervous, and he wondered if coming here had been a mistake. It had been many years since he had last been to Malen, and the chances of their customs changing were not something he had considered when he thought to bring all these people here.

"What do you think will happen?" Nora asked, and Shaw looked at her.

"I don't know. We can only hope for the best."

The man returned to the wall and took another look at the crowd gathered before the gate. "We will honor the treaty, but we do have conditions that all must abide by." Shaw smiled as hope began to return. "First, before any pass through the gate, all weapons must be forfeited, or no entry will be granted. Second, you all will be confined to a section of the city and must remain there until we confirm there is no threat. Lastly, you will be given food, water, and medical aid if necessary. If anyone violates these conditions, becomes a threat, or makes notions of deception, we will remove or imprison any and all violators. I speak on behalf of his majesty King Ahven. Do I make myself clear?" the man asked.

"We will follow any and all terms while we are given shelter in your city. Your conditions will be met," Shaw replied. The men locked eyes, nodding in agreement.

Loud movements came from behind the gates, followed by men shouting, "Open the gates!" The giant wood swung inward, splitting the carved sequoia emblem into two, revealing dozens upon dozens of Malen soldiers standing on either side, ready to receive the people of Meno. Shaw took the lead with Nora following behind, and the crowd began moving forward. Nora felt Grant squeeze her shoulder softly, and he tried to say something, but when Nora turned her head to look at him, he fell off the horse, striking the ground.

"Grant, Grant!" Nora dismounted quickly, picking up Grant's head as she cradled him. His eyes were closed, his skin was pale, and a cold sweat clung to his body. Nora put her ear to his mouth only to hear shallow breathing. "Shaw, we need help."

The old man came to her side as soldiers rushed to her and Abby pushed to the front of the crowd. Then Nora pulled her hand back, and saw it covered in dark blood.

Chapter Fifteen

Among Enemies

Three raps to the door woke Ron from a dreamless sleep. He didn't know how long he had slept for, but the sun was trying to break its way through the red curtain covering the window. Sitting up and placing his feet on the floor, he could feel his body react as it should. His toes wiggled between the fibers of the rug on the right side of the bed. Looking around the room, Ron saw his clothes folded neatly on the desk and his boots on the floor. Seeing his clothes made him realize he was only wearing his undergarments; he must have been asleep for some time if someone was able to come in the room, undress him without waking him up, leave, and return with clean clothes.

After getting dressed, Ron looked at the bloodstains that clung to his white shirt. Then he heard another rap on the door. Looking around unsuccessfully for a weapon, Ron stood away from the door, bracing himself for a fight. The door cracked open, and a small voice came through. "May I enter, sir?"

Surprised to hear someone ask instead of just barging in, Ron slightly lowered his hands, though he remained suspicious. "Come in."

A servant walked into the room with his hands folded in front of him, then gave a slight bow. "May the wielders of the flame guide us through the darkness as one."

Ron frowned. "What is that? What you just said."

The servant was puzzled, as he was sure everyone knew the words. "It's what we say to the wielders. They're the ones who will bring us all together and make us one through the power of the flame, sir."

Ron lowered his arms as any sense of danger dissipated. "Why would you say that to me?"

"You're a wielder, aren't you?" the servant said.

"I am. I mean, I guess I am. Not a good one, that's for sure."

"Either way, it's our way to show respect to the wielders."

Ron stepped back and took a seat in the wooden chair at the desk. "What do you want? Um, what's your name?" he asked.

"My name is Conrad. I've been sent up here to take you to see someone. I was told to escort you and that you would want to see this person, sir."

Getting back to his feet, Ron stepped closer to Conrad. "Who am I going to see?"

"I'm not sure, sir—I only know where they are. They are in a cell in the Ark of Redemption. I was instructed to tell you it would be in your best interest to go with me without fighting or trying to escape. If you comply, you can walk on your own accord without being shackled. Although, just in case, there will be two guards following us. You won't need to worry if you follow the instructions."

Ron paced around the room, trying to think of who he could possibly visit here, wherever here was, let alone who he could know in a place called the Ark of Redemption. Thoughts started swirling around in his head. What if Nora, Grant, or Shaw had been captured while he was imprisoned? What if they were just using them as leverage to get him to cooperate? Ron knew he could not fight his way out or try to escape, but he was running out of options for what he could do to save himself. He also couldn't try escaping if it was someone he knew locked in the Ark of Redemption. "Okay, I'll go with you, peacefully."

"It will make this much easy, sir, I assure you," Conrad said with relief.

Ron was holding on to a small strand of hope that it wasn't any of his friends locked away. Stepping out from his room, he walked to the railing and looked down, seeing the green grass lit up by the rays of the sun. He took a deep breath and held the fresh air, letting it linger in his lungs. Slowly, he let the air out, happy not to have the heavy musk surrounding him like it had in his cell.

Ron saw two guards standing down the right corridor, blocking the path; Conrad was a little way to the left, calling for him to follow. With the kitchens being below the rooms in the east wing, the smells of savory meats and fresh loaves of bread found their way to Ron's nose. He could feel his stomach long for a meal that wasn't old or covered in mold. Taking the stairs to the first floor, Ron heard the servant talking and hurried to catch up.

"This is the courtyard of Oroze—it was one of the few places to remain intact after it was taken over. As a sign of goodwill toward the people, the lord agreed to leave this place untouched," Conrad said with a sense of pride.

"How kind of him."

Conrad could sense the sarcasm in Ron's voice but continued anyway. "The lord is not as bad as some people think. He has very few guidelines to follow, and if we do, we have nothing to worry about."

"So attacking villages and killing hundreds of innocent people is just a side effect of not following his rule?" Ron asked in indignation.

"It's not for me to say, sir. I just know that if I do my job well, then I am provided for—taken care of, if you will."

Ron gave Conrad a sidelong look. "Right, and I'm sure that burn on your cheek was just one of the many ways this lord shows his appreciation for his people."

Conrad touched his hand to his cheek, feeling the burn and the pieces of skin that had begun to peel off while it healed. "This was my fault. I haven't been a servant in the courtyard for very long, and I made the mistake of forgetting the creed as one of the lords walked by," he admitted.

Rounding the corner at the bottom of the stairs, moving past the pillars toward the city, Ron was amazed at how big Oroze really was. He overlooked the kingdom. The courtyard stood atop a sloped hill angled just enough to give a full view of its vastness. Ron could see the more prominent, wealthier houses closer to the top, and then the houses and shops got smaller and more compact closer to the bottom, by the gate. Smoke rose from the lower end of the city while daily life continued.

Ever since the First Born occupation, life had returned to normal for those who chose to stay and submit themselves. Several buildings had been rebuilt within the year, but only if the owner had enough money or compensation to afford new materials. Still, much of the destruction remained in the lower half of the city as there were no means to rebuild. Half-burned houses were still being occupied and lived in, the owners doing their best with what was left. Other shops were left to ruin, and farmlands with unusable soil still remained. The homes and belonging of the people who chose to leave were fought over during the first few weeks of the occupation, with the soldiers taking the first pick and leaving the rest to be taken by those whose greed and opportunistic leeching knew no bounds.

Conrad was urging him to move, and Ron turned away from the sight of the city. He trailed behind by a few paces. "Why are you here, Conrad?" he asked, wanting to know what would drive someone to be a servant to these murderers when other choices could have been made.

"I've known Oroze as my home my whole life, and when the First Born came, my family and I chose to leave with all the other deserters. I thought that would have led to a better life—I mean, being able to get away from all the fighting would have been the ideal choice—but it didn't turn out that way for me. My family didn't mind living out of a tent in Meno, but I did. I missed my home, the friends I had that stayed here. My family thinks I'm weak for coming back and letting myself be ruled, but the way I see it, I'm protected. I get a bed to sleep in, food to eat, and time to myself where I'm not constantly afraid of what is going to happen next," Conrad said.

Ron didn't know what to say.

"You probably think I'm weak too, but it doesn't matter to me. I chose to be here, and I feel I made the right choice."

"At least you had a choice, Conrad. Mine was taken from me." Ron understood what Conrad was saying, but it didn't mean he had to agree.

Walking behind the east wing toward the base of the mountain that made up the rear defenses of Oroze, Conrad and Ron came to a double door built into the face of the mountain. There were no markings, no distinguishable emblem carved into the stone. "This leads to the Ark of Redemption." Conrad pounded on the doors. Ron heard people remove the wooden beam holding the doors closed on the other side.

Two burly, thick soldiers pushed the doors open, muscles tensing and straining. Once Conrad, Ron, and the accompanying soldiers were inside, the two behemoths in charge of the door pulled it closed behind them. Wooden beams, spread roughly twenty feet apart, held the ceiling, supporting the hollowed-out tunnel built into the mountain. The soft orange glow from over a dozen candles hung on the walls lighting the tunnel.

"These tunnels were built just after the First Born arrived. The prisoners who still attempted to fight were forced to build them, with many dying in the process. There are multiple tunnels and more than one entrance, even with entrances leading into the lords' quarters. I'm not sure how extensive it is, though. I would just get lost in here if I wandered from the path I know," Conrad said.

"Why is it called the Ark of Redemption?" Ron asked.

"From what I have gathered, this place was the father's idea. This is where people are taken and given a chance to change their beliefs, to learn to follow the ways of the First Born, to submit themselves and their will. If they resist, then things happen to them. I believe you already know what they do to people down here."

Ron shuddered at the thought of being strung up again, having his body relentlessly dropped and lifted upon several spikes until he was close to the point of unconsciousness, his skin ripping and tearing open anew after prolonged hours or days left on the spikes. He remembered more than he wanted to.

After taking a series of turns throughout the tunnel, they came upon more doors less imposing than the first set carved into the mountain. These were a simple wood construction hanging on hinges with a sliding bolt and keyhole. Conrad once again knocked, and soldiers opened. Beyond, more doors lined the tunnel walls, with guards pacing back and forth along the way—doors that had not left Ron's mind, as he knew all too well what the other side looked like. Distant screams and howls found his ears, as they had when he was down here before.

"Where are those screams coming from?"

"They say there's a place where the lord keeps the people he personally tortures, but that is all speculation. It's not our place to ask. Hurry along. We are almost there," Conrad said, walking faster.

Walking toward the end of the hall, turning to face the last door on the right, Conrad signaled for a guard to come over. Ron paid close attention to where the keyring was pulled from as the guard took out a set of keys. He knew people were creatures of habit, just like he had been when he lived in Greyland, so it was not out of the question to assume a guard's keyring would be put in the same spot time after time. Ron's eyes were quick to snap to the door when the key turned the bolt, as it reminded him of each time the father would open the door to his cell, repeat the same question, and continue the torture he was forced to endure.

As Ron expected, the guard put the keyring in the same spot as before after unlocking the door. Conrad then turned to him. "Once you go in, I will close the door. It will remain unlocked, but if you try anything, and I mean anything, the lord has given the soldiers permission to take you back to the father."

As much as Ron wanted to try to escape, he knew there was no possibility of that, not for now. The only question on his mind was who was behind the door. His heart sank as he thought about Nora being the one in there, having been subjected to the same torture he had.

Conrad grabbed a candle from the small dish attached to the wall and handed it to Ron. He drew a deep breath, then opened the cell door, trying to prepare himself for who was on the other side. However, no amount of mental fortitude could have prepared him for who was waiting.

The door closed, and Ron's eyes were transfixed. He could not believe who he was seeing in the light of the candle. There was no way for it to be possible; no reasoning was to be made within his mind. He stood there frozen, not able to form a thought, not able to utter a word. He didn't know if his eyes were lying to him or if he was just imagining what was happening, but the tears felt real enough. There was no chance this could be another dream, but standing there in disbelief, Ron waited for the flames to start their consumption of his surroundings. He stood there and waited, but nothing happened.

"Is this real?" he muttered as he regained his voice.

"Yes, Ron, this is real." The voice was deeper than the last time Ron had heard it, but he disregarded such a trivial thought and rushed forward, extending his arms.

"Nathill, I can't believe it's really you. I thought you were dead. I saw you die," Ron cried.

The man stood up and hugged his little brother. No other words were said for a time, just silence as Ron's emotions poured out of him. For eight years, Ron had thought his brother was dead, always returning to the memory of them running for their lives when Regis was attacked. Seeing Nathill get shot with arrows and run through with a sword, unable to help all the while, was the most challenging memory for him to process, besides the death of his parents. But now, Ron was finally able to let go of some of the pain he'd carried since that night.

Nathill broke from the hug and pulled back. "You've gotten bigger. It seems I can't be calling you little brother anymore." They both laughed, seeing how Ron was roughly the same height as Nathill now; although his brother's hair was shorter and more cleaned up, his eyes were brown, and they shared the same muscular build. Ron wiped the tears from his eyes and finally took in his surroundings.

Nathill's cell was quite different than the one Ron had been so lucky to inhabit. A small desk with a row of books placed on top sat in the corner with a chair. A bed, an actual bed with sheets, was what Nathill had been sitting on when Ron entered the room. Ron looked at his brother and saw that while he was only wearing pants, he had not yet put on a shirt, making the scars that ran up his arms to his elbows visible, along with the scar of where the sword had been driven through him. Nathill's face had seen better days as well. He had a black eye and busted lip.

Ron was unable to hide his confusion about what had happened over the last eight years. He started rambling off questions faster than Nathill could try to answer them, so Nathill grabbed him by the shoulders.

"Ron, slow down. I know this is a lot, and trust me, I had no idea it would be you when I was told I had a visitor. I know you want answers, so why don't you sit down and we can talk?" Nathill pulled out his desk chair for Ron and motioned for him to sit while he reached under his bed for a folded black shirt that fit loosely once he pulled it on. Sitting back on his bed, Nathill leaned against the wall.

Ron took the initiative and asked the first question. "How are you alive?"

"You know, for the first few years, I asked myself the same thing. I asked, how and why am I alive? At first, I didn't understand what was happening. Everything seemed fuzzy, and the last thing I remembered was the pain of the arrows and my hands glowing blue. After that, I felt a sharp pain rip through my body, and then nothing. I woke up weeks later, as I was told, and my wounds had been healed. I didn't know how or by who, but it was a miracle.

"I was happy to just be alive, or so I thought. But, soon after waking up, I learned the gravity of my situation—I was a prisoner. At the time, I didn't know why, but after the first year, I understood. I was kept alive for the power I possess, the same that you possess. I was locked in a cage worse than the one we are in now, believe it or not." A small smile of comfort ran across Nathill's face. "I was starved, beaten, forced into labor whenever it seemed necessary. That was better, though. Seeing the outside and breathing the fresh air was something else. I'm still not sure where I was kept for the first few years, but it didn't really matter due to my conditioning not being complete."

Ron took the opportunity during a pause to ask. "What kind of conditioning?"

"I kept being asked by someone called the father to accept what the lord had to offer, to be taught. I refused time and time again, but that only resulted in more beatings, more torture. Finally, after some time, I eventually gave in. I know it makes me sound weak, but . . ."

Ron's eyes grew wide.

"I take it you know who I'm talking about. By the look on your face, that answers the question of why you are here. They got to you too, didn't they?" Nathill asked.

Anger flashed on Ron's face at the memory of the father. "I am their prisoner."

Nathill's expression saddened. "Figures. They want the same thing from you."

"I don't know what they want—the father, the lord, they . . ."

Nathill blurted out. "You met the Lord of the First Born?"

"Yes," Ron said.

"Where? When did this happen?" Nathill's tone was beginning to worry Ron.

"I met him here, after I was captured, but I met him before as well when I was being followed through the woods around Greyland. He wore a mask, and he was able to use the flame. He talked about being a wielder and how I'm not strong enough," Ron said.

Nathill's expression loosened. "I see." Breathing a sigh of relief, he looked at Ron. "You didn't meet the Lord of the First Born. You met his second-in-command."

"His second-in-command? Do you mean there are more of them? More than one wielder out there?" Ron couldn't believe the masked wielder wasn't the lord. Every encounter Ron had had with him ended poorly. How strong was the Lord of the First Born if even his second-in-command was so much faster and stronger than Ron?

Nathill stood up, breaking Ron's train of thought. "I hate to admit it, but being a prisoner for just about the better part of a decade does have some advantages."

"How so?" Ron didn't understand how being anyone's prisoner could have a bright side.

"In the first few years, I was slowly told more and more about the reasons I was kept alive. There was also a time when I was ready to die. I was so tired of being hungry all the time. My body hurt everywhere, and when I was showing signs of improvement, the father would do it all over again until I said yes and let the lord teach me," Nathill explained.

Ron's heart was breaking hearing about what his brother had been forced to go through while he was happily living in Greyland making friends, falling in love, living a life. He had never entertained the idea that Nathill could be alive—and now to hear that he had suffered for years alone, maybe even hoping Ron would try to find him, try to rescue him, or send somebody, anybody? Nathill was truly isolated for all those years. How long had it taken for the hope he held to die? How long did he wish for help, for his brother to help him?

The sound of sniffles had Nathill stop pacing. "I'm sorry. I'm sorry I didn't look for you. I'm sorry I didn't try to find you."

The man went to Ron's side and knelt down, taking his head against his chest. Nathill held him with his scarred arms while he quietly sobbed. "Shhh, it's okay, Ron," he said comfortingly.

"No, maybe I could have done something."

"There was nothing that you could have done," his brother reiterated.

"What if there was? I could have tried. I should have tried."

Nathill held up Ron's head and wiped the tears away. "It's okay. There was nothing you could do. You thought I died. How would you look for someone who was dead? I don't blame you. You did exactly as I told you."

Getting back some composure, Ron sat up straight. "What do you mean?" he asked.

"I told you to run, and you did. I saw our people take you to safety. If I'd died that night, I would have died knowing you were okay." Sitting back onto his bed, Nathill ran a hand through his hair. "Whatever burden I have tolerated is mine to keep. It's a weight on my shoulders, not yours, but I'm afraid some burdens have to be shared." He paused. "So, Ron, what do you know about wielding?"

"Besides the fact you and I can do it, I heard about the wars. The War of the Wielders and Battle of the Storming Mountains. Other than that, not a whole lot. Before I was taken, my friends and I met a man—what was his name? Collins, that was it. He told us a story of some old wielders, Taroth and Thalom. I don't know what that had to do with me, but we only went there . . ." Ron paused, his mind finally working. "We only went there because of what I found in your room behind the false wall. What was all that? The papers, the pictures, it didn't make any sense."

Nathill put a scarred finger to his lips, tapping and looking off to the side. "I put that wall up a long time ago. It's an easy explanation, though. I can understand that not knowing what was going on in that room, it might look a little crazy.

"A long time ago, I started seeing someone hanging around that I didn't recognize. It wasn't any of my friends or yours, so when I saw them, I tried to remember what they looked like. The only way to do that was to draw a picture. Although, it didn't help that they wore a black cloak with the hood covering their face. Anyway, that's where it started. I asked Mom and Dad if they'd seen this person. After I asked, they started acting differently around me, cutting off any conversation they were having when I entered a room or having discussions and arguments behind locked doors.

"Then, all of a sudden, I didn't see this person anymore. It was only after a few months that I received the first letter. At first, I threw them in the trash. I didn't know who sent them, and they had a bunch of gibberish in a language I couldn't read, so I figured it must have been a mistake. I didn't know it at the time, but whoever sent the letters must have been watching, because the next letter I got was about learning to translate the language. It took a lot of time, but I was able to read it, and that's when I got the letters you took to this Collins person. I put the wall in place so Mother, Father, and you wouldn't find any of the letters. I was able to go in and out through the left side where I hollowed out a space in the house."

Ron scratched his head, feeling more confused than he felt at Collins's house. "So what about the letter talking about your hard work and a meeting of two worlds? What was that about? It was even signed 'FB' for First Born."

"You need to understand, I was young. I didn't know what I was doing. I didn't know about the First Born—I didn't even know I was a wielder. When I read the story of Taroth and his power, I felt as though it would be impossible to have a power like that. I couldn't even send letters back to ask why I was getting these letters in the first place. The day I got that letter was the day they came." A grim look fell over Nathill's face. His eyes grew unfocused and he held a cold stare. "But like I said, being a prisoner has its advantages. I didn't know exactly what the merging of the two worlds meant, but I do now.

"It took time, but eventually the beatings stopped, and I was fed real food. I still refused to let the lord teach me, but I stopped fighting and resisting everything else. Once they saw that I was ready to die, they let me go outside and read. The guards assigned to watch over me let me into a library, and it was in there that I found my solace. I have never seen so many books in my life; you could have filled a whole house with them. I spent all my time in there, reading, until one day the lord approached me. He asked me how I was doing and if these books were able to pique my interest. I said yes, obviously, why wouldn't they?"

Ron shrugged his shoulders.

"Anyway, he asked if I wanted to read from his personal collection. I was too scared to say no to him, so I said yes again, and he walked me to the back of the library. We passed through a locked door, and inside were books that looked older than time itself. He must have spent years searching for and collecting these books. He told me to remember to close the door on my way out, and then he left me there, no guards, no one to watch me. So I read, and read, and read. Half of the books were in the language of the Essenti."

Ron stirred at the name.

"Have you heard that name before?" Nathill asked.

"I have, but only a little. They are the essence of life, of creation," Ron said, trying to remember.

"Very good, Ron. That's right, but it's a little more complex than that. What else do you know?"

Ron thought about what Shaw tried to tell them when they were in his home at the Canopy. "There were five of them, but only one gave power to people.

After that, the Essenti chose a champion and performed something called the awakening to give the people power. Then I guess the people liked the champion more and didn't want to follow the Essenti any longer," Ron recited.

"Yes, that's the simplistic version of the story, but it's true nonetheless. Overall, what I learned from the letter was the convergence of two worlds is about the forge, where the Essenti was banished. From what I understand, the Lord of the First Born wants to bring that world and ours together, so learning the language was in preparation to speak with the Essenti if it was still alive and use whatever is in the forge for his own gain," Nathill explained.

"Okay, but wouldn't the Essenti be free? And if it's free, wouldn't it be angry after being banished?" Ron asked.

Shrugging and leaning forward, Nathill interlaced his fingers. "I don't know. From what I've read, the forge has not been opened for a long time, so as far as anyone knows, the Essenti could be dead. According to the books, it takes a massive amount of power to open the forge, and the only ones strong enough to do that were the Essenti itself, its champion, and Taroth."

Ron's head was spinning in multiple directions with all this information he had no idea what to do with, but somehow he was still involved. He felt overwhelmed, as if it were too much to take in. Ron stood up and paced around the cell, but his mind was full. He needed something else to talk about so he could clear his head.

He looked over at his brother, who was sitting on his bed with his fingers laced together.

"Nathill, what happened to your arms? Why are there scars all over them?" Ron asked.

Unlacing his fingers, Nathill held his hands out in front of him. "This is what happens when wielders use too much of their power."

"That's from the flame?" Ron was speechless. He knew the power of the flame could heal, but to see that it could also permanently scar the body stunned him.

"You really don't know anything about the flame of the Essenti? Have you ever called the flame before?" Nathill asked.

"I've tried, but I have only been successful a handful of times. I don't know how to do it, and when I can, I can only hold it for a few seconds," Ron admitted.

"Okay." Nathill stood up and moved in front of him. "When you called it, what did it feel like?" he asked.

"My hands hurt, like needles stabbing all over. Then they go numb."

Nathill took Ron's hands in his and looked them over. "That will happen every time you call forth the flame, no matter how many times or how well versed you are in its use. Now, when I asked what it felt like, I meant when the flame was in your hand, what were you feeling?" Nathill inquired.

"I'm not sure. I know I called it once when I was upset, and it . . . it felt good. Kind of like being weightless and warm. Almost like I was all that mattered, and everything else melted away," Ron said, thinking about the feeling of the flame.

Then the door to the cell opened, and Conrad leaned his head in.

"I can only give you another five minutes, then we have to get back."

"Wait, can't you give us more time?" Ron asked.

"It's not up to me," Conrad said, closing the door.

"But—" Ron started.

"It's okay, Ron. They let you come see me, and that's more than I could have hoped for," Nathill said calmly.

"It's been eight years! Can't they give more time? I have so many questions."

"That's the thing about being a prisoner. They don't care much for what you want. But I will tell you this before you leave. These scars, they are a result of pulling too much power. The power is not limitless or without consequence. Using it is dangerous, it's seductive. Pull too much, and your body starts to break down, and your power can destroy you. In the library, I read that before the Essenti was banished to the forge, it bestowed a curse upon the people of this world.

"The curse of the flame is how inviting it is to use, how it captivates you, how it makes you feel the need for more. Once you go too far, there is no coming back. I had seen it before when the lord was attempting to open the forge. He used prisoners that were capable of using only a fraction of this power and forced them to fall into its seductive grasp until it consumed their minds and scarred every inch of their bodies.

"All that was left to them was madness, rage, and an insatiable hunger for the flame's power all at the same time—every feeling, every want, every craving. Just wanting even for one more drop of power, bringing the person to insanity. I tell you this so in the event you try to use the flame, you know to be careful."

The door swung open. Conrad stood in the frame with the two escorting soldiers behind him. "It's time to go."

Nathill saw Ron about to protest and spoke out. "Go. I'm sure they will let us meet again." He grabbed Ron's shoulder and smiled. Ron turned and gave his brother a parting hug.

"I've missed you, brother," Ron said. Nathill let him go, holding his smile, and Ron made his way out the cell door. Hundreds of thoughts were running through his head as he was herded back through the labyrinth of tunnels, with the distant screams fading the farther he went, not paying attention to where he was going until the slam of the bolt brought him back from his thoughts. Once again, he was alone in his room with the soft glow of a solitary candle. Ron lay on his bed; he was amazed at everything that had transpired in the last few hours.

To think that Nathill had survived all this time—maybe now that he was here, Ron could escape with Nathill's help. It had seemed impossible just by himself, but Nathill knew how to use the flame. Perhaps all Ron had to do now was bide his time, learn from Nathill, and together they could get away. Plans began to form while Ron lay on his bed, longing for the next time he could see his friends and hold Nora in his arms.

For the first time during his capture, Ron fell into a peaceful sleep with the hope of freedom, the hope of being reunited, and the hope that tomorrow, he could set his plan in motion.

Chapter Sixteen

The Meaning of Control

R on may have fallen asleep peacefully, but during the night, his dreams were anything but. While sleeping, he tossed and turned in bed, kicking his legs under the sheets, whispering unintelligible words. Ron knew he was in another dream, but this one was different. This time, he wasn't in a memory he knew. Ron had never seen this place before, and he was pretty sure it did not exist within the Alumma Biyar kingdoms.

Without a cloud in the sky, the sun was shining with a burnt-orange glow, but Ron couldn't tell if it was dawn or dusk. Regardless of the color of the sky or how long the dream lasted, he couldn't figure out what time it was. A dry, hot wind blew dust constantly at his back, threatening to break his body into a sweat, but Ron just looked around at the jagged rock formations littered throughout the dehydrated dirt, stretching for miles. Most of the rocks were manageable to navigate moving forward.

But there were spots that at a glance looked walkable, then only as he got closer to the rock ledge, he could see led to a steep drop-off instead of a gradual decline.

Getting to the ground from his position took patience and energy. Finally descending to the bottom, he heard his name on the wind. Ron turned around, looking everywhere, but saw no one. Maybe he just heard things; this was a dream, after all. Considering the last time he'd had dreams, this should have come as no surprise, but something was different. Why wasn't this a memory like the others?

He kept walking forward despite not knowing where he was headed. It didn't matter. He could see nothing for miles in any direction except for the rocks he'd had to climb down behind him. The wind continued to swipe at his back, forcing beads of sweat to roll down his face, and he could swear he heard his name being called again, just above a whisper. Yet walking faster into the open foreground, Ron knew he was alone. *It's just in my head, that's all. It's just a dream, just another dream.*

Ron walked for what felt like hours, but when he looked into the sky, nothing had changed—no sunrise, no sunset, just the same cloudless orange.

A strong urge to stop walking shot through Ron's body before he took another step. Moving his eyes from the sky, he looked out in front of him. If his body hadn't stopped, he would have fallen to his death, as the ground came to a sudden end, dropping down hundreds of feet. He took a step back. It was no wonder why Ron could see for miles; he couldn't see what lay on the ground from a flat surface, but he was awestruck at what he was witnessing.

In a ring extending outward in a roughly three-mile radius by Ron's guess, a hole with one descending pathway on the other side led to a city nested hundreds of feet down. Its tallest tower didn't even reach the midway point of the encircling walls. From what Ron could see from above, the city walls were comprised of dust-beaten stonework that made up the structures below, all covered by an encompassing aqua-green dome. He was too high up to make out if any people were there, but it was a city, so there had to be someone.

Following the edge, Ron made his way to the only entrance visible. Then he stopped abruptly. He was so enraptured by the city that he didn't feel the change in the wind as it blew. The wind was more than dry or hot this time as it whipped at Ron's clothes and skin; he could feel it starting to burn as the intensity grew. His name came again, but he knew this time it wasn't in his head. He heard it as clear as someone standing right next to him, but still, he was the only one around. *Where is that voice coming from?* Ron looked down at the city. *It can't be coming from there, can it?* He didn't know what to think, and quickened his pace almost to a run before coming to a stop once more.

It was not the wind that stopped him this time but a tremble in the ground. With the path to the city more than a mile away, Ron looked in front of him to see dust rising from the direction he was going. A simple dust storm was one thing, but for the ground to shake was another; Ron knew something was coming, and fast. He looked at the path entrance and knew it was too far away to try to run toward, and there was nowhere else to go even if he wanted to flee.

In a panic, Ron stood there, trying to see what was coming. He thought if he saw what it was, he could figure out what to do. With the swirling dust coming closer, Ron could hear wild roars and cries, but one roar broke through the rest, one that Ron had heard before. As it came into view, Ron confirmed what he knew he'd heard—the roar of the Ybarra.

But what Ron saw next made his stomach drop, for it was not one Ybarra, it was dozens, charging full speed toward him. And other creatures mixed among the Ybarra, creatures that should not have existed.

They were otherworldly abominations, some with unmatched legs, one more extended than its twin, and arms protruding from the body in unnaturally contorted positions. Eyes bulged from faces with mouths that held razor teeth in rows of two or three. Shrieks rang out. Ron regained his footing, turning to run, but the wind came again, shouting his name loud enough to cause an echo that repeated across the empty plain until it faded out. Ron felt what he had to do but doubted he could. There was no place to run or hide, so he thought of the only thing he could do—conjure the flame.

Ron understood where he was, but how he got there, he did not know. He cast his thoughts away and focused on his hand. Closing his eyes, he put all his thought into having a flame in his hand, but nothing came. No needles, no numbness, and no flame. Trying to remember how he pulled the power before seemed impossible; the only times he could pull it were when he was in a fit of rage or sadness, but maybe that was how it worked. Perhaps he needed an outlet, a way to channel the power with what he was feeling at the time. Ron closed his eyes and thought back to when he watched his parents die, seeing his town on fire and witnessing his brother being murdered. He thought about how angry he was that he was now a prisoner to the First Born and how his brother had been their captive for years. Ron could feel his anger, his hate manifesting into something else. It was something he felt he needed, and it felt good. He used that feeling and pushed his focus to his right hand; it felt as if needles were piercing his skin, thousands at a time, the pain growing greater and greater.

And then nothing.

Ron opened his eyes and saw that his hand held the blue flame, the flame of the Essenti. The dust cloud had vanished, and he saw no creatures, no Ybarra. They were just gone. Ron stood looking at his hand, turning it over, seeing the flame remain. He felt the power, he felt the warmth, and he wanted more of it. Closing his eyes, he reached further into his hate and tried to pull more power. The need for more continued to grow. Then, just as he was about to focus the flame into his left hand, his eyes burst open. He lost control of the flame as he covered his ears from the deafening sound of his name being called on the wind.

Holding one hand to cover his face, he strained to see through the wind and dust, and he heard his name again. Ron became frightened, freezing in place. Then he saw the face of a man screaming his name. The force from the wind smacked into his chest, knocking the air from his lungs and throwing him over the ledge into a free fall toward the city below.

Ron screamed as he shot up in bed just when he was about to hit the city's highest tower. Breathing hard, he noticed his sheets were soaked with sweat, and he was burning up. His skin still felt the heat of the wind. He could feel his heart racing in his chest as he tried to control his breathing. Sitting up in bed, he noticed that a small serving of food and water had been placed inside the door while he was asleep. Ron downed the cold water, leaving just a small sip left to swirl around his dry mouth. He was surprised to see that the food was different today.

Most days, he was only allowed to enjoy some bread, cheese, and the occasional fruit, but today was different. He picked up the bowl and smelled the savory aroma of basil and pepper that drifted from the lamb stew.

He began eating immediately. The taste was something to behold—the savory spice of the broth, the small, diced carrots, and the potatoes hidden within the dark liquid only making themselves known when they found Ron's tongue.

It felt like he was eating a feast made for kings. After savoring each and every portion of the stew, feeling the warmth spread throughout his stomach, Ron set the bowl down, only to realize his body was becoming cold with the sweat still on his clothes. He surveyed the room and saw a neatly folded pile with a note placed on top. It read:

Clothes to be worn, as anything less would be unbecoming of a wielder. Place the rags you currently have in your possession by the door. They will be collected and discarded appropriately.

Ron begrudgingly changed into the clothes the First Born had provided for him. Granted, the ones he currently wore were blood stained and had numerous holes, but they were his. Once he got dressed, he was surprised to find that the clothes fit. They must have measured his other clothes when they cleaned them.

The color scheme was not to his liking, as he preferred more earth-toned colors like the ones he wore in Greyland as opposed to the black pants and gray long-sleeve undershirt with ruffled wristlets and a three-button collar. Nevertheless, he put them on. Like Nathill had said, no one cared what a captive wanted.

Ron sat on the end of his bed, looking at his hands, thinking about his dream. Had it been real? It sure felt real. Did he actually invoke the flame? He remembered the needles, the numbness, and most of all, the want for more. Nathill had told him to be careful when trying to use his power, but had he fallen prey to the flame that easily?

Ron took a deep breath. *Who said my name?* He felt that he was just amassing more questions than answers throughout his whole journey, always being told about what he was or how the past came to be. It was time for him to get the answers he wanted—and time to get Nathill and himself free from the First Born.

Then a knocking came on Ron's door, followed by Conrad's soft voice. "Are you awake, sir?" It was a nice gesture, despite him unlocking and opening the door anyway before Ron could respond. "Good morning, sir, glad to see you're awake. You were making a lot of noise during the night—I hope everything is okay."

"Yes, everything's fine." Ron decided he would keep what happened during the dream to himself. "You know, Conrad, you don't have to call me sir. You can call me Ron."

The man stood there with his hands folded in front of him. "I will try, but sometimes it's hard to separate customs and courtesies, even when talking to prisoners, high-ranking servants, or the soldiers. It's just easier to say it to everyone."

"I can see where you're coming from, but if I am going to be here for an extended time, then I think being able to talk to a friend would help." Ron wanted to be rid of this city as quickly as possible, but in the meantime, he thought it would be best to try to make friends with who he could. Knowing people around the grounds could help him in the long run.

Conrad's face lit up at the sound of having a friend. His family had disowned him for coming back to Oroze, and the other servants knew he'd chosen to leave the first time. He was not viewed by the others as a strong supporter of the First Born but as a weak man, only choosing to save himself. "I would like to be able to talk to a friend too. Thank you, Ron."

Ron smiled before asking, "So, what brings you to my neck of the woods today?" Standing more comfortably than when he entered, Conrad moved his hands behind his back. "I am to take you to see your brother."

Ron was happy to hear this, as he had questions that needed to be answered. He also wanted to take another look through the tunnels and memorize the way from the stone door to the cells within. Ron wanted to see as much as possible to plan a possible escape. "Sounds good to me. Are we taking the tunnels?"

"Not today. You will be seeing your brother in the courtyard outside the east wing here. I have been permitted to let you walk around the patch of grass but no further. You are not to leave the courtyard," Conrad emphasized.

"I understand, but I was wondering, how extensive are those tunnels? Didn't you mention they also lead into the lords' quarters?" Ron asked.

"I'm not too sure how far into the mountain they go, but they do go deep from what I have heard. But, like I said, I would get lost if I wandered around them.

This was not what Ron wanted to hear, but at least he would get to see the layout of the courtyard. So, along with digging for a little more information about the tunnels, he figured he might as well know his immediate surroundings just in case. "Okay, but what about the tunnels in the lords' quarters?"

The man looked visibly uneasy, and Ron didn't know how much he would get before Conrad shut down. "Well, the tunnels are there, but I have never used them. Guards are put at the doors to the tunnels, so I just steer clear when I work in that building. Why do you ask?"

Ron answered quickly, hoping to avoid any suspicion. "I'm from a small town, and I have never heard of tunnels built into a mountain before, so when you took me down there, it made me wonder how many there were. I was just curious, but I'm ready to go."

Ron held his wrists up, waiting for Conrad to put on the restraints, but the man said, "I wasn't given any restraints today. Seeing as how you're just going downstairs and being watched by the guards outside, I guess the lord didn't see the need for them."

Ron was genuinely flabbergasted. He still felt like a prisoner, but within the last few days, his treatment had been getting exponentially better.

"I mean, I could ask the guards for some restrains if you want them," Conrad jested.

Ron lifted his hands in protest. "No, no. I'm quite fine, really." They both let out a small laugh and exited the room, making their way to the courtyard.

The sun was shining bright on the lush green grass when Conrad and Ron exited the east wing. Ron now understood why restraints were not necessary; guards were posted at every entrance to the courtyard, and Nathill was already there, sitting on a marble bench in the center pathway between two soaring pillars near the east wing. He stood up when Ron approached, and gave his little brother a hug. "You look tired. Didn't get much sleep, I take it?"

They sat down together. "It was just restless. I haven't had a good sleep since I got here," Ron wanted to tell Nathill about his dream, but a part of him felt he should keep it close for now.

"Yes, well, after a while, it won't matter if it's good sleep or bad. Sleep will be sleep. So take it when you can."

Ron felt foolish comparing his time in Oroze to Nathill's eight years as a prisoner. "I'm sorry, I don't mean to complain. I mean, what I've gone through pales in comparison. Almost sounds like I'm whining about it."

Nathill gave a small laugh. "It hasn't been all bad. Being a prisoner, that is."

Ron didn't know how to respond to that. He assumed that after so much time, his brother had just learned to accept what was happening. That was the only way he could understand how it got better. "Nathill?" Ron asked, staring at the vibrant patch of grass.

"What is it?"

"Can you teach me to wield?"

A small smile grew on Nathill's face. "Of course I can. There are some rules, though, and it's not as easy as it might seem. The scars show how difficult it can be." Nathill held out his arms, turning them over front to back. "There is a cost for indulging in the flame, and I will do my best to try and keep you from wanting more."

Ron knew exactly what he was talking about. Even in the dream, he'd wanted more power from the flame. Ron didn't want that feeling to happen again, so he convinced himself that if he felt the pull, he would let it go. But the theory was always harder than the act.

"First, before I can teach you anything, we need permission from the lord to even think about using the flame." Nathill stood up and looked around, and upon seeing Conrad standing by the south end of the grass, called him over with a sharp whistle.

"What can I do for you, sir?" he asked.

"If it's not too much trouble, could you ask the lord if it's alright that I begin to teach Ron to use the flame?"

Conrad got nervous at the thought of talking to the lord by himself, but replied, "Yes, I—I will go ask at once."

They watched as he walked quickly to the lords' quarters and up the stairs. Conrad hesitated before knocking on the great doors before him, and once they opened, he disappeared inside.

It didn't take long for him to come back, scurrying out of the door faster than he entered. "The lord gives his permission for you to teach, sir, but only while the sun is touching the grass. Once the sun has passed, time will be up."

"Well, that gives us most of the day. We should be able to get some basics down. Thank you, uh. . . . uh." Nathill snapped his fingers, trying to put a name to the face.

"Conrad, sir. My name is Conrad."

"Ah yes, thank you, Conrad." Once Conrad took his leave, Nathill motioned for Ron to walk with him. "Okay, so first, how have you called the flame before?"

Walking along the pathway on the edge of the grass, Ron answered, "I've called it when I've been angry, and once when I was sad."

"Good, so now I need you to understand that the flame that's in you, as it's in me, can feed off our emotions, making them stronger or weaker. But that is a dangerous way to use the flame. Pulling power from such an unstable source as emotion can trap you in its grasp. That is how I used it early on when I first woke up after the attack. I was angry at feeling so helpless, like I couldn't do anything, but I no longer felt helpless when I called the flame. Strength was at my fingertips, my body flooded with power—I felt invincible.

"So I pulled more and more, trying to fight my way out. I killed so many people that day that the lord came to stop me, but I tried to pull more power. I didn't know that without control of the flame, control of myself, the more power I pulled, the more my body couldn't handle the amount. It was the first time I felt my body burn. It started with my hands. The feeling of wanting more became too overwhelming; it became unbearable, like my body was being torn apart or burned from the inside out. After the lord stopped me, I began to understand how the flame is a double-edged sword in some regards," Nathill explained.

"How can someone control the flame, then? If the pull to power is too great, then how can anyone control it?" Ron asked.

Nathill drew a long breath. "I don't know. I fear the lord doesn't know, either. That is the curse of the Essenti, but instead of control, it has become about moderation. Using the flame for short periods of time or using it until you begin to feel the need for more power and then stopping has been the key so far."

Ron understood what Nathill was saying, but it seemed crazy to him. If the lord couldn't control the flame, how could he?

They'd walked around the grass twice at this point. Nathill stopped and turned to Ron. "I want you to call the flame."

"Right now? I thought you were going to give me some advice about trying to call it first." Ron sounded nervous, not about calling the flame but about the possibility of failing to.

Nathill grabbed his hands. "I could, but I need to see what you know so I can gauge a starting point."

He wasn't wrong. Ron didn't want to start at the beginning, but he didn't want to embarrass himself either. He closed his eyes and thought about his dream, how he brought the flame into his hands. It had felt real, so he should be able to do it while awake. Thinking of the night the First Born attacked was the quickest way for Ron to get his most intense feeling to call the flame. Just like in the dream, he felt his anger and directed it into his right hand. He pushed harder into his anger until he felt the needles. Pain soared into his hand, and then it was numb. Ron opened his eyes and saw the flame waving in the gentle breeze coming up from the valley passing over the city below. He smiled, looking into the flame.

"Now, very carefully, without pulling too much, put the flame into your other hand," Nathill said, watching carefully.

Holding up his left hand, Ron pulled more power, slowly. When he was in the dream, he'd rushed to pull the power, overindulging in its influence, but this time he had a chance to focus, so he pulled slow, holding on to the anger fueling the flame. His left hand seized with pain as the skin was stabbed repeatedly by unseen needles until the numbness washed over it and the flame emerged. Ron successfully called the flame to his hands, for the first time not by accident, not reactionary, but by choice. He felt happy about his accomplishment, but as soon as he did, he felt the power of the flame start to waver.

"Easy, Ron—hold on to whatever thought helped you call it. You don't know enough to be able to hold the flame at will yet. Just focus on one thing at a time." Nathill was right. Ron brought back the rage, the hate for the First Born, and the flame stabilized. But that was not the only thought in his head—another had crept in.

The thought of him not knowing enough, not knowing enough to be able to help. His thoughts took him back to the night in the forest when he was attacked by the masked wielder. His thoughts circled around what that man said about not being a wielder, about being weak. Ron also remembered how he was afraid that night and how angry it had made him, anger at being too scared and vulnerable, unable to protect the people he cared for—it made him feel shame. Not being able to protect Grant or Shaw, sure, but not protecting Nora was a fear he couldn't live with.

Would she even want to be with someone who was too weak and afraid? Nora could handle her own, and Ron knew that, but he was fixated on the idea he might not be strong enough. A wave of new anger grew inside him, and he felt his body pull more power. The flames upon his hands doubled in size; no longer were they waving in the breeze. Instead, a ferocity took over, and the flames rapidly burned with an intensity that seemed to surprise Nathill. Ron could feel himself giving into power. He thought with this, he would be strong enough. With this power, the flame, he would have no need to be afraid or weak.

Ron looked away from his hands and saw his brother shouting something at him, but heard only a muffled sound. The sensation of power consumed Ron. He felt the pull and was giving in as he closed his eyes only to be suddenly gasping for air, letting the flame go from his hands as he toppled over, holding his stomach.

Once he caught his breath, Ron raised his head to see what happened and saw Nathill standing over him with the flame. He watched the flame slowly fade away from his brother's hand. Then, Nathill offered the same hand to help Ron to his feet.

"What happened?" Ron asked, still taking short breaths.

"You were losing it. I don't know what you were thinking, but you took too much power. If I didn't punch you hard enough to pull you out of the flames' grasp, you would be gone by now."

Ron had fallen victim to the power again. Even though he knew what signs to look for and not pull too much, the power of the flame still got the better of him. "How? How can you hold the flame and do something else without losing the original thought?"

"Time, Ron. It takes time and practice. No one can do it all in their first day. You need to crawl before you can walk. Walk before you can run. Remember when we would spar at home? The first time you picked up a sword, you thought you could fight like the knights in our bedtime stories. Do you remember how that turned out?"

Standing up straight but still holding his stomach, Ron said, "I remember. I remember getting smacked around by that damn stick, but I get your point."

"Good. Now, just like our sparring matches, do you want to go again?" Nathill asked.

Ron smiled. The thought of sparring gave him a sort of comfort. Even just talking to his brother brought back fond memories. This time, the only difference would be that they were using the flame instead of sticks or wooden swords. "You're damn right I do."

"Just remember, if you pull too much, I'm going to hit you again."

"Deal." Ron smirked, letting go of his stomach as he shook out his hands, ready to go again.

* * *

Gritting his teeth, sweat dripping from his face, growling between each strained breath, Ron stood to his feet only to stagger to the left. Nathill grabbed hold of his shoulders, catching him before he toppled over to the ground. "How about we call it a day, huh? You look exhausted, and the sun is just about to pass over the last corner of grass."

Ron was panting for breath, leaning over, resting his hands on his knees. "Okay, I guess. I don't think I could handle another hit to the stomach." Letting out a brief laugh accompanied by a wince of pain, Ron saw the last bit of sun leave the grass. The shadows of the evening engulfed the patch.

"Who would have thought it would only take half a day for you to be able to call the flame, hold it steady, and have a conversation at the same time? I only had to bring you back four times," Nathill teased.

"I'm sure I'll be feeling those reminders for the next few days." They both let themselves laugh, just as they had when they were kids. Nathill was astounded that Ron was learning so quickly. It had taken him weeks just to be able to hold the flame still in his hand, so to see Ron accomplish such a task in a matter of hours was a real feat.

"We can keep practicing for the next few days if the lord permits us, and depending on how much he will let me teach, I will show you how to defend yourself. But we will not start until I know you can keep the flow of power in check. If I have to keep hitting you to bring you back, then we will continue with the basics." Nathill's tone was serious.

"That sounds fair." The pain began to subside in Ron's abdomen, but his legs were weak, and his body felt heavy. Making his way over to the marble bench in front of the east wing with his brother's assistance, he let out a relaxing sigh as he sat. "Nathill, how do you call the flame without using an emotion? I've seen you do it, but where does it come from?"

"It actually took a long time for me to figure that out. Unlike you, I didn't get to have someone guide me through the process. The lord only brought me back if I pulled too much, but he never helped me find a limit, hence all the scars. I guess after using the anger I felt for so long, it's like a part of me had done away with it. The pain over the loss of our home, our parents, didn't fuel me anymore. But then, one day, I went to call the flame, and I felt something.

"Not an emotion, but it felt like a part of me was wanting to call the flame. So I held on to that, and all I had to do was find that part of myself from that day. I think it comes down to control. Even though I don't have full control of this power, a part of me does, and that is where I pull the power from."

Ron nodded in agreement, trying to make sense of it. "There is something else I want to know. When I fought the masked wielder the first time, he was fast. I mean, I know my limits with a sword, and I've trained for years, but his speed was incredible. I wasn't able to keep up with him. Is that part of the flame as well?"

Nathill remained silent for a long while, then spoke. "Those that can conjure the flame have a wide range when it comes to what they are capable of. The books from the lord's private collection touch on what the flame can do for other people. They didn't explain why or how, but the flame manifests itself differently in each person. Other than that, the books described a time when there were great healers among the people. Some wielders had strength that could rival that of multiple men. My guess is that the power is used differently by each person's body, as no two people are alike. I assume that goes for how long people can use the flame as well."

Ron interjected, "What do you mean?"

"From personal experience, I have seen two things happen when drawing power from the flame. Either you draw too much, and your body and mind start to break down, or you build up your ability to control the flame, pulling more power, little by little, increasing the limits of how much you can control until your body becomes too physically exhausted to continue producing the flame."

No wonder Ron felt so fatigued every time he tried to use the flame; his body had not been conditioned for that kind of power. His face took on a melancholy expression. "Did the First Born attack our home just to get to us?" It was a question Ron had been afraid to ask ever since he began learning more about the power of the flame. Was he partly responsible for all the deaths that had occurred that night, just because he and Nathill were wielders?

"It appears that way, Ron."

"It doesn't make sense. We didn't even know we had this power. The chances of this lord knowing we did should have been less than none," Ron snarled.

A severe tone gripped Nathill's voice. "There are some things I am yet to understand, little brother." A lingering, somber silence held the air as the brothers sat on the bench, recalling the night that had changed everything.

Conrad soon strolled over to the two brooding brothers. "Both of you are being requested to attend a formal banquet held by the lord tonight. I have already had clothes sent to your rooms in preparation for this evening. I suggest getting washed and changed beforehand. Dinner will begin shortly." Conrad's eyes shifted to Ron. "I will escort you back to your room and then to the main hall where the banquet will be held."

He addressed Nathill. "You have been given a room in the west wing for the time being, just as long as you do not cause any further trouble that requires you being sent back to the ark."

Ron arched an eyebrow out of curiosity. "Why am I requested? I want nothing to do with this lord or his offerings." He was ready to reject the offer, but Conrad cleared his throat.

"I was not given a reason, just orders for what to do. However, upon refusal to attend, I was told that either one of you would receive a punishment from the father. Furthermore, if a flame is raised in hostility, by either of you, or toward the lord's guests or the lord himself, permission will be granted to the father to deliver retribution for the acts committed. Lastly, if a punishment for violating the rules must be carried out, the transgressor will not be the one to receive it. Instead, it will affect those that are relative and chose to abide by the rules."

Anger gripped Ron as he tightly squeezed his fist. Ron was starting to understand that this lord's cruelty knew no bounds and would be extended to anyone within his reach if it suited his purpose. "Fine. If he wants us to follow the rules, then we will," he said through gritted teeth.

Nathill slapped his knees, rising to his feet. "Well, it beats having to sleep in the ark, that's for sure."

It was still strange for Ron to see Nathill just shrug off what Conrad had said, but after being the lord's captive for so long, he must have been accustomed to what the lord chose to do.

Before Ron followed Conrad and Nathill was escorted by the guards, one more question still remained. "What is the lord's name?" Ron asked, looking to his brother.

The words came with a snarl of disgust. "Lord Hadal."

Chapter Seventeen

Dressed for the Occasion

Pushing open the door to his room, Ron noticed the clothes folded neatly on the bed. The stitch of the fabric created a grander look than any garments Ron had ever worn in his life. The only times that had required him to dress in something nicer than pants and a pullover shirt were the Arena students' advancement ceremonies, when they completed all mandatory tasks in their given training level. Students had to advance through three distinct ranks for their chosen weapons, culminating in an intense, six-year process working their way from the rank of novice to journeymen and finally expert.

Two years in each rank offered the students enough time to understand their weapon, build the foundation, start with basic concepts, and instill respect for their weapon. They were also taught to treat the weapon as an extension of themselves, instead of just another tool to be used and discarded. Greyland held much pride in the students who completed their training for becoming experts not just with their weapons, but also the tactics and knowledge gained over the years.

During Ron's time in Greyland, Nora had introduced him to Grant after healing from his wounds. Within the first few weeks, Nora and Grant had convinced Ron to apply at the Arena to being training. Nora had already been accepted and was awaiting an official start date, while Grant had been sitting on the idea, unsure if he wanted to commit so many years to training. All he needed was one more push to commit, and once he heard that Ron decided to apply, they applied together.

Grant's idea wasn't to train in the Arena, but his parents wanted him out of their house since he had finished his schooling months prior, and Grant was deemed old enough to move out. Being accepted to train at the Arena afforded its own privileges. Each group of students was housed in different dormitories, according to their individual skills. Ron, for instance, had a room in the dormitory for swordsmen, or as they liked to call it, the sword dorm. Grant's dormitory named themselves the dagger dorm. All the nicknames for student housing had been passed down from class to class.

On the other hand, Nora was not required to stay in a dormitory, seeing as she owned a house left to her after her parents' passing when she was in her last year of schooling. She spent plenty of time in the dormitories anyway with her classmates in what they referred to as the high staff dorm. Two other houses occupied Greyland for the students who preferred hand-to-hand fighting and the art of the bow and arrow. Those two kept to themselves mostly, always thinking they were superior to the other ordinary houses.

Ron had only had to dress for two ceremonies, since he skipped the graduation ceremony scheduled later in the week after he passed his final exam. However, he regretted not standing up on the raised wooden platform in the center of the Arena, arranged by the new group of students excitedly awaiting their own training. He remembered when he'd had to set up the platform with Grant and Nora, looking out into the stands where parents or relatives gathered to watch as their loved ones stood tall with pride, listening to Cap commend each graduate on their achievement. Ron wanted that moment. Even though there would be no family to hear the tales of what he had accomplished, he wanted to be able to picture his parents and brother in the stands watching.

The only other time he'd had to dress for any occasion was one fall, and it was definitely an occasion to remember.

When the fall harvest came, the town was always in an uproar. It was an event the townsfolk looked forward to every year. Once the leaves changed color on the trees, people knew it was time for the fall festival. Men and women wore their best suits or dresses, some even pulling out decorative hats, handcrafted themselves with leaves of every color to signify the event. Children would run through the streets around the carts placed alongside each other for the market, selling freshly picked crops, fruits, and harvested nuts.

Music was played, songs were sung, and the local pub made a special ale every year just for the festival, changing the name each time. That year, the ale was called the All Fall Ale. Regardless of the owner's taste in jokes, everyone enjoyed the brew, and the people danced for hours to enjoy themselves.

Ron hadn't cared for the first few festivals he partook in upon his arrival in Greyland, mainly due to the fact that he sometimes had to watch from afar as the woman he had been saving up the courage to ask to dance had been asked by another. As the years came and went, though, one year stuck out the most to Ron, especially now as he looked at the clothes folded on his bed in front of him.

The clothes reminded him of the year he'd finally asked Nora to dance. It was only after Grant had invited Ron to stay at his parents' house while on break from the Arena. Ron met Grant's parents, and when they asked him what he was planning to wear to the festival, he just shrugged, telling them he might skip this year's festival altogether. Ron knew that withholding details from Grant's mom was like trying to hide a six-foot man under a three-foot bed. It wouldn't work, as Grant had explained to him multiple times before their introduction. After all the years Grant's parents had had to put up with him and his so-called trickery, trying to get away with whatever mischief he was up to, both were able to deduce reasoning from almost anyone.

Grant's mother was much more involved than his father, always wanting to know the juicy details. She figured out right quick just by looking at Ron that it was about a girl. Considering Ron's age, it wasn't a tough mystery. After he told her he didn't have anything as nice or fashionable as the others who danced in the festival, Grant's mother told him not to worry about it and to just be ready to ask the girl to dance when he saw her.

When the day of the festival arrived, Ron returned to his room from the kitchens downstairs and saw a package on his bed. He thought it must have come during breakfast, but it had no name on it. Ron picked it up and felt how soft it was. It was held together by string wrapped around the four sides, coming together in the center with a knotted bow. He pulled the string, and the light brown canvas wrap fell to the sides, revealing an outfit.

Taking the coat off the top, he held it up, gazing at the fabric, seeing the red body that matched the leaves that had fallen off the trees. The coat ended with the sleeve cuff breaking the red and taking in the brown of the collar, which resembled the trees themselves. Each button on the coat looked wooden, hand-carved acorns with no detail spared.

Even the cuffs at the end of the sleeves each held an engraved image of a leaf. The pants were equally as impressive as the coat, the same soft brown color of the collar with cuffs and an inch-and-a-half-wide red stripe running down the outside of each leg.

Smiling wide to himself, Ron tried to think of who could have brought this to him, and moments later, he put the palm of his hand to his head, knowing it was a stupid question to ask. He knew who'd made this. It must have taken Grant's mother a week, and by the look of it, it was a perfect fit.

During the festival, Ron made it a point to find her and thank her for all the hard work she put into making the outfit as it was completely unnecessary, but he was happy she'd made it for him. Once he found Grant's parents drinking ale by the House for Ale tavern, he gave Grant's mother a hug and thanked her, adding that if there was a way to repay her generosity, he would. Flattered, she simply hugged Ron once more and said that asking the girl to dance would be payment enough.

Seeing Ron's face convey reluctance as he looked around the crowd, Grant's mother took his shoulder and told him that not trying was worse than failing. By failing, Ron would know it didn't work, but how would he know if Nora would dance with him if he never asked? She added that it would be crazy for any girl to not want to dance given how handsome he looked. Ron wasn't accustomed to so much flattery, so he blushed and took his leave.

Finding Nora did not prove challenging as she and Grant had been friends before Ron came to Greyland. Ron knew that once Grant saw him, he would make a scene. He was the most outspoken person Ron had ever met, and took great pleasure in that fact. As Ron expected, Grant saw him approach. Once within speaking range, Grant got up and circled Ron, pulling lightly at his fancy new clothes, asking questions he knew Ron wasn't going to answer. But after having a few ales, Grant was behaving as anticipated.

Seeing Nora made Ron nervous even after knowing her for a couple years. He had always thought she was the most beautiful woman in Greyland, since the moment he woke up in the ward of healers. Here, the light of the bonfires reflected off her light brown skin from behind, encompassing her in a warm glow. Her dark hair fell straight down, stopping short just above her bare shoulders. Thin straps held her tan dress, which clung snugly to her body with a red cloth tied around her waist and hanging off her left hip, swaying inches above the ground.

She looked magnificent. Ron didn't know if it was his renewed confidence from his outfit that caused him to ask Nora for a dance, but his nerves got the best of him, and his words stumbled out of his mouth, resulting in audible gibberish. Nora laughed and used her hand to cover her mouth so it wouldn't be as apparent. Ron quickly composed himself and asked again. This time, he spoke like a normal person and not a blubbering fool.

Now, glancing at the clothes on his bed, Ron's face soured at seeing the mismatch of blue and black fabrics. Conrad instructed Ron to grab the clothes and follow him to the washrooms located down the hall. Inside, two servants prepared his bath, adding pitchers of scalding water, heated over a roaring corner fireplace to keep the bath at temperature.

The curtains were drawn closed to block the sunlight and create a relaxing ambiance and cast shadows with the help of the fire reflecting off the steam floating in the air from the bath. One of the servant girls approached him, taking his clothes and setting them on a bench pushed up against the left wall. The other took Ron by the hand and led him to the center of the room before an oversized, copper-stained bath.

Ron had a hard time looking at each woman as they stood before him in sheer, dark blue dresses. Even in the dim light, the clothing was bordering on revealing every intimate detail about them. The women removed Ron's gray shirt, slowly running their hands affectionately along the ridges of his muscles, which glistened with tiny beads of sweat from the mixture of heat from the hearth and steam.

Each woman circled him as a vulture would circle above the remains of its meal, caressing his shoulders, moving over the solid muscles that tensed in his arms. Ron could feel his breathing and heartbeat quicken as they moved. Finally, two pairs of hands made their way to his belt, pulling the strap from the first loop, holding it in place when Ron grabbed the woman's hands. They were taken aback when Ron put an end to their advances, helping him undress.

Ron looked to each as they waited to see what he would do next, since most men in his situation would have gladly accepted and let them continue. "I think I can handle the rest of this myself."

The women glanced at each other, then moved to each end of the bath. "We will help wash you then, if you wish." They beckoned their hands over the bathwater, inviting him in.

"I'll manage just fine, thank you. I don't even know your names."

They stood clasping their hands together in front of themselves, and spoke one after another. "My name's Erin."

"And I'm Diane."

Erin continued talking. "It is our charge to make sure you get bathed and cleaned before the banquet. The lord has given his orders, and we will carry them out."

"I understand you have orders, but can't you just tell him you did as required? I don't see a need for you two to do something I am fully capable of doing myself."

The women shared an uneasy look. "If the lord ever found out that we lied to him, even over something as trivial as a bath, we would not be alive in the morning."

A deep frown settled on Ron's face. "He would really do that?"

"He expects one hundred percent loyalty from all of us. If he suspects any form of betrayal or distrust, whether it's the form of a lie or a half-truth, he will make an example," Erin recited.

Ron thought for a moment. He couldn't just send these women away. What if a guard or another servant saw them leave the room without him shortly following? Could he condemn them just because he didn't want them taking off his clothes and bathing him? They were captives themselves, just like him. Whether they chose to be safe in Oroze or not, they still had to follow the rule of a mad man. "Okay, here's what's going to happen. First, both of you turn around while I undress and get in the water. After that, if you feel the need to bathe me, you can, but nothing below the shoulders. I don't see the need for you two to get punished for something I don't want," Ron said as the two women nodded.

He turned to make sure the door was locked and then back again to confirm Erin and Diane had indeed turned around. Not that Ron was bashful, but these women were on orders, not their own volition. Most importantly, his heart and affections belonged to another. He longed to be with only one woman, and he would wait for the day he and Nora would be reunited.

While he was unhooking his belt and removing his pants, Erin and Diane took turns slyly grinning at one another, trying to get a look without fully turning around. None of this caught Ron off guard, but he did pick up the pace of undressing to get through with it.

After getting into the water, he cleaned himself, for the most part. He allowed Diane to soap and rinse his hair, and provide a needed shave to his face while Erin massaged his neck and shoulders—begrudgingly, as he told her it was not necessary. He had to reiterate that they keep their hands above his shoulders, as he felt them trying to maneuver their fingers down below several times.

Before stepping out of the bath, Ron asked both women to leave, as they had completed what they were sent there to do. Upon closing the door, he wrapped himself in a towel and proceeded to dry and get dressed. Ron brushed his fingers through his hair, looking himself over in a mirror secured to the wall by the fireplace.

Seeing himself wear the clothes of the people he despised the most sent ripples of anger through his body. But he had to remember to remain calm during this evening's dinner; he didn't want to do anything to upset the lord and cause Nathill to suffer any consequences. So before Ron left the washroom, he gave himself one last look over. The black boots and pants fit well enough, and given the fact that the First Born had his old clothes to use as a guide in getting the sizes right didn't surprise him.

A thinner, deep-blue, almost-black pullover shirt was provided for him to wear under the embroidered blue coat that completed the set of clothing. Seeing the coat on himself and the work put into it reminded him again of his fall festival coat. The stark difference was that the blue coat he now wore was tainted with hatred. The blue was a lighter color than he'd expected. After folding the collar down, Ron put each of the three silver buttons through their respective holes to close the coat, leaving enough of the top open to show the darker shirt above and draw attention to the silver buckle of the belt below.

Conrad knocked, opening the door to check on Ron and ticking his head in to make sure he was dressed. "Does everything fit properly?"

"It does."

The servant walked into the washroom. "You will fit right in. I don't think anyone will be able to tell if you are a prisoner or not."

Ron finished looking at himself in the mirror. "Well, I don't plan on being a prisoner for much longer."

He caught on to what he'd just said, not having meant for the words to come out as they did. Conrad seemed worried by his declaration.

"You aren't trying to escape, are you? I've heard of people trying to do it before, and it always ends the same. They are either burned alive or torn apart piece by piece. I don't want to see that happen to you, Ron—I don't want to lose the only friend I have."

Seeing the sincerity in his eyes, Ron placed a hand on Conrad's shoulder. "I didn't mean it to sound that way. I just thought that maybe if I listen and learn, I can be afforded privileges like the ones my brother has. He was able to go to libraries and who knows where else. That's all I meant. You won't be losing a friend."

Exhaling with relief, Conrad nodded his head.

He led Ron through the east wing, passing the courtyard, and into the main hall of the lords' quarters. They walked by the other arriving guests. Men and women wore variations of blues, blacks, and other colors embroidered upon their clothes. Some had red-cuffed coats, others dark blue pants and black jackets, the reverse of what Ron was wearing. Women wore elegant, long dresses that dragged behind them. It seemed the women had more leeway to use other colors than the men did, as Ron had seen red and black dresses and green ones with brown accents.

These were all manner of sophisticated-looking people, but Ron couldn't help but wonder whether these people made up the First Born's higher-ranking officers or most valued supporters. They had to be of some note to be invited to a banquet held by the lord. The main hall had been fitted with tables three rows deep, with chairs to each side stretching all the way to the elevated tables where the lord and his closest officers and advisors would be seated. All these people mingled with each other as Conrad walked Ron to where he would be sitting.

While migrating through the crowd, Ron caught bits and pieces of conversations, such as the news of a small camp called Meno being destroyed and the First Born hunting down the rest of the deserters. Sifting through the crowd was slow going, and the people were loud, talking about how some had still fought to save the deserters, even pushing back the First Born soldiers and reaching the safety of the kingdom of Malen.

Conrad showed Ron to the first seat on the left row of tables, telling him not to move and to do as instructed. With Conrad gone and two soldiers standing a few paces behind him, all Ron could do was sit, wait, and listen. He overheard people talking about when they thought the lord would reveal his grand plans for the takeover of Baddon due to the fact that they were expected to cease all forms of trade, and expressing the desire to stay neutral while the First Born tried to acquire all five kingdoms. Others spoke about how they have been tasked to go out and find more wielders that had been in hiding, and what would be the best way.

Ron placed his hands on the table, getting ready to stand and talk to these people regardless of the guards. Then the door on the far right of the lord's line of tables opened. A silence filled the hall, and the guests took their seats. First came the officers, filling the seats at the farthest end, followed by the father wearing his traditional white robes and belt. Once all the seats were filled, only the lord's chair and the chair on his right remained empty. Then the father stood up and spoke. "All rise."

In unison, the men and women in the hall rose as one and began to speak together. "May the wielders of the flame guide us through the darkness as one." The creed had been spoken, and the lord walked through the door with the masked wielder in tow.

It occurred to Ron that this was the first time he'd laid eyes on the Lord of the First Born. The lord walked to his chair, standing in front of it in clothes very similar to what Ron was wearing. The only difference was that his coat's embroidery was gold, and a sword hung off the left side of his belt in a brown, polished leather scabbard. This Lord Hadal looked younger than Ron had thought he would, especially for having amassed such an army and being able to take an entire kingdom. It seemed as though someone older and with more experience would have been in charge of the First Born.

He looked young, but his face was weathered, mainly by the scars visible on the left side—two lines, just like the masked wielder. Lord Hadal's short brown hair was kept neat and proper, giving off a sense of pride in how he carried himself. Ron could feel his desire to call the flame but had to suppress the thought when he caught a glimpse of Nathill sitting two rows over to the right.

Once Lord Hadal had given everyone the go-ahead to start eating, the talking resumed, and the guests were roaring with laughter as they drank wine and mugs of ale while pulling meat from a roasted pig gleaming in its own cooked juices. There was more food on these three tables than Ron had seen in his entire life, and these people, these guests or officers or whatever they were to the First Born, were fixed on devouring it all with glutenous intent.

Despite how hungry Ron was and how magnificent the food smelled, he managed to lose his appetite after eating a small portion, when he heard an older man go into detail about how he was down in the city square the other day when a family asked for a few coins to feed their children. Hearing the man tell the others how he kicked dirt and spat in the parents' faces, telling them to do more work or provide something of value to earn money like everyone else, was hard enough to hear. Then he had to listen to the man laugh when he recounted how he told the father, in front of his children, that he could always make a few coins if he sold his whore of a wife for a night or two. It was too much for Ron to handle. He slammed his fists on the table, trembling with anger for this man.

The hall went silent.

The man looked at Ron, noticing his rage. "Do you have a problem, boy?" Ron saw the two guards step closer to make sure he didn't jump the table and start beating the man senseless, but they backed away when they saw Lord Hadal raise his hand. Ron decided that since he was being watched anyway, he might as well say what he wanted. The rules Conrad had told him didn't seem to apply to Lord Hadal's guests or the manner he spoke in, so he went for it.

"Treating people like trash, even those that are less fortunate than you, shows character, real top-notch quality. What reason could you possibly have for that, besides being full of yourself?" The old man's face reddened, and he opened his mouth to speak, but Ron dismissed him and continued talking.

"I don't really want you to answer that—I already know the answer. You must have felt threatened, right? You must have, or could it possibly be that the only way for you to have a woman, let alone see one, is to pay for it? Don't bother answering that either. Look, my point is, it must be hard for you, being who you are and all, which isn't much of anything. Let alone possessing the ability to please another person intimately. So you boast with your money and act all important, but in all honesty, you're just worthless."

The old man looked ready to burst as he shot to his feet, grabbing a meat knife from the roast pig. "I'll gut you here and now, boy. Think you can insult me? Do you know who I am? I'll—"

"Do nothing," a voice declared. The old man and Ron both turned their heads to see Lord Hadal standing at the table, watching them.

"But my lord, this boy has—"

Using a commanding voice and igniting the flame within his palm, the lord spoke. "The boy has gotten the better of you with just a few simple words. And I must agree with him. You have made yourself look foolish in my hall, and for what? A few words and opinions of a boy, and here I thought a man in high standing such as yourself would be better composed when faced with such an opponent as the spoken word. Perhaps you are as he says you are: worthless." The old man's jaw drooped as Lord Hadal continued, "You shouldn't talk so carelessly about your exploits among the citizens of my kingdom. You never know who could be listening. If word were to reach certain ears about your affairs with my people, I might need to step in, as unlikely as that would be. Now put the knife down and calm yourself before I feel the need to make an example out of you."

In an instant, the man was sitting in his chair, sticking the knife back into the pig. His face was red as he stared at Ron. The flame evaporated from Lord Hadal's hand, and he returned to his seat. "I suppose now would be a good time to introduce our newest guest. This, ladies and gentlemen, is Ron. He may not be here on his own accord, but he is my guest and will be treated as such unless I deem otherwise. I would also like to inform you that he, like myself, is a wielder."

A noticeable gasp cascaded through the room. Then silence fell over the hall, except for the old man muttering to himself, not paying attention to Lord Hadal's introductions. The man was lost in his own thoughts.

Lord Hadal moved with grace as not to make a sound when he approached the table again. "Do you still have a problem?" he asked, standing with his hands behind his back.

The man stood to his feet with perspiration accumulating on his brow. He began to shake. "No, my lord."

"Are you sure? Because it looks to me like you have something to say, so by all means, voice your opinion; I'm sure we are all dying to hear it."

Looking around the hall at the other guests for any sort of reassurance, and receiving none, the man spoke weakly. "My lord, I don't understand why we should treat him any differently than the servants or the prisoners. We are the First Born. We can do what we want with these people. They are ours to use—we took their city. We—"

Lord Hadal put a finger to the old man's mouth, shushing him. "Words spoken by a man who has held a high position his whole life. Allow me to clarify something for you."

The lord addressed the room. "And this goes for everyone, so listen well. First of all, we did not take their city. I took their city with my army; you celebrate in the spoils of such and act as if you had a hand in it.

"Second, these citizens that I let stay here are not yours to use, they are mine. They do not bow to you—they bow to me, to my will." Lord Hadal's tone grew more menacing as he talked through gritted teeth. "We are not the First Born, I am! You are my subjects. All of you are my subjects." Pointing around the room at the guests too afraid to make a sound, the lord continued. "Lastly, and do take note—" Lord Hadal's posture relaxed as he untensed his muscles. "He is a wielder, and even as my prisoner, he is better than you. He is better than all of you, as wielders should be."

Then, igniting the flame to cover his hand, Lord Hadal thrust his fist into the old man's stomach, continuing to look him in the eyes. "Wielders will forever surpass ordinary people like you. It's the right of power, and wielders will always rule over the powerless."

A quick, satisfied grin appeared on the lord's face. The old man let out a scream of agony as Hadal twisted his hand inside the man's stomach, tightening his grasp on his insides before ripping them out of his body for the old man to see, then letting his intestines fall to the floor. The lord moved faster than Ron's eyes could keep up with, and before the old man fell to his knees, Hadal used the flame, covering the man in what looked like liquid blue fire.

His clothes melted as his skin bubbled and burst; his screams were drowned out as the fire flowed into his mouth. The old man collapsed on the ground, falling flat on his face while he burned. The guests moved out of the way as the heat radiated from the burning corpse. The stench of hair and flesh burning was enough to make more than a few guests nauseous, sending them running for the door to empty the contents of their stomachs. Then, with a wave of his hand, the flame ceased, leaving the charred remains of a First Born subject.

No one was safe. The women from the washroom were right. The lord wanted complete devotion and nothing less.

Soldiers removed the dead man from the hall, leaving the main doors open for fresh air to circulate around the room, airing out the smell. Normalcy returned to the hall with people continuing to drink and eat, acting like a man had not just been killed a few moments ago in the same room. Lord Hadal had not taken more than two steps before he stopped and turned to Ron.

"I don't believe I have introduced myself. I am Lord Hadal. If you prefer, you may address me as Hadal. Seeing as you're a wielder, you hold higher station than most of these people."

Ron locked eyes with the lord, seeing the man who'd uprooted his life standing right in front of him. "I know who you are." Ron was seething, trying his best not to call the power of the flame. He knew if he did it now, not only would he be putting Nathill in danger, but himself. If he set his power loose, he would pull more than he could handle and get consumed by the flame; he would fall into the enchanting power and be lost forever.

Trying to calm himself, he thought of Nora. He needed to get himself and Nathill free. Then he could find her, and hold her in his arms. He could have that safe and comfortable feeling that had been missing for so long. No more would he shy away from his feelings for her as he had before. Instead, Ron found his calm with her; she was his peace, she was his world, and when he returned to her, he would love her until the end of days. So with that thought, Ron relaxed his fists against the table.

"You're angry. I can see it. Please tell me why." Lord Hadal smiled to himself, almost pleased that Ron was angry.

"You just killed a man, your subject, and for what?"

The grin on Lord Hadal's face grew more prominent. "No, Ron, I didn't kill that man. You did."

Ron didn't understand. He was beginning to think all these people were genuinely following a madman. "What do you mean I killed him? I saw you—everyone saw you," Ron objected.

"I may have committed the act, but you are the one that set the events in motion. You are the reason he is dead." Ron couldn't make sense of what Lord Hadal was talking about. "You look confused—let me explain. The second you decided to open your mouth, you chose that man's fate. If you said nothing, he would still be alive to see another day, but you didn't. You caused him to make a scene, which in turn forced me to step in and reveal who and what you are.

"You set him on the path of questioning my orders, challenging the real power in this world. I have given all my subjects a choice, and if they question that, they are dealt with. So now his blood is on your hands, not mine. Everything you do has a consequence, no matter how small it may seem, and unfortunately, the bloodshed will not stop with this man. You will have more on your hands by the end of tomorrow."

Ron was at a loss for words. Was it really his fault Lord Hadal had killed that man? It couldn't have been, could it? "What do you mean, more blood? He's dead. How does that mean more people have to die?"

The grin stayed firm on the lord's face. "The family, if they catch wind that someone from the lords' quarters defended them and caused the death of the man who treated them as such, what do you think would happen? Do you think they would just go on about their lives, or would they see what happened as some sort of justice? Well, I will tell you what they will see. They will spread the word that the First Born are becoming soft, that we are putting them, people of lower stature, above the First Born, my people, and that just isn't true."

Ron stood. "That's insane. You can't just go killing people because of what you think they might do. You can't condemn people for things they haven't done. That family has done nothing to deserve what you are talking about."

"Insane, is it? Is it insane to keep order, to keep everything I have worked so hard to build? No, I don't believe it is. What's insane is that you don't seem to understand the family will die because of you. Remember, they chose to stay under my rule. And now, because you caused the death of the man who wronged them, they may see fit to question their place in my kingdom. Do you see now how these events have unfolded? One small choice has now led to five deaths, and all the fault lies on you." Lord Hadal let his gaze linger upon Ron's eyes, taking in every bit of anger aimed at him.

* * *

Throwing his coat into the corner of the room, Ron paced, running his hands through his hair. He couldn't believe what had happened. How could he have let his temper get the better of his judgment? Ron had retreated to his room after his conversation with Hadal; nothing had turned out as planned. He was chastising himself for being so overwhelmed at the thought of the family he had inadvertently sentenced to death that he failed to look for doors that could lead to the tunnels through the mountain.

He told himself he hadn't meant to get the family killed. He knew Lord Hadal could let them live, but suddenly, Conrad's words raced back into his mind: *"If a punishment for violating the rules must be carried out, the transgressor will not be the one to receive it. Instead, it will affect those that are relative and chose to abide by the rules."*

Ron thought about those words over and over, trying to find how it applied to the blood of the people he'd gotten killed, and then it hit him.

Ron realized it was the wording. The rules stated punishment would be given to those in relation and who abided by the rules. Ron grabbed the sides of his head with his hands, wishing he had seen it earlier. He had taken the words only at face value, but the only word that would have saved those people was "relative." Ron had only thought of Nathill, his actual relative, his brother, but the word held more meaning than that.

Thinking of all the ways the word could be used, Ron's heart twisted with anguish. There were many forms the word relative could take, and he'd missed them all, such as those who were involved in a current situation. Lord Hadal had been using the word as an extension not only to Ron's immediate family but to the people who would become involved if Ron violated the rules.

It was Ron's fault. If only he had listened, no one would have had to die. Ron felt his anger bubble to the surface—anger at himself for being foolish, anger at Lord Hadal for his brutality, anger at being unable to save an innocent family. Bringing the flame into his hands, holding it steady, he let the power flow with fervor, pulling at a tolerable rate until he could feel the want for more beginning to draw him in.

The second he felt it, he withdrew the flame. Hours of the night dragged on, during which Ron continuously called upon the flame only to smother the power once he felt the craving for more. Each time he summoned the flame, he held it longer than the last; every endeavor to find his threshold of power took longer to come to him. Finally, Ron could feel his body giving way to fatigue. Letting go of the flame, he panted with rapid, shallow breaths.

He had been calling the flame for hours. His shirt was soaked through with sweat, the muscles in his arms ached from power coursing through them all night, his chest was tight, and his head was throbbing. Ron knew it was time to stop before he blacked out; driving himself to the brink of unconsciousness would serve no other purpose than stoking his self-loathing.

Discarding his sweat-soaked shirt and falling to the bed, Ron wished he could go back and stop himself from saying a word, but as he lay there, he came to the conclusion that he had to accept the reality that the family was going to die tomorrow, and he couldn't save them.

In the morning, when Ron opened his eyes to the light coming in through the sheer curtains, listening to the bird's harmonies outside, he decided that once he could use the flame as a weapon, he would make his escape.

Chapter Eighteen

Kingdom of Malen

U shering the refugees from Meno into the city was a smooth process. Gathering the weapons at the gate took little time since the people only carried makeshift weapons anyway. Unfortunately, Nora's staff was broken in two, so its usefulness had run its course. Grant's daggers were taken from his waist when Nora checked for other wounds and ultimately given to the soldiers as he was taken to the healers. Shaw had to gently place his bow in a waiting soldier's hands.

The city streets ran both left and right upon entry. Cobblestone roads were worn by foot traffic, horses, and wagons from suppliers throughout the years. Homes of varying materials were built along each side, making the city feel broad and complex.

The people of Meno gazed upon wooden homes built two stories tall with shops on the bottom and living quarters above, while some residents in turn watched them enter the kingdom. Others went about their normal business, hanging clothes outside their upper windows, paying no mind. Signs hung above businesses, and inns were littered among the streets, offering much to gander at as the crowd walked farther into the city. The most noticeable and busiest inn was the Stay for a Seq Inn.

Whitestone homes, built brick by brick, were intermingled with the wooden structures, although paling in comparison to the size, with most being residential in nature. Clothing lines strung between neighboring houses occupied the smaller streets that wound through the buildings. The Malenites' curiosity brought men and women to look out their windows, cracking their doors open to get a look at the procession walking through the streets. Children ran through the crowd and among the soldiers, chatting about who they could be and where they came from.

Nora's concern was placed with Grant when he was taken away after he fell from the horse outside the gates. Looking at her hands painted red with her friend's blood, Nora was worried and angry that Grant had lied to her about being injured. If he'd told her, she could have done something, used a salve or the green oil from Loa's shop. Granted, the oil's was meant for minor cuts and lacerations, not deep slashes from swords. Nora was angry regardless. She was mad that he made her worry so much. To her, losing Grant would be losing her best friend from childhood; they'd practically grown up together.

Shaw leaned over, whispering to her. "Do you think Grant will be alright? His wound looked pretty serious."

Nora looked back at her hands. "I hope so—he lost a lot of blood. I'm not sure how much of it was his or from the First Born soldiers. I've never seen him act like that. Collins's death was one thing, but . . . I guess those men must have done something at the bar in Noic to really set him off. Although with Alas dying next to him, I can understand how he felt anyway."

"We are all wound up too tight. Having to save these people, find Ron, and on top of that stay alive is a lot to ask of anyone. So perhaps a break, with some rest while he heals, will be good for him." Shaw gave a hopeful smile to Nora.

"You're right, and now that we're here, we can rest ourselves. Truth be told, we need it. Somewhere to sleep other than the ground would be nice."

Putting an arm around Nora's shoulder, Shaw said, "Yes, a bath even, or better yet a meal that we don't have to cook." The smiles slowly faded from their faces during the walk to the sectioned-off part of the city.

Nora's mind kept coming back to Ron. It had been weeks since he was taken from Collins's house, and at this point, the odds of finding him were getting smaller by the day. With Noic not being a prisoner camp and Abby talking about the Ark of Redemption in the mountainside of Oroze, the odds were quickly stacking against them.

Taking a left turn from the main road, cutting through houses in the southwest district of the city, they came to an opening that had been recently cleared out to accommodate the refugees. From its looks, the clearing was usually a meeting place for the Malenites to gather, but to what purpose, no one knew.

Finally, the last women and men from Meno came into the clearing, marking the end of the line.

Some sat down, removing their boots and shoes, taking the weight of the journey off their bodies. The clearing had homes around its border; most were the white stonework, continuing along the southern section of the city wall until the wall met the lake. The stream branching from the Red Band River gave life to Malen's lake, spreading out behind the city.

Given where the refugees had been placed, it was not the only accessible part of the lake, but the other side rested at the foot of the forest. Malen was built in front of the lake, choosing to use it as a clean water source and protection. The tree line was a natural defense for Malen, as the forest was too dense and dark to navigate without getting lost or being attacked by wild animals. If someone had the luck to make it through the forest, their next challenge would be to swim across the lake, which was no easy task either. The unknown depths of the dark blue waters dissipated any desire to cross.

The sounds of boots and shuffling armor made their way to the clearing; dozens of soldiers came from the small road, then split to the left and right, forming a line. Bringing up the rear and standing in the center was the man from the gate, brandishing the yellow plate of armor on his shoulder. Holding the sword's hilt as it hung from his hip, he paced in front of the refugees, looking at their faces, taking in each intricate detail of every person.

"My name is General Sydell; I am the one in charge of the protection of this kingdom that our majesty King Ahven has so graciously opened to you." The general reiterated the conditions that needed to be followed if any were to stay in Malen, making sure that everyone understood. "Now, as far as what we can provide, as stated by the old treaties, we can provide food and shelter. Once we have the first two sorted out, we will send word to our healers to come and evaluate those who are sick or injured."

Excitement built within the crowd; none had been expecting to be granted such accommodations. The general held up his hand to still the noise. "You will be housed within this area. This is where you will remain unless you are summoned by myself, another soldier, or the king. None shall go past this wall." His hands glided from left to right. "I have asked the residents of these homes to lend them to you during this time. Treat these homes like your own, with care and respect. While they are being compensated for their generosity, the owners expect to return to their homes just as they have left them. If there is any thievery, broken items, or destruction of property while you are here, those associated with such crimes will be tried and sentenced accordingly by King Ahven."

Once General Sydell finished his announcement, he posted guards and walked among the people.

A clapping of hands rose from the crowd, and the people of Meno found their way to Nora and Shaw, hugging them and extending kind words of gratitude for risking their lives to save them, their children, and their families. Then, the crowd slowly dispersed, eagerly discussing among themselves which home would suit them best. Abby was the last one remaining, waiting to see Nora and Shaw. She walked up, giving each a hug. Nora let go, waiting for Yulis, but she didn't see him.

"Hey Abby, where's your boy?" Nora asked, looking over her shoulder.

"I sent him with Gretta to find a home. I thought he would get some enjoyment out of getting to pick."

"I'm sure he will find the perfect one," Shaw said, smiling at Abby.

"I'm sure he will. I actually wanted to ask you two something."

Abby looked nervous, but pressed on after Nora said, "Of course, anything."

"I was hoping I could come with you when you go check on Grant. I saw him fall off his horse—I just want to make sure he's alright." The woman was clutching pieces of her clothes firmly in her fist, anticipating the answer.

"That would be great. I think Grant would be thrilled to see you when he wakes up."

"Do you really think so?"

"I do. He's told me how much he enjoys your company. It will be a nice surprise for him."

Giving Nora another hug, Abby told her and Shaw thank you, and said that once Yulis picked a house, she would find them.

General Sydell made his way toward Shaw and Nora. It was easier to find them now that the crowd had thinned. "King Ahven would like to have a word with you two. He seems very intrigued by the man who invoked the treaties of old. It's not every day someone comes to Malen asking for such a thing to be honored."

Shaw bowed his head slightly. "It would be our honor, General." The general eyed them both with a high eyebrow, and Nora felt he was trying to figure out what to do about their appearance since they were about to stand in front of a king.

Just as Nora thought it, the general said, "Before I have you stand before the king, I will have some of our people show you the proper etiquette that is required in his presence. Also, perhaps have the royal tailor find some new garments, preferably ones not covered in blood and dirt. Both of you will need to be washed before meeting his majesty. Follow me."

Nora made a quick detour before departing with the general. She found Abby letting her know what they were doing just in case they were not back in time, alleviating her worry if she thought they went to see Grant without her.

They took a maze of winding streets throughout the city, eventually coming to a wide main road; as long as it was, it had a clear view of the palace at the end of the cobblestone. Citizens made way as Nora took in just how big the palace looked. Shaw, on the other hand, had seen much in his travels, with palaces low on his list of impressive sights.

The closer Nora got, the larger the palace became. Seeing the finer detail within the architecture was a sight to behold. Yellow banners hung from the walls, with a brown sequoia in the center, its extended, leaf-filled branches reaching the upper borders. Polished stonework caught the sun to an almost-blinding effect. Now Nora understood why the city was so hard to see during the day.

Nearing the palace doors, she noticed more soldiers with the yellow armor upon their shoulder. Others had different colors, and some brandished the armor on the right instead of the left.

She looked to Shaw for an answer. "Why do these men have the different armor plates?"

Glancing around, Shaw began to notice as well. "I can only assume it has to do with their rank structure; other than that, I'm not sure. The general has one, so I believe it applies to the officers."

General Sydell overheard their conversation and thought he would clear up the matter. "That is correct, but not entirely. You see, those who wear the yellow on their shoulders are higher-ranking officers like me, mostly generals. The ones with the brown are captains, and the green armor represents our lieutenants. Our infantrymen wear no colors but have the sequoia tree emblem on the back of their breastplates to show they possess the strength to defend their kingdom. It's all structured around our banner. The leaves need the tree's branches to grow, the trunk of the tree gives the leaves the ability to grow, while the yellow in our banner represents the sun in which the tree can thrive. The king uses this structure to enhance each and every member who fights to protect our kingdom."

The archway into the palace was vast, and then the doors opened. Spiral staircases to each side wound upward, connecting to the four floors, each containing numerous rooms. The main hall was not as long as Nora had expected it to be, given how grand every bit of the outside was. At the end of the hall stood two double doors with guards posted by each one.

A single door to the left was constantly being paraded through by what appeared to be kitchen staff, hustling back and forth with trays of food. Bickering came from beyond the door about how a meal should be prepared and how the cooks couldn't make the food any faster. The aroma of fresh-baked bread drifted through the hall; alongside the sounds of the kitchen staff and boots walking across the polished marble floor, Shaw's stomach made itself known.

General Sydell sent a guard to the door on the right, only gone momentarily before he returned with three women trailing behind. Each wore their hair braided on both sides, leading to a bun tied with a yellow ribbon. From the looks of their dresses, it seemed as though the pattern for officers applied to the palace staff as well. The heads of the women's staff wore yellow dresses, with straps over the shoulder and a deep plunge to accentuate their features. The gowns were form-fitting around the waist only to flow gracefully above the knees. Each woman after the lead wore a similar dress, changing in color and length due to position.

"These ladies will help you get ready for your appearance before His Majesty," General Sydell said.

The woman in yellow gave a slight bow. "Welcome to Malen. My name is Lilly. If you could come with me, we will get you prepared." Lilly took Nora by the hand and led her through the door to the right.

General Sydell turned to Shaw. "These two will take you to get cleaned up as well," He signaled to the two escorts. "I will see you back down here shortly, and then we will go over a few customs before you see King Ahven." Nodding his acknowledgment to the general, Shaw followed the women through the same door on the right.

* * *

Coming to a halt, Lilly opened a door and led Nora through. Candles had been lit inside, engulfing the room with the fragrance of cinnamon. Nora breathed deep, taking it in, thinking how much better it smelled than the dirt, horse, and blood she had grown accustomed to.

"Alright, dear, let's get you changed." Lilly had an almost motherly comfort about her. Older than the other two women who went with Shaw but having lost none of her beauty, she carried an air of kindness.

Nora's clothes peeling off one piece at a time felt like a weight being lifted from her body. Each item had conformed to her body, hardened by dirt, sweat, and blood. Once she removed her undergarments, the women in brown and green dresses took Nora to a tub on the other side of the room.

Dipping her feet into the hot water sent goosebumps all over her body. Inch by inch, she settled in, feeling the grime wash away. Lilly had instructed Nora to close her eyes and lean her head back. Hot water rushed through her dark hair while fingers massaged her scalp. "What brings you this way, dear?"

Nora kept her eyes closed, letting the heat sink into her skin. "We have been trying to find someone." She paused, opening her eyes; she wondered what she was doing. Enjoying a hot bath while Ron was still out there—it didn't feel right to her. A tear fell down her cheek before she continued. "We have been looking for someone, but during our search, we got swept up in helping the people of Meno. If we didn't help, they would all be dead by now."

Wiping the tear with a hot cloth, Lilly said, "I see. This person must be important to you." The years of working at the palace had given Lilly insight about all kinds of people, from the ones that came and went to the permanent residents. She has seen much in her years, becoming very perceptive.

"It's just been one challenge after another. I know it was the right thing to do, but I can't stop thinking we should be out there right now looking for him instead of sitting here. This feels selfish. Anything could be happening to him right now, and I'm just here."

Lilly took up Nora's hands and gently scrubbed the blood off. "It's okay to feel that way, but don't blame yourself too hard. There are times in life that are out of our control, and sometimes the only way to get where you need to be is to follow the path that's set before you."

"What do you mean?" Nora asked.

Lilly had Nora stand up, handing her a towel to cover herself and dry off. "Take, for example, those people you brought here. I don't know what happened, but like you said, without your help, they would have died. Your path crossed with theirs. Now your path is to meet King Ahven, so the feelings of selfishness you hold for what is happening now are not of your choosing. It is required by the king. If anything, you are allowed to enjoy the small things, even when you feel you shouldn't, as long as you don't forget what your purpose is."

Lilly took Nora's hand and sat her down, slowly bushing her hair. Each brush stroke reminded Nora of when her father would take the time to brush her hair as a child almost every night before she went to bed. He would tell her to always look ahead to the path she wanted to choose. That if anything were to stand in her way, she would become a force to be reckoned with. Her parents had instilled confidence in her that she had forgotten in the past couple of weeks. But talking to Lilly reminded her of her father's words and brought back the certainty in herself she had almost forgotten.

"Alright now," said the woman, "let's get you something to wear."

* * *

Shaw was led down the hall in the opposite direction of Nora, coming to a very similar room with a tub of warm water ready and waiting. While Nora had the kindhearted Lilly to tend to her, Shaw had the opposite. Once inside, he was greeted by two women who wore yellow dresses but looked nothing like the ones he'd seen earlier. They were older, and much rounder in the middle, with less grace than the others.

The pair hurried toward Shaw, giving him little time to react before being stripped down and tossed into the tub. With rough, callused hands, Shaw was scrubbed clean from head to toe. Try as he might, he could not even ask the women to be gentle as they finished in record time. Finally, Shaw was wrapped in a towel, sitting up in a chair without the comfort of the warm water or gentle care. The women looked at him, talking and snickering to each other before moving in on him once again. Only this time, they had a pair of scissors in each hand, and Shaw knew what they would do. He stood, trying to turn and run, but the large, callused hands had a firm grip on him. He was flung back into the chair, and the women proceeded to cut his hair and give his beard a much-needed trim despite his struggle to get away.

* * *

Nora saw Shaw talking as she was escorted back to the main hall, waiting for General Sydell to show. "You look nice," Nora said, seeing that he was dressed in brown pants and a green pullover long-sleeve shirt with a folded collar. Pull strings hung loosely around the cuffs, letting the bracelet on his left wrist move freely, as Shaw preferred the airflow through the shirt.

Shaw only grumbled as he ran his hand through his shortened white hair that had once been long and flowing. Gone were the days of stroking his long beard in thought; now, he would have to hold his chin since the hair was only an inch long. He rubbed his sore bones from the manhandling he'd received and put on a smile. "You look nice as well," he said.

"Thank you." Nora pulled slightly on the yellow shirt she'd received as the sleeves didn't go all the way down to her wrists, ending halfway below her elbows, and the upper portion of the shirt was lower cut than she would prefer. Nora chose to wear the brown pants over a yellow dress since it would be easier to move around; she'd never cared too much for dresses, only wearing them for special occasions.

General Sydell came through the kitchen door, bringing the aroma of food with him. "You both cleaned up nicely. I hope everything was satisfactory,"

Nora answered first. "It was, thank you."

Shaw didn't have the same response. "I don't want to talk about it."

Nora looked confused but didn't have time to ask. "Before you go before His Majesty, there are customs you need to be mindful of. First of all, before you speak, you must enter and bow like this." General Sydell demonstrated by placing his right hand in the middle of his chest, bending low at the waist, then keeping his head down as he slowly rose back up. "It's not complicated, but it is important. Once you bow, you may introduce yourselves. After that, King Ahven will ask you what he deems necessary, and you are required to answer."

Nora and Shaw practiced bowing just to make sure they were doing it right.

"Walk behind me, and bow when I bow. I will take my leave after. Then, introduce yourselves." The double doors swung open, and General Sydell led the way into the throne room.

The throne room was vastly different from the palace's main hall; it was noticeable the moment they set foot inside. Portraits were spaced evenly on the walls, showing each king and queen during their rule of Malen throughout history, starting with the inception of the kingdom as the walls rounded to meet each other. Not all portraits remained pristine and untouched; during the rule of certain kings and queens, there had been times where they had to contest with civil uprisings, wars, and keeping the favor of the people—not to mention the War of the Wielders, which nearly decimated Malen altogether.

The last remaining rays of light shone through the intricate wooden frames holding the glass dome above the throne while the guards lit candles placed next to each portrait, preparing for the night to spill in from the dome. The king sat on his throne, observing Nora and Shaw's approach, hoping to assess the people who had called upon the old treaties. The king wore a brown coat fixed with two yellow-buckled straps sitting high on each shoulder, following the brown pattern until it reached his elbow, then shifting to yellow that ran down to the cuff. The collar went as high as his jawline, staying open before finding the next three straps pulled tightly across his chest, leaving an opening below his waist as the coat fell to either side of his legs, which were covered by black pants with brown boots. The king wore a crown of silver with what looked like a gold sequoia tree etched into the front center of the crown. The crown sat atop a brown-and-gray head of hair falling only as far as his ears. Wrinkles imprinted along his forehead showed a weight behind his hazel eyes.

General Sydell placed his right hand in the center of his chest, bowing low, and Nora and Shaw followed accordingly. "Your Majesty," the general said after he stood tall. Then he took his leave. Nora and Shaw stepped forward, introducing themselves as planned. King Ahven looked at each, settling on Shaw when introductions were over.

His gravelly voice took over the room.

"For a man to come to my kingdom, barring title, allegiance, and with a mass of people, no less, raises my suspicion. Then I hear you have invoked the treaties of old, treaties not talked about for ages, and now all of a sudden you show up." He scratching at his clean-shaven face, thinking before speaking. "It brings two thoughts to mind. One, how does one such as yourself know about the treaties of old?"

"Fabled stories, your Majesty. I was young when my parents would tell me the tales of the five kingdoms coming together to join forces against the enemy of the land. Stories of when each kingdom would give aid to one another while fighting back against the destruction caused by the wielder Taroth. I didn't know if the treaties were real, so I took a shot in the dark, risking not only my life but the lives of the people we brought," Shaw answered.

Dropping his hand from his face, King Ahven shifted his weight in his throne. "Why risk the lives of so many on something you were told from a story?" The king's demeanor changed; his tone grew just a hair more excited.

"Our options at the time were limited, and seeing as how we had little time to come up with another plan, it was either do nothing and be killed or come to Malen," Shaw replied.

"Yes, I was told of how you all arrived. Which brings me to my second thought. Who have you brought to my kingdom, and who wants you dead?" King Ahven asked.

Shaw told King Ahven all about their travels with the people of Meno, starting with when they first rode through the village.

"So the First Born wanted to kill the deserters—nothing to be surprised about. My men have heard the First Born do not take kindly to deserters even if they let them go. They are a brutal lot." King Ahven now gave his full attention to Shaw and Nora; their answers had proven worthwhile.

The man was a good king, but over the years, ruling had become tiresome. It was the same thing day after day, with no end to the monotony of submissions for requests, monetary inquiries by his officials who oversaw the populace of Malen, or the judging and punishment of crimes. So King Ahven, at times, more than once, took the opportunity whenever it presented itself to get out of the palace and walk among the people, anything to break the cyclical flow of bureaucracy.

"You took a big risk coming here. Not many know of the old treaties from before the Battle of the Storming Mountain. I'm not even sure the other kingdoms know. When I became king of Malen, my parent's advisors told me about the treaties, how they still stand and should be honored even if only a story to most. It's exciting to have it come to fruition," King Ahven said.

"Your Majesty," Nora said, breaking the long pause. "You knew the First Born took Oroze; why not send help or send a message to the other kingdoms?"

Easing back into his throne King Ahven said, "Resources, simple as that. I do not have enough men to send to Oroze and defend my kingdom at the same time. My first responsibility is to my people. The fate of Oroze is unfortunate, and regretfully, there was nothing I could do."

"What about sending a rider to the other kingdoms? They could have—"

King Ahven raised his hand. "The First Born took Oroze swiftly, so sending messages to the other kingdoms would have been in vain. It would have been too late."

Nora knew the king was right. Trying to take back an entire city, especially one with a wielder, would be suicide. Her expression dampened, but she wondered if the king even knew that a wielder was within the First Born. He didn't mention anything about it. Surely rumors must have spread by now?

King Ahven continued, "While nothing could be done about Oroze, you two have done well. You saved a lot of lives, and as long as they follow the rules, they will be safe here—as will you."

"Your Majesty, what do you know about wielders?" Shaw asked abruptly. Nora had wanted to keep that among themselves.

"I know enough. Why do you ask?"

Nora looked at Shaw, not knowing where he was going with his question, hoping it wouldn't reveal too much of their intent. "Are you aware there is a wielder within the ranks of the First Born?"

"I have heard rumor among the people, but that's all it has been. No proof of such a person has been found. The last wielders ever seen were Taroth and Thalom, and we all know that story." King Ahven's tone was growing bored again, as the conversation ran its course.

"I'm sorry, Your Majesty, but the rumors are true. The First Born is led by a wielder."

That brought the king to the edge of his seat. His eyes doubled in disbelief. "How do you know this?" he asked.

"Before we went through Meno, we had an encounter with the First Born. A wielder led the soldiers, wearing a white mask with two black markings on the left side."

The king stood up, walking to Nora and Shaw for the first time. He wasn't as tall as the throne had made him look. Standing almost eye-to-eye with Shaw, King Ahven now had a slight but noticeable tremble in his voice. "What do you mean you had an encounter?"

"We were attacked, and a friend of ours was taken. During the fight, the masked wielder put up a wall of flame, boxing us in with his men while he took one of ours."

Turning around, King Ahven paced in front of them for a moment before asking, "Why would they take your friend? What business would a wielder want with you?"

Distrust ran across his brow, but before Shaw answered, Nora spoke. "We don't know why they took him, but we are trying to get him back. That's how we found Meno—we heard about a prison camp and went looking for it, only to get caught between helping the people of Meno and the First Born."

King Ahven listened intently but was not pleased with what he heard. "So you have turned the First Born's attention to Malen, to my kingdom? You would call upon the old treaties for protection—only to bring a possible war to my doorstep."

"I believe the war would come regardless of the part we played. If the First Born took Oroze with such speed and efficiency, what would stop them from trying to take another kingdom?" Shaw asked, agitated at the king's attempt to place blame.

"Reports indicated Oroze had little to no warning of an attack, so if this wielder is leading the First Born, at least we will be ready to defend ourselves if need be. They would not have the same element of surprise as they did with Oroze. I still maintain the fact you are safe here, even with Oroze having a wielder. Given the lack of surprise, I believe the First Born would not risk sending soldiers to attack Malen. I will do as I must and inform the other kingdoms of this wielder, but other than that, there is nothing more I can do for you, besides provide what the old treaties entail," King Ahven said, walking away again.

Nora's jaw clenched, but Shaw gave her foot a kick, meeting her eyes to get her compliance. They both bowed, thanking the king for his time.

"Before you leave, tell me—what are you to do now?" King Ahven stood awaiting an answer, but Nora and Shaw paused, trying to collect their thoughts.

"Once our friend is better, we will continue our search to find who was taken from us. We have a lead, but we still need to put together a plan," Nora said, her voice trailing off. Shaw put a reassuring hand on her shoulder. "Once Grant is better, we will figure something out."

The king's interest rose once more. "What lead do you have?"

"We have learned of a place called the Ark of Redemption, built into the mountainside of Oroze. We don't know much else, but if our friend is alive, we suspect he will be there," said Shaw.

Walking back to his throne, King Ahven said, "I have heard of that place. I do not envy your journey, but if war is to come based on this wielder, I will provide you with what I can within the kingdom. After I contact the other kings and queens, more might be possible, but only time will tell."

Taking their leave of the throne room, Nora and Shaw were led by General Sydell back to the sectioned-off quarter in the southwest. There, they met up with Abby. Nora asked General Sydell to bring them to their healers to visit Grant before returning to his post. He agreed, and they followed him through the streets until they reached a stone building reminiscent of the inns around the city. "I will leave a guard with you to accompany you back when you are done. I have some things I need to attend to. Farewell."

Inside the building, healers walked back and forth, only stopping to talk to the sick or wounded in beds separated by white curtains. Vials of multiple colors were stacked in cabinets, and herbs the likes of which Nora had never seen before were placed next to pestle and mortars. Clear vials full of dark liquids stood in locked cabinets behind a desk with a healer seated in front. Nora thought it would be best to approach the seated woman instead of trying to stop one of the busy ones.

"Can I help you?" asked the healer.

"We were wondering if you could tell us where our friend is. He was brought in with a wound to his right side. Do you know how he's doing?" Nora asked.

The healer's look lingered before she said, "You must be the people from the gate. The young man you're looking for is going to be down the hall on the left. He lost a lot of blood with a wound like that—I'm surprised he made it to the gate. His side was almost split wide open. Took the healers several hours to stop the bleeding and stitch him back up. I don't know if he's awake or not, but you can go see him." Abby's hands quickly shot to her mouth, fearing for Grant's well-being.

Reaching the end of the hall, they found Grant lying in bed with the sheet drawn to his waist, a large bandage six inches wide wrapped around his right side with blood staining through. Abby rushed to him, grabbing his hand in hers, whispering soft prayers.

A healer came walking up behind Shaw, moving him to the side. "Please make space. I need to change his bandage." Slowly peeling the corners of his bandage from his skin, the healer exposed the stitched flesh. Gently rolling Grant to his left side, she pulled the bandage off. His side, held together by an inch of skin, had not been separated after the sword entered his body.

The healer irrigated the wound, keeping it clean to prevent infection. Then, before reapplying a fresh bandage, she pulled out two vials, one clear with the dark liquid Nora had seen behind the locked cabinet doors and the other containing a green salve. Gently applying the salve over the stitched skin caused Grant to respond for the first time since they'd arrived; a sharp wince came when it touched his wound.

The healer then used the vial with the dark liquid, pouring some into Grant's mouth. Shortly after he swallowed it, his posture relaxed. Nora knew a good amount of medicinal applications, but she had never seen something work so fast at calming someone with a wound of such severity. "What is in that vial? It doesn't look like it has any calendula flower or coniferous resin mixed in."

"You seem to know your way around a salve or two," the healer said, looking at Nora.

"I spent time in a healers' ward for a few years where I grew up."

Genuine interest guided the woman's words. "This is a mixture of a few different ingredients. Most are common, like those you mentioned. The only difference is that this one has refined poppy seed, mainly to remove the pain while the wound heals. It is also the reason we keep it locked away." Nora tried to not let on that she wasn't familiar with the seed, but the healer could tell. "It's a rare flower that is only cultivated here in Malen. One of our herbalists discovered it when he was testing the effects of different flower salves."

"That's amazing. The most I've ever used was willow bark and feverfew for most headaches or aches and pains, but nothing like this," Nora said.

"Well, I see you have a knack for this sort of thing. Why don't you come by and visit later? Perhaps you could learn something and bring it back to your home."

Nora was eager to learn about new medicines and ways to help treat people. "Of course, that would be great." Nora's parents were both medically inclined. They were the reason she'd volunteered at the ward of healers in Greyland. They both treated people, constantly bringing Nora with them when they had the chance. They were always willing to go help others. That was what they'd told her when they left Greyland—only they never came back.

Finishing with the bandage, the healer rolled Grant onto his back. "It's no use staying here. Your friend is going to be sleeping for a while. Might as well get some rest—he should be awake in the morning." She turning to leave before adding, "Oh, ask for Healer Henna when you come by. Someone will come and get me." Nora nodded, and Healer Henna was gone.

"Guess we should listen and head back. Let Grant get some rest." Shaw agreed with Henna; there was nothing for them to do. The best idea would be to rest.

"If it's alright with both of you, I would like to stay with him. I don't want him to be alone if he wakes up before morning," Abby said, sitting at Grant's side.

Shaw smiled, putting a hand on her shoulder. "That sounds like a good idea. Take care of him for us." Abby's reassuring smile was all they needed.

Nora and Shaw went to the front and found the guard who was supposed to be escorting them engaged in a flirtatious entanglement with a healer. They went over to him, seemingly interrupting his smooth conversation. The guard growled as the healer walked away, but he begrudgingly brought them back to the others.

* * *

Low moans and the rustling of sheets woke Abby; lifting her head off the white sheet, she could see Grant tossing and turning in the luminous candle-light. Rubbing her eyes while they adjusted to the soft glow, she could see the light reflecting off the precipitation gathered on his forehead. Reaching next to the bed, Abby picked up a small cloth, dipping it in a bowl of water left by one of the healers. She gently dabbed the cloth above Grant's eyes and felt the heat from his body.

She thought he might have a fever; the healer had said he could develop one while his wounds healed, leaving the cloth and bowl of water for Abby to cool off his skin. Using the cloth to gently stroke the side of Grant's face, she saw that his eyes had opened slightly. Grant reached up subtly, lacing his fingers with hers, holding the cloth close to his cheek. A small smile found its place on the young man's face as he closed his eyes. Then he just held her hand and whispered, "I'm glad you're here. How is everyone?"

"They will be okay, thanks to you. Everyone is talking about you. They want to hold a celebration in your honor for saving them."

Abby saw the hurt written across his face.

"No, I don't want anyone to thank me or honor me. I don't deserve it," he said weakly.

"Why not? You could have died."

A tear rolled down Grant's cheek. "What about the people that did die? They were fathers and husbands. They gave their lives knowing someone was waiting for them to come home, and now they never will. They are the ones who should be honored, not me."

Abby moved her hand to dampen the cloth, patting it along his brow, tenderly moving the coldness to each side of his neck. "We will honor the ones who have fallen and grieve when the time is right. I don't think they could handle dealing with everything they lost these last few days. Some just needed to feel hopeful again."

Grant's hand tightened on Abby's. "It's my fault." Grant shook his head. "If only I could have made them listen and leave sooner, they would be alive, Alas would be alive. Why didn't they listen?" His wet eyes locked onto hers, looking for an answer that would help ease his guilt.

"I don't know. Maybe they were scared. Maybe having to give up everything again was too hard after Oroze, but it's not your fault. You did everything you could." Abby set the cloth down, knowing the answer was not what Grant was hoping for, so she cupped his hand in both of hers, bringing it to her lips and kissing his fingers.

"I should have pushed harder. Maybe if I tried harder, they would have listened," Grant said.

She brought his hand to her lap. "It was their choice. You tried, but—"

Anger gripped Grant's voice. "Maybe they shouldn't have had a choice. What's the use of having it if it's the wrong choice?"

Finally, after a long silence, Abby spoke. "Perhaps you're right. Maybe they shouldn't have had a choice, but let's not talk about this right now. You still need to rest. Your friends will be here in the morning, and when you're able to walk, I know Yulis will be excited to see you."

Grant knew she was right. His body still felt weak. The simple act of lifting his arm was draining; the most he could do besides talk was keep his eyes open, and even that was beginning to prove difficult.

"Why don't you go to sleep? I will be right here when you wake up," Abby said, leaning in close to kiss his forehead. She held Grant's hand as he closed his eyes and fell asleep.

Chapter Nineteen

Delayed Plans

T he days came and went, turning into weeks while Nora and Shaw visited Grant during his recovery, seeing him getting stronger each day. After seeing Grant, Nora would visit with Healer Henna; she enjoyed learning the new medical techniques that were not practiced in Greyland. They built upon her preexisting knowledge, such as new salve mixtures, including beeswax as a supporting base, finding mixes of herbs brewed into teas to relieve stomach pains, applying the most appropriate salve to ward away infection, and a new skill of stitching a wound properly.

In the back of Nora's mind, despite improving upon her natural skills as a healer, she kept thinking about the passing days, wondering what Ron had to endure while they waited for Grant to get better. Like an itch, Nora couldn't scratch the thought; it continued to gnaw at her. Did she need to wait for Grant? If it was only her and Shaw sneaking their way to the Ark of Redemption, they could have less chance of getting caught. How difficult would it be to find this place, and what would she do once she had found it?

After spending another afternoon with Healer Henna, Nora decided she was tired of doing nothing. She couldn't just wait around for Grant anymore, so she made her way to the home provided by the Malenites as part of the old treaty. Shaw was inside getting a fire prepared for the stew he was planning to cook for Nora, but she came back earlier than expected.

"Shaw, we need to do something. I can't keep waiting day in and day out."

Stoking the flames of the fire, Shaw said, "I know, but what do you plan to do? Storm the mountainside? There are a lot more of them than there are of us."

Nora pulled a chair out from a table a few feet from the fire. "I know, but we need to do something. Make a plan, I don't know, anything more than what we are doing now."

"I agree, but we need to be patient. It will take time. If we try to rush this, who knows what could happen," Shaw said calmly.

Nora slammed her fist on the table. "It's been weeks, and we are no closer to finding Ron. We have been patient, but you know good and well that Ron would be out there still looking if it were anyone of us. He wouldn't be sitting around waiting for others or pretending to play house."

Setting down the poker he used in the fire, Shaw let out a deep exhale before sitting in a chair opposite of Nora. "I have no doubt he would be. So tell me, what are you thinking?"

Nora cleared the table of the cups, bowls, and utensils Shaw had arranged earlier. Grabbing a couple candles from a nearby dresser pressed against a wall, she put them on the table.

"So if we are here"—she used a candle to indicate their placement—"Oroze is here. When we left Collins's house, the mountain didn't look to extend any farther into the northeast; it didn't have any markings, guards, or anything of note to imply a prison being built on that side. My guess is this Ark of Redemption is on the other side of Oroze."

Placing more candles where she thought the ark was located gave Shaw an idea of what she was talking about. "Okay, so if it's on the far east of Oroze, how are we going to get around to find the exact location? Between Noic to the south and the other villages surrounding Oroze, how would we remain undetected by the First Born? Surely at this point, the First Born know what we look like." Shaw tore pieces of bread apart, placing them on the table to symbolize the surrounding villages of Oroze. "How do you plan to get around this?" he asked.

"It wouldn't be easy, but if we were to go at night, we could get past most villages unseen." Nora traced a line with her finger, showing a route that led around the villages farther southeast.

"Hold on, Nora, that seems too risky. We don't know the layout of the land over there. Not counting how long it would take to travel. It took multiple days just from Meno; it could take over a week to reach Oroze, let alone the far east side. What happens if we get spotted during the days we travel? How much time would we lose, and once we're there, then what?" Nora remained silent as she thought, but Shaw continued, "It also may still be a few days before Grant can ride, and at best, it would be slow going."

Nora shot Shaw a stare that held his tongue in place. "Grant will not be going with us," she said decisively.

"I don't think he would be too happy about the idea of us leaving him here. You know he wants to get Ron back just as much as we do, but—"

Nora held her stare, bringing Shaw's words to an abrupt end. "Grant doesn't have a choice in this. I'll tell him myself when the time comes. We can't keep waiting for him to get better, but to come back to the points you made, you're right. We can't just go there and figure it out once we arrive. What if we just scouted it out first?" She pointed to the pieces of bread. "We know where Noic is, and from what we've seen, that's as far south as any villages go. If we stay far enough away, maybe we don't need to get so close. If we can get a clear view of the mountains' east side, we can come back and make more definitive plans on what to do next."

Shaw rubbed his trimmed beard, mulling over Nora's plan. "That will take up a lot of time. Are you sure?"

Nora ran her figures through her hair in a frustrated fashion. "Yes, I'm sure. It will give Grant the time he needs, and I will be able to feel like I'm actually doing something useful." Nora paused and let out an irritated groan.

"What's wrong?" Shaw asked.

"The First Born know we are here, and we destroyed one of the two bridges coming this way. So they could be waiting anywhere outside the city or just on the other side of the bridge." She stood up from the chair, walking over to the fire, wandering back and forth. "It's always one thing after another, isn't it?" she said. The sarcasm was holding back the anger she felt in her rhetorical question, but a soft sob made its way through.

Shaw knew how she felt. It was grating even to him, how since the start of their journey, every step had become more and more complicated. Shaw felt it, but he also couldn't help but think of all the good they had done along the way.

"Nora, come have a seat." Shaw took a deep breath before he started. "Remember when you asked me about my wife?" Nora nodded her head. "After my daughter passed, my wife Thea and I decided to start over somewhere new. There were too many memories, too many ghosts, for us to stay where we were. I would hear Thea cry herself to sleep each night. I would hold her throughout most nights. Some days were better than others for the both of us. We would talk like we used to, even share a laugh. To see her smile like that again was wonderous. Seeing her happy again began to mend the broken pieces within me. Then we decided to move to Regis, where Ron grew up.

"Back in our younger years, Thea and I would go all over, never settling on one place for very long. She liked to get different jobs everywhere we went. Everything fascinated her. She worked for merchants, fishermen, tailors, butchers—you name it, she did it. I pursued academic studies, and with not being nailed down to any one place, I got to learn the histories and teachings of the different kingdoms. But Regis—we fell in love with Regis. The beautiful countryside expanding out in all directions. It was where we wanted to go as our last adventure.

"Once we were all packed and got our horses ready and saddled, I told Thea I would be back after I visited Allurin one last time. So I went to the mountain to pick the lady's thimbles before going to where we buried her. I told her that her mother and I were going away and how we would try our best to make it out once a year to see her and bring her more flowers. I told her I loved her, and I always would, before heading back home.

"I was gone for a few hours, and when I got home, I couldn't find Thea. Her horse was still hitched to its post, but the front door was open. I searched the house, and there was no sign of her," Shaw took a deep breath. Then, steadying his voice, he continued. "Thea and I lived next to the Red Band River, a hundred yards or so from the banks. I looked over, and she was there at the river. I started to walk over, but then I saw Thea going into the water. I screamed her name as loud as I could, but she didn't hear me. I ran so hard to the river that I couldn't tell if my lungs were even getting air. By the time I reached the river, Thea was gone. I couldn't see her." Shaw cleaned the tears from his face. "I got in the water, trying to swim to the bottom, but it was too deep. The current kept pulling me away. I looked along the river for hours, but she was gone—I lost her."

Taking a pause to collect himself and regain composure, Shaw walked to the fire to warm his hands. "Do you know why I am telling you this, Nora?"

Nora hadn't the slightest idea, especially now. Going through losing his daughter and his wife also must have been unbearable. "I don't know," she said.

Shaw turned from the fire. "I'm telling you this because if I gave in to the sorrow, or the feeling of hopelessness, the anger I felt, or the irrational thoughts that plagued my mind, I would not be here today. The repercussions would have changed the entire outcome of not only your life, but Ron's and Grant's as well. I know you feel like you have lost Ron, like he is gone forever; I'm sure Grant feels the same. I know I do as well sometimes, but you cannot let that feeling consume you. You need to keep fighting, keep pushing, take in the victories we have. It's not what we intended or set out to do, but our path led us here. And look at the good we've done, the people we saved. Take the victory when you can and keep having hope that we will find Ron and get him back. That is the only way to survive."

Nora had a puzzled look on her face, and Shaw didn't know why until she said, "How did you have hope?"

Those words dug deep into Shaw's heart as he recalled how he'd been on the border of losing hope altogether. "I almost didn't, but I started small. When I decided to stop searching for Thea, it was almost like I felt myself die inside. That was when I understood why she did what she did. She must have felt that way ever since Allurin died. I almost followed Thea into the river over the next couple of weeks, but that was when I knew what I had to do.

"I was never going to be able to get rid of my ghosts if I stayed, so I left and set out for Regis just as Thea and I had planned. I had the clothes in my saddlebags, Allurin's flower in my pocket, and something to keep Thea with me until I see her again."

Shaw rolled up his sleeve to reveal the bracelet Nora had seen him spin on his wrist every now and again. It was simple, made of silver, with blue kyanite stones circling the center. Thea had found the stones during their travels, so Shaw had paid a blacksmith to make a bracelet with them, to surprise her with the bracelet before Allurin was born.

"When I got to Regis, I was still a broken man, but slowly, as time went on, my ghosts faded and hope came back. I started teaching. That's how I came to know Ron and his parents. I began educating the children of Regis. That's where my hope was rebuilt. Every small victory and every person I met gave me something to hold on to. If I hadn't gone to Regis, I never would have been there to pull Ron away from the First Born when the town was attacked."

He took Nora's hand in his. "The point is, we will find him, and we won't give up, no matter how long it takes. So you don't give up either, not for one second, no matter how difficult it may seem." Shaw got up and walked back to the fire. "So, when do we leave?"

A smile came to Nora's face. "We should leave tomorrow night. That will give us enough time to gather any supplies we may need. Do you think we should tell King Ahven what we are planning on doing?"

The king's guards still followed them everywhere, not allowing any of the people from Meno to venture through the city except for a select few that accompanied Nora and Shaw or people needing medical treatment that could not be performed within the confines of the sectioned-off quarter. Nora didn't know if the king would let her and Shaw come in and out of the city as they pleased, given that the trust between the two peoples was thin at best.

"What do you think he would say?" Shaw asked, trying to see how she had gauged the king.

"I'm not sure. I mean, he did say he would help us within the city itself. So I don't see him being unreasonable in letting us leave as long as we don't bring the whole of the First Born army back with us. Also, I think it would prove difficult to get out of Malen without someone opening the gate."

Shaw nodded in agreement. "True, it would look quite suspicious if we tried to leave during the night, and getting caught in the process wouldn't be ideal. I guess in the morning, we should ask if one of the guards could take us to see the king."

Now that they had a rough outline of a plan, the only thing left to do before the morning was to reset the table and get ready to eat the food Shaw had prepared.

The sun's rays dove over the mountains stretching across the valley, reaching into every window within the Kingdom of Malen. The city was slow to wake. The early risers placed signs outside their doors to draw the crowd of soon-to-be customers. Livestock was shepherded into respective pens; chickens strutted from their coops, with the rooster announcing that morning had arrived.

Nora and Shaw decided it would be best to ask for an audience with the king early so as to have the rest of the day to get whatever supplies they needed. Nora also wanted to wait to tell Grant they were going to leave without him. She was going to tell him just before she and Shaw made their way to the gate. That way, Grant would have no grounds to argue or insist on going with them. She knew he would be upset, but he was a liability to take in his current state, and as much as it would hurt to tell him, she knew it was the right thing to do.

Getting an audience with the king was not as hard of a task to accomplish as they'd expected. Coincidentally, General Sydell had come to the closed-off residential quarter to summon Nora and Shaw to see King Ahven before they could even ask him themselves.

"General, do you know why the king wants to see us again?" Nora asked.

"I do not. All I was instructed to do was bring you before His Majesty." So, through the streets, they made their way into the palace, which still looked as grand as the first time Nora had laid her eyes upon it.

In the throne room, King Ahven sat, and after receiving the customary bows from each, he began, "I have received word from the other kingdoms. Apparently, word has spread, and everyone knows about the fall of Oroze. The First

Born have made a name for themselves with its taking. Even more troubling is that I sent out three messages and have only received two in return. I tell you this because you have turned my attention to a situation I may not have seen otherwise with your coming here. I thank you for that."

Shaw bowed again, feeling it was expected. "We are honored we could be of service. But, if I may, which kingdom has yet to respond?"

King Ahven sat mulling over the idea of what information needed to be withheld and what these two should be privy to. "Baddon has yet to send a message, but with it being the closest to Oroze, I can understand they may be more guarded than usual as to the sending of information. I will continue to discuss matters with the other kingdoms, but I wanted to tell you personally that I appreciate your help."

This time, both Nora and Shaw bowed. "Your Majesty, I was wondering if I could ask a favor?" Nora asked.

The king raised an eyebrow. "I suppose a favor may be in order depending on what is being requested."

"Shaw and I were hoping that, with your permission, we could leave Malen for a few days, and after such time return."

King Ahven looked quizzical, pondering the possible reasons these two would have for leaving the safety and protection of the kingdom. "You may have my permission on one condition—tell me the honest truth as to why you want to leave. If I find it to be false, I can personally guarantee the only thing you will be seeing is the inside of these walls for the foreseeable future."

His words made Nora's choice clear. There was no point in lying. "We would like to go and scout out the mountain that contains the possible location of the Ark of Redemption."

Shaw added, "We need to gather as much information about the mountain and surrounding areas as we can if we want to have any chance of getting our friend back."

A small chuckle came from the king. "Well, that sounds too dangerous to be a lie, but is that all you are planning?"

"Yes, Your Majesty. All we want to do is figure out our next move while our friend heals. We are wasting too much time sitting idly by, so once we return, we can construct a better plan and leave once Grant can ride." Nora was nervous telling King Ahven so much of their plan, but it was the only option to convince him.

"Alright, you have my permission to come and go as you see fit. But know this: if anything happens to you, there will be no help coming. I will not risk my soldiers' lives to save yours." The king had a grim expression. Once Nora and Shaw left the walls of Malen, they were on their own. "I will have General Sydell draw up a pair of letters stating your privileges. Upon leaving, your weapons will be returned to you as well."

Nora remembered that her staff had been broken during her last encounter with the First Born. "Your Majesty, before we leave, is there a blacksmith or merchant I could purchase a weapon from?" She hadn't had the opportunity to look around the city.

"Yes, there are a few, but if you so choose, you could also look through my armory. The weapons made by the palace blacksmith are the best in Malen. On the other hand, the price is much higher than what is found in the shops, but being as helpful as you two have been, I will reduce the price of one item for each of you. Does that sound fair?"

Bowing for a final time, Shaw said, "Yes, Your Majesty. Thank you for your hospitality. We hope we can be of service again."

General Sydell escorted them out a side door to the left of the throne, leading them down a busy hallway, filled with servants carrying bed linens to be beaten and cleaned alongside guards making their way toward the barracks. Taking a left at the end of the hallway only to take an immediate right, they found themselves standing before two guards, each with a double-bladed battle ax held across the entrance of the next room.

General Sydell held the letters he had drawn up for them while King Ahven finished talking. As the soldiers stood aside, he pushed the door open to reveal the armory. Weapons were stacked upon multiple racks. Swords, long and short, rested in mounts along the walls. Round shields of iron and steel, wood shields encased with an iron border, and long, heavy iron shields all hung from the walls, showcasing skill and craftsmanship.

Arrows bundled in several leather quivers lay on a table alongside different bows. Shaw lifted each bow, pulling the string back, feeling for the right amount of tension until he found the perfect fit. Finally, he found a dark brown bow with hints of red lined into the wood. Leaves were engraved from top to bottom, and in the middle, little ridges were carved on either side, so when Shaw held it in his hand, he had a firm grip. Holding it tight, he pulled the bowstring back, placing his right hand next to his cheek; he then eased the tension on the bowstring and admired the exceptional craft of the bow.

Nora looked around the room, seeing the engravements upon each piece. Shields had sequoia trees etched on the front, and the swords had carvings on the hilt that resembled twisting branches climbing up toward the blade. Nora spotted what she was looking for on the other side of the room.

Toward the back corner was a rack of staffs five deep. Simple wooden ones were placed on the bottom, but she wanted something stronger, thinking about how the other staff had been cut it in two. Going to the other side of the rack, Nora saw a staff and picked it up. It was about the same size as her, but made of full metal.

It looked as though its shine had been purposefully buffed out, leaving a rough, dulled exterior engraved with crisscrossed markings along the middle, each endpoint sharpened for lethal intent. The staff felt light in her hands. Nora spun it around as she would have in training to get a feel for its balance; with the metal being denser than the wood, it took Nora a few spins to get the rhythm right in her hands.

"I hope you are finding everything to be satisfactory?" Nora and Shaw turned in the direction the voice came from. The blacksmith walked toward them with his hands behind his back. The man was old, with thinning gray hair, wrinkled skin, and a slight hunch in his back. "Everything I have here I made myself. That bow you are holding right there is made of young oak and red pine." He looked over to Nora. "I see you are proficient with a staff. That one is made from our strongest steel. It won't bend or break. The weight is distributed evenly throughout to maintain perfect balance, and you're in luck—that particular piece comes with a backstrap."

"How much for both?" Shaw asked as General Sydell handed the letters to the blacksmith.

"Seeing as you have this letter, it will be twenty silver for the lot, ten apiece." Their eyes widened, and Nora placed the staff back on the rack, wondering if the price had indeed been lowered. They collectively had seven copper coins and twelve silver coins. Even if they could haggle the price down to their last coin, they would not be able to procure any supplies from the other shops.

General Sydell eyed the coins in their hands while they whispered about which one weapon they should buy. Nora argued that since her staff was in two pieces, she needed something stronger that could not be split. Shaw countered with the fact that a new bow could increase the distance and speed of his arrows. His old bowstring was worn and had lost a lot of tension.

While they discussed, General Sydell approached the blacksmith and engaged him in low conversation. The blacksmith soon left the room. Moments later, without Nora or Shaw noticing, he returned with the backstrap in hand, placing it on the table next to the bow. He also grabbed the staff from the rack.

The backstrap on the table looked simple, with one leather strap to sling across a shoulder. Coming together with an adjustable buckle, the clasp on the back swiveled left or right, locking in place with a loud click when positioned off-center. The blacksmith made sure the staff fit in the clasp, as he had other straps for the smaller or larger staffs.

Shaw looked disheartened. "We won't be able to purchase both weapons today, I'm afraid, so we will just take the staff." Nora was genuinely surprised, but Shaw looked to her and said, "I don't need a new bow—as nice as it would be, the old one works just fine."

The old blacksmith waved his hand at Shaw dismissively. Taking the bow off the table, he checked the drawstring, pulling it back to his cheek with ease to see if the string held up to his standards after sitting in the armory since its creation.

"Seeing as how I've been paid, these weapons belong to you. Do take care of them now. Took me quite some time to make those just right." Before Shaw or

Nora could raise questions as to how he had been paid, General Sydell thanked the blacksmith and handed the weapons over to their new respective owners.

Walking into the bright sun with the palace door closing firmly, General Sydell turned to face them. "King Ahven figured the armory would be too expensive even with the price reduced, so as my way of thanks for the information about the First Born, I covered the cost. It was the least I could do." A thanks was in order, but General Sydell waved it off. "My father has a keen eye for when someone finds their perfect weapon. Even if I didn't cover the cost, I'm sure he would have made a deal."

Nora and Shaw never would have guessed that the blacksmith was General Sydell's father. Before they could say anything, the general said, "Now, I must be going. Here are your letters to get in and out of the Malen, and I will leave one of my lieutenants with you to help guide you to whatever shop you need."

Without so much as another word, General Sydell went about his business; the lieutenant that was left to guide them had a familiar face, but Nora couldn't remember where she had seen him last. In a salty tone, he introduced himself. "I'm Lieutenant Lario Basset. You may call me Lieutenant, Basset, or Lieutenant Basset. Any is fine by me." He was a tall man with sandy-blond hair and light brown eyes bordering on hazel; he maintained a short, trimmed beard and wore his green left shoulder piece on top of polished silver armor. Shaw told Lieutenant Basset what items they would need to find, and before long, they arrived at the first shop. The lieutenant told them he would wait outside until they found what they needed.

Inside, it didn't take long to find food that would not spoil over multiple days. Shaw purchased dried fruits, as he was fond of sweetness. Nora found dried venison; she felt it would be just fine, though not her favorite. Upon exiting the shop, she looked for Lieutenant Basset, and once she spotted him, she remembered where she had seen him earlier.

It now made sense why he was not the happiest person to be escorting them. The last time they'd met, Nora and Shaw had interrupted his attempts to swoon one of the healers in between treatments. This time, instead of approaching Lieutenant Basset, Nora and Shaw waited until he looked in their direction, giving him time to finish sweet-talking the woman he was conversing with. When he asked where they were going next, a slight change in his demeanor became noticeable. Nora and Shaw shared a laugh with each other and moved on to the next shop.

* * *

Abby held tight to Grant's hand. He slowly raised himself up in bed, moving carefully to not rip any stitches. His wound was healing well, allowing him to walk for a short time before he had to lie back down due to his side feeling like it would split open. Over the weeks, Abby had helped him walk around the room among the other healers, but today, Grant felt better and wanted to get out and see the city. The last he'd seen of it was the gate before he lost consciousness and fell from his horse.

Grant felt if he stayed in bed any longer, he would become a part of it and never leave. Even when Abby told him they would only be allowed to walk from the healers' building straight to the residential quarter, he didn't mind. Anything would be better than seeing the same white hanging sheets or listening to people moan from whatever was ailing them.

Abby went to get Healer Henna to check his bandage; she peeled the corners off, checking for any residual bleeding, and found none. Grant's wound had begun to scab over. Healer Henna told him he could have the stitches removed tomorrow so it could scar over properly, but that he still needed to take it easy. Grant moved his legs to the side of the bed, relieved that his body no longer felt heavy or drained. He was ready to get going before Healer Henna stopped him, giving him a few drops off the black salve in the clear vial, so he could enjoy being out on his feet without the pain returning for a few hours. Abby put her arm through Grant's on the left side, leading the way out of the building. Grant squinted as he stepped outside; he felt his eyes burn from the bright light of the sun. After staying in a bed with little to no natural light surrounding him, his eyes had become used to a darker setting.

Walking on the mismatched, colored rocks that made up the cobblestone road, Grant breathed in the fresh air, filling his lungs with as much as he could. He smiled to himself, enjoying the peace he felt with Abby. He looked to her as the breeze gently pushed her long, red hair back, revealing tiny freckles running across her nose from cheek to cheek.

She caught him staring. "What? Do I have something on my face?" She lifted her hand, brushing her face where she thought something might be.

"No, you don't. I just thought you look nice, is all. I don't think we have been able to just talk to each other without any problems bearing down on us, and I don't think I've properly thanked you for taking care of me."

Abby held her gaze on Grant. "You don't need to. I wanted to be there for you. That's what you do for someone you care about."

Grant put his arm around her and pulled her close while they walked. He had almost forgotten what it felt like for someone to care for him. Over the years, he'd dated and mingled with the women of Greyland. Still, since he had training at the Arena, he hadn't had time to partake in any outside engagements that lasted nearly long enough for him to develop real feelings for anyone.

Besides the occasional fling, even Ron had had more luck than Grant in that department. Grant had watched his friend go through the motions with other women throughout the years, always wondering why he never directly asked Nora. It was beyond his reasoning.

Now, seeing how Abby looked at him gave him a feeling he didn't want to lose. Just being around her brought a smile to his face. "I wanted to ask you—when I was still in and out of sleep, I could have sworn I heard you whisper something."

"Oh, you heard that, huh?" she blushed, just on the verge of sounding shy.

"I did. What was it?" Grant asked,

"It was an old prayer my parents would say to me whenever I was sick or in need of help. It's a silly tradition, but it's a small comfort," Abby said, pushing a strand of hair behind her ear.

"I wasn't able to hear the words, but it sounded nice," Grant said with a smile. Going through a narrow alley, he saw the guards standing at their posts at the entrance to the residential quarter. Once inside the grounds, he was met with smiling faces who came to say their thanks and show their gratitude with congratulatory pats on the back or shoulder, or intimately long hugs. Children ran by, shouting over their parents to see the hero who saved them from the First Born. Grant's smile faded. A quiet fell over the crowd. All eyes were on him, and he figured he had to say something.

"Please, I am no hero. The real heroes are the ones who are still out there, the ones who gave their lives, the ones who stood next to me." He paused, thinking of the last moments before Alas took his final breath on the bridge. "Remember them, and remember what they fought for. In their memory, we will honor them."

A slew of voices rang out in affirmation to the truth of Grant's words. He continued making his way through the crowd, still receiving the thanks he felt he didn't deserve. One child ran into his right side, forcing him to fall to a knee. He gritted his teeth to keep from shouting, grabbing hold of his side.

The pain tore through his body, radiating to his stomach and chest. He tried to catch his breath; it felt like the wind was knocked from his lungs. Abby helped stand him to his feet. Stepping to his right side, she lifted his shirt to look at his bandage briefly so as to not worry the crowd. Blood had started to soak through. "It looks like a stitch might have torn."

"It definitely feels that way." Grant tried to make light of the pain to take his mind from it, but it wasn't working.

Grabbing his hand, Abby moved through the crowd. "Let's go this way—I know someone who might be able to help." Looking to the right, Abby found a path through the crowd toward a smaller, wood-paneled house close to the border of the lake.

She tapped lightly on the door before pushing it open and announcing herself. A voice echoed back, "Come on in." An older round woman came walking around the corner to greet them. It was Gretta, but this time she was not wearing an apron. She had on a modest blue dress and looked very reminiscent of a grandmother. "It's nice to see you, dear, and you as well."

After giving Abby a long hug, she went to give Grant one as well. Then she saw him holding his side.

"Gretta, I was hoping you could help Grant. We were outside, and one of the boys ran into him." Abby lifted his shirt so Gretta could take a look at the wound.

"What makes you think I can do more for him than the healers?" Gretta asked, giving Abby a look that conveyed a secret only shared between them.

"I know we aren't supposed to talk about it, but he needs your help, and after all he has done, I think it's the least we can do," Abby said.

Gretta moved past them with a slight sigh of reluctance, making sure the bolt on the front door was locked in place, then shuffled over to the window and pulled the curtains closed. "Alright, come into the common room, away from the windows. Can you lay him down?"

Helping Grant to the floor, Abby cradled his head in her lap while Gretta lifted his shirt to remove the bandage. "This is more than a little tear—the front of the wound is almost reopened completely. I will try my best, but once it's done, I won't be able to do anything more for a while. Also, I'm going to have to remove the stitches. I've done it before, so don't worry."

Gretta then asked Abby to grab a knife from the kitchen and a pillow from one of the chairs in the common room, and she instructed her to have Grant bite down on a corner of it. Gretta began to remove the stitches slowly, pulling gently on each one to avoid separating the skin further.

"That wasn't so bad," Grant said, relieved that taking the remaining stitches out hadn't caused too much pain.

"I have yet to start, but when I begin, it's going to hurt something fierce. Try not to scream," Gretta said, focusing on his stitches.

Grant looked confused. "What are you going to do?"

Before he had time to asked again, Abby put the corner of the pillow in his mouth. Once Gretta saw him bite down, she placed her hands on Grant's side, covering the back and front where the stitches held the skin together. Grant's eyes went wild as the pain soared through his abdomen. He could feel his skin stretching. The air smelled of hot iron, and his insides burned while his teeth bared down on the pillow, threatening to tear it apart as he held in his screams. In the next instant, the pain was gone. Grant was breathing heavily. Sweat beaded off his head, and he looked down at Gretta and only saw thin streams of smoke rising from his injury—and from her hands.

Grant rapidly moved his hands to touch his side, finding only warm flesh and a thick scar. "What did you—how did you?" He thought faster than his mouth could form words. Gretta slowly raised her hands to calm him.

"Easy. Just relax, and I'll explain." When she stood up, Grant noticed she had to quickly find a chair to brace herself as her legs couldn't hold her up for long. Whatever she had done had taken its toll on her. When she sat down, she whisked the sweat from her forehead. "How do you feel?" she asked as Grant was still trying to catch his breath.

"Good. I mean, the pain is gone."

With a satisfied smile, Gretta said, "Good." Before explaining, she asked Abby to get her some water. Grant stood on his own, inspecting the new scar, then sat back down as Abby returned.

"How did you do that?"

Once she finished drinking, she explained.

"When I was a little girl, my mother taught me how to do it. My mother was a gifted healer when I was young, and she normally tended to the injured. One day, I decided to try and do it as well, but the first time I did, my mother said she found me unconscious. I stayed that way for a few days. When she gave me lessons, she said that in order to heal, I had to picture what I wanted to fix in my mind. Once I had a clear picture, there would be a moment of clarity, and I would know what to do. It's almost like an impulse. I can feel it, and I just knew when to let go."

Grant still didn't understand. "Why would you hide that? That sounds like it could help a lot of people."

"I hid my gift out of fear. One day, strangers came to our village saying they heard rumors of what my mother and I could do. They didn't know it was us they were looking for, so they took people, torturing them until they got what they wanted. My mother and I ran—we left before anyone gave our names. I've used my gift sparingly ever since, but it always takes a lot of energy from my body, especially the older I get. There are also limitations to what I can do. I can't heal someone if they are close to death. As I told Abby, I tried to heal her late husband, but he was too badly injured. I didn't have enough strength to help him."

Grant reflected on this. "I think I understand what you mean." Thinking back to when he was on the battlefield after Alas died, he remembered feeling something as well. He remembered how he knew when to let go. Grant decided to keep that information to himself; it would be best if he understood exactly what he did before telling anyone about it.

Gretta looked at him. "I hope we can keep what happened here today between us." She used a more authoritative voice now, one that implied she wasn't really asking him to keep quiet about her ability but telling him.

"Of course. Thank you for healing me. It really is a gift—it's a shame you have to hide it. It should be something you're allowed to embrace. I promise I will keep it between us."

Gretta gave Grant a hug. "You two should be on your way now; I need some rest. Like I said, healing takes a lot of energy when I use it."

A thought came into Grant's mind at that. "What am I going to tell Healer Henna when we get back? She is probably going to want to check the stitches."

Abby cut in, "How about you stay here, and I'll go back and tell her I will keep an eye on your stitches. I've watched her do everything else, so she should feel comfortable with me caring for you." Grant smiled at how fast she thought of that. "We should get going. Thank you again, Gretta," Abby said, giving her one more departing hug; Gretta followed and closed the door behind them.

* * *

Late in the afternoon, Nora and Shaw heard a complaining sigh from Lieutenant Basset. They'd been to multiple shops, searching for odds and ends that may help them on their journey to Oroze. Finding all the items they needed used up most of the day, and most of the lieutenant's patience. Basset wasn't so vocal about his distaste for being their chaperone anymore, but still, his constant grumbling and eye-rolling were enough to indicate he felt he had better things to do.

"Do you have everything you need? The shops will be closing soon, and I have to tend to my other duties. It's not like anyone else will do them for me, so the sooner we finish, the sooner I can get my work done."

Shaw passively waved him off while thinking through if they had everything they required. "Yes, yes, I do believe we have gotten all we need."

"Alright then, let's head back to your quarters." Lieutenant Basset started walking.

"Before we do that, could we make one last stop? We need to talk to a friend that was taken to your healers."

The lieutenant reluctantly assented.

The roads were becoming more and more empty as the sun set. Lights poured out the windows into the encroaching dark, filling the streets and alleys. Music filtered out from the inns; most had musicians who played for coins or a hot meal. The tenants would eat, drink and sing along to the songs they knew. The loudest inn with the most people coming in and out, some stumbling but laughing nonetheless, was the Stay for a Seq Inn.

"Lieutenant, why do people like this inn so much? There seems to be plenty of others around," Nora asked.

"The Seq Inn has a lot of history. It's one of the founding buildings that has been preserved for generations. Granted, it has had some renovations made and was almost burned down during one of the wars many years ago, but it's a cherished landmark among the people. Even the other officers and I frequent the Seq Inn for a drink or a song every now and again. Also, people mostly behave themselves in there. Some of the other inns have gained a reputation for the kind of people that hang around.

"Most respectable people tend to stay away from the inns farther east in the city. Things can get rough there after dark. People have been found beaten and bloody in the streets, and when we try to investigate, no one says a word. We have tried to place more palace guards around the troubled areas, but no good has come of it. Unfortunately, that's how it is around here sometimes."

Listening to Lieutenant Basset, Nora realized that was the most she'd heard him talk all day, and without sounding snarky, no less. "Where are you from, Lieutenant?" she asked.

"Me? I'm from here, Malen. I was born here, but my parents were from Sonnalin, on the other side of the mountains in the south. Have you heard of it?"

"No, I haven't." Nora had never been outside the walls of Greyland, so everything she has seen and heard since she left has been new to her, especially the kingdoms and the people. She'd learned a bit about the kingdoms when she was younger, as all the children did, but seeing them was entirely different.

"I've heard of Sonnalin," said Shaw. "During my younger years, when my wife and I would travel, we went past the outskirts of the kingdom, only catching a glimpse of its massive walls."

"Ah, yes. My parents told me the kingdom is impenetrable, its outer walls harder than any stone touched by man—unbreakable, even. They said it was a kingdom built by the Essenti." Lieutenant Basset let out a laugh. "The tales people tell."

All the talking had distracted them from the time it took to reach the healers' building, and just as Shaw went to reach for the door, it swung open, almost crashing into his chest. "Oh my, are you okay?" a startled Abby asked, coming through the door, hoping she didn't just slam it into Shaw.

"I'm fine, dear, just a little surprised is all." He straightened the ruffles in his shirt. "Is Grant awake in there?"

"He's awake, but he's not with the healers."

Bewildered, Nora asked, "Where is he then?"

"I talked to Healer Henna, and she said I could care for him in the residential quarter as long as I changed his bandage regularly, but I think he will be fine. He is a fast healer," A sly smile touched the corner of her mouth. "I'm headed back if you want to walk with me."

Abby stayed close to Nora and Shaw as they followed Lieutenant Basset to the residential quarters.

Once there, the lieutenant was about to relieve himself of his escort duty when Nora called to him. "Lieutenant, we wanted to give you this as a token of thanks for today." She pulled out a small silver ring with a flat top engraved with Malen's signature sequoia tree. Lieutenant Basset held it in his hand. "Shaw pointed out that some of the other officers had this ring, and we thought it would be a nice gift to show our appreciation. Also, when we bought it, the shopkeeper said it doubles as a seal for any letters you send out." Nora smiled.

Lieutenant Basset was staggered by their generosity, knowing he hadn't been that kind to them throughout the day with all his grumbling and reluctance. "Thank you. I honestly hadn't expected anything. I haven't been the most gracious host to you," he said, turning the ring over in his hand. "There is a reason not every officer wears one of these. Do you know what this ring symbolizes?"

"No, but the shopkeeper was very adamant about selling this particular ring. Why is that?" Nora asked.

Smiling to himself, he looked at the ring. "These rings were made for any soldier to wear, although we are not permitted to buy them ourselves. They can be given from soldier to soldier or by any resident within Malen. They symbolize the commitment made by the soldier to the people of the kingdom. Please, accept my apologies for how I acted. As gratitude for such a gift, I want you to know that if any of you ever need anything while in the kingdom of Malen, please ask for me by name. I will be more than happy to tend to your request."

"We'll take you up on that offer," Shaw said, extending his hand.

Abby knocked lightly before pushing the door open, looking around to see if Grant or Yulis were in the house. She held the door as Nora and Shaw made their way in.

"Where's Grant?" Nora asked, looking around inside the home. It wasn't the biggest house on the row, but it was the closest to the water, and cozy enough with a small fire in the fireplace.

"I'm sure he and Yulis are somewhere. The boy hasn't given Grant a moment to himself since he walked through the door. Those boys." Abby laughed to herself and smiled as she walked over to a light brown wooden table along the far wall. "By the way, one of the soldiers came by and dropped these off for you." She handed Shaw and Nora a small, folded pile of clothes.

"I never thought I'd see these again, especially with how rough the ladies at the palace were with them," Shaw said, looking in amazement at his folded clothes until his thoughts were broken by Nora.

"What do you mean, rough?" Nora had immensely enjoyed her time with Lilly at the palace, as brief as it was. Shaw, however, turned a little bit red in the face.

"Oh, it's nothing. Forget I mentioned it," he said.

Faint laughter came from outside the house. "That sounds like my Yulis. It sounds like they're out back by the lake."

Going through a back door that led to the lake, Abby, Nora, and Shaw saw Grant and Yulis playing by the water. Abby just smiled, but Nora and Shaw were concerned, seeing the boy run full speed toward Grant, jumping just as he was about to collide with him. Grant hoisted him into the air, spinning around a few times before they both laughed and fell to the ground. Nora and Shaw rushed over to Grant to see if he was okay—they thought his wound may have opened again, or maybe he was in pain.

With Abby following behind slowly, Nora and Shaw were within earshot and heard Yulis say, "I'm getting dizzy—I don't think I can go anymore."

Grant giggled. "Me neither, buddy. I think if we do any more spinning, I'll get sick." Grant patted Yulis's hair as they lay on the grass, looking at the lake. Grant was happy. He was taking in the sights and the calm of the closing day, wishing to himself life could stay this way, but he knew better.

He knew he had to find Ron with Nora and Shaw, but he wanted to cherish this moment. Then he heard someone walking up behind him. He thought it would be Abby, but to his surprise, Nora stood over him, looking worried. The last time she'd seen Grant, he was still being nursed back to health. It perplexed her to see him walking around, and playing no less.

"I thought you were supposed to take it easy. What about your wound? You can't be reckless like this. What if it reopens, gets infected, or worse?" she scolded.

The edges of Grant's mouth curved up. "It's strange, isn't it?" he said. Then he turned, sat up, and sprang to his feet. Nora and Shaw both winced and moved to catch him as they thought he may fall, but he didn't. Lifting up his shirt, Grant exposed the scar that had taken over from the injury.

"I don't know how it happened, but I woke up this afternoon and felt much better. Last I remember, those healers put something on me, and it scarred over—must be some kind of magic." Grant looked over to Abby, giving her a little nod, keeping hers and Gretta's secret.

Nora scratched her head. "This doesn't make any sense. What could they have possibly used that would have worked so fast? I can't believe it."

"Neither can I, but whatever they did, I'm glad they did it. I didn't want to be in that bed for another second."

Nora was at a loss for words, but she was glad Grant was better. The how of it all started not to matter as much as she saw the way Grant kept looking at Abby; it reminded her of how Ron would steal looks when he thought she wouldn't notice. Nora had noticed every time Ron would look her way. She let him think his gaze went by unseen, but she was just waiting for the right moment to tell him how she felt. The only thing that had held her back from expressing herself sooner was the timing of events that always seemed to get in the way when she thought she had the perfect opportunity.

Clearing her mind, Nora knew she had to tell Grant about the plan she and Shaw had made, although she had to make some adjustments with him being better now. She'd only accounted for herself and Shaw in every scenario she planned, though adding a third wouldn't hurt any. It would actually be nice to have another pair of eyes, but Grant wasn't prepared. He didn't even have a weapon. By the time she was ready to talk, Grant had walked over to Abby with Yulis at his side.

"Listen, Shaw and I need to tell you something."

Grant looked puzzled for a moment. "What's going on?"

"This won't be easy to hear, but we have decided we are going to scout the lands around Oroze for a way to enter the Ark of Redemption. So we came here to tell you we're leaving tonight, and we will be gone for a week or so, depending on how far we can go with our horses." Nora waited to see Grant's reaction.

Grant didn't like what he heard, just like she had predicted. "You two were going to leave without me? You can't. I want to find Ron as much as you. How could you just leave me here?"

Shaw could hear the anger growing in Grant's voice. "We knew you wouldn't be able to make the ride in your condition. What if we came across more First Born soldiers? There would be no way for you to fight."

Grant interrupted, "But I'm better now. There's no way I'm going to stay here while you go out there. That's out of the question."

"We didn't know that," said Nora, "so you still don't have any supplies or weapons. We can't wait any longer—we need to do something."

"I can pack quickly. I don't need that much. What happened to my daggers?" Grant asked, not remembering what had happened after falling off his horse, losing consciousness, and entering Malen. He had no recollection of the people having to forfeit their weapons to get inside the city.

"We had to surrender them up at the gate. That was one of the conditions of entering," Nora said.

"We can stop by a merchant before we leave, and I can buy a weapon." Grant began padding his clothes to check if he had any coins in his pockets, only for him to realize the clothes he was wearing were not his own but those the healers had changed him into upon his arrival. "What happened to my clothes and my pack?"

Abby touched his shoulder. "I have your pack here in the house, but your clothes are gone. They were torn and covered in blood. There was no way to salvage anything you were wearing."

Grant thought frantically about how he could get a new set of clothes and weapons before Nora and Shaw left without him. "Look, just give me some time, and I'll get what I need."

Nora sighed. "It's not just that. You also do not have permission to leave the city. Shaw and I had a meeting with the king. We discussed our plans, and he gave us letters to allow our coming and going. So even if we got what you need, the guards wouldn't let you leave with us."

Grant's eyebrows bent inward. "I don't understand—why would I need permission to leave?" He was getting frustrated.

"That was another condition we had to adhere to. Everyone is restricted to this one residential quarter while under the protection of the treaty," Nora explained.

Grant looked at the fading sun lowering itself below the trees beyond the lake. "What if I try and see the king? Maybe I can get one of those letters—it shouldn't take long. If I leave right now, he might see me."

"I don't think the guards would bother the king this late," Nora reasoned.

"Then we can all leave tomorrow night. I know you said tonight, but you can't leave without me. Just give it one more day, I'll get a letter. I have to go with you—we can find a way to the Ark of Redemption together," Grant pleaded.

"Grant, I . . ." Nora began, but Grant cut her off.

"Nora, Ron's like a brother to me. You can't just leave me here to do nothing. What good will I be if I can't help? We've come all this way. Please don't leave me behind." Grant's voice slightly cracked as he pled.

Shaw remained silent. This was not his decision to make. Nora had to decide if she would wait another day and leave with Grant or tonight without him. An uncomfortable silence lingered while Nora thought of what to do. The only sound came from a light evening breeze brushing against the gentle, lapping water of the lake.

"If I was in your position," Grant said, "I would not leave you behind."

Nora wasn't happy about her decision, but she knew in the end she couldn't leave him. So she agreed to wait one more night.

Grant wasted no time trying to get an audience with the king. Once morning came, Nora and Shaw asked one of the guards to call for Lieutenant Basset. The lieutenant wondered why they were still in the city, but Nora explained that Grant needed a letter as well.

Lieutenant Basset took them to the palace, and Nora saw the same wonderous look she'd worn when Grant laid his eyes on the palace. Once inside, Lieutenant

Basset had them wait in the hall outside the throne room while he went to see if the king would grant an audience. Nora and Shaw showed Grant how to bow appropriately, low and with their right hand in the center of their chest.

Lieutenant Basset came back. "King Ahven is very busy this morning, but he's willing to see you, although you must make it brief. If what you need takes too long, he will dismiss you and ask you to come back at a later time. When that may be exactly is anyone's guess."

The lieutenant looked Grant up and down, seeing his dirty clothes and over a week's worth of beard growth. He was rather unfit, appearance-wise, to stand in front of the king. However, since the king was in a rush, the lieutenant figured it didn't matter all that much.

They entered the throne room and stood before the king, bowing low and reintroducing themselves along with Grant while the king was signing papers with a feather quill. His advisors read aloud what was being signed. King Ahven looked up briefly and gave a grumble. "What can I do for you?"

Nora stepped forward and quickly explained why they needed a letter for Grant. King Ahven looked at him standing behind her. "I will approve a letter for you, young man, based on the merit of these two, but if you come into this room again looking as you do now, this will be the last time you ever set foot within my palace." King Ahven looked to Lieutenant Basset. "Write a letter for him, and be off. I don't have time for such petty business." Then, with a wave of his hand, the king dismissed them, and they followed the lieutenant to the main hall.

"That went better than expected." Basset said. "Wait here while I draw up a letter for you." He came back with the letter stamped with the official seal of the king. As they were headed out of place, Nora asked if they could stop by the armory, seeing as Grant had no weapons. The lieutenant obliged.

Grant was amazed when they entered the armory. He had never seen so many finely crafted weapons before. He walked around, admiring the craftsmanship that had been put into each weapon until he became awestruck at a pair of blades that stopped him in his tracks. He picked up each blade in his hands, feeling the lightness of the weight. Each had a dark silver hilt with a circular handguard. The blades themselves were an opaque black, running roughly ten inches in length from tip to hilt.

"Back for more, I see." Grant turned to see an old man shuffling around. "I see those caught your eye. Can't blame you." He shuffled his way toward Grant. "These here are made of blackened steel, folded onto itself more times than I care to repeat. Each fold increases its strength, with a full tang to balance the weight. This is a fine set," the blacksmith said, admiring his work.

"How much?" Grant was hoping he could afford such well-crafted blades as his fingers turned the coins lining the bottom of his pocket.

"They are going to cost quite a few coins, seeing as how I am not ordered to allow a price reduction, but as you are with these two," the old man said, looking at Nora and Shaw before continuing, "how about you give me what you have, and if I deem it enough, then you may take them."

Grant felt the coins in his pocket, counting only two silver and five copper pieces. He knew it wouldn't be enough, and felt it would be insulting to the old blacksmith if he offered it. Grant walked over to Nora and Shaw.

"I don't think I have enough to offer. Do you have any coins?" he asked.

Nora and Shaw dug around their own pockets, but they'd run low on coins themselves after purchasing all the supplies the other day. Nora held out her hand. "I have six coppers."

Shaw held out his hand and produced another two silvers. Grant hoped it was enough as he presented the coins to the old blacksmith. The old man eyed the coins in Grant's hand, pushing them around his palm with his finger. "Alright, that looks like it will do. Let me fetch the sheath from the back."

"Wait, really, that was enough?" Grant stammered, but the old man didn't reply. "I can't believe it."

Nora and Shaw were surprised as well. "That was all the coins we had left," Nora said, looking at Grant's clothes.

"I'd rather be able to help fight than look appealing." Grant laughed to himself under his breath.

The old man returned with the sheaths for the blades. "Alright, I'll show you how to put this on, then you can be on your way."

The sheaths were made of dark brown leather, appearing to have a worn texture to hide any tears or scuffs they might suffer during use. Two release hooks attached to the openings, securing the blades, and a belt was fashioned to the back of the sheath. The old man placed the sheath on the small of Grant's lower back and fed the belt strap through the clasp, pulling it tight before fastening.

"Looks like you are all set to me. Although now you stick out like a sore thumb with the brown belt and those white clothes of yours."

Nora and Shaw couldn't help but smile as Grant's face became somewhat flushed from embarrassment. Lieutenant Basset ushered them out of the armory, and put a hand on the old man's shoulder as he left. "Thank you."

His father smiled. "I'll be seeing you soon for the rest of the coins I'm owed." He eyed Lieutenant Basset's hand and the ring he wore. "You have earned that ring."

The lieutenant caught up to Grant, Nora, and Shaw as they stood outside the armory waiting for him. "Is there anything else you need before I escort you back to the residential quarter?" Shaw shook his head, as did Nora. Grant just looked down at himself, taking in how ridiculous he looked in the healers' clothes and his daggers. "I'll take that as a no then."

They followed Lieutenant Basset as he led the way back to the residential quarter, but as they walked, the lieutenant deviated from the path they'd commonly used since being in Malen. Instead, he led them through the streets before stopping at a small shop at the end of the cobble-stoned road. "Here, take this and get yourself something more fitting." Lieutenant Basset held out his hand and dropped three silver coins into Grant's palm.

"I can't accept this—it's too much. Why are you giving me all this?"

The lieutenant looked at Nora and Shaw. "Some people reminded me that as a soldier of Malen, I must tend to the protection and wellbeing of its citizens. Even if those people do not live in the kingdom, I will do what I can for them while they are here."

Grant shook Lieutenant Basset's hand, thanking him for his generosity.

Once they returned to the residential quarter, Lieutenant Basset took his leave, and the trio made their way to the house where Abby and Yulis were staying by the edge of the lake. Grant was happy to change out of his dirty clothes and put on the new ones from the shop. Even though the selection was limited, Grant found what he wanted to wear. He chose faded black pants and a light brown, long-sleeved pullover shirt. Grant didn't take long to have his pack ready, as it still had food left in it. Now, all that was left was to wait for nightfall.

When it finally arrived, their packs were stocked with provisions, and they'd added a clock to each since the wind had picked up over the last few hours. Nora and Shaw stood by the door with their packs while Grant took a moment to say goodbye to Yulis. He picked the boy up, giving him a big hug. "You take good care of your mom while I'm gone, sound good?"

Yulis nodded his head in agreement, wrapping his little arms around Grant's neck once more. Grant set him down and went into the next room to say goodbye to Abby.

The woman pulled Grant close, holding him tightly in her arms. "Promise me you will be safe out there. I understand you have to go, even though I wish you could stay. So please just promise me you will be safe and come back."

Grant backed away from Abby without letting go of her waist; he stared into her eyes, seeing her desire for him to stay. He took to memory the features of her face, from each freckle that sat across the bridge of her nose to the way her mouth curved when she smiled, and the tears he saw building in her eyes.

Finally, he said, "I promise I'll come back. When all this is over, I'll stay, and we can be together, all of us—you, me, and Yulis."

A tear rolled down her face, but Grant caught it with his thumb as he caressed her cheek. Abby stepped closer to him, pulling him toward her until their bodies touched; she reached a hand behind his head, running her fingers through his shaggy blond hair. Then, lifting herself onto her tip-toes, she kissed him as though she would never see him again.

Grant felt the passion and the longing she had for him to stay. He gave in to what he knew—his heart longed for Abby as they shared their embrace. After a minute, they pulled away when they heard the pitter-patter of tiny feet thumping closer. Yulis popped his head from around the corner, smiling at them before taking a hand from each. Grant walked with Abby and the boy to the front door, where he picked up his pack. "You take care, little man."

Yulis smiled; Grant gave Abby a look that needed no words for what he wanted to convey. She knew he was telling her he would be coming back.

The streets were almost barren at this time of night, with the occasional drunk stumbling out of an inn and making their way home. Guards were posted along the street corners as usual, with only one or two stopping to ask what they were doing this late and so heavily armed. It was easy enough for them to be on their way—all they had to do was show the letters. No further explanation was needed. Following the cobblestone road coming up on the north gate, they stopped and gathered their horses, which had been placed in the stables after their arrival. The north gate was less used by most as it was smaller, allowing the width of a wagon to barely fit through. Malen's main point of entry relied heavily on the northeast gate.

Still, since the only bridge crossing the Red Band River had been destroyed during the fight with the First Born, it was best to go through the north gate instead of wading through the stream.

Once the gate closed behind them, the dark seemed to endlessly stretch for miles with no light in sight. The only source of light came from the moon and stars, reflecting off the water, giving them their heading as the horses trotted along the riverbank.

Chapter Twenty

A Message for the King

A lmost three full days had passed since Nora, Shaw, and Grant departed from Malen, and business continued as usual. A young, innocent-looking woman watched as merchants woke early to open their shops, farmers unloaded fresh-picked fruits and vegetables, and town officials were busy rushing back and forth with business they felt was necessary.

All the trivial things the common folk did around the city would amount to nothing once the woman's objective had been met. If the king met with resistance or any form of pushback, it wouldn't matter; all avenues had been considered and planned.

Now all that remained was the last part of the plan.

She would accomplish that tonight, as she'd watched her prey since his arrival in Malen. By now, she understood his habits, likes, and dislikes, and the routes he preferred to take on his coming and goings.

Being able to blend into a crowd had always been easy for her, and she was quite good at it, if only because of her deceptive appearance, non-threatening and diminutive. The job would be handled this night. If there was any hesitation left when the time came, it was only because this would be the first kill she had committed in total, by themselves. She had been involved with murders before, but never responsible for ensuring the act was done entirely. All she had to do was get who she needed in the right place at the right time, and the others finished the job.

This time, the responsibility fell on her, and she didn't want to squander the opportunity to prove herself on this first official task.

Every detail of the plan was ready—the amount of waiting it took for the day to end was mind-numbingly tedious. The orders came from one of the messengers known around Malen, Oroze, and Baddon. It wasn't uncommon for city officials to have messengers make deliveries for them. The king alone had a handful of trusted messengers. Lord Hadal had said once before that he had eyes and ears placed where he wanted them, all he needed to do was bide his time—and once she received the orders, she understood the time had come.

The lights in the city grew brighter and the shadows drew longer until the darkness filled the streets and alleyways. The time was almost upon her to slip out into the night and find her intended target. Pulling a hood to cover her head, the young woman moved slowly through the shadows, as she had done many times before, sneaking past a guard as she clung close to a wall that rounded onto the street. The sound of songs spilled out from several inns as drunken men and women cheered and hollered for another song or more ale. The noise was more than helpful in the event the man she was after turned out to be a screamer. The woman didn't care too much for the screaming; to her, what mattered most was the promise of the position that was to be secured once she proved herself and her unconditional devotion.

It didn't take long to track the man down; he was a creature of habit, as she'd witnessed over the previous weeks. He walked by himself most of the time, stopping by the inns that held a less-than-favorable reputation, ensuring the patrons kept themselves in order. Most did, and the ones that didn't only provide a small distraction. The woman followed quietly behind him and recognized the route he was walking, as she'd committed to memory most of his nightly routes. She broke away from following him, taking side allies and narrow streets that could be moved through swiftly and unseen until she came to where he would draw his last breath. All that was left was to wait for his arrival. The woman checked for the knife tucked inside her right sleeve for reassurance; it was still there. Then she sat in a dark corner where the wall met the main gate of Malen.

During the day, the gate was one of the most heavily guarded areas in the kingdom besides the palace, but at night, the only guards were the ones put in charge of patrolling different sections of the city. Tonight, her target was charged with patrolling the northeast section of the city. She heard footsteps coming, growing louder against the cobblestone. Seeing him come into view from around the corner, the woman let out a moan, not so distressing as for him to try and acquire more guards for help, but just enough to catch his attention. The moaning continued, but she added the act of dry heaving, giving off the impression she'd had too much ale, and before making it home, drunkenly tried to sleep it off at the gate.

He approached cautiously. "Is everything alright?"

Playing it off as best she could, the woman slurred, "I'm fine, just trying to get a nap before heading home."

Huffing to himself, he walked over and prepared to lend his assistance in getting the drunk back to their home. He had done this on more than one occasion, so this was nothing new. "Alright, let's get you up and get you home." He reached down and pulled her up to her feet while she swayed from side to side. He threw her right arm around his shoulders, steadying her to take a few steps. "There you go. Just lean on me, and we'll get you home."

No more than three steps were taken when he stopped; he began to frantically clutch at his throat while the warmth of his blood poured over his hands. He fell to the ground, trying to breathe, but every attempt failed. He gasped for air, holding his throat with one hand reaching out with the other as he grabbed handful after handful of the woman's cloak, watching her above him, holding a small knife covered in his blood.

The blood began to ooze out onto the street, his breathing slowed, and the panic that was once in his eyes started to fade. His hand held tight to the piece of the cloak he was able to grab, but it slowly released its grip and fell to the ground.

The woman stood staring at his body on the ground, watching the blood flow in between the cobblestones. She heard no screams as she watched him die; it almost seemed like a peaceful way to She hadn't realized it could be done so easily; if she had known that this way was an alternative, she could have performed the other tasks as well, without the need of others. A sense of pride swelled within her chest; she'd done it, and she knew the lord would be pleased to hear of her success, but she still had one thing left to do. Kneeling down beside the body, the woman dipper her fingers in the warm blood along the cobblestone.

* * *

It wasn't until morning that he was found. Alarms rang throughout the kingdom, and guards encircled the area, keeping the gate shut, letting no one through. General Sydell ordered a lockdown on the entire city before making his way to the palace to inform King Ahven. When he reached the palace, he wasted no time with customs or courtesies, for he knew the matter at hand far exceeded such pleasantries. As the general pushed his way into the throne room, King Ahven met his gaze.

"What is the meaning of this, General? You know better than to barge in unannounced."

"I beg your apologies, Your Majesty, but I came as quickly as I could—one of our officers was murdered inside the main gate last night. It is of great importance that you come with me. There is something you need to see."

King Ahven stood with fury in his eyes. "No one leaves the city. I want you to put out a mandatory curfew and have three guards stationed at every post until we can apprehend this murderer. As such, you will take every single one of those refugees from Meno and throw them in the holding cells. I did my part and stood by the treaties of old, but until we know who committed this crime, they are all to be locked away."

"Yes, Your Majesty." General Sydell bowed slightly.

"Tell me, General, who was murdered?"

* * *

King Ahven stood next to the general as they looked over the body. He hadn't wanted to believe it when he heard it was one of his officers who had fallen victim to such a crime, but he confirmed it with his own eyes. Lieutenant Basset's body had been propped against the gate; bloodsplatter covered his once-green-shouldered armor plate.

"Who would do such a thing?" King Ahven spoke aloud to himself.

Lieutenant Basset's breastplate had been removed along with his chainmail and shirt, leaving his chest exposed, showing an FB carved into his flesh. King Ahven broke his gaze from the lieutenant's body and looked at the gate. A message was written there in blood.

Submit and be rewarded. Resist and suffer, for the light of the breaking day will be your ruin.

Chapter Twenty-One

The Impending Storm

T he cold bite of the wind found its way through Nora, Grant, and Shaw's clothes, requiring them to unpack their cloaks. Alongside the sounds of rustling grass and rushing water from the river, not many words were shared between them. Each of them was on edge as they expected the First Born to be waiting somewhere either before or after the bridge. Nora had stressed before leaving that while it would be difficult to travel during the day, they would if need be. Most of the day would be used for resting and waiting until the sun was low enough that they could continue.

The night sky began to brighten, revealing treetops in the distance. Shaw pointed. "We should make camp by those trees—they should give us a good amount of cover during the day. Another hour or two of riding, if I had to guess."

There was no sign of the First Born during the night, and while the sun rose, the way ahead looked clear for the time being. They dismounted their horses, leading them by their reins into the trees. Shaw stopped and found a spot with a small clearing buried within a cluster of trees, allowing them to rest and have enough coverage to be safe. Shaw pulled some vegetables from his pack and fed each horse, giving their thick necks a pat before sitting down to rest.

"So if we find a way into this place, this Ark of Redemption, then what?" Grant asked openly, not directing the question toward either of his companions.

Standing up, Shaw walked over to a shrub at the base of a tree, breaking off a small branch before sitting back down on the ground. "Before we can even think of reaching the Ark, we need to figure out how we are going to get around these." Shaw dug the tip of the branch into the ground, marking their position in relation to the river, the bridge, Oroze, and the surrounding villages he knew about. "This is the best-case scenario, so bear with me—if we make it to the bridge with no interference, we can make our way past Meno, or whatever is left of it." Shaw marked an X in the dirt. "We know Noic is here, Oroze is here, and the Ark is somewhere around here." He marked an X for all the areas he knew about before continuing. "What we don't know is what is around here." Shaw drew a circle covering a wide span of the map drawn in the dirt. "Even if we avoid detection all the way through Noic, this area is going to be our biggest challenge. Depending on how close we want to get, we will have to leave the horses behind and go on foot, but like I said, that's if all goes according to plan."

Grant looked at the map, thinking of other possible routes they could take. "This would be risky and certainly dangerous, but what if we went this way?" He drew a line in the dirt with his finger. "What if we head back toward Collins's house, and once we get close to Oroze, we leave the horses and skirt alongside the outer walls until we reach the east side? It's so close I don't think anyone would expect us to be there, and going along the wall at night would make things easier as well."

Shaw rubbed his trimmed beard, contemplating Grant's idea.

Nora only found one issue with his plan. "The only problem is that we don't know what is around the wall. What if guard posts or sentries are patrolling the outer walls at night? I do agree it's the last place they would look for us, but it seems like too big of a risk, and without the horses, if we were spotted so close, it would be near impossible to get away."

Frustration loomed over them as they looked at the dirt map, contemplating the best option. Besides being detected, they all were struggling with the same problem—they all had no idea of what was on the east side of Oroze. That was the only unknown, the one piece to the puzzle they were missing. Shaw sighed as another idea came to mind, but he only chose to voice it because he wanted more options, even if the ones presented were not the best.

"There is another way, but it may prove ineffective. If what I'm thinking doesn't work, then we would have wasted more time by backtracking, and we would end up being in the same position that we're in now. If it works, then we would be extremely lucky, but the problem is the same as the one we face with the east side or Oroze." Shaw dragged the stick through the dirt. "We could try to go around the back side of the mountain and avoid detection altogether, but like I said, we don't know who or what occupies that area. It would be a shot in the dark, but it's a shot nonetheless."

Every idea appeared to come to the same conclusion—no matter what they did, they would have to face what lay in the unknown areas around Oroze, as well as any First Born soldiers they may encounter along the way. They all knew one thing, though. They knew they had to pick a plan and stick to it. Ron's life depended on it.

Nora spoke after a long bout of silent thinking. "I think we should take this way." She pointed to a route on the dirt map that would take them past Meno by Noic and have their approach come from the northeast side.

"Why that way?" Shaw asked.

"I thought about it, and do you remember when we rode from Collins's house to Meno?"

"I do," Shaw replied, wondering where she was going with this idea.

"Well, before the valley becomes flat, you know how it was when we were in Meno and Noic? What if we round the valley using the depressions in the land to our advantage? It may take longer, but it would give us cover, and if we're lucky enough during the day, we should be able to see what lies ahead."

"That's not a bad idea, not bad at all." Shaw smiled at Nora. They all knew what could go wrong with her plan, but no one had to voice it. It was the best option they had; it was also the only one they could agree on. As much as they wanted this strategy to work, they knew it would not go exactly as planned.

"Alright, now that we have an idea of how to get closer to the Ark, what are we going to do once we reach it?" Grant asked.

Shaw scratched his beard. "That question is a different beast entirely."

"Say we do manage to find a way inside," Grant said. "We won't know where we are or where Ron is being held. I'm sure the place is going to be full of First Born soldiers." Then a thought came to him. "Do you think if we found a way in and came back to Malen, the king would help us?" Of course, Nora and Shaw already knew the answer to that.

"We talked to King Ahven about the First Born already, and while he has helped us so far, he said he would only do so within the walls of his kingdom. Other than that, we're on our own." The hope they'd felt after agreeing on a plan quickly faded as another problem mounted on top of an already-heavy load.

Shaw stood up, stretched his legs, and yawned. "Why don't we pick this back up after we get some rest? Perhaps we can think of a solution after a few hours' sleep."

There was no argument from Nora or Grant. Shaw took the first watch, spending his time tending to the horses, making sure they had water and another carrot or stick of celery to hold them over through the day. He woke Nora for her watch when his time was up, and she did the same to Grant. Once the sun had set below the trees, they finished eating, gathered their packs along with the reins, and guided the horses from the trees back toward the Red Band river.

The bridge was still a few hours away after a few days as the steady trot of the horses continued along the riverbank. A persistent wind whistled in the air; thankfully, the wind did not have a chill to it this night. It wasn't until it shifted direction that all three became alarmed at what they smelled. Even though they saw no light in the distance, they could smell the smoke of a campfire.

With the bridge coming into view, they needed to decide if they wanted to cross over tonight and forgo the cover of the remaining trees or wait to cross and use a full night cycle the next day. They agreed to stop and wait until the next night to continue.

Throughout the following day, during each watch, Nora, Grant, and Shaw would slowly creep to the tree line to see if the bridge and the immediate area stayed clear of First Born soldiers. Being able to smell the smoke from a campfire told them the First Born was on the other side of the bridge, but since the wind picked up, there was no way to be sure about how far they actually were. Checking every few hours gave them reassurance that, in the meantime, they were safe.

Dark clouds moved in as the night began to overtake the sky, but it wasn't dark enough for them to leave the cover of the trees. While waiting, Grant had reopened the discussion of what should be done once they found and possibly entered the Ark. But again the question remained unanswered, as no one had any good ideas.

"I guess the best we could do would be to not get caught—once we get caught, it's over," Nora said. Grant and Shaw looked at one another, knowing that what she said was true.

It was a hard truth to hear, and even harder to come to terms with, but Shaw spoke up. "It may seem like this could all be in vain if we fail, but we can't just give up based on a maybe. I've said it before, and I'll say it again—there is always hope. Even if it's just a small sliver, it's still there."

Nora had heard Shaw's rallying speeches before, and each time, his words helped her regain her resolve. This time was no different. If Shaw could keep hope alive after losing his daughter Allurin and wife Thea, then surely Nora could too. Ron still had a chance to be saved, and there was no giving up on that chance. Grant knew that he couldn't give up either. He knew Ron would do the same for him without a moment's notice.

Ever since they'd met, they'd been inseparable; every day for eight years, they were side by side. Ron was the brother Grant had always wanted. Even his parents behaved as if Ron was one of their own. There was no way Grant would let his brother down, not in this life or the next.

A low rumbling echoed across the sky with quick flashes of light from the northwest breaking over the Storming Mountains. The wind picked up and brought with it the bitter cold. Shaw looked out from the tree line, straining his eyes to see if the way was clear.

Once he approved, he led the others toward the bridge, only pausing for a moment to fasten his cloak, pulling over his hood as he said, "There could be a storm coming."

Light rain began to fall as the storm gained momentum and moved outward from the mountains. Thunder chased after the rainfall, increasing in intensity, masking any sound of the horses' hooves, allowing them an opportunity to gallop and cover more ground. Nora knew it wouldn't be long until they reached the first depression within the valley, not far outside where Meno used to be. They slowed their horses to a halt as they looked out and saw the glow of fires burning within the remains of the town.

Grant could feel his anger in the pit of his stomach, but he calmed himself when he saw Nora pull her horse away and move on. Nora felt her horse slow without her pulling the reins and wondered what was wrong. She gently spurred the horse to continue forward, but all she got was a whinny and a step back. Then thunder erupted above their heads, frightening the horses. Next, lightning struck, giving light to their surroundings. Nora now understood why her horse refused to go any farther.

Another bolt shot through the sky. Nora, Grant, and Shaw saw the horses' legs covered in thick, slippery mud a quarter of the way past their hooves. It was no longer an option to go through the depression until the storm subsided. Yet the rain continued to come down harder. "We need to find another way," Nora shouted over the rain and thunder.

"The only other way would bring us to close to Meno," Shaw said. "It's either that, or we go back and wait for the storm to pass."

Nora was no more than five feet from Shaw, but her voice barely carried that far through the rain. "Let's go back—we don't know how many soldiers are in Meno!"

Turning the horses back the way they came proved complicated; the winds and rain pushed against them with the cold of each drop seeping through their clothes and into their bones. Glancing over through the rain as they passed Meno once more, they saw a fire still lit inside a tent that remained intact. Thunder cracked, and Nora spun her head to look forward. Her eyes grew wide as she felt a strong, rapid pulse rush through her body. Then, jolting back on the reins, she had everyone stop. Lighting flashed, revealing what was up ahead. Squinting her eyes, Nora was able to make out two wagons and what looked like a small battalion of soldiers heading toward the bridge they desperately needed to cross.

"What should we do? We can't go back that way," Grant said. Shaw wondered the same thing. Nora knew what to do, but she wished she could avoid it.

"We need to go through Meno. We can't fight that many at once." Her voice broke against the wind and rain.

"There could be more than a dozen First Born in Meno. It's too dangerous," Grant shouted back.

"There must be another way," Shaw said, voicing his concern.

"There is only one fire—it's late, cold, and loud. If we have any luck at all, most of the soldiers should be asleep. This may be our best chance," Nora shouted.

"Alright, if it's the best way." Grant didn't like the idea, but he trusted her.

"When we get closer, we will need to leave the horses. If we can clear the camp, we can come back for them." Nora pulled her horse to the right, slowly trotting toward the glow emitting from inside the canvas of the tent.

Nora saw what very well could have been the last remaining hitching post left within the ruins of Meno. Luckily, it wasn't so close to the tents to arouse suspicion, not that there was much movement within the camp. Nora, Shaw, and Grant pulled their cloaks tight, approaching the tents with weapons drawn. Mud caked around their boots while the rain and thunder drowned out the squelching of each step. Each lightning strike gave them a brief opportunity to catch a glimpse of what was left of Meno. Half-burned tents and piles of wet black remnants littered the grounds.

Nora approached the tent, putting her ear to the canvas, hoping she could discern any words over the downpour of rain. Fortunately, she was able to recognize a word or two between the booms of thunder. She held up a hand, motioning for Shaw to take the right side. He understood, slowly stalking to the right and placing his bow back over his shoulder. He removed two arrows from his quiver, one for each hand, as he grabbed just behind the steel tips. Grant followed behind Nora, adjusting the grip on his blades. Grant was glad they had the element of surprise, but a part of him wished the First Born soldiers were more awake. He could feel the anger build with every step he took. He knew he wanted to fight, but he wasn't ready to admit that fully to himself yet. Standing just around the opening of the tent, Nora took a deep breath while Shaw and Grant waited to follow her lead.

They moved fast and silent. The soldiers had no chance to react to the swiftness and force of the onslaught that ended their lives. For the few soldiers still awake, their wide-eyed looks of panic became the last expression their faces would ever make. Shaw smothered the fire, while Grant and Nora looked for the next tent housing any more of the First Born soldiers. The only noise from the tent was the indistinguishable drops of blood dripping steadily into the pools collecting under the dead soldiers

Then, soundlessly, using whatever cover they could to conceal themselves, they made their way deeper into camp, moving as carefully as possible, getting closer to the center. Suddenly Grant tripped, falling to a knee in the mud. He didn't know what he'd tripped over, but as he looked back, lightning struck.

His eyes took in the sight of a human leg; he turned his head, following the leg up to the body of a dead, mud-covered woman, clothed only from the waist up. Another bolt of lightning ripped through the blackened sky. It became apparent that the piles of what they thought to be burnt tents or belongings were, in fact, dead bodies stacked on top of each other. They looked around, not understanding how they didn't see it before; perhaps they were too focused on reaching the tent to notice, or it was too dark to make out the bodies that plagued the streets.

No one had to guess anymore what had happened to people who stayed behind. Shaw held his head, heavy with sadness for the dead. Nora covered her mouth with a hand as shock set in. Grant felt a solitary tear fall down his cheek mixing with the rain. Men, women, and children carelessly stacked upon one another was a sight they had never seen before. Grant closed his eyes, wishing he could go back in time and convince these people to come with him when they had the chance.

He knew he should have tried harder, and remembered the conversation with Abby when she told him he'd tried, but it was the people's choice to stay. He kept thinking, though, what if he'd taken their choice away? If he'd forced everyone to go with him, they would all be alive. Finally, he opened his eyes as the thought of what the women and children were forced to suffer through before the graciousness of death relieved them from their tormentor's grasp.

Grant couldn't stomach picturing such images in his mind, but having his eyes open was no better. He looked upon the aftermath of what the soldiers had done, seeing the stripped bodies of the ones left behind. Again, hatred filled Grant; he let it flow through him this time, giving way to it, to the rising heat coursing through his body.

Grant noticed a larger tent in the distance that looked to have endured the destruction better than the others. They moved toward it. The dim light from a flickering oil lamp marked the bodies of sleeping soldiers as the light cast shadows around each body. More than ten soldiers slept on the floor.

Nora, Grant, and Shaw spread out among them, crouching low. Grant struck first and fast. He plunged a dagger into two men's chests, leaving the blades in place as he covered their mouths with his free hand, feeling the muffled screams soften against his palm as the life drained from them. Grant felt a sensation of calm during the soldiers' struggle to live, and only when their struggle stopped did he remove his daggers and move on to the next victim with unmatched speed.

Nora moved from soldier to soldier rather quickly as well, using the sharpened point of her staff to stab each soldier where the top of the sternum met the base of the neck, severing any chance to scream. Nora didn't linger with each kill as Grant did—she knew she had to kill them, but she derived no pleasure from doing so, even with the anger she held for the First Born.

Shaw was much more meticulous; he simply cut each carotid artery with his arrow tips, barely waiting for the soldier to bleed out before moving on. When Nora and Shaw looked to see if any other soldiers remained, they saw Grant standing at the back of the tent with the last First Born soldier. Grant stood there holding him at the tip of his blade with the soldier's hands bound behind his back. He then dragged the other blade across the soldier's cheek, smearing the blood of his comrades without breaking eye contact.

"Tell me why you did this. Tell me why, and once you do, I'll allow you to join the rest of these animals, understand?" Grant said, seething. The soldier was trembling, opening his mouth to speak until Grant cut him off, pressing his blade harder against his throat. "You had better give me a good answer. I don't want to hear anything about, 'oh, I was ordered to do it, it's not my fault.' Be honest."

The soldier nodded in agreement.

Nora and Shaw stood at Grant's side. "Grant, what are you doing? We need to keep going," Nora said, trying to hurry him along, but he held his gaze on the soldier.

"I want to know why. I can't find a reason as to why someone would do this to defenseless people. So before he dies, he's going to tell me."

"Does it matter? What's done is done. We can't change that. What happened here is terrible, but we need to move now." The words hurt, but she said them anyway.

"Does it matter? Of course it matters, Nora. Did you see what they did? How long did these people have to suffer, and for what? That's what I want to know, so yes, it matters. It matters to me." Nora saw the intensity in Grant's eyes and realized whatever she said, he was going to stay until he got his answer.

"Go on," Grant said.

"We were ordered to . . ." Grant pushed the tip of the dagger into his skin. "But, but, but the others they went on a rampage, taking whatever they wanted, whoever they wanted. That's what they do when taking over. The spoils of war have no boundaries," the soldier said.

"So that's it? The spoils of war is your reason. The spoils of war, when there is no war being waged except by you? No one else wants a war, but that doesn't matter to the First Born since you are the ones creating it, right?" Grant said, trembling with anger.

The soldier didn't have anything else to say. Grant was right in his assessment, and the soldier knew it. The trembling stopped as a crooked smile took form. "Lord Hadal will take this land over, and when he does, it will be a freer land than ever before. You think we are starting a war? No, no, you haven't even begun to see a war. The forge will be open. It's only a matter of time now until Lord Hadal succeeds as he has promised. Then you will have your war, and trust me, it will not be a war you can win. And this, this is just a taste of the hell the First Born will rain down upon the people."

"What do you mean the forge will be open? How is that possible?" Grant said through gritted teeth.

"I don't know, but it will happen. The lord has said so." A maniacal laugh grew in the soldier's throat, but Grant had a smirk of his own.

"Well, it's too bad you won't be alive to see it then. Now let me hear you scream." Nora and Shaw looked at each other in confusion at the last words Grant spoke.

"Grant, what are you—" Nora stopped talking when Grant sheathed one blade, freeing his hand and moving the blade of his other dagger from the man's neck to his chest. He placed it just above his heart while his hand gently covered the soldier's mouth. The smile faded from the soldier's lips as he braced for a quick death, but this death was anything but quick. Grant slowly inserted the tip of the dagger into his skin, feeling the separation of flesh as he pushed deeper. The soldier held his screams for as long as he could, but they erupted out only to be caught by Grant's palm. While the blade moved forward inch by inch, Grant never looked away.

The soldier realized at that moment what was happening to Grant, much like the man from the bar in Noic had. The look in Grant's eyes was unmistakable, but Grant didn't know what it was, and the soldier would never speak it. The muffled screams felt prolonged to Nora and Shaw, who stood by, watching him slowly kill this man until Shaw had his fill and placed his hand upon Grant's, shoving the dagger the rest of the way in.

"What are you doing? I wasn't finished."

Shaw didn't recognize Grant's face. The anger had contorted his features. "Yes, you are. We are not here to torture these people, regardless of how much they deserve it. We are not like them. We need to do what we must and move on. We can avenge the victims of Meno in other ways, but not like this and not at the expense of getting caught."

Grant breathed in deep when he felt a hand on his shoulder.

"I understand how you feel, but Shaw is right," Nora said calmly. "We need to move. We have bigger things to worry about now. If there really is a war coming and this Lord Hadal can open the forge, we need to be ready."

Grant took another breath, then slowly exhaled, feeling his anger slip away. He looked to Shaw. "How can someone open the forge?"

Shaw rubbed his beard. "I'm not sure. From what I know, only a very powerful wielder can open it. There hasn't been a wielder that strong since Taroth, so I doubt this lord can open it, but we will be in trouble if he can. Remember that letter Ron found in his brother's room? I recall it said something about a convergence of two worlds. The only thing I can think of is that he plans to bring whatever is in the forge into this world, but it still doesn't make sense."

"Well, at least we got something out of that guy. Too bad it just makes things more confusing." Grant retrieved his dagger from the dead man's chest, hooking the blade back into its sheath. "Let's try and get through the rest of Meno quickly, okay? We still have some ground to cover, and night won't last forever."

Nora shot Shaw a concerned glance; they had seen Grant become increasingly unstable, and they both worried about him. They walked behind him to the front of the tent, but he stumbled onto his knees.

"Grant, are you okay?"

Nora and Shaw were at his sides, helping him to his feet. "I'm okay. I just feel really tired all of a sudden. Must be traveling during the nights—I'm more of a day person if anything." He laughed to himself. Grant knew he'd felt this before but didn't want to say anything. The last time he'd felt this exhausted was when he fought the First Born with Alas on the bridge. He didn't understand it, but he was starting to see a connection.

The rest of Meno contained at most another three or four soldiers, who were dispatched quickly. Nora reasoned it wouldn't be practical to have a large force all waiting in one spot where they could possibly be bypassed altogether. Instead, it would make more sense to be spread out, covering a larger area in hopes of cutting off other potential routes. After retrieving their horses, they came up with a plan to ride alongside the hills they originally wanted to use. Since the storm wouldn't allow them to hide within the depression, they chose to ride along the face of a hill, swinging wide to avoid roads and Noic altogether.

There was plenty of night left, but the storm was relentless, never seeming to ease up. Their clothes were soaked, the cold penetrated their skin, and they knew it would take another few hours to reach Noic's encampment. Noic was a much larger, more established village, with people having lived there for almost an entire year since the occupation of Oroze by the First Born. Unlike Meno, Noic was made up of supporters who followed the First Born ideals, although some of its people had only pledged their loyalty to survive and live in whatever peace they were being offered. There would be more soldiers, and they knew they would not get as lucky as they had in Meno.

Leaving behind the small amount of safety the hills provided, they cut through the valley. Through the darkness, rain, and thunder, Nora was able to see dim-glowing clusters of fire in the distance, giving them a good indication of how far they were from Noic. "We will have to swing around to the right—that will bring us closest to where the Ark's entrance should be," Nora said as Shaw pulled his horse alongside her.

"We will need to take extra caution. We don't know what's out there."

"Like you always say, I guess we will hope for the best."

Besides the rain and thunder, the only thing they could hear was the rattling of their teeth as they shivered in the cold. Nora patted her horse's neck, giving it the comfort and reassurance she felt it needed. The outskirts of Noic were visible with each strike of lightning, along with the glow of the fires remaining in the village; Nora knew they were far enough away to slip by unnoticed.

Unfortunately, they came across two paths leading farther to the left and one straight down the middle with a makeshift signpost at the fork as they continued forward. The wooden arrow pointing north read "Oroze," and the arrow pointing east read "Lalin." A pulse suddenly ran up Nora's spine, jolting her in her saddle. She spun her head to the right, then left, not seeing anything. She knew something happened, and she felt it, or at least she thought it did. Shaw noticed Nora's movements. "Everything alright?" he asked.

"No, something's not right—I'm not sure what, but something's coming," she said, trying not to sound too worried, but her voice conveyed it anyway. Shaw and Grant looked around in all directions, but they couldn't see anything in the dark.

"Is it the First Born?" Grant asked.

"I don't know."

Faint shouts traveled with the rain on the wind. As the voices got louder, another bolt flashed, striking the ground not far from where they stood. It illuminated the soldiers walking along the path, heading east away from Noic and west away from Lalin, soldiers escorting wagons full of supplies to be traded between each encampment by the looks of it. Each wagon looked to have roughly a dozen men guarding each side.

The sky cracked with thunder and flashed with lightning, frightening Grant's horse, which let out a succession of whinnies. Grant tried to regain control, pulling the reins in, shushing the horse, hoping to calm its fright, but it was too late. The soldiers were close enough to hear the horse's cry. The First Born slowed their wagons and grouped together, drawing their swords as they advanced.

Nora was lost in thought. Another pulse jolted up her spine—she saw the soldiers coming, but that wasn't what concerned her. She didn't know what it was, but something else was coming, something more dangerous than soldiers, something worse.

"Nora, we need to go," Grant said despite his desire to kill the soldiers; he knew there would be too many, so he shook her shoulder, trying to rouse her from her thoughts. She looked at him, seeing his mouth move, but she wasn't listening to the words. Another pulse shot through her, stronger. She looked around, trying to see what was coming, but there was only dark.

"Nora, Nora!" Grant shouted, inches away from her. "What are you doing? We have to go."

Pulse after pulse hit her spine until her eyes widened with fear. "It's here," Nora said.

Grant looked at her like she was crazy. "We know, the soldiers are right over there, that's what I've been trying to tell you."

"No, Grant, the First Born doesn't matter—something else has come."

"What are you talking about? There's nothing else out here." Grant was getting frustrated that she wasn't listening. But another part of him wanted the soldiers to come—he wanted to unleash his fury upon them.

Grant unhooked his blades, preparing to fight. Nora spoke again. "It's here." She turned her head around, looking back the way they came; Shaw and Grant looked into the dark with her while the soldiers continued advancing. A shimmer appeared there, almost like heat waves rising from the ground with a crackle that sounded like sap bursting in a new fire.

"What in the world?" Grants jaw dropped at what he saw.

Shaw looked on in horror. "This can't be possible."

The soldiers continued marching toward them, but Nora, Shaw, and Grant sat still atop their horses, watching the shimmer in the dark. Then an ear-deafening crack rang out through the night, dropping the oncoming soldiers to their knees. They clutched their ears, screaming in pain. Nora, Grant, and Shaw held their own ears as the ringing engulfed the world around them. Nora looked toward the shimmer, seeing a dark orange glow solidify in front of them. The shimmer had torn open, exposing a rift that flickered unsteadily. The First Born's attention was now entirely on the orange fissure in the darkness.

"Shaw, what is that?" Nora asked, feeling her voice shake.

"That is a forge gate."

They were all mesmerized by the glow. Water dripped from mouths hanging open; no one had yet seen an opening to the forge, not even Shaw. He had only heard the stories from his childhood and during his studies over the years. To actually see a forge gate in front of him was something he'd never fathomed would happen in his lifetime. Nora could still feel a pulse racing through her back, the same pulse that warned her about the direction in which the forge gate would open, but she knew there was something else coming.

A high-pitched shriek broke through the storm's persistent rain and thunder, jolting all who bore witness to the awe that was the forge. A long, hairless leg protruded from the dark orange opening, the glow of the gate detailing the tight, gray, wax-like skin wrapped around the freakishly long, boney leg. Sharpened fingers wrapped the edge of the forge gate, pulling the creature forth into full view.

Horror filled Nora's mind as she looked upon the emerging monstrosity. Rows of sharp teeth its mouth as it let out another shriek into the night, eyes moving around wildly, trying to adjust to the sudden onset of darkness it had just come into.

Nora's eyes were pulled back to the forge gate as she saw another hand come through. Two creatures now stood in front of the forge gate, the light illuminating their wet, distorted bodies. Then the gate vanished, and they were plunged back into the surrounding darkness. "Where did it go?" Grant asked, looking at the creatures during each lightning strike.

"I don't—" Before Nora could finish answering, another ear-piercing bang ripped through the sky. Farther off to the left, another forge gate appeared in the dark. It was too far away to make out any detail of what was coming through, but the shapes they could see were not human. Howls and shrieks filled the air around them as the forge gate vanished yet again, only for another to appear moments later in a different location.

"We need to run," Nora shouted, pulling the reins and turning her horse around.

"Run where?" Grant asked, knowing there was no safe place to flee to.

Nora looked at Grant. "Anywhere but here." With a swift kick, the horses took off, running in the opposite direction; Grant looked back only to see the creatures running full speed toward the First Born remaining in the area, tearing them apart once contact was made. Screams of dying men rang out against the clashing of steel and claws. Shrieks echoed from the creatures, slowly fading out of earshot with each gallop.

Dread gripped Nora, Grant, and Shaw as their horses drew them closer to the walls of Oroze, but Nora hoped the dark would conceal them from the guards. Fires in the distance rose to life in response to the shrieks, roars, and howls from behind them. The entirety of Noic was now awake with the sudden movements of soldiers preparing for an enemy they were not ready to face. Following the path between the two camps, Nora was able to see the ominous mountains that contained an entrance to the Ark of Redemption.

Her back pulsed, stiffening as her body reacted on its own accord. She reached behind her, pulling her staff free of its clasp and seizing the etched lines tightly, and in a powerful backward motion, stabbed at the dark behind her. A screech cried out, drawing Grant and Shaw's attention to Nora.

She turned her head to see the creature from the forge gate fall from the tip of her staff. Only its blood remained behind as it tumbled to the ground, clutching at its sunken, boney chest as it struggled to regain its footing. Shaw tightened his legs to his horse's midsection and unshouldered his bow. He readied an arrow and let loose, then fired at the four other creatures that pursued them, hitting one in the shoulder with little effect. The speed at which these creatures ran was unlike anything they had seen. The legs covered more than twice the gait of a regular man. Even given a head start, the creatures were bound to catch up with the galloping horses, just as the creature caught up to Nora.

More fires grew in the night while silhouettes of soldiers fought in Noic against the creatures from the forge. A fire then erupted within the village, large and uncontrolled by the look of it. The only way for the fire to become so intense in the rain was from the oil lamps breaking upon the canvas of the tents, catching fire as the First Born battled what had emerged.

Nora looked ahead, seeing two more small fires appear in the air to either side of the path. The fire reflected off the black armor of guards as the posts came into view. Wooden guard posts with slanted roofs sat on either side, reaching upward about fifteen feet, high enough to get a clear view of all surroundings on a warm day with space enough for two.

"Guard posts!" she shouted while Shaw fired another arrow at the encroaching creatures, turning his head to look. They saw the guards ready their arrows as Shaw did the same in anticipation, hoping they would miss as it would be nearly impossible to dodge or deflect an arrow in the dark. The guards fired, and Nora, Grant, and Shaw prepared for the worst, only to feel the displaced air rush by their faces ending in dull thuds behind them. Each arrow had hit its intended target.

Whether it was the rain and the dark that concealed who they were or the lanky deformities that followed, it didn't matter. What did was that when Nora looked beyond the guard posts, she saw the kingdom of Oroze come to life. Beacons were lit, shadows moved along the walls, and a bell began to ring. She didn't need to know a lot about Oroze, but she knew that was an alarm, and now this path could very well be a one-way trip.

The horses raced along, arrows continued to zip past, sinking into the creatures biting and clawing at their hooves. Then, just as they were about to run between the guard posts, two long, gray bodies leaped into the air, crashing into the guard posts. Wood beams snapped and splintered, collapsing down into the mud and trapping the First Born guards underneath the slanted roofs and debris. The horses grunted and pulled at the reins in fright, jumping over the broken wooden beams that landed in their path.

Grant looked back, seeing the creatures crawl on top of the fallen debris, eyeing their prey, opening their mouths, exposing the rows of razor-sharp teeth. He focused through the dark and through the rain, watching as the First Born soldier tried to free himself. The creature's head jerked up, locking orange eyes with Grant. Fear ran through him, but he knew the fate that awaited the First Born soldier. A grin found its way to Grant's face before he broke eye contact. His attention was brought back to the fact that they were still being chased by two of those things from the forge. He yelled through the noise. "Nora, where are you taking us?"

"As close to Oroze as possible. Maybe this way, these creatures can create a distraction, and we can get away from here."

Panting hard, running through the mud, the horses were being pushed beyond their limits. Stopping was not an option, as it would most certainly lead to their death. The outer walls of Oroze loomed as they drew closer, trying to stay more to the east of the mountain, hoping to see any opening that would lead to the Ark. The horses abandoned the road, cutting across the fields where the mud was thicker, but the terror drove them forward, though they still gained little ground ahead of the creatures.

Finally, at long last, Nora saw what looked to be a door of stone in the mountain. She felt hope grow the closer they got to it, but the joy was short-lived once she realized they had no way of opening the door. She glanced back to see how far behind the creatures were, and found herself looking into the orange eyes as they covered the lost ground and built more speed.

Nora's thoughts raced through her head, trying to find a way to get inside and avoid being torn apart. Then, loud shrieks cried out in tandem from behind. Turning her head, she saw the creatures leap in the air, and she suddenly felt weightless. Her eyes dashed wildly, looking to Grant and Shaw as they flew through the air, striking hard into the ground, sliding through the mud, and tumbling to a halt while the creatures passed overhead and crashed into the stone door of the ark.

Nora looked to the horses in a daze, not knowing what had happened. Then she saw that they'd stepped off a knoll with pooled water below. As much as she wanted to make sure the steeds were okay, she knew there was no time. "Shaw, Grant, are you okay?" she yelled out, trying to stand in the process.

"We're fine," they shouted as they regrouped, clutching their weapons, and turned quickly toward the mountainside. They heard a shriek and watched as one of the creatures pulled itself forward in the mud with its long, bony fingers. The creature's movements caused a slab of stone to break free from the cracks in the stone door. It fell to the ground, crushing the monstrosity beneath the rubble.

"We have to get inside," Nora said. No one hesitated or questioned what needed to be done. They sprinted as fast as they could toward the pitch-black opening to the ark. Forgoing their packs and supplies left behind with the horses. Nora, Grant, and Shaw were within mere inches of the opening when the rubble shifted, revealing the second creature was still very much alive. Wet stone rolled off the shoulders of its gray skin as a deep growl rumbled from its throat.

"Get through the door," Shaw shouted. "Run! Run!"

Chapter Twenty-Two

Before the Storm

The harmonious chirping of birds ended, and Ron's attention was drawn from their enchanting song to the knock on his door. Of course, no one needed permission to enter his room, but Conrad thought it was a nice formality to abide by, showing that not everyone had to uphold the same rude mannerisms as the First Born.

"I'm here to take you to the front of the courtyard, where you will then be escorted by Lord Hadal's personal guard," Conrad said, holding his hands behind his back, waiting for Ron to finish pulling the blue shirt provided for him over his head.

"Where am I going this time?" Ron asked. He saw Conrad become uneasy at the question. "Conrad, where am I going?" Ron's brow showed his growing concern as to what the answer could be, but he waited patiently for his friend to speak.

"The lord has decided since you are the one responsible for the execution of a family, he deemed it necessary for you to witness the consequences of your actions you displayed last night." Ron's stomach sank, but before he could try and form words, Conrad spoke again. "It's time to leave—come with me."

A brashness surrounded the man's words. He was still polite, but the words were shrouded in disapproval. Conrad had every right to be upset with Ron; he'd relayed the lord's message and told him explicitly what his actions could bring. Ron accepted the fact that he had not only disobeyed Lord Hadal's orders, but that his actions had betrayed Conrad.

Ron's mind raced, trying to think of a way to save these people while he followed Conrad down halls and through corridors. He thought about using the flame but quickly discarded the idea—he wasn't strong enough. Regardless of if he could hold the flame and pull more power into himself, he still had no clue how to use it as a weapon or protect himself with it. He thought about the possibility of trying to reason with Lord Hadal, perhaps telling him the whole situation was a misunderstanding, but that idea fell through.

If the lord was willing to murder a family over a few choice words, what chance could reasoning have? Then again, maybe if he asked for forgiveness and offered to take whatever punishment the father could concoct in his head, Lord Hadal would change his mind, instead of the family being on the receiving end of such cruelty. Ron decided he would go with that idea—it felt like the only real possibility.

Before he knew it, Ron was at the entrance of the courtyard, standing before the vibrant patch of grass, waiting for the lord's personal guards to arrive. He looked at Conrad. "No restraints this time?" Ron questioned, rubbing each wrist.

"No, not this time," Conrad said, knowing why Ron didn't have his wrists in chains. Conrad has seen Lord Hadal do this with other people he'd captured before. It was something so simple, but to Lord Hadal, it was a statement of power. "Do not be deceived by the manner in which Lord Hadal allows you to walk freely. He has done this before—I've seen it go both ways." Ron waited until Conrad continued. "It's an illusion. The lord lets you believe that you have gained some sort of freedom, or the possibility of fighting back, or in your case wielding your power. I've seen men try to run, fight, escape. It always ends the same. Whether you are chained or not, it doesn't matter. There is nothing you can do either way. Some men can't see the trap set right before them until it's too late."

"Thank you for telling me, Conrad." The man nodded. Ron thought about what he'd said about how the other people had been captured, and a question came to him. "These other prisoners, were any of them wielders?"

Conrad scratched his head. "I'm not sure. I know that since I've been here, you and your brother are the only ones capable of covering your hands with blue fire. Besides Lord Hadal, of course. Without the physical presence of the flame, it would be difficult for anyone to tell who might be a wielder."

"Have you seen anything that looked out of the ordinary or anything that didn't seem possible?"

Conrad didn't quite understand the question. "What do you mean?" he asked.

"Nathill told me some people are not strong enough to produce a flame, but they are still capable of using what power they have. He only gave me one or two examples, but if you saw someone do what I'm talking about, it would have been memorable."

"The only incident that comes to mind is when one of the prisoners tried to escape. This man, he came running out of the courtyard in nothing but his pants—no shoes or shirt. His body was beaten up something fierce. He must have been tortured for a long time."

"Why do you say that?" Ron asked.

"He was covered in scars, across both his arms and half his chest. He ran out, grabbing his head, screaming nonsense like 'get out,' or 'no more,' but the guards weren't anywhere near him yet. The strangest thing about this man was that when the guards finally caught up to him, he killed them all."

"All of them? How many were there?" Ron was stunned to hear that one man had killed multiple guards right in front of the courtyard.

"There must have been six or seven. They circled him, but it was like he knew what they were going to do before they did anything. He was able to get a sword from one of the guards, and once he did, he killed them very quickly. I've never seen anyone that fast before, except for the lord."

"What did the man do next?" Ron asked.

"That was another strange thing. After he killed the guards, he started screaming again, dropping to his knees. I don't know what happened, but smoke started to rise from the skin on his chest. It looked like the rest of his unmarked skin was burning. I thought it was Lord Hadal doing something to him, but he had only just exited his quarters."

Ron whispered softly, pacing in front of Conrad. "It must have been the curse of the Essenti. Just like Nathill said, he must have pulled too much power. But why does Lord Hadal need these people?" Ron stopped pacing when he heard his name. "What?" he asked.

"I said I couldn't hear you—what were you mumbling?"

"Oh, sorry, Conrad, it's nothing."

Facing the courtyard, Ron saw eight of Lord Hadal's personal guard approach, clad in their black armor with the insignia Ron hadn't seen since the night the masked wielder, Regis, found him in the woods. Lord Hadal followed behind with a smile on his face.

Conrad was ordered back to his duties by the lord. Two guards were placed in front, two guards standing to each side, and two more followed behind Ron. They guided him toward the lower half of Oroze. Lord Hadal walked beside him as they went through the streets of the upper quarter. Large homes, much grander than any Ron had seen before, lined the streets, constructed of masonry materials and wood to give the residents a feeling of luxury. They most likely belonged to a city official or family with status or wealth, much like all the other homes along the streets.

Ron wondered how many of the homes were still occupied by the original owner; after the First Born's attack on Oroze, it would make sense if the homes had been repurposed and given to the higher-ranking officers in the First Born army. Ron was surprised, however, as they continued walking, to see that there was little to no destruction among the high-class homes. The fighting must not have reached this far into the city, despite how bad it must have been in the lower quarters.

"It's quite a lovely kingdom, isn't it?" Lord Hadal asked, the first to speak, walking with his fingers laced behind his back.

"I'm sure it would have been," Ron said, regretting the words as soon as they left his mouth. He needed to keep control and guard his speech, not knowing how Hadal would interpret his words. It was impossible to predict what the lord would choose to do. After witnessing him disembowel one of his own followers, Ron had to assume anything could change Lord Hadal's disposition, even a slight breeze.

The lord laughed. "Yes, I suppose your right, but it will be. Once it's rebuilt, Oroze will return to its former glory." Ron stayed silent, not wanting to reply; Oroze wouldn't have had to be rebuilt if Lord Hadal had never invaded. "You must think I'm a monster. Do you think I'm just some cruel man bent on destruction?" Lord Hadal asked.

Was he kidding? Did Hadal really expect Ron to answer a question like that? Ron felt the question itself was a trap; anything he said could be wrong no matter what answer he gave. The lord continued, "I get it—you do not want to talk because of what happened at the banquet. It's completely understandable, but rest assured, for the time being, there will be no consequences for what you have to say. You may talk candidly. There will be consequences, however, if you choose to remain silent."

Ron didn't care for Lord Hadal's game, but thinking back to what Conrad had said, he realized this could be a trap to get him more comfortable—giving him the illusion of speaking freely, just like the freedom to walk unchained. Ron was going to have to maneuver through this game very carefully if he planned on winning his freedom. "From what I've seen, I would say yes."

Ron worried his answer was too forthcoming, but Lord Hadal seemed to be amused by it. "That makes sense. From your perspective, I can see why you would think that. But, for the most part, others think that as well. You share a commonality with like-minded people, which I don't blame you for, but collectively speaking, what you all have failed to do is to see the actions I have taken from my perspective."

Granted, Ron had never considered what Lord Hadal's perspective was in all this, but if it came at the cost of all the lives he had taken, then he would never see its worth. On top of that, how did his way of thinking involve what

happened to Regis eight years ago? Ron opened his mouth to speak, but Lord
Hadal wasn't done talking. "The way I see it is the Alumma Biyar kingdoms
needs to be unified, to have one central, focal point, instead of being divided,
ruled by kings and queens with no common goal. Why not be united in peace?"

"There is peace within the kingdoms. No one else is fighting."

"Ah, but you don't see it, do you? People are fighting all over the kingdoms.
It's just not a fight that's as noticeable as war. People constantly fight for shelter
when it's not afforded to them or within their means to acquire. People fight off
the hunger pains or die of thirst as they are discarded, deemed useless by those
with more than enough to give. People fight to feel protected and secure in their
homes, regardless of whether they live behind walls or in the open countryside.
I offer a solution to all these problems."

"What about the people who will oppose you? What will happen to them
or the kingdoms that don't share your perspective of peace? Will they all be
subjected to the same treatment that's been shown to Oroze, or will they be
destroyed in the same fashion as Regis?" Ron asked.

Lord Hadal grinned. "I was wondering when you were going to want to
discuss Regis. I will say yes—the same fate will follow those who choose to go
against me. I present a fair choice, just as I did for Oroze. I was kind, I was patient,
and I gave them adequate time to consider my offer, but as you can see, they
declined. I offered the people of this kingdom a chance at prosperity, a chance
to become something greater than they could imagine. I offered long-lasting
peace."

As they walked down the sloped streets, more common-style homes occupied
the area. Some were fully rebuilt, while others were nearing completion. The
shops were open, the markets busy with the foot traffic of the local populace.
For all intents and purposes, it looked like life had returned to normal despite
the attack a little less than a year ago. Soldiers still patrolled the streets though,
bowing when they saw the lord's procession passing by. Ron could hear the
whispers from the people as they bowed and recited, "May the wielders of the
flame guide us through the darkness as one."

It pleased Lord Hadal to hear the words of respect come from his people. "We will discuss Regis another time. That subject is a little more complicated than you can understand."

Ron watched the lord as he waved to the people they passed while weaving through the crowded streets. He wondered if the people actually recognized and respected Lord Hadal as their leader, their king, or if they were just too frightened to raise a voice. With that thought, Ron remembered why he was walking through the city with Lord Hadal in the first place. He didn't know how long it would take to find this family or if he had enough time to try and convince the lord to spare their lives, but he had to try. "I would like to ask you something."

"What would that be?" Lord Hadal said, sounding interested.

"Is there anything I could do, or is there any possibility this family doesn't have to die today?" Ron asked.

"No. You were given a chance to avoid this, to avoid all of this. I extended an invitation for you to willingly meet with me, and you refused. Time and time again, you refused. So tell me, do you think we would be here right now, on our way to execute this family, if you chose to accept my invitation?"

Ron took some time thinking of how to answer, but Lord Hadal answered for him. "No, we would not be here. We are here because every choice you decided to make was the wrong one. Every opportunity presented to you from the very beginning was to help your situation. Now your actions have affected the lives of people you don't even know. I had given clear instruction before the banquet, and now you will experience firsthand the outcome of your actions."

Ron understood he'd made some mistakes, but he knew Lord Hadal was wrong in his justifications. "Those were my actions—I'm the one that should be held accountable, not an innocent family that had absolutely no reason to be involved. You're the lord. You could stop this right now unless this is your version of the peace and prosperity you bring to your people. The repercussions of last night should fall on me and me alone. I understand what I did wrong, and I can tell you it won't happen again," Ron said, trying to reason with Lord

Hadal, but he realized his words were falling on deaf ears. The man remained silent, walking to the sounds of the soldier's footsteps and murmuring crowds.

Turning off the main road, the procession curved to the right, continuing down a narrow street lined with small shops. Ron couldn't change the wrinkles in his brow over the fact these people looked happy, except for the split second of fear that struck when they caught a glimpse of Lord Hadal and his guards walking by. After a quick recital of the creed, life returned back to normal for them. Ron's lack of understanding didn't slip by unnoticed; Lord Hadal was just waiting to see his reaction at the livelihood of Oroze. Then the lord spoke.

"Do you know the difference between an absolute ruler and the freely governed? An absolute ruler makes all choices for his people—the easy ones, the hard ones, and the ones that no one else could be able to stomach. Decisions that would break the hearts and souls of men and women. An absolute ruler takes that weight off his people, placing it all upon himself, shouldering the burden, you could say. Knowing their choice is best for the people, even if they don't know it themselves.

"The freely governed are given more choices than they know what to do with. More than half the time, they don't choose correctly, causing someone or, in your case, multiple people to suffer needlessly." Lord Hadal sighed apathetically. "People say they want the freedom to choose their own path, their own lives, but they don't. Time and time again, I have seen it. Too many choices will always lead to people making no choice, or worse, making the wrong choice, rendering the person worthless. What good is someone that can't make up their mind?"

Ron had a few thoughts about all the nonsense Lord Hadal had just said, but he didn't get the chance to speak them. Instead, the lord raised his hand, dispersing his guards as they came to a four-way street. Two were sent to each intersecting street, blocking the way for anyone to enter or exit. All eyes became fixed on Ron and Lord Hadal as they backed away from the guards.

"A man came this way not long ago—he was from the upper quarter. This man displayed unjust and unwarranted behavior based on what he thought to believe his status provided him. I am here to tell you that I have dealt with this individual personally, and he will no longer be frequenting this area. Or any other area, for that matter." Lord Hadal scanned the crowd, looking for the family the man had mentioned before he died. "I would like to offer my apologies for his misguided behavior to whomever he slighted. So please, come forth and make yourself known."

Whispers ran through the crowd of people, anxiously waiting to see who would come forward. A man emerged, followed by a woman holding his hand, while the other hand gently pushed back against two small children, hiding them within the crowd. The man and woman stood meekly in front of Lord Hadal, barely making eye contact. They bowed and recited the chant together.

A pleased smile hung on Lord Hadal's face. "I was told there were two children with you as well. My apologies are extended to them, too. Are they here?"

"I'm sorry, my lord. After our run-in with that gentleman, we thought it be best for our children to stay home," the man spoke softly.

"Good choice. You wouldn't want them to be exposed to that kind of behavior, now would you?" Lord Hadal asked.

"No, my lord."

"Well, on behalf of the First Born and their people, I offer you our deepest apologizes." Lord Hadal bowed slightly.

"Thank you, my lord, but we hope you were not inconvenienced by such things. You didn't have to come out of your way on account of us." The man and woman bowed.

"It's quite alright. I had some business to attend to in this area anyway," Lord Hadal said with a smile.

Ron didn't like seeing the false sense of security Lord Hadal was giving these people. Why would he go through the trouble of apologizing to them if he meant to kill them? Why was he acting as a kind leader? What if that was what he was doing the whole time? Maybe he had no intention of killing them. Perhaps everything Lord Hadal had said while they walked through Oroze was to get inside his head, make him believe something so horrible to be his fault. Lord Hadal must have known that the pain of guilt would have consumed his mind since the night of the banquet. Just making Ron believe in his intentions was a way to damage him. Even without the physical act of violence, Lord Hadal was able to cause him pain.

The lord began turning back toward Ron only to pause midstride. "Actually," he said, raising a finger to the man and woman, "the other business that needs attending does involve you."

Panic spread across their faces.

"What—what do you need with us?" stuttered the woman.

"Do both of you see this man?" Lord Hadal asked, pointing directly at Ron.

He'd allowed himself hope, hope that Lord Hadal was only trying to mentally tax him, but the panic Ron saw in their eyes reflected his own. "He's the reason I am here. It's no fault of your own, I assure you, but he is undeniably responsible for the forfeiture of your lives," Lord Hadal said calmly.

The man and woman looked at Ron. Tears streamed down their cheeks. "What does he mean? We didn't do anything wrong. Why would you do this to us?" they pleaded.

"No, it's not like that. I didn't mean to. This shouldn't be happening. I don't want this. Lord Hadal, please, you don't have to do this!" Ron shouted.

Lord Hadal raised his hand, silencing Ron and the hysterical man and woman. "He was given a choice not to involve you or anyone in this matter. Yet he broke the rules I gave him, knowing full well what would happen."

"No. I didn't know he was going to do this. I swear I had no—" One of Lord Hadal's guards rammed the bottom end of their spear into Ron's chest, knocking the air out of him. Ron gasped for breath as he fell to his knees, holding his stomach.

Lord Hadal made his way over, grabbed his chin, and lifted his head. "Here's where your next choice comes in. You get to choose how they die." Everyone in the crowd heard what the lord said and began shuffling their feet, trying to make way for an exit. Lord Hadal shot up. "If anyone tries to leave, I will kill all of you where you stand. I want all of you to bear witness to his punishment as a reminder." Suddenly, a blue flame burned bright, covering Lord Hadal's right hand. The people stopped moving, and only the quiet sobs and cries could be heard.

"I won't do it," Ron said with hatred burning in his eyes.

"Are you sure?" Lord Hadal asked.

"I won't do it. You're insane. There has to be something else. Kill me instead."

Lord Hadal scoffed at Ron. "You already know I'm not going to kill you. But there is something else." He motioned for the guard closest to Ron to bring him to his feet. "If you refuse to make a choice, then a choice will be made for you. As it rightly should, seeing as how you can't decide. Either you choose how they die, or I let my men here have their way with them. After my men get their hands on them, there is nothing I can do. They will be their property at that point, and trust me, that fate is much worse."

Ron couldn't bring himself to decide which manner they would be killed in, but he didn't want them to suffer whatever brutality awaited them if he didn't think of something.

"Time is running out." Lord Hadal paced back and forth. Images flashed through Ron's mind about the least painful ways to kill a person, but each made his stomach turn. Just looking at the man and woman staring at him, waiting for his judgment, waiting for whatever method of death Lord Hadal would deliver, made Ron's stomach twist into knots.

His mind raced. Lord Hadal began to speak once more. "Well, I guess we have our . . ."

"Wait!" he shouted. Ron was out of time, so he did the only thing he could. Lord Hadal stopped pacing. "I'll do it." Ron hung his head. "I'll do it."

"Do what exactly?" Hadal asked.

"I'll say yes. Alright? Yes. Just let them go. Please."

Lord Hadal's twisted smile returned more pronounced than ever. "This is certainly unexpected. If this is all it took, I would have done it a lot sooner, but—" He was interrupted as the sound of galloping hooves pounded the stone streets; a First Born soldier rode into the small square. "What is the meaning of this?" Fury coated the lord's every word.

"Lord Hadal, your presence is required at the ark." The soldier must have ridden fast, as he and his horse were out of breath.

"What for? Speak!"

The soldier looked around the crowd, unsure if he should speak aloud, but he did as commanded. "One of the scarred escaped. He has killed maybe a dozen men, but we have him trapped in the tunnels for now."

Hadal's temper unleashed itself. "How is that possible? I have said countless times, no one is to go near them unless I am there." Then his voice took on a softer but deadlier bite than before. "Give me your horse. Now." The lord mounted the horse and looked at Ron. "I will hold you to your word. If you go back on it in any way—" A cruelness took over his face. "This will happen again and again until you commit."

Lord Hadal pulled the flame into both hands, basking in the glow as it burned; then he shot two streams of blue fire at the man and woman, covering them from head to toe. He pulled the reins around, and the horse galloped through the street toward the lords' quarters.

Ron couldn't take his eyes off the man and woman burning alive. Their screams faded away, their bodies slumped to the ground, but not once did they let go of each other's hand. Ron watched their bodies burn while the crowd ran, scattering in every direction. Then his ears caught the high-pitched crying of the children being carried off, away from their dead parents. Ron felt the cold tears run down his face as silence filled the small square; only the shuffling of soldiers' boots broke the stillness. Their hands pulled and pushed Ron back down the street, forcing him to leave.

It was a long walk back to the lords' quarters. The soldiers slowly marched Ron through the streets as people watched and whispered among themselves. He overheard some of the conversations. He knew why they were watching him the way they were. Word quickly spread throughout Oroze about what had taken place.

Ron had become the talk of the kingdom. Glares and curses were propelled his way by the angry citizens, blaming him for the murder of the man and woman. Yet, given what had just happened and the guilt festering inside him, Ron found a small silver lining within the tragedy of the day. Even though the children would grow up without their mother and father, Ron was just happy they'd lived. He whispered a solemn thank you to no one in particular, since he didn't worship a god or deity, but he still said it just in case someone or something was listening.

Then, in the blink of an eye, Ron found himself lying on the ground. His vision was blurred, his head throbbed, and he felt a steady wet drip roll along the side of his face as he breathed in the matting dust off the stone road. Sounds grew dull, and his vision was slow to return, but he saw Lord Hadal's personal guards pushing back against a screaming crowd, holding them back with their spears to make a barricade. He glanced at a large, rough, jagged rock lying before him, covered in what he assumed was his blood.

Strong hands lifted Ron to his feet, but his legs were too wobbly to hold all his weight.

The shouting and yelling of the crowd grew louder. His hearing was returning to normal. The more lucid he became, the more his head throbbed from the sound. The guards helping him walk cursed under their breath as Ron was then pelted by numerous items. Fruits, vegetables, or anything that wouldn't cause a debilitating wound was thrown at him, with the occasional item hitting a guard.

If it hadn't been for Lord Hadal wanting to keep him alive, Ron knew the guards would have let the people tear him apart right in the street. They were out for blood, and despite whatever truth Ron knew to be right, the people of Oroze believed otherwise.

The shops became fewer, the homes and shouts of the people in the lower quarter dwindled, and as he walked past the extravagantly larger homes, Ron bathed in the silence. The throbbing in his head calmed, and the dried blood stuck to the side of his face pulled on his skin, but it was more pleasant than the aches in his body, which were slow to subside. The blue of his shirt and the black of his pants were now stained. They were covered in a dried extract from fruits and vegetables that smashed open from the force of hitting his body. Ron was tired and thirsty, so much so he could still taste the dust clinging to his tongue from the street.

Walking back seemed to take a lot longer than when he'd left in the morning. Looking up at the blue sky filled with white clouds drifting along, Ron knew it was later in the day than it should have been. The guards must have taken a different route, subjecting him to the people's anger for as long as possible before they returned. Ron thought he must have been out of touch with where they were going ever since he was hit in the head by the rock, but it didn't matter—it was over now, and he just wanted to be alone.

He was escorted back to his room in the east wing of the courtyard, feeling relief once the door shut behind him. But unfortunately, in his solitude, the overwhelming feeling of relief let slip the other emotions he was not allowing himself to feel. All of it came flooding out, the pain of guilt for the death of two innocent parents, the screams of the children he was responsible for orphaning. The humiliation he felt for letting Lord Hadal manipulate him over and over. The false sense of hope he held on to, the longing for his friends, for Nora, and most of all, the anger at not being able to help protect anyone.

He couldn't believe that all of his training, all the time he'd sacrificed to not feel helpless, to defend others in times of need, had been for nothing. Everything that had transpired since he left Greyland mounted higher and higher, piling on top of him. Ron collapsed to his knees, holding his head in his hands as he wept. Finally, he couldn't hold it back any longer. The lowest moment in his life had arrived, and he knew it. He felt completely and utterly defeated.

Bit by bit, he pulled himself together. He regained control of his breathing, his eyes dried, and he wiped his face with his hand, smearing the moist blood across his face. His heart still ached, but he felt more in control, more capable of rebuilding the wall that had ruptured, encasing his emotions. Then Ron heard a light tapping on the other side of his door. He stood up and turned around. "Come in, Conrad."

With a turn of the knob and gentle push, Conrad stepped into the room. The man froze in place at the unexpected sight. Dirty, stained clothes, an open wound on Ron's head, and blood spread along his face. "What did you do?" Conrad asked, closing the door.

"I didn't do anything. I tried reasoning with Lord Hadal, but it was no use. I did everything I could think of to save those people. I even said yes to allow him to teach me how to be a wielder, but he—" Ron felt his voice choke the more he spoke; he took a breath to calm down. "He killed them anyway. He told the people it was my fault. I tried to tell them it wasn't, and Lord Hadal could stop, but they blamed me anyway. So this is the result of that."

Ron lifted his arms, showcasing their handiwork.

"I see," Conrad said solemnly.

"One good thing came from today, though," Ron said.

"What good could possibly come from a day like this?"

"It stays between us."

"Of course," Conrad agreed.

"The children are alive. Before the parents stood before Lord Hadal, they hid their children in the crowd. I don't know how they knew to do that, perhaps just instinct, but it was the best thing they could have done."

Ron walked to the desk, staring vacantly. He pulled the chair out and sat down, leaning back with a small ounce of satisfaction, knowing Lord Hadal had not gotten everything he wanted.

"That's good to hear."

"Yes. Now I just need this day to end." Ron sighed.

Conrad stood fidgeting with his fingers. Ron reached down to pull a boot off but stopped as the servant spoke. "I wouldn't get too comfortable yet."

Ron's body tensed. "Why not?" he asked.

"I know you said you want this day to be over, but I'm afraid I have some bad news."

Ron stood up and slammed his fists against the top of the desk.

"It's always something, isn't it? There's always more. Why can't it just stop?" Ron looked to Conrad and saw his wide, frightened eyes. Unclenching his fists, he sat back down. "What more could they possibly want?" Ron asked, running his fingers through his dirty hair. "I'm sorry Conrad, I'm—I'm not mad at you. I'm just . . ." Ron sighed. "I'm just exhausted."

"It's okay, I understand. However, sometimes being the messenger means taking the brunt of the yelling when others don't like what I have to tell them." Hearing Conrad's understanding was a breath of fresh air.

Ron sat for a couple minutes before asking, "What is it you have to tell me?"

"Your attendance is being requested tonight for another banquet. As Lord Hadal put it, it is an opportunity for you to prove you're a man of your word. He also said you already understand what the consequences are if you do not follow through."

Ron shook his head, talking out loud but mostly to himself. "Of course, of course. It's another banquet. Should have guessed."

"What was that?" Conrad asked, not able to hear all of what Ron said.

"It's nothing. When does the banquet start?"

"In a few hours. I'm the one in charge of making sure you are presentable. So, just like the first time, we will go to the washroom, get cleaned up, then see about some stitches for your head, and lastly get dressed in something that doesn't smell like it's rotting."

Ron had nothing else to say, so he got up and followed Conrad to the baths.

Walking down the halls unchained, unshackled, but no less a prisoner than the ones locked in the ark, Ron felt the weight of defeat. The illusion of freedom was worse than being locked away, being so close yet knowing any attempt would only lead to others' pain and death, which he could not live with. Lord Hadal still had the upper hand.

Upon opening the door to the washroom, steam rolled along the top of the doorframe, escaping to a cooler climate when Conrad closed the door behind Ron. A new set of clothing was folded and placed on the same bench along the wall. Erin and Diane stood beside the copper bath, the dim light from the candles reflecting off their flowing hair, wearing only their sheer blue dresses.

However, when they looked at Ron's condition, there was no giggling. They just stood by the steaming bath. Ron dragged his fingers along the hot water, skimming the surface before he stood close enough for Diane and Erin to lend him assistance. Concern seized both their faces. His eyes looked forward as if looking through the women standing in front of him. They shared a glance of sympathetic understanding. Something was missing when they looked into his eyes.

They cautiously pulled his shirt off, trying not to brush against the open wound, only to gaze upon the newly formed welts and dark bruises littering his arms and torso. Erin attended to Ron's rigid and aching muscles, applying gentle pressure along the back of his neck, shoulders, and arms. Ron could feel the muscles loosen and relax. Sweat beaded down his face, stinging as it moved across the damaged skin. The humid air dampened the dried blood, and every soothing touch Erin provided, while comforting, left the muscle tender and sore. Diane reached to unbuckle his belt, waiting for Ron to stop her, but he didn't move. Instead, he kept his eyes straight ahead, watching the steam hanging in the air.

He placed his feet in the water, taking his time as Erin and Diane provided him some privacy by turning away. Ron slowly lowered himself, feeling the heat sting his skin as the water covered overtook his body, helping to release what little tension his muscles had left. Both women proceeded to bathe Ron. He moved only when Erin used more pressure to scrape off the remaining blood from his face and stitch his wound. They took their time, giving Ron's body and mind a chance to mend.

The fire in the hearth burned slow, giving a peaceful glow to the room and filling it with the scent of pine. Ron cleared all thoughts from his mind. He needed time to be still, to let go of his worry just for a little bit. He needed a moment of peace and tranquility. Closing his eyes, he pictured Nora. He sat still, feeling the water, feeling the gentle touch of empathy from Erin and Diane, and let his mind wander.

Then he heard the soothing, mesmerizing music. It was a song he had never heard before, but it made his heart remember what it was like to be with Nora. He found his moment of peace, for in his mind, he held Nora close, in the embrace of a warm blue flame, never wanting to let go ever again.

Erin and Diane were humming their favorite song they'd memorized from a traveling musician who frequented the Harbor Inn long before the First Born took over. Their voices slowly intertwined, harmonizing their tones as they came together to form a hauntingly beautiful melodic masterpiece, allowing Ron to remain in the world he created where it was only him and Nora.

It felt like an eternity had passed since he closed his eyes, yet once the last enchanting, rhythmic hum faded away, the time in his head felt all too brief. He wished the song could be sung till the end of time. To live in a world where pain did not exist and worry was a thought long forgotten. A world where his heart could be happy and content with the one he loved. Ron opened his eyes to see that Erin and Diane had finished their duties, making him clean and presentable. They stood off to the side of the copper tub, waiting for him to order them away or to help him get dressed. Instead, he said, "Thank you."

Both women smiled. Ron's body continued to ache, and his heart was still heavy, but he didn't feel as broken down as before. He felt a certain clarity, almost as if the time spent in his head, the time he'd spent with Nora, had reinvigorated his resolve.

"What was that song?" he asked.

"Did you like it?" said Erin.

"I did. It was—I'm not sure how to say it. It felt like I was living inside of the song. How is that possible?" Erin and Diane beamed with joy. As far as Ron could tell, it was the first time he'd seen them express a genuine feeling that didn't come ordered from Lord Hadal.

"Let's just call it a little gift from us to you," Erin said.

"I don't understand,"

"It's our gift, our power. We may not be able to make a flame like Lord Hadal, but our power allows us to help others heal in other ways than just the physical. I'm willing to bet your body still hurts, but now you no longer have the same look in your eyes as when you walked in here," Erin explained.

"So it's true then? People can have the power of the flame without actually calling it?" Ron said, more to himself.

"I guess. I mean, we don't meet many people like us. It was only by chance we met each other, and once we started singing, we found our voice had a soothing effect on people. That's why Lord Hadal has us stay in the washroom, to make his guests happy in every aspect of the word." Eric didn't hide the contempt for the lord in her voice.

"We rarely sing this particular song, though. It doesn't have the same effect on everyone, but every once in a while, we will see someone like yourself who it looks like it would fit perfectly," Diane said as she reached to grab Erin's hand.

"What's the song about?" Ron asked.

"Traditionally, it's about a man searching for his long-lost love. Going to the ends of the world to find her." Diane paused, letting Erin take over.

"The second part of the song is sung from the women's perspective. She is also searching for her love, but never getting any closer to finding him. Then, at the end, when all their searching seemed in vain, they find each other. Separated by only one room at the same inn. They went to the same place every time, but as fate would have it, time was the only thing keeping them apart. They missed finding each other, sometimes by minutes, sometimes by hours, but they were always close by."

The song was special to Erin and Diane, as it spoke about how they'd found each other. They were always close by but never together at the same time until finally they ran into each other, and hadn't parted since.

"Wow, I don't know what to say, but thank you," Ron said sincerely.

"Like I said, it was our gift to you. You're not like the other guests that come in and out of here. Most just take what they want and leave, but you didn't. Why is that?" Erin asked.

The expression on Ron's face said it all.

"I see. Well, in that case, don't give up on trying to find her. Just like in the song, she is probably out there searching for you as well."

Ron finished getting dressed after Erin and Diane left the room. He was thinking about what Erin had said, how people could have power without the flame. Nathill and Conrad had told him about these people, but he'd never expected to actually meet them. Ron was glad his first encounter was with Erin and Diane. It comforted him to know other wielders existed, ones who did not seek to conquer, kill, or control.

It made him wonder how many other people were out there like Erin and Diane. How many people could use the power without drawing upon the flame? How many different abilities could people have? What were the limitations of said power besides not being able to create the flame? Ron shook the questions from his head. Best to focus on what was in store for the rest of the night, and ask Nathill more questions whenever he saw him again.

Opening the door from the washroom, Ron stepped into the walkway to see Conrad leaning against the wall, waiting. The man straightened. "You took quite some time in there. I take it everything was to your satisfaction?" The meaning in his words was not lost on Ron, and he knew the answer his friend was looking for.

"It was." That was the best answer Ron could give. The time he spent in the washroom was not something he wanted to share with anyone else. It was a personal moment, only to be remembered by Erin, Diane, and himself. To reveal it to anyone would be to tarnish the sincerity of the gift he was given.

"Good, let's get you seated at your table. The banquet will be starting soon."

Following alongside Conrad, Ron couldn't help but wonder why Lord Hadal was having another banquet so soon. What was the purpose behind it? There had to be a reason, perhaps some other motive Ron couldn't see yet. No matter—tonight, Ron figured he would do as instructed, and if that meant keeping his mouth shut, so be it. He was not willing to risk the lives of others, knowing anything that spilled from his vile lips carried more than one meaning.

Men and women were amassed in the dining hall. The men were dressed in their best suits, and the women wore a wide array of dresses. The groups chattered on about the status they wished to achieve once Lord Hadal secured the Alumma Biyar kingdoms or who would be in charge of each thereafter. Each seemed to have personal stake in who they wished to lead under Lord Hadal.

Ron heard no mention of the family that was killed earlier in the day, which brought two thoughts to his mind.

It could just be they were too far removed from the event to hear about it. Or, they considered it of little importance, not giving it a second thought as they considered only what they could obtain by supporting and following the First Born in their conquest. Ron didn't need to overthink the options—he had already decided it was the latter. Moving in and around the groups of people, Ron continued to follow Conrad.

Along the way, he smelled the scent of the suckling lamb presented on each table, accompanied by a savory brown gravy sauce with bits of onion and whole roasted mushrooms mixed in. Bowls of pureed green mint jam were set beside each tray. Roasted potatoes, melted butter, and freshly baked bread made up the rest of the feast. The food made Ron's stomach yearn for a taste, but he had no natural desire to eat after the day's events. As Ron approached the same seat he'd occupied the night before, a guard stepped in front of Conrad.

"There has been a change of plans. He will not be seated here tonight." The guard's raspy voice was grating to Ron's ears.

"Yes, sir. Where would you like me to take him?" Conrad asked, standing nervously in front of the guard, awaiting his reply.

The guard towered over him, making him look small. "I will take him from here. Your services are no longer required. Head back to your quartermaster."

"I will at once, sir." Conrad turned, giving Ron an apprehensive look, and disappeared into the crowd of people.

The doors on the far right opened as the First Born officers took to their seats. The guests quieted and sat down. The father entered the dining hall and stood next to his seat. "All rise."

Again in unison, the men and women in the hall rose as one to recite the creed.

Then Lord Hadal came through the doors, joining his officers and the father as he took to his seat. He looked in Ron's direction and waved at the guard to bring him over. The guard walked Ron over to the line of tables, bringing him to an empty chair placed right next to the Lord Hadal.

Ron didn't understand what the lord was doing. He'd never thought he would be seated up front with them. Ron stood still, trying to discern the lord's reasoning, but he couldn't come up with an answer. The guard's large hand clamped down on his shoulder and forced him into the chair. The men and women in the dining hall whispered, stealing looks at the head table.

"Go ahead and plate yourself some food. Who knows the next time you will have the opportunity to enjoy such a delectable feast," Lord Hadal said.

Ron had already committed to doing as he was instructed, so he plated a sample of the lamb with a ladle of gravy. He slowly ate while maintaining a slight frown on his face. He didn't want to show how much he was enjoying the lamb.

At no point did he want to give Lord Hadal any reason to think he was pleased with his time as a prisoner.

Lord Hadal continued to eat, glancing first at his people and then at Ron. Upon noticing Ron's discontent, he asked, "If you have something to say, go ahead and say it. Remember, you are allowed to speak freely unless told otherwise."

Ron put his fork down and swallowed his bite. "What am I doing here? Why am I sitting up here?"

"That's simple. I wanted you to get an idea of what it's like from up here. This is what it could feel like to look over your subjects. Just think of how you could lead these people. And you already know why you are here, as you agreed earlier." Lord Hadal bit into a piece of lamb smothered in a mint jam.

"I may have agreed, but that doesn't mean I want any subjects. I don't want any part of what you offer except for what I agreed to."

Lord Hadal nodded. "Well, seeing as how you are a wielder by birthright, it kind of puts you above all these other people, regardless of if you choose to exercise that right or not. These people already pledged their loyalty to me, to the First Born. In doing so, they have agreed to follow the wielders I place in command."

Ron had nothing else to say that would be beneficial, so he went back to eating his lamb.

Lord Hadal then stood up and called the attention of the dining hall. "Ladies and gentlemen, thank you for coming. You may not know the exact reason I have asked you all here tonight, but let me assure you it's for a special occasion. You have seen him before, but allow me to properly introduce Ron as our newest wielder." Applause filled the dining hall as all eyes locked onto Ron. "Go ahead, Ron—stand up," Lord Hadal said, motioning him to his feet.

Ron reluctantly rose, showing a brief acknowledgment to the people. Hadal raised his hands to quiet the crowd, but a voice called out. "How do we know he's a real wielder?" A flash of anger dashed across Lord Hadal's face and left just as quickly. But Ron could see it lingering in his eyes.

"You're right. I don't want you to believe he's a wielder just because I said so. He's going to give you a demonstration." Ron's heart began to race as he felt his face get flush. Lord Hadal stood next to Ron. "Alright, go ahead and show them."

Ron froze. "I don't know if I can—I've never had so many people watching me." Ron was committed to following what he was ordered to do, but all the times he'd practiced calling the flame, besides when Nathill was teaching him, were in the quiet solitude of his room.

"I'll make this easy for you then. Either call the flame, or I will have your brother sent to the father for his failure in teaching you how to control your power. Hopefully, that will be enough motivation for you."

Ron could feel his anger boil to the surface as Lord Hadal stepped away with an arrogant grin. He closed his eyes, trying to focus his anger. Ron started to feel the pain in his right hand, but he couldn't hold on to it. He tried again with the same result. Finally, he opened his eyes to a quiet crowd staring at him, waiting to see the flame.

Lord Hadal looked to Ron, then to the father. Ron closed his eyes and tried with all his strength to call the flame, using every ounce of anger he could gather, but nothing more than a few seconds of pain traveled through his hand. He was failing.

Ron needed to call the flame if he wanted to keep Nathill from the father, but he didn't understand why it wasn't working. Each time he trained with Nathill, he used the exact same method to conjure the flame. With Nathill, Ron was able to achieve it in seconds, but why was this different? Sweat rolled down the side of his head. The crowd grew to a dull roar as they called out.

"Liar."

"Imposter."

"False wielder."

Ron glanced at Lord Hadal, and his anger came back with a vicious intensity. He was close to losing the chance to call the flame and save Nathill, so he closed his eyes one more time. Using anger wouldn't work, so he tried to think of something else, and that was when he heard it.

In the back of his mind, he heard a faint humming, the beautiful notes coming together, forming the space in his mind where he was able to find his peace. The humming grew louder as he felt a warmth spread throughout his body. He pictured Nora with him in the space he created, and could feel the warmth of his body manifest itself into the blue flame that surrounded them. Then the melodic humming began to crescendo, and he felt it. Thousands of needles stabbed his hand all at once, coming to a point where he could no longer tolerate the pain.

His hand went numb. Ron opened his eyes and saw the blue flame swaying as it burned bright. The room fell silent, staring in awe, and Ron looked around only to catch the menacing gleam in Lord Hadal's eyes as the fire burned in his hand.

Chapter Twenty-Three

Manipulation of the Flame

The morning began just like every other, with the sun burning bright in the new day's sky, but for Ron, the night and day melded into one. He lay awake in his bed, unable to sleep; his hands were stained with blood from the night before. Ron kept wondering how far Lord Hadal would go to prove he had control over Ron and control over the people who remained loyal to him. Last night proved one thing for sure—the people who joined Lord Hadal and the First Born had indeed given themselves over to him completely. In mind as well as body. Ron had replayed the events of the banquet over and over throughout the night. Though he'd done everything right and followed every order, Lord Hadal had still found a way to force Ron into doing something he never wanted.

Soon after Ron summoned the flame into his hand, he let it drift away, feeling he'd provided enough proof of his capabilities as a wielder. The people in attendance ceased shouting their accusations, looking sheepish as they quieted down.

Ron sat back down as Lord Hadal spoke. "As you can see, he is, in fact, a wielder. I told you this and offered proof as such. For those of you that deemed it necessary to be outspoken and voice your opinions otherwise, I have to ask—" His voice held its restraint. "Did you think I was lying to you? Did you truly think you knew better? I mean, you must have thought well enough, seeing as how there are those who question my judgment."

Lord Hadal spoke louder. "If I tell you he is a wielder, then I expect each and every one of you to show the proper respect and do as commanded, whether I have him prove it or not." Taking a deep breath, Lord Hadal eased his temper. "But I don't blame all of you. No, it appears as though most of you were following the judgment of the person that took it upon themselves to question me in the first place."

Lord Hadal snapped his fingers, and the guards on the far end of the dining hall grabbed a man seated at the end, hoisting him by his arms to his feet and walking to the front while he stuttered his apologies.

Lord Hadal turned to Ron. "This man thinks he is allowed to question if you are a wielder or not. In doing so, he willingly violated the oath he swore when becoming a follower of the First Born. All who choose to follow are to commit themselves to the rule of wielders. Now we must remind him that his true place in life is beneath us. Such punishment will serve as a warning to the others who think as he does."

Ron made no notion of answering. He had to remain indifferent to what Lord Hadal was saying. The man was brought up the small set of wooden stairs leading to the platform. They let him go and returned to their posts while he trembled, begging for forgiveness.

Lord Hadal quieted the blubbering man. "So you think you know better than I do?"

"No, my lord, I would never presume such things," the man quickly answered.

"Perhaps you would like a seat at the table. You know, better yet, why not take my chair? Here, you can have my sword as well." Lord Hadal began to unbuckle his baldric when the man thrust his hands out to stop him.

"No, my lord. It was my mistake; I should never have spoken out of turn. Please, I beg your forgiveness."

"There is a chance I could forgive you, but it isn't just my forgiveness you need to ask for. You did not just insult me when you could not keep your mouth shut—you insulted another wielder. Maybe you should ask him as well."

Lord Hadal turned from the man and spoke to Ron quietly so their conversation could not be overheard. "An example needs to be made of this man, and you're the one who's going to do it."

"What? I can't," Ron said, too shocked to get anything else out.

"You can, and you will—or need I remind you of what will happen if you do not follow through?" Lord Hadal smiled, pulling away from Ron.

As much as Ron hated the lord, he was committed to following any given orders; he did not want Nathill to suffer because of him. He couldn't say no.

"Fine," Ron said, trying to act as though this was going to be a trivial matter until he found out the extent of what Lord Hadal would have him do.

"Here's what you are going to do." Lord Hadal whispered to Ron what he wanted to be done, and Ron's eyes widened. The lord bent down and unclipped a single button stitched on the outside of his boot. He removed a small knife from a leather slit inside the boot, placed it in Ron's hands, and stepped aside.

Lord Hadal said, "Remove your shirt."

"My lord?"

"I said remove your shirt." The man quickly took it off and discarded it on the floor as Lord Hadal snapped his fingers.

Two guards came to each side of the man, holding his arms firmly in place. Ron did not want to do this, but he was already committed; the consequences would be severe if he backed out now. Ron stepped up to the bare-chested man, hearing him mumble his regrets under his breath, but Ron could not stop.

He had to rationalize his actions, telling himself the man had made his choice the moment he joined the First Born. He knew the rules and what repercussions would follow should he break them, and with that in mind, Ron whispered, "I'm sorry."

He gripped the knife's handle tightly in his fist and dug the blade deep into the man's upper left breast, carving the first diagonal line. Blood ran down the man's exposed chest as his cries of pain echoed within the dining hall. Ron removed the knife, giving the man a chance to breathe before burying it back into his flesh, making a second diagonal cut that connected at the top. Reluctantly, Ron pulled the knife across his flesh, lacerating the skin to connect each line, forming a bloodied upside-down triangle on his chest.

The man breathed heavily. Bright blood ran down his torso, dripping onto the floor. He breathed a sigh of relief as Ron took a step back, holding the knife in his blood-soaked hand. Ron looked to Lord Hadal, who then motioned for Ron to finish.

The man saw the silent exchange and said, "Please no more, I beg you. Please stop." Ron knew he couldn't. The screaming became strained and hoarse while Ron's head pounded from the prolonged sound, but when Ron stepped back, he dropped the knife on the floor and watched as the man's body shook from the pain.

"Let this be a reminder to you all. You serve me—you answer to me. It will never be the other way around. If anyone else has any problems or concerns, please come forth now, and we can discuss what bothers you," Lord Hadal said, then waited. The people in the dining hall had become morbidly silent. "Now that we understand each other, let's get back to the feast."

Picking up his knife, Lord Hadal looked at the man's mutilated flesh. A bloody "FB" lay in the center of the freshly carved triangle; he now bore the mark of the First Born.

Ron didn't have the stomach to eat much after helping in the butchering of a man, so he was escorted back to his room, ending the day he so desperately wanted to be over.

Now, as he lay in bed waiting for Conrad, Ron once again entertained the idea of escape. If he was presented the chance, he knew he would have to find a way to free Nathill as well. He couldn't leave him again, not after they'd just reconnected. This time Ron would save him. He just needed a plan.

Ron's eyelids felt heavy as he planned multiple scenarios of how he would escape, letting his eyes close on their own, only to be startled by a knock on the door. As usual, Conrad entered the room, saying good morning. He was always one for pleasantries, but then he saw Ron's hands.

"What happened this time?" he said, sounding concerned yet carrying a hint of disappointment.

"Nothing. I did everything as commanded. This—" Ron held his hands up. "This was Lord Hadal's handiwork."

"What did he make you do?" Conrad's tone lightened.

"One of his guests was too outspoken, and as a punishment, Lord Hadal had me brand the man with the First Born symbol. I didn't want anyone to get hurt, so I did everything as commanded, but it didn't matter. All that matters is how Lord Hadal chooses to interpret what happened." Conrad was silent, knowing full well what the lord was capable of. Ron cleared his throat, "So, what brings you here today?"

"I have been given instructions to take you to see your brother. Apparently, Lord Hadal has given the orders for him to continue your training."

Ron breathed a sigh of relief at the fact he would get to see Nathill, and that Hadal would not be the one to train him. "Well, what are we waiting for? Lead the way." Ron's excitement about seeing his brother outweighed how tired he was. There were more questions he wanted to ask. He also needed to let out some of his mounting frustrations. What better way than to use the flame in hopes of learning how to use it to his benefit, advancing his plans for escape?

Once outside in the courtyard, Ron wondered where Nathill was. The sun was shining bright on the vibrant patch of grass while the caretaker methodically trimmed each blade. He moved slowly, adjusting the grass to its original place as he inched back.

Conrad took Ron up the steps of the lords' quarters and through the double doors after explaining to the guards where they were going. Stepping onto the red carpet, Ron looked around the large room, examining how many guards were posted and at which doors. He tried to commit to memory the layout of the hall, just in case. Next, he looked beyond the large desk, toward the end of the red carpet and the door leading to the tunnels inside the mountain. Ron figured his best chance of escape would be through the tunnels. Seeing as how he didn't know any other way in, besides the large stone door built into the mountain, the option of using the door in the lords' quarters was the most appealing.

The next obstacle would be finding the right time to access the door. Since his arrival, Ron had always seen a guard posted by the door, so it was safe to assume it was guarded at all times. If he could get out of his room during the night, he would have a better chance at sneaking into the lords' quarters, but a foolproof plan was needed first. Ron had an idea that if he could make it to the tunnels, he would be able to escape, as long as he didn't run into a dead-end. The First Born soldiers would be funneled almost in a single file line, trying to catch Ron in the tunnels. It was the best idea Ron had, and the last thing to do was get Nathill and reach the tunnels.

Ron focused back on Conrad when he turned from the carpet and made for a door on their left. They walked down a long hallway with few rooms attached to it. Some rooms were closed, while others were large open areas filled with desks and chairs for when First Born officers held briefings with their lower-ranking soldiers. The hallway bent to the right, bringing Conrad and Ron to another door. It led outside to a large empty dirt field that continued until it met the base of the mountain.

And there was Nathill, not far off on the right, sitting on the ground patiently waiting. Conrad stopped a few steps from the doors. "Alright, it looks like I'll leave you to it. I'll be back later this evening to take you to your room. Lord Hadal expects progress, so you'll be training out here all day."

"Of course he does," Ron said. "Thank you, Conrad. I'll see you later then."

Conrad took his leave, shutting the door after him. Hearing the door close, Nathill rose to his feet and waited for Ron to make his way over. Ron scanned the area, and to his surprise, no one else was outside with them. It was just him and his brother. Ron had thought there would be guards placed at the doors or someone watching them at least. This might allow him to get the answers he hoped Nathill had. They could talk without feeling the need to guard their speech or tip-toe around questions.

Ron met Nathill in the middle of the field, embracing him in a brotherly hug that had been missing for far too long. "Glad to see you're doing well, given the events from last night," Nathill said, glancing at Ron's hands. Ron briefly looked down as well.

"You heard about that, huh?" he said.

"I did. Sorry you had to go through that. Lord Hadal can be quite extreme in his methods. I also heard you agreed to his offer. Is that true?"

A slight sigh of defeat escaped Ron. "Yes, it's true. I only did it because I thought it would have helped. I tried to save those people, but I couldn't."

"This may sound harsh, but I don't believe there was anything you could have done to help them. They were going to die no matter what you did. Lord Hadal has a way of making people believe they have a choice, then showing them they never did—that's what breaks people the quickest." Nathill spoke from personal experience.

"I can believe it. It almost broke me," Ron said.

Nathill could feel the pain Ron was expressing, and at that moment, he wanted to comfort his little brother, but the day was not getting any younger, and they had a lot of work to do. Nathill placed a hand on Ron's shoulder. "Well, let's put that in the past for now. Lord Hadal wants to see results so let's give him something to see."

A smile returned to Ron's face. "Sounds good."

Nathill paced before him as he began the lesson. "Before you can use the flame as a weapon, you need to harness its power without the influence of the curse, forcing you to draw more power than you can handle. That's why we spent so long just becoming able to call it forth. Once you manage to hold the flame steady in your hand, we will learn to use it as a weapon. Now, show me the flame."

Ron was ready to show Nathill he could hold the flame. All the nights he'd spent awake in his room, drawing the power into his hand, bringing himself to the edge of the flame's temptation, only to let it go and start over until his body was too exhausted to continue was about to pay off. Closing his eyes, Ron looked deep within himself for the rage that once channeled his power, but a thought came before he could find it. He'd tried using his anger last time, during the banquet, but the only sensation he'd felt was the brief stabbing of needles. Ron knew he had to try a different approach, so he took a breath, closed his eyes, and cleared his mind.

FLAME OF DECEPTION

Just like before, he heard the song hum softly in his head. He stood in the dark emptiness of his mind, holding Nora while the light of the blue flame surrounded them. Then the pain came to his hand, with thousands upon thousands of needles piercing his flesh all at once, but Ron held on to Nora, to the warmth spreading in his mind, until the numbness washed over him. Then he opened his eyes, seeing the burning blue flame waving gently in the soft breeze passing over the walls from the valley. He watched the flame; he didn't feel the desire to pull more power, only calm control.

"Very good," Nathill said. "That's the fastest I've seen you call it yet. What do you use to bring the flame into being?"

"I can't say." Nathill looked confused. "It's not that I don't want to tell you, but I'm afraid if I do, I won't be able to use it anymore."

Nathill gave Ron an understanding smile. "It's okay for a man to have his secrets. Sometimes they can be in the best interest of others, and often in the best interest of yourself. Now, how long can you hold the flame?"

Ron held the flame in the morning sun for over an hour before his brother said he could let it go. "If I didn't know any better, I'd say you've been practicing on your own. This long and not even a drop of sweat—that's surprisingly good. You're a fast learner. Go take a quick break, drink some water. Then we will start learning how to use the flame as a weapon."

A wooden barrel was sitting alongside the stone wall next to the door Conrad had opened for Ron when they first stepped outside. Ron must not have noticed it by the door. After drinking a couple handfuls, Ron turned back toward Nathill, running his wet hand through his hair to cool himself off.

"This is going to be more difficult than holding the flame, but once you understand it, it will come just as naturally. Now, if at any point you feel the pull is too great or your body is getting tired, you need to tell me so we can take a break. I don't think you want scars like mine." Nathill lifted his long sleeve so Ron could get a good look at what the flame could do to someone's body.

"Okay, I'll let you know."

Nathill began the lesson. "First, you need to understand that to use the flame, you must view it as an extension of yourself. You control it—you are the only one that can determine what to do with it once you have called it. In other words, visualize what you want the flame to do. So what I want you to do is call the flame to your hand, and then, while pointing your hand to the ground in front of you, produce a steady stream of fire. I will show you."

Nathill summoned the flame to his hand within the blink of an eye and extended his arm out in front of him. Ron observed him as he held his open palm toward the ground. The flame on his hand grew larger until it burst with a barrage of fire flowing out. Ron felt the radiant heat as it burned the ground before him. Nathill then turned his palm upward and made a fist, cutting off the flow of fire from his hand. "It may look easy, but be careful—it's more draining than you may realize."

Nathill stepped back, watching as Ron brought the flame into his hand. The flame came with ease once the humming of the song brought the world he created for only him and Nora into his head. The needles stabbed violently, then were immediately followed by the calming numbing. Ron imitated what Nathill had done by facing his open palm toward the area on the ground he intended to burn, but nothing happened. He tried to push the flame forward, but it just wafted softly in the wind. *Okay, it's an extension; that should be easy. Just like my sword, it's a part of me.*

Ron already knew the fundamentals of understanding his weapon. Cap had spent many months making sure it was ingrained in each and every student during the first two years of training in the Arena. The flame and his sword were one and the same, with the exception of appearance. Both served the same purpose. Looking at the flame surrounding his outstretched hand, Ron focused on the warmth in his head encircling him and Nora. He took that feeling and redirected it to his hand. The sensation moved quickly through his body.

The flame burned with greater intensity as it got bigger. "Alright Ron, good. Now, just visualize what you want the flame to do," Nathill instructed.

Ron pictured himself creating a stream of fire from his hand, and for the first time, he felt the flame as a tangible object. He looked at his hand, turning it over and back again. The flame didn't feel solid, but it had a weight to it. First, he closed and wiggled his fingers, feeling the sensation of pressure. Next, he held his open palm forward, preparing his muscles just as if thrusting a sword, feeling the weight until the pressure built in his hand. Then he forced it through his palm to the ground in an uncontrolled eruption of liquid fire.

The flame rushed out of his hand, consuming the dirt in front of him. Ron felt the rapid pace as he tried to reel it back and regain control, but it proved difficult. He had never used this much unrestrained power before. When he let the warmth spread to his hand, allowing it to grow, he had control, but the power of the flame became too much.

Ron lost focus in his mind, losing the hum of the song, losing Nora and the warm embrace. All he felt now was the pull for more power, the seductive grasp to let the flame flow freely. Ron collapsed to his knees, trying to restrain the flow of fire as Nathill's muffled shouts filled the soundless void he had fallen into.

Ron opened his eyes, staring at the blue sky with small white clouds scattered throughout. He was lying on his back in the dirt with a headache that would have toppled any grown man. He sat up slowly; his body felt tired and heavy, almost like it had been drained of energy. Sitting upright, he saw his brother leaning against the wall by the barrel. Nathill came to Ron's side, helping him to his feet.

"What happened? Why wasn't I able to control it?" Ron asked, rubbing his head.

"I wanted you to see for yourself what it feels like the first time you try to manipulate the flame."

Ron's brow wrinkled. "You knew this was going to happen? Why didn't you tell me?"

"If I told you, you would have been able to prepare for what the flame would do. By having you experience it on your own, you now have a better understanding of how much control is needed. It's easier to find out how it feels the first time so you can understand your limits." Nathill smirked.

"But I thought I had control. Everything was working. I held the flame in my hand, I made it larger, and then . . ."

"And then you felt it, didn't you?" Nathill interjected. "You felt the life of the flame."

"What is that?" Ron asked.

"That weight you felt, the pressure, it felt like you were holding something and nothing at the same time. That's the life of the flame. It burns in every wielder. In some people, it burns far stronger, like you and me. While the flame is a part of you, it also carries the Essenti's power and curse. I'm sure you felt that as well."

Ron rubbed his head, trying to alleviate the throbbing. "I did—I felt the want for more. When the flame was flowing out of my hand, it felt good to let go, but a part of me also wanted it to stop."

"That's where we must learn to control and manipulate the flame to our benefit. If you let the flame course through you unchecked, it will destroy your body and mind, but the more control you have over the flow of power, the stronger you will become."

"So what you're saying is, if I want to control the flame, I need to make some sort of barrier until I can handle more power?" Ron asked.

"Yes, exactly. Taper the power of the flame so you can gradually start using more."

"Okay, I'm ready to try again."

"Are you sure? You were out for quite a while," Nathill said, though he had no intention of stopping Ron.

"Lord Hadal wants results, right? So let's give him some."

Ron held the flame as it grew in his hand. He felt the weight and pressure build as before, but instead of letting it all rush out at once, he relaxed his hand, pulling back some of the weight, easing the pressure. He could still feel the life of the flame surrounding his palm, but the intensity had subsided. He took a breath, envisioned what he wanted, and forced the flame from his hand to the ground. A bright, stable stream flowed out, igniting the ground. Ron looked at the flame as it poured forth, amazed at what he was doing. He pulled more power, slowly feeding the flame just enough so that he didn't feel the need for more.

* * *

Turning his palm up, Ron made a fist, snuffing out the flame; the simple task of holding his arm out became tiresome. He had been alternating between his right and left hand, getting more comfortable using both so as to not have his dominant side become more familiar with the feeling of power. Nathill had had Ron practice using the flame well into the afternoon, waiting for him to take a break or show signs of slowing down, but he continued harnessing the flame. Nathill was more than impressed—he'd thought Ron surely would have taken a break by now.

Controlling a stream of fire wasn't the only use Nathill taught during the afternoon. One of the more straightforward attacks was to throw the flame as if throwing a ball.

Nathill explained, "Throwing part of the flame is different than pushing it through your body to your hand. This takes a little more control in that when you feel the flame become heavy or dense around your hand, you need to sever all ties to the flow of power. The important part to remember is that if you oversaturate the flame, increasing its density, it becomes more powerful and destructive. Once it leaves your hand, depending on how much power you put into it, the damage it causes can extend to anything and everything around you. I want you to only put a small amount of power into the flame and throw it at that rock at the base of the mountain."

Ron called the flame to his hand, feeling the piercing needles for only a moment as the numbing warmth spread through his body. He channeled the warmth to his hand as the weight and pressure escalated. Cutting off the flow of power so abruptly sent an unexpected jolt through his body, but Ron maintained his control.

He held the weighted flame just like he held an old ball of yarn he once snuck out from his mother's sewing kit so he and Nathill could play a game of catch when they had nothing better to do. Then, drawing his right arm back, he heaved the ball of fire at the rock. The flame found its mark and exploded upon contact, sending pieces of stone and dirt flying in all directions. When the dust settled, and the smoke faded, Ron saw the barrel-sized crater blown into the mountain.

"Maybe that was a little much for the first one." Nathill smirked.

"I think you're right, but it didn't feel that way." Ron gave a slight laugh.

He told his brother he needed to take a break. It wasn't only the use of the flame that made him overly tired, but also the lack of sleep. They each drank a few handfuls of water from the barrel by the door, then sat on the ground, leaning their backs against the stone wall.

"Hey, Nathill, can I ask you something?" Ron asked as he picked up a piece of rock from the crater in the mountain, rotating it around with his fingers. Nathill leaned his head against the wall with his eyes closed.

"Sure, go ahead."

Ron twirled the rock in his hands a moment longer before asking, "What are the scarred?"

Nathill opened his eyes slowly without turning his head, watching from his peripheral as Ron stared at the rock. "How did you hear about them?" he said calmly.

"After Lord Hadal took me through the city, and I agreed to learn how to wield, one of his guards came through the crowd. He told the lord that one of the scarred escaped. It was strange how worried Hadal got once he found out. Seems like the scarred are something important," Ron said, rotating the rock.

"Remember when I told you Lord Hadal tried to use people to open the forge?"

"I do." Ron stopped moving the rock.

"Well, the scarred are the people he uses that get consumed by the flame. Every person he has tried using to open the forge is not like you or me. They have the gift of the flame but are not strong enough to wield it. Lord Hadal forced them to pull more power until they became lost in it and, in turn, fell to the curse of the Essenti. I'm not surprised he was more than concerned after hearing one escaped. I have seen one myself over the years, and from what I gathered, they are difficult to deal with."

"How are they difficult? Couldn't he just lock..." It finally came to Ron. The screams he heard within the Ark of Redemption, the howling—it all came from the scarred, but how many were down there? He'd heard overlapping screams one after another while he was locked in his cell. The more he thought, the more questions came to mind. Ron cleared his throat. "Why would the scarred worry Lord Hadal?"

"It's my assumption that after falling to the flame and the madness, they don't fully lose the ability to use their power."

Ron looked confused. "But I thought you said it consumes them."

"It does, but the way I see it, the flame now runs rampant throughout their body uncontrolled, keeping them wanting more power, driving the madness further. There is no way to reason with them. They attack at random, trying to find the flame. When the guards had one surrounded, they were very much unprepared for the fight they entered into. The scarred are fast, strong, and relentless. They do not die like everyone else. I believe they don't feel pain like we do, and if the flame courses through their body, then they might not feel anything at all except for the madness from the curse. But that's just what I think. Who knows for sure."

"If that's true, then why would Lord Hadal keep them alive?" Ron asked.

"I don't know, but whatever the reason is, it can't be good."

Once their break was over, they continued training until the sun began its decline. By the time it drifted behind the mountains, Ron was panting with his hands on his knees. Sweat dripped from his face while he tried to catch his breath.

"If you keep training like this, you'll be stronger in no time. You're adapting to wielding much faster than I did. Just remember not to push too hard." Nathill's words were encouraging, but Ron was drained. His body ached, his head pounded, and all he wanted now was the chance to lie down and sleep. Nevertheless, the training hours helped Ron become more comfortable with manipulating the flame to his will. While he still struggled at times, the difference between when he first started and now was substantial.

Ron heard the door behind him open and saw Conrad step out onto the dirt.

"Tomorrow, if permitted, I will teach you how to use the flame in a different manner. It should be no more difficult than today was, but it's different," Nathill said.

"How so?" Ron asked.

Nathill smirked. "You will just have to wait till tomorrow to find out."

Conrad escorted them back toward the courtyard. Then Nathill went his separate way while Ron and Conrad continued toward his room. "I must say, Ron, you look terrible," Conrad joked.

"Thanks." Ron shook his head, and they both laughed. "I'm just exhausted—this has been a long day."

"I believe it has, but I have some good news for you."

Ron's eyebrows drew down as the thought of good news seemed out of place. "What could that be?" he asked suspiciously.

"I've been instructed to tell you that upon starting your training, you have been granted certain liberties."

"Liberties?" Ron scoffed.

"You are now permitted, with an escort, to be allowed in the dining hall for meals, have the washroom prepared upon request, and access the library within the lords' quarters. It may not seem like much, but it's better than being in a cell or locked in a room all day."

Ron didn't care to eat in the dining hall, let alone step foot in there ever again. The last two liberties held his attention, though. "You're right. Do you know who will be escorting me from place to place?"

"I do—you will be escorted by the lord's personal guard," Conrad said.

"What?" Ron looked to Conrad only to see him unsuccessfully hold his laughter.

"I'm joking. I'll be the one to escort you. You should have seen the look on your face."

"Very funny. You had me worried for a second, but I'm glad I'll be able to have a friend by my side while I'm here."

Ron entered his room, but before he closed the door, Conrad said, "Did you mean that? What you said, that is? About being friends?"

"Of course I did. You're the only person here I can trust." Ron could tell this simple thing meant a lot to the man.

"Thank you, Ron. I'll let you get some rest now. I'll be back in the morning."

"Sounds good, Conrad—see you in the morning." Ron closed the door, took off his boots and shirt, and fell into bed, falling asleep within minutes.

The next morning arrived quickly. Ron woke up feeling rested and content for once. No dreams had invaded his sleep, no unease or restlessness had taken his body or mind, and he'd slept through the night uninterrupted. The aches and pains had ceased; his anticipation for the day of training swelled, bringing him one day closer to his inevitable escape. There was much he still needed to learn, and at the rate he was able to control his abilities, Ron felt he would be able to make his move within a week's time.

Besides considering his escape plan, he also thought about how to get Nathill and possibly Conrad out of Oroze. One idea came to mind—that if he continued to comply, he would be allotted more privileges and use those to his advantage. However, nothing could take place until he learned how to use the full extent of the flame.

Conrad arrived, and after a quick exchange of morning pleasantries, he led Ron along the hall, down the stairs, and through the courtyard, making small talk along the way. Ron thanked Conrad and went to Nathill, standing in the dirt before him.

"I hope you slept well," he said.

"I did," Ron replied. "So now that we're here, perhaps you can tell me what makes today's training so different than yesterday."

Nathill grinned. "You just want to get right down to it. Alright then. Today, we will focus on using the flame to enhance abilities you already have."

"So we are just improving upon what I learned yesterday? That doesn't sound any different."

Nathill continued to explain. "No, it's not quite the same. Over time you can incorporate today's training with any form of flame you decide to make, but today I will teach you how to strengthen your body, as well as double your speed and heighten your senses. I'll also explain how to heal if there's time."

Ron was more than ready to learn how to use the flame in this manner. After multiple encounters with Regis, Ron saw the strength and speed he possessed with his own eyes. If Ron could learn to increase his natural abilities, then the thought of fighting Regis or Lord Hadal didn't sound so daunting. The gaps between their respective skills would begin to close, leaving them on an equal playing field. Everything Cap had taught him during his six years of training would be of use once he could match the speed and strength of Regis.

Hopeful thoughts flowed in his head—how much easier it would be to escape, especially after his training.

"If we can become stronger and faster, how come you never tried to escape years ago?" Ron asked.

Nathill had planned for this question. "I did. I tried to escape once many years ago, and as you can see by me standing before you, it didn't work out in my favor. You need to understand, this power grows—the longer you use it and control it, the stronger it becomes. I found out very quickly that someone like Lord Hadal has unmatched strength. His power runs deep. Even now, I would not be strong enough to fight him alone."

Nathill saw the slight shift in Ron's disposition.

"What about Regis? Is he as strong as Lord Hadal?" Ron asked.

"No, he's not, but he's still more skilled than you or I." Ron's face brightened up ever so slightly, and Nathill saw the change. "Why do you ask, Ron? Are you planning on escaping?" Nathill smiled and turned away, allowing Ron to think he didn't see the terror in his eyes at the mention of escape.

"No, I was—I was just curious." Ron wasn't trying to hide his plans from Nathill; he would tell him when he was ready, but couldn't believe how obvious he was just by the questions he asked. If Nathill could put the pieces together so quickly, then perhaps so could anyone else he talked to. Ron took a deep breath, thinking maybe Nathill was only able to guess as fast as he did because he had been in the same situation. That made more sense, but either way, Ron decided to guard his speech and be more careful in how he asked questions.

Nathill faced Ron again. "So, are you ready to begin, or do you want to talk instead?"

Nathill brought the flame into his right hand. "I want you to see this up close, so come at me as if you were going to attack. I won't hit back, but I want you to try and follow my movements."

Moving toward his brother with his fists raised, Ron was well within striking range. He observed Nathill, focusing solely on him standing inches away. Ron jabbed with his left, not taking his eyes off him, but his punch never made contact. In the seconds it took for Ron to extend his arm, his brother had already moved. Ron looked to his left to see Nathill standing there, waiting for his next move.

"How did you do that? I didn't take my eyes off you, not once." Ron was astonished.

"That's the difference between using the flame as an external offense and an internal offense. The time it took for you to lift your arm and bring it forward was more time than I needed to see what your body was doing. When you use the flame to increase your speed, it's as if time slows down around you. For example, have you ever dropped something, maybe a cup or plate, and watched it fall, knowing you were not fast enough to catch it even though it looked to be falling slowly?" Ron nodded. "Okay, so now picture the cup falling slowly while there is nothing you can do to catch it. Except now, with the power of the flame coursing through you, you can reach down and grab the cup, as it's still moving slowly before it shatters to pieces on the ground. It takes some time getting adjusted to it, but I'm sure you will do fine."

Nathill paced in front of Ron as he listened intently. "Now strength, on the other hand, is more straightforward, meaning it doesn't involve any physical changes. The biggest change you will experience is centered around what you come into contact with. If you lift an object, it will obviously feel lighter. If you exert more force onto an object that normally could not be moved, you will then feel the power within your muscles expanding beyond your normal limitations, down to the very fibers. That's really all there is to explain regarding strength. It's basic, but it's beneficial.

"Lastly, to heighten your senses, there's not much I can tell you. It's the one ability you will have to feel for yourself. What I can tell you is when you use this power, you need to trust your body and trust what you feel in here." Nathill placed his hand over his stomach. "Once you trust yourself and learn what each feeling may represent, you will understand how the senses work. All of these can be used in conjunction with offensive attacks using the flame itself.

"However, you must remember to not overexert your capabilities. The flame can be controlled by using the power you need sparingly, especially when using it both internally and externally. It requires a lot of control. Never constantly use the flame, or you will risk scarring your body or being consumed by your own power. I don't think you want to end up like the scarred."

Ron was familiar with the irresistible urge. Still, his determination to learn and control his power outweighed the risks. He knew Nathill would stop him if he pushed too hard or fell to the seductive tendencies of the flame. Knowing he had someone to watch him allowed Ron to push his body to its limits.

Still, the thought of escape was not the only one to run through his mind. He desperately wanted to be back with Nora, to hold her in his arms instead of in his mind. He also wanted to see Grant and Shaw again, and to know they were all safe. Those thoughts never left him.

Ron tried to clear his mind; only the song's gentle hum filled the darkness where he pictured himself with Nora. The warm light of the blue flame surrounded them, and before Ron called the power, he felt it build inside his body. The sensation was different. He hadn't expected to feel anything until he called the flame into his hands, but he understood what was happening. As Nathill explained, Ron's body was able to contain the power of the flame without the need to pull more, now it became clear to Ron how a wielder could become stronger and use the flame for more extended periods of time without destroying their body or mind.

His body was a vessel to contain the amount of power he was capable of using. Ron lingered on the feeling for a moment before calling the flame to his hands. The stabbing needle sensation lasted for a few short seconds, but the pain never changed, no matter how fleeting the feeling was, until his hands became numb.

"Alright, let's start with speed. What I want you to do is focus on one arm only. For now, think of using the flame as a reflex." Nathill bent down and retrieved a rock. "I'm going to throw this rock at you, and I want you to catch it."

He walked a good fifteen to twenty feet from Ron and then threw the rock. Ron caught it with no trouble.

"Nothing changed," Ron said.

"Good, that was just to make sure you could still catch." Ron threw the rock back, shaking his head. "Alright, this time, it will come much faster, so be ready." His brother raised his arm, ready to throw.

"Wait, if the power of the flame is in my arm, how will my eyes be able to see the rock if it's moving too fast?" Ron asked.

"Simple—if you are sending the power to your arm, where do you think it's coming from?" Ron thought for a moment until he saw Nathill tapping the side of his head with his finger. Now he felt foolish. "Ready?" Nathill shouted.

"Ready."

Ron watched his brother bring the flame to the hand holding the rock, waiting for him to throw. In the blink of an eye, the rock went flying through the air. Ron could see the rock, so he reached out to catch it. It soared past him, hitting the stone wall.

"Did you see it, or were you just trying to grab the air?" Nathill mocked.

"I saw it, but it went by too fast. I couldn't catch it. Let's go again." Ron saw the change for himself. He'd been able to keep an eye on the rock, but it was still faster than he was. He decided he didn't want to play it safe and wait to see the rock. He called out to Nathill. "I want you to throw the rock directly at me."

Nathill was baffled. "What? Why? No, that's ridiculous. A rock at this speed could cause a serious injury or worse. So no, I'm not going to do that."

"You're just afraid I'll catch it and make it look easy, just like yesterday," Ron said, knowing the comment would stir his brother.

Ron had heard the jealousy in his voice during yesterday's training when Nathill told him that Ron was learning to wield much faster than he had. Even growing up as kids, Nathill and Ron always had a competitive side, a sibling rivalry. They were always to better one another, whether it was racing home, collecting wood for the fireplace, or even something as ridiculous as who was taller.

During their sparring sessions, their competitive sides would get the better of them. Most times, Nathill would be the one to come out victorious against Ron, as his size and strength offered him the advantage, but as they got older, Ron began learning at a faster rate. He even began to surpass Nathill in skill. That was when Nathill stopped sharing his techniques and studied on his own just so he could beat Ron in a sparring match.

Ron was right—by the look on Nathill's face, they were right back home, ready to spar.

Chapter Twenty-Four

Revelations

Another rock hurled toward Ron. His breathing was labored, and sweat soaked his shirt, but he saw it coming toward him. Ron felt the air around him as the breeze slowed down; he looked around, noticing the almost-stagnant particles of dust in the air, the delayed swaying of trees in the distance. Then, just as the rock was about to smash into his chest, he reached out and grabbed it. He held the rock in his hand as the world around him resumed its natural pace.

Ron dropped it. "I think it's time for a break."

They both drank some water and sat down leaning against the stone wall. Raised welts throbbed across Ron's body from each failure. He'd caught more than he expected to, but also missed more than he hoped. "See, I told you," Ron teased with a light chuckle.

"You did, but from the looks of it, it definitely wasn't easy. What gave you the idea to have me throw the rocks at you?" Nathill wondered.

Ron tilted his head back against the wall, "Do you remember when we would spar at home?" he asked.

"Of course I do. I won so often how, could I forget?" Nathill boasted.

"Each time we would spar, I got better with the wooden swords we used. I could practice by myself all day long, but I learned the most by actually fighting against you with the sword. I just thought I could apply the same reasoning I did back then for today. Turns out it was a good idea. A little painful, but worth it in the long run." Ron laughed to himself. "She would think I was foolish," he said mindlessly.

"Who would?" Nathill asked.

"What? Oh, just a friend."

"Who is she? Sounds like she may be more than a friend. Are you and this woman close? Go on, tell me," Nathill said, nudging Ron with his elbow.

Ron shook his head, letting out a sigh. "Her name's Nora. The last time I saw her was weeks, maybe a month ago, before Regis brought me here. She's partly the reason I'm pushing myself so hard. I just want the chance to see her again. Not a day goes by where I don't think about her."

Nathill looked at Ron as he rested his eyes and head against the wall, seeing the longing wash over him, his voice reflecting the ache in his heart. "Seems to me you're in love with this girl, little brother," he said with a genuine smile.

"I am. The only thing is, I haven't been able to tell her. I wasted so much time holding my tongue, waiting for the perfect moment."

"Does she share the same affection for you?" Nathill asked.

"She does. The night before I was brought here, we expressed how we felt, but we fell asleep before I could tell her everything."

Nathill patted Ron's knee. "I'm sure you will see her again. Just make sure you tell her next time."

The sound from the breeze filled the quiet until Ron asked, "Have you ever felt this way about someone?"

"I have." Nathill pressed his back higher up the wall. "For a short, fleeting moment, I shared this feeling with another, but . . ." For the first time, Ron heard his brother's voice softly break. "Being a prisoner doesn't allow for such wishful things."

"I'm sorry to have asked. I didn't mean to bring up any—"

Nathill interrupted. "It's okay. It's in the past, many years ago. But what do you say we continue training? I think this break has been long enough."

Ron found that enhancing his strength came more naturally than any other form of manipulation involving his power. Each time he sent the flame through his body, he could feel each of his muscles contract momentarily before reverting back to normal.

"Just to test your strength, I want you to use one hand and push as hard as you can against the mountainside. Don't worry, you're not going to move the mountain." Nathill laughed. Ron placed his right hand on the steep rock of the mountainside and pushed. Nothing happened. He pushed again, feeling the strain in his arm the harder he pressed his hand to the rock. Ron focused more power into his muscles, and still, nothing happened.

He placed both hands onto the mountain's rough surface as his frustration grew and forced more power from the flame into his arms. He didn't let up as he continued to push against the mountain, but then he felt the need to pull more power. He gradually let the power of the flame flow into his body, but even at the rate he was going, the desire for more came faster. Ron knew he needed to let the flame go, but he wanted to show some form of progress, so he let the flame rush in before cutting off the flow of power and used that last burst to push against the mountain.

Fissures scattered in all directions from where his palms touched the mountain, but Ron sank to his knees, looking at his hands. Searing pain ripped through each hand as they shook before him.

Nathill rushed to Ron's side, taking his hands. "Let me see." He turned them over and back again, waiting for something to appear, but nothing did. Ron's hands stopped shaking, and the pain dissipated.

"What was that?" Ron asked.

"That was you being foolish." Nathill helped him to his feet. "You let yourself take in more power than you could handle even though I told you what could happen. Well, now it seems like you've finally gotten a first taste of what it feels like when your body can't maintain that much power."

"I thought if I drew a large amount and then cut off the flow, I could manage it," Ron said, feeling disappointed.

Nathill shook his head. "There is no other way to go around it—either your body suffers or your mind. What do you think would have happened if you didn't have an outlet for the power you took in. If you were not able to release that much power, it would tear through your body; you could have been scarred or worse." Nathill sighed. "Look, I know you want to learn wielding quickly, which is fine, but there are consequences if you're not mindful of the power of the flame."

Ron knew his brother was right. But, even though he wanted to justify his actions, he refrained from arguing. It had grown late. Nathill began teaching Ron his last lesson of the day.

"Heightening your senses is all about you trusting your body and allowing it to take control to your benefit. Like before, you need to direct the flow of power from the flame to each sense. That's all the instructions I can give you. Once you're ready, let me know." Nathill walked behind him. "Then we will see if you have figured it out."

Ron called the flame into his hand, but instead of feeling the entire store of power inside him, he felt empty; he felt as if a void had been placed in his body where something should be. Ron realized he'd used all the power his body could contain during the day's training; the only way to use more power would be to pull from the flame and risk the consequences. Holding the flame steady, directing it to where it needed to be, Ron closed his eyes. He decided to let his body take what was required.

The gentle wind sounded crisp, the plain, muted colors of the dirt and mountainous rock popped with a new vibrancy, and a hint of the soon-to-fall rain caught Ron's attention. He felt as if he was just witnessing the world for the first time. Everything seemed new, bright, and exciting. Then suddenly, he felt a twisting knot in his stomach, an imminent feeling of danger. Ron kept his eyes closed as he followed Nathill's instructions of trusting his body; he let his body react, giving way to movements he did not control.

Ron ducked, spinning around only to rise up and seize his brother's open right hand. Had Ron not listened to his body, he would have found Nathill's palm firmly planted on the side of his face from behind. He opened his eyes, staring in wonder that he could dodge Nathill's attack and grab him without knowing what was happening behind him.

"Well done. For a moment, I thought I had the element of surprise. I honestly thought you weren't ready yet. Looks like I was wrong." Ron smiled, but his face went pale, his eyes rolled back in his head, and he collapsed to the ground.

* * *

The shock of cold water on Ron's face forced his eyes open while Nathill continued to dump handfuls on him from the barrel. "Alright, alright, I'm awake," Ron said, gasping for air. "What happened?"

"You pushed your body past its limits. You passed out."

"I had a feeling I did too much. I guess we can be done for today."

"I would think so. Perhaps tomorrow we take it slow, huh?" Nathill suggested.

"Sounds good."

Nathill helped him to his feet. His knees were still shaking a little, but with his brother's help , Ron would be okay. "You stay here, and I'll ask a guard to get your escort." It didn't take long for Nathill to return with Conrad; after leaning against the wall for a while, Ron was able to walk unaided back to his room.

Along the way, after Nathill had departed, Ron asked, "Conrad, who do I ask if I want to get cleaned up in the washroom?"

"I could arrange that for you; it wouldn't take too long. I can drop you off at your room before I get everything prepared, then come back once it's ready."

"Okay, and do I get a choice of who is to help me once I'm there?" Ron asked.

Conrad scratched his head. "I don't see why not; do you have someone specific in mind?"

"As a matter of fact, I do. If it could be Erin and Diane, it would be much appreciated."

Conrad laughed slyly. "Taking a liking to those two, have you? I will see what I can do."

"Thank you." Ron had taken a liking to Erin and Diane, but not for the reasons Conrad suspected. Despite actually needing to clean himself up, he wanted to ask them some questions that had been on his mind.

Conrad brought Ron to the washroom and then returned to his duties. Ron closed the door as the steam swirled around the dim-lit chamber, a fire adding to the warmth already supplied by the steaming water in the copper tub. Erin and Diane stood by the tub, waiting for Ron to make his way over to them.

Ron undressed as they turned around; once he was in the water, they poured hot water over his head. "We were surprised to hear we were requested by a wielder. Usually, we only attend to guests, but you sure know how to make someone feel special, don't you?" Erin said coyly.

"To what do we owe this honor?" Diane added.

"Honestly, there are a select few people I can trust, and you two are not like the others here. So I feel the trust I have in you is not misplaced," Ron said, hoping he made the right choice.

"Well, you can rest assured. If there were ever to be someone we wished to be requested by, it would be you," Erin said, smiling at Diane.

"There's another reason why I asked for you two."

The pour of water slowed. "And what might that be?" Uncertainty filled Erin's voice.

"I wanted to ask you about your gift. After the last time I saw you, something changed, and I don't understand why. Also, I don't have any other way of seeing you two, so asking for you to be here was all I could think of."

The thoughts drifting through Erin and Diane's minds left, and they both breathed a sigh of relief. "Tell us what happened, and we may be able to offer a solution."

Ron explained that after their last visit, he tried to call the flame using his anger as he had in the past, but to little effect this time. Once he explained, he asked, "Have you ever used your gift on a wielder before? A wielder like me."

Erin and Diane thought for a moment. "Can't say we have. We don't know who could be a wielder, but we have never been told of something like this happening," Erin said.

"If your power has the ability to heal the mind, do you think it's possible that ..." Ron trailed off in thought. What if their power somehow healed part of the curse or suppressed a part that feeds off raw anger to amplify the flame inside a person? Could their power be capable of countering the curse of the Essenti?

Or did it create a new pathway for the flame to flow through a wielder's mind, allowing a more controlled use of power?

Ron didn't want to run the risk of sounding like a ranting lunatic if Erin or Diane didn't know about the curse of the Essenti, so he didn't ask. There was also the fact he had no way to confirm what he was thinking; if they didn't know who was a wielder, then there would be no way to see if their power affected others in the same way it did him.

"What do you use to wield now, since anger is no longer an option?" Diane asked.

"I use the song you sang and the images inside my head from the last time I was here."

"Really? We are flattered, but may we ask what you were thinking of?"

Ron didn't tell Nathill how he'd conjured the flame, but there couldn't be any risk involved with telling Erin and Diane. After all, they were the ones who helped him create it.

Ron closed his eyes. "I empty my mind, and I hear your song, then I picture her. I picture Nora with me, in my arms, in her arms, and we're together. Then I let the flame embrace us both. There's no pain, no sadness, just warmth like there is now. I can hear your song." Ron was back in the world he'd created for Nora and himself; it sounded as if they were singing to him at that very moment. They were, in fact, softly humming.

Peace and comfort washed over him. Happiness found its way to Ron, a joy he hadn't felt in some time. He looked at Nora, not wanting to miss another chance, and said, "I love you."

She simply smiled at him, a smile he could never forget, a smile he wanted to see for the rest of his life. Ron didn't care if what he said was just in his mind. For him, it felt as natural as holding Nora in person, but then the song started to fade, and as it did, he could hear Erin and Diane whispering to each other with concern.

Ron opened his eyes to see a look of fear in each of their eyes. He didn't understand why until he looked down and saw that both his hands were engulfed in flame. He was right— something about their power created a new pathway, allowing him to bypass the pain associated with the flame, but how?

Ron let go.

"It's okay. I didn't think that would happen. Usually, I get a painful feeling in my hands every time I call the flame, but I think your power mended a part of mine somehow."

Erin and Diane stopped whispering. "We didn't realize we could do that; we just saw your hands catch fire and didn't know what you were doing," Erin said, stepping forward.

Ron took on a look of worry. "Don't tell anyone about this. I'm afraid if Lord Hadal or Regis find out, they may try to use your power for themselves. I don't want anything terrible to happen to you two. This needs to stay between us."

"It will stay between us. We will make certain it does not leave this room," Diane said. "But who is Regis? Is he a new wielder here?"

Ron was confused; why wouldn't they know who he was if they had been under the lord's service for almost a year. "He's the other lord besides Lord Hadal; I thought you would know him—he's the one that wears the mask," Ron said, hoping that would clear up the confusion.

"No, we have never heard of a Regis. There's only Lord Hadal, and the one that wears the mask is Lord Nathill."

Ron couldn't believe what he had just heard; there was no way that could be right. "No, no, no, that can't be right. Nathill is my brother; he's a prisoner here just like I am. There's no way he could be a lord working with the First Born. That's just not possible." Ron's mind raced with questions and uncertainties. How could Erin and Diane know his name if what they said wasn't true? How could Nathill be a lord if he was locked in the Ark of Redemption? Why would Nathill lie?

Ron got out of the water, dried off, and proceeded to get dressed. "I have been with Nathill for weeks now, and he has been treated just as I have. It can't be true. He wouldn't lie to me, not about something like this." Ron's emotions were getting the better of him, but he didn't know what to believe. "Tell me, what does he look like?" he said, raising his voice, thinking Erin and Diane were simply confused and mixed him up with someone else. Then Erin described Nathills exact build, hair color, eye color, and the scars marking his arms.

"Calm down, we didn't mean to upset you. We didn't know he was your brother. Besides, we have no reason to lie to you. Whatever you were told outside of this room is unknown to us, but we are telling you the truth." Erin said calmly.

Ron slowed down, took a breath, and realized he was acting without thinking. "I'm sorry, I didn't mean to shout at you. I just . . . It doesn't make sense. Why would he lie to me? Why would he do any of this?" Erin and Diane stood silent as Ron recognized the confusion in their faces. They had no idea what he was talking about. Ron ran his fingers through his hair, "I'm sorry, but I have to go. Please keep all of this between us, and thank you for everything."

They smiled warily as Ron left the room.

Conrad was waiting outside, leaning against a wall, when Ron burst through the door.

"Everything alright?" he asked.

Ron had to keep himself calm; he didn't want to cause any concern. "Yes, I just want to go lie down."

Once he was in his room, he thought of all the reasons Nathill would keep this from him. If Nathill was part of the First Born, why did he want to make Ron believe he was a prisoner? Why would he have joined in the first place? And the thought Ron could not ignore no matter how hard he tried was: What if Nathill was part of the attack on their home?

Ron couldn't make sense out of any of it. The only thing he could do would be to wait until after training tomorrow and ask Nathill outright. But Ron still needed to learn how to defend himself using the flame, and if he angered Nathill, he might not get the chance to complete his training. Ron lay on his bed, and eventually fell into a restless sleep.

In the morning, he walked hurriedly to the training grounds where Nathill would be waiting. Once Conrad left, Ron met his brother and put on a guise of eagerness to finish training while hiding his true feelings.

"Morning! Are you ready to start?" Nathill asked.

"I'm more than ready." Ron wanted to learn as quickly as possible so he could ask Nathill to tell him the truth.

Nathill began, "First things first then—your defense is only as strong as you make it. That's how one wielder's guard can cancel out an oncoming attack. For example, if I were to throw a ball of fire at you and it was stronger than the shield you put up, your shield would be destroyed, leaving you vulnerable. Now, if your shield is stronger than the attack, then the attack will be nullified. I'll demonstrate. Go ahead and throw a ball of flame at me."

Nathill walked a reasonable distance from Ron and brought the flame into his right hand. He lowered his hand, palm up, and when he raised it again, a shield of flame stood before him. He then placed his hand on the raised wall of flame protecting his body.

Ron remembered seeing this when he'd fought Regis outside of Collins's house. The shield was raised in the exact same fashion as before, but a part of Ron still refused to believe it was Nathill. Perhaps all wielders raised a flame shield in the same fashion. Then Nathill's words broke Ron's thoughts, "Hey, are you still with me?" he asked.

"I am sorry, I was just thinking of something."

"Well, now that I have your attention, go ahead and attack." Ron cleared his mind and called the flame to his hands. He was still amazed when no pain ripped through his hands; the only sensation was the numbness that came before the flame. Ron flowed the power of the flame into his hand before cutting it off. Then, feeling the flames' weight, he looked at Nathill and hurled it forward. He watched as the ball of flame flew through the air and smashed into Nathill's flame shield, only for his attack to burst against it and disappear.

Nathill dropped the shield and returned to Ron. "Your hand must stay on the flame shield just in case you need to add more power to make a stronger defense. You will never know how strong an attack will be, so it's better to make your shield stronger than you need it to be. Now go ahead and raise a shield. Let's see how strong you can make it."

Ron mimicked Nathill's movements, and once he raised his palm, a shield the length and width of his body appeared in front of him. He placed his hand on it held it steady. Nathill called the flame to his hand as Ron braced himself for the imminent impact. Nathill threw the ball of blue flame; it crashed against Ron's shield, pushing his feet back a couple inches as he held his guard. Ron pushed more power into the shield as a loud, bright burst erupted before him. Breathing heavily, Ron dropped his shield.

"I'm impressed. That attack had some strength behind it," Nathill said.

"I know. I felt it." Ron looked down at his feet, seeing how far back he'd slid.

"Once you get better, you will be able to raise and drop a shield if you are attacked from multiple angles. Quick shields are effective as long as you make them strong enough. It just takes time to become proficient. Healing, on the other hand, isn't hard to get a handle on, but it does have its own rules," Nathill said.

"What kind of rules?" Ron asked.

"Well, for starters, if someone is dead, there is nothing we can do to bring them back to life. No power in the world can do that. Also, if too much time goes by or if someone is fatally injured, there is nothing our power can do."

"So we can heal people who have moderate to severe injuries but nothing that could kill them unless we get to them in time?" Ron asked.

"Yes, exactly. It doesn't sound like much, but it comes in handy. To heal someone, you need to place your hands on the wound, then picture what needs to be fixed in your mind. The power of the flame will heal what your hands feel, what your eyes see, and what the flame comes into contact with while you send it into their body."

Ron was listening, but his mind went back to when Regis had healed him after removing him from the spikes in the ark. All he could picture was Nathills face beneath the mask. Nathill paused and looked at Ron. "Is everything alright? You seem distracted."

Ron was indeed. All he could think about was what Erin and Diane had told him the other night.

"I am," Ron replied.

"Tell me, what's on your mind?"

Ron smirked, shaking his head. "You want to know what's on my mind? Okay, but first, why don't you tell me the truth?"

Nathill's brow wrinkled. "Truth about what?"

"Tell me why I'm here. Tell me why you are working with the First Born, working with Lord Hadal. Tell me why you lied to me about what happened eight years ago."

Nathill was caught off guard by the number of allegations.

"Where did you hear all this?" he asked calmly.

"It doesn't matter where I heard it. Just tell me if it's true." Ron's eyes felt wet, hoping he was wrong, hoping Nathill wasn't the monster that had ruined his life.

Nathill held Ron's gaze. "It's true."

They stared at each other as the words settled into Ron's mind; his worst fears had been confirmed. How could his brother do this? Why would he have? There had to be a reason, so Ron mustered one word.

"Why?"

"You must understand, things are happening that have been in motion for almost a decade. I was going to tell you about everything when the time came. I wanted the chance to explain why all this has happened and the purpose behind it. Just know that I'm not the enemy." Nathill insisted.

"If you're not the enemy, then why are you with the First Born? Why did you follow me from Greyland and take me prisoner only to have me tortured? My friends could have been killed; Nora could have been killed." Ron collected himself before he asked his last question. "Why did you have our parents killed? You loved them just as much as I did. They never did anything but love you. Tell me why?"

"Now is not the time to—"

Ron shouted at Nathill, interrupting him, "Now is the perfect time to tell me! Do you think I'm going to just let you walk away and tell me later after all this time? You're going to tell me right now!"

Nathill held his hand up. "You're right. I owe you an explanation. So let's sit down, and I'll explain."

They leaned against the wall and sat down. "I want you to know, none of this has gone the way I planned. In the beginning, when Lord Hadal first contacted me with the letters, I was genuinely curious about this power. He told me about the flame of the Essenti, taught me the language, and he taught me how to wield as well, but I wasn't able to wield yet. I'm not a fast learner like you are. However, once I learned of the forge and his plan to bring the two worlds together, it sounded like we would be liberating the people that were banished unjustly because of their beliefs."

Ron cut in, "What does that have to do with the attack?"

"Just listen. He told me that in order to open the forge, he needed to find wielders like me. He wanted to rule his own kingdom and have people willingly offer to help. So he had me talk to our parents, the councilmen, and the mayor. He wanted me to convince them that they should become loyal to the First Born army. He must have known they would not comply because I didn't even have time to write a letter back with an answer. So that night, he attacked."

"But the note you had said whatever plans were made were going to happen that night." Ron countered.

"I was under the impression we were going to find the third piece of what we needed. Then when Lord Hadal sent those soldiers into Regis, I figured out what the third piece was," Nathill paused. "The third piece was you, Ron. I don't know how Lord Hadal knew you were a wielder; I didn't even know you were, but somehow he did. So that's why I killed those soldiers and tried to help you escape."

Nathill shook his head. "Lord Hadal destroyed both our lives that night. I loved our parents, and if I had known what he was really going to do, maybe I could have stopped him. But, after the attack, I knew I couldn't let him get to you,"

"Then why did his soldiers make it look like they killed you? How do I fit into the three pieces of whatever he needs?" Ron asked.

"He needed to confirm you could wield, so his soldiers stab me to elicit the flame lying dormant inside of you." Nathill sighed and continued, "As far as you being the third piece is concerned, Lord Hadal needs your power to open a forge gate."

"I thought he's been trying to open the forge with other gifted people; why does he need my power? What makes him think I can do what the others can't?" Ron asked.

"The people who become the scarred are not strong enough to open a stable one. When he uses them, the forge is only open briefly, and they don't always show up where he wants them to. Lord Hadal has tried for years, and all he has to show for it is thunderous sounds in the sky and people becoming the scarred. That's why he needs your power, the power of a wielder who can conjure the flame."

"How does my power help him open a forge gate?"

"During the years I was with Lord Hadal, the years after you escaped, he searched relentlessly for something called the last Orb of Ember. You see, since he knew you were a wielder and you escaped, he didn't need to keep searching for you. That's why you could live in peace. So instead, he searched for the Orb of Ember, only to find it three years ago, far north of the castle ruins deep in the Storming Mountains.

"After he found it, he began to use people while he sent out others searching for you. In my studies of the old books, I learned of what lies in the forge. Wielders of immense power from long ago, storied beasts and monstrous creatures that should never have been brought into existence. Once I knew what was in there, I knew he could never find you."

Ron ran his fingers through his hair. "Why did you stay with him for so long? Why didn't you fight or try to escape?"

Nathill looked away, ashamed. "I stayed because I was afraid. I'm not strong enough to fight him. After the night he attacked and healed me, I knew as long as he didn't have you, he couldn't fulfill his plans, but I also knew I would never be able to live a life free from Lord Hadal. Over the years, I learned he is a man who only looks after his own ambitions, and in learning that, I was able to keep him from you. Every time he sent messengers to the other kingdoms, villages, and towns in search of you, I intercepted them. I made sure they would never find you, even though I didn't know where you were. I just thought the longer it took, the better off you would be."

"What did you do to the messengers?" Ron knew the answer but asked anyway.

"I freed them," Nathill said.

Ron saw the pain in his brother's eyes. "So, how did Hadal find me?"

"He changed his tactics. He used a weapon from a time long ago. He attached what looked like a lantern to one of his messengers. These lanterns are, in fact, more like explosives. A wielder can put a powerful flame inside without it breaking, and a trace of that flame can be felt by the one who placed it. The only way to trigger an explosion is for another wielder to come into close proximity of the lantern."

Ron couldn't believe it—it was his fault the blacksmith had died that day. If he had only known, if he hadn't let his anger take control of him, none of this would be happening. "It's my fault. I ran toward him. I'm the one that caused all this," Ron said.

"No, Ron, there's no way you ever could have known. These weapons are from the first War of the Wielders; they are barely even written in history, let alone people's knowledge."

Ron shook the thought from his mind even though it hurt. "So, how did you find me if Lord Hadal put the flame in the lantern?"

"I followed the messenger from a distance, and when I saw the explosion, I knew he'd found you. So when I questioned you in the woods, and you told me you knew nothing of wielding, I was hoping you would abandon what you were doing, but you continued to go forward. I knew Lord Hadal gave the messenger something to tell you, but I didn't know what exactly. The closer you got, the less control I had, so I was out of options when I reported back to him. That's when he sent me to apprehend you at Collins's house. I had no choice."

Ron frowned and raised his voice. "You had a choice. You could have told me in the woods who you were. You could have told me all of this back then before any of this happened."

"No, I couldn't. If I had, then what? Even if I did tell you, and you believed every word I said, we would have the whole First Born army searching for us. Where would we run? Lord Hadal already knew you were somewhere in the Greyland region. If he sent his army out in full force, we would have both been captured, your friends would be killed, tortured, or worse. I would have had no time to train you, and Lord Hadal would have gotten what he wanted. At least this way, we can try to stop him."

Ron's temper flared, but his brother's reasoning was sound; he'd put a lot of thought behind his actions since the beginning. Ron slowly came to terms that Nathill was right. He needed to have a level head as he thought through this.

"Okay, so how are we going to stop him?" Ron asked.

"Like I said, I'm not strong enough to fight him on my own, and you are not strong enough either. So the only way I can think of stopping him, for now, is to destroy the last Orb of Ember."

"You have said that a few times now. What is an Orb of Ember?" Ron asked.

"There are three Orbs in total; they were made centuries ago by the Essenti's champion. He created these Orbs for his successors to open the forge. It takes an extreme amount of power to open the forge, but it can be achieved with the three Orbs of Ember and three wielders of the flame. He needs your power to activate the third and final Orb so he can have unlimited access to a stabilized forge gate," Nathill explained.

"How do we destroy the Orb?" Ron asked.

"That's the only problem—to activate the Orbs of Ember, you have to flow the power of the flame into it, and in the books I've read, the text says they are nearly impossible to destroy."

"So if we can't destroy it, we just need to make sure I don't put my power into it."

Nathill shook his head. "It won't be that simple. Lord Hadal will force you to—he will find a way and make you do it." The lord had already forced Ron's hand in many situations, and Ron knew he was capable of making him do it again.

"We need to take it from him then. Get rid of it."

"And go where? The only chance of getting it away from him is if you were to escape. If you can manage that, he will require my help to recapture you. I would only be able to give you so much time before I had to join in the search."

"How long do you think he will wait until he tries to make me active the third Orb?" Ron asked, hoping he had time.

"I don't know, but I can buy you a few more days and tell him you're not ready until your training is complete. That will give us a few days, nothing more. In the meantime, practice what you can on your own, in your room. While you are doing that, I will think of a plan." Nathill's voice trailed off.

"None of this is what I expected. I thought you were dead all these years, while you were here trying to keep me safe. I don't even—"

Nathill placed a hand on Ron's shoulder. "I would do it all over again if I had to."

Ron and Nathill quickly rose to their feet as they heard the door open. A First Born guard walked through the doorway. "Lord Hadal requests your presence." He pointed to Nathill.

"I will be right there. Just let me finish today's lesson."

"Make it quick." The guard let the door close and waited in the hallway.

"My work is never done, I suppose." Nathill chuckled.

Ron hugged his brother, relieved that he could trust him. Although he hadn't wanted to believe what he'd heard from Erin and Diane, he now knew the truth. A new sense of hope washed over him.

When they were finished, Nathill went through the door just as Conrad passed through.

"So, where would you like to go?" Conrad asked Ron as he approached.

"How about the library? There's something I want to check."

He took Ron down the corridor back to the main hall in the lords' quarters, then led him up the left side staircase to the second floor instead of leaving through the main door. Passing four other doors, Conrad opened a plain, brown door, easily missable.

When Ron entered, he was amazed at the number of books the room held. Tall bookcases wrapped around the walls, running five columns deep and three rows wide. He didn't know how he was ever going to find what he was looking for. Ron looked aimlessly for the oldest books he could find, pulling out a few and flipping through the pages.

"Conrad, are there any books in here that cover the War of the Wielders or any time before that?" Ron asked.

"I think so, but I'm not sure. I could ask the bookkeeper to find some for you."

Ron didn't want to arouse suspicion about what he was searching for, but he wanted to find these books. "Is there a way you could get these books and not tell the bookkeeper who they're for?"

"Of course, I'll just tell say they're for an officer."

"That's perfect. Can you do that and bring the books to me?"

Conrad agreed, then took Ron to his room. After an hour or so, he knocked on Ron's door holding six books.

"Thank you, Conrad."

"What are you looking for?" he asked.

"It might be best if you didn't know." Ron didn't want his friend knowing just in case something went wrong in the next few days and he was brought in for questioning. Conrad got the hint and left Ron to look over the books. He opened the first book's cover, hoping to find what he was looking for within its pages.

Chapter Twenty-Five

Uncovering Answers

Three Orbs sat cradled side by side, placed on a fine white silk cloth. Two glowed a bright, luminescent blue as the flame within them swirled around. The last Orb was a dull, lifeless, opaque gray that yearned to glow bright with the light of the flame. Lord Hadal locked the Orbs away in a private room guarded day and night by only his most trusted soldiers, personally handpicked. No one came close to the room, let alone inside it.

The Orbs were Hadal's most prized possessions. Not only because once he was able to activate the third, he could control the opening of the forge, but for the fact he'd spent the better part of a decade searching for each one. From north of the ruins in the Storming Mountains to the peaks of the northernmost snowcapped foothills to the depths of the great caverns located in the far west amid the roaring seas, Lord Hadal risked life and limb for his prize, and tonight he was going to attempt opening the forge once more.

The day progressed for him just as any other would have. From his chair in the center of the grand hall, he doled out menial tasks to the multitude of servants and messengers he had at his disposal. Common inquiries were brought to his attention if they were deemed necessary by his supporting advisors. Letters of trade agreements that needed his official seal required his attention. With Baddon continuing their trade with Oroze even after its occupation, businesses still needed to be run, and goods needed to be sold. Lord Hadal made good on his word that prices would not increase, and the regular scheduling, along with trade routes, were to go as usual.

His official seal was required, as he was seeking to acquire men with skills in specific trades he felt could help bolster his army and raise the morale of his men by providing new weapons and armor. Of course, the reasoning for wanting these men did not need to be included in his letter, but if he were to conquer the kingdoms, he would need the best for his army. It was all pleasantries anyway, as he had no intention of letting any king or queen keep their seat of power after he conquered. Lord Hadal heated the blue wax, dripping it on the envelope, and pressed his seal down.

Now that the tedious work was finished, Lord Hadal cleared the table as he unrolled a map showing the locations of the other kingdoms as well as towns and villages his scouts had reportedly found. Looking over the map, as he did many times during the day, he planned various ways to acquire each kingdom. First, he considered large-scale troop movements, calculating the risk involved and the possible casualties his army would suffer. In a head-on attack, even though thousands of soldiers manned the First Born army, a strong defense could dwindle his numbers drastically.

He would then gauge the other kingdom's outer defenses, based on the reports from his soldiers, and try to find weaknesses he could exploit. He thought about attacking with the cover of darkness, impregnating the kingdoms with his men by slowly sneaking them in over time, or breaching the defenses himself and letting his soldiers run rampant. Many different ideas came and went, some better than others, so when he held meetings with the appointed officers, the discussions lasted hours as they debated best strategies.

Now, Lord Hadal rose from his chair, walked down the hall, and exited through the doors. He stood at the steps overlooking the vibrant patch of green grass in the courtyard as a chill clung to the breeze blowing in from the Storming Mountains. A storm was coming tonight; he could feel it in the air. Lord Hadal liked how a storm's sound masked the screams of the people he used while trying to open the forge.

Nathill approached from the west wing of the courtyard as the lord stood at the top step just beyond the doors of his quarters, watching. He'd requested Nathill's presence earlier in the day, but due to the trivial work he needed to complete and the time it took for Nathill to get cleaned up, it slipped into the late afternoon. Nathill reached the bottom stair, giving a quick informal bow before he ascended the steps.

"How is Ron's training coming along?" Lord Hadal asked.

"He has learned wielding quicker than I thought he would, but he pushes himself too hard. He doesn't allow his body to recover fast enough before he starts wielding again," Nathill said, telling Lord Hadal the truth but embellishing certain aspects.

"Will he be ready for tonight? Is he able to produce enough power for the Orb?"

Nathill paused, thinking about how to answer without arising suspicion. "Not yet, my lord." That was not what Hadal wanted to hear. A look of disappointment crossed his face, but Nathill continued. "He will be strong, perhaps more so than we have initially thought, but he needs more time to grow his strength, to harness it."

Looking displeased, Lord Hadal said, "How much more time?"

Nathill knew he was on thin ice and needed to tread carefully. "Only a few more days, three at the most. When Ron wields the flame, he uses his power too quickly; his control and reserves of power need to be cultivated a bit more before he's ready."

When Nathill told Ron he could only get him a couple days more, he wasn't just grabbing at a random estimation of time. Lord Hadal's patience was known to fly off the handle when it came to things he wanted.

"You think you can have Ron ready in these extra couple of days? You do understand if he's not ready on time, you will suffer the consequences of your failures?"

"Yes, Lord Hadal, I understand. Ron will be ready in the next few day, you have my word." Nathill understood well enough the punishment for failure. Hadal had a propensity to remove the things Nathill cared most for when he failed him. Only this time, the thing Nathill cared most for was Ron. Granted, Lord Hadal did not know of the scheme they were hatching, but that only meant he would find something else. Nathill had learned to hide what he considered most valuable ever since he lost the love of his life.

Three years after Nathill left Regis, he found someone who shared his views and interests. Her name was Lucett, and she tended to the kitchens, overseeing meals, ordering food supply, and hiring cooks with superior talent. She did everything from breakfast to dinner, grand feasts, banquets, and even the prisoners' feeding. She ran her kitchen staff well, with respect and gratitude, only showing a harsh side when First Born officials, officers, or the lord himself would come down and visit to see how well the operations were running. Nathill became entranced the moment he laid eyes on her. Her sun-kissed blond hair, her lustrous green eyes that could pick him out of the procession while he walked through the kitchens, and a smile so infectious it followed him into his dreams.

When Nathill was done with his duties, he would find any excuse to go down to the kitchens. Even if he wasn't hungry and didn't have any reason to be there, he would find a way. His status as a wielder, second only to Lord Hadal, gave him more confidence than he would've possessed if he lacked title, but she was able to see straight through his façade. Something about Lucett made him nervous; perhaps it was her beauty, the way she presented herself, or the fact titles meant little to her. It was almost as if her gaze pierced through him, showing her the person he wished he could be.

He knew he was falling for her the moment they spoke to each other. Shortly after their first conversation, a new romance began to bloom. They both were able to be themselves around each other, always finding time to sneak away to have secret rendezvous during the night. Lucett shared stories of her youth and how she came to be in the employ of the First Born. Of course, these stories did not always end happily, but Nathill felt more connected to her than anyone else he'd ever met.

Perhaps it was their shared bond through tragedy that connected them so. His feelings grew stronger for her over time, as did hers for him. They talked and dreamed about a life together far removed from the First Born. They both knew it was only a fantasy they shared, but as long as they were together, they were happy.

Over the next couple of months, Nathill made sure to see Lucett every day, even if it was only for a passing glance, a passionate hug, or to simply steal a kiss. Just seeing her gave him a brighter disposition and helped him get through even the worst of days. As long as she was there, he knew where his happiness was, but everything changed when he came to understand the repercussions of failing Lord Hadal.

Now, Nathill tried clearing his mind, but thoughts of Lucett lingered as he listened. "Alright then, you have two more days." Lord Hadal turned, walking back toward the entrance to his quarters. Then he stopped. "Oh, there's one more thing, Nathill." Hadal turned to face him. "I need you to go to the ark and find four capable prisoners. Once you have found them, bring them to my private chamber. I have a message I need to send, so let's see if anyone is strong enough to open the forge." A smile curved on his face as he took his leave.

Nathill walked along the borders of the patch of grass as he headed to the ark. His thoughts were consumed with Lucett. It had been some time since he last thought of her; some of the memories were too painful to remember. He recalled the last time he was unable to follow the orders Lord Hadal had given him.

He'd been supposed to go to smaller outlying villages that had received the lord's messages about joining the First Born. He was to get their answer and take the willing men and women back to Lord Hadal to be trained as new recruits. As for those opposed to joining the First Born, Nathill was charged with killing them. He did as he was ordered, but on his way back with the new recruits, word must have spread to the other villages that the First Born were coming. An ambush was set, and Nathill walked right into it.

Men from the neighboring villages surrounded him, the recruits, and the First Born soldiers on the road. Steel rang as swords were drawn, by First Born and villagers alike. The men shouted death threats at the soldiers while others could be heard calling the recruits cowards and betrayers. The next thing Nathill knew, a battle broke out. Soldiers and men charged at each other, clashing violently.

Scents of blood and death filled the air; men and soldiers lay fallen on the ground as some of the recruits ran for their lives.

Nathill had had enough killing for the day, but his power was not fully restored after he razed a small village to the ground. With what power he had left, he wielded the flame into his hands, yelling for his soldiers to stop fighting and regroup. Unfortunately, less than half of the First Born soldiers were left standing. Nothing was left of the recruits, as they'd either fled during the battle or died at the hands of the villagers. The men who ambushed them now had the greater numbers.

Nathill offered to let the men leave with their lives if they would only turn and walk away. He wished they would, but they wanted to fight as his luck would have it. They were tired of the First Born's raids, senseless killing, and taking of their people. Nathill stepped in front of his soldiers, holding the flame in his hands, watching as the men ran toward him. Then, with a sigh, he unleashed the flame in two steady streams of liquid fire. It clung to the men's flesh as they fell to the ground, writhing and screaming. Nathill cut the flow of power, and a shocking pain shot through his fingers to his palms, ending at his wrists. He screamed as he watched his skin crack and split, releasing smoke while lines of scar tissue burned through his hands.

He returned to Lord Hadal with fewer men than he left with and no recruits to speak of. He explained what had happened, and as Nathill learned, the lord did not tolerate failure, especially at the cost of his own men. Lord Hadal explained there would be consequences, and over the next few days, he waited for his punishment, but it never came.

Now, Nathill turned a corner and headed straight for the large stone doors of the ark. His mind drifted to the last day he saw Lucett. He'd already said goodbye for the night and left out the side entrance of the kitchen when he forgot he still had a small gift in his pocket he wanted to give Lucett. Nathill pushed the door open but backed away as he heard the main kitchen door open. He pushed gently on the door, trying to see who would've been going in the kitchen so late at night. He couldn't see their face or hear what they were talking about, so he pushed the door open just a bit more. He saw long white robes with a belt of woven rope fixed in the center. Nathill wondered why the father would be talking to Lucett at this time of night; he would have to ask Lucett about it the next time he saw her, but as he watched, the father took her by the arm, and they left the kitchen.

That was the last time Nathill laid eyes on the woman he had fallen in love with. The following day, she was nowhere to be found—she just disappeared. Nathill knew the father and Lord Hadal were the ones responsible, but there was nothing he could do. He didn't know why the father would take her, but then it made sense.

Lord Hadal had somehow found out he was spending his time with Lucett. He'd thought they were careful not to get seen or discovered, but the lord knew.

Nathill reached the entrance to the ark. A guard tapped the stone doors, and they split open as two hulking guards pushed from the inside. Nathill walked through the tunnels, hearing the distant screaming of the scarred locked away in the deep bowels of the mountain as he wound his way to the prisoners' cells. He knocked on the door and waited for the patrolling guard to let him in.

Once inside the dim-lit hallway, he said, "Bring me four prisoners that still have the strength to stand." The guard nodded and walked off to find the prisoners. There was no way for Nathill to tell who had more strength, no one had that sort of ability, but he figured if they still had a will to fight, they would be stronger than the rest. He'd never understood how Lord Hadal found these people, but it was of no concern.

While Nathill waited by the door for the guard to round up the prisoners, he reached into his jacket's inner pocket, pulling out a piece of paper. He stared at it fondly—the drawing he'd made of Lucett, the picture he'd meant to give her the night she disappeared.

The four prisoners, each shackled, walked behind Nathill, keeping pace as he led them through the tunnels. None of them spoke a word, too afraid to even whisper to one another. All prisoners were kept in single cells within the tunnels, never seeing or talking to the others. Some went insane just from being isolated for so long. Others begged for death so they could have some form of release or escape from the nightmare they were trapped in. Little did they know, each and every one of them had a purpose, and tonight these chosen four would find out what it was.

Nathill came to a wooden door, pushing it open and leading the prisoners into the main hall of the lords' quarters. Each looked amazed at the sheer size of the hall, though their eyes winced from the natural light that flooded the room. It was the first bright light they had seen in months. A group of guards were waiting to receive the prisoners once Nathill selected them.

"You know your orders. These men are to be fed, bathed, and left to rest until it's time to wake them later this evening. Once the sun has fallen, bring them back here, and I will take them to Lord Hadal."

"Yes, sir," the guards said in unison as they went to the task at hand. Nathill left the lords' quarters and felt the cool breeze brush against him. He walked toward his room in the west wing and decided that now was the right time for him to figure out how to help Ron, with only two days left before Hadal saw to it personally.

* * *

Putting aside another book that contained no helpful information, Ron opened the next one. The books Ron requested were fascinating. If he had time to read them at his leisure, he would, but as time was of the essence, he was looking for very specific writings—anything regarding the Orbs of Ember. He hoped to find something about how to destroy them, but nothing turned up. Still, he had unopened books stacked five high. The covers all looked the same. Each book was old, fragile, and worn to the point the words on the covers were faded and unreadable.

Turning another page, Ron continued reading. He felt he had already read this exact passage before. The wording seemed different, but he didn't realize it until a name appeared that he recognized. Ron knew what he was reading the second he found the name Taroth.

The first few pages were similar to the story Collins translated for them. There were subtle differences, but nothing that varied greatly. Once he found where the story left off in the translated papers he collected from Nathill's room, he focused intently on what was written.

After Taroth had vanished into the night, leaving Thalom to grieve over the bodies of his dead mother and father, Thalom never saw Taroth again. Reports steadily came in during the first year since Taroth murdered Thalom's family, reports of a wielder murdering innocents in a rage, burning their homes, and taking what was left of the spoils for himself. Panic ensued for the people living in towns and small villages not protected by city walls, as no one knew where Taroth would go next.

Then, one night, as a report claimed, Taroth unsuspectedly arrived in a small mining town as the people slept. Before they knew it, he set fire to all the mining equipment and outlying homes, and made his way through the town. As the report stated, this was the first time Taroth had appeared wearing a white mask with black lines above and below the left eye. Word began to spread throughout the kingdoms. The destructive power of the flame was enough reason for people to fear him, but the mask elevated him too much more; after that night, Taroth was no longer referred to by his name. Instead, he became known as the Demon Wielder.

The attacks became less frequent, but continued sporadically. Most people thought that since there was a price on his head in all the kingdoms, he kept the attacks random to avoid leaving a pattern, only attacking when he needed provisions. With a substantial bounty on his head, men from all regions within the kingdoms went looking for the Demon Wielder. Most never returned, and the ones that came back were never the same.

Ron turned the page.

Months turned into years, and the story of the Demon Wielder continued to strike fear throughout the kingdoms. However, no one could find him, and people continued to die as they searched. With the help of their respective kings and queens, townsfolk and villagers fortified the borders of the outlying towns and villages. Walls were constructed, watchtowers built, and soldiers were placed in each settlement within the kingdoms, but the attacks still came.

Everything changed when one man called for an audience with all the kings and queens within the lands. When they all gathered, he introduced himself in front of them—his name was Thalom. He proposed to the council of royals seated before him that if he were provided with an army, he would seek out and destroy Taroth, once and for all ending the Demon Wielder's reign of terror.

When pressed about how he would accomplish such a task, he revealed to the council that Taroth was not the only wielder left in existence. Thalom gave a grand spectacle, showcasing the power of the flame, the likes of which the royal council had never witnessed before. They had only ever experienced the aftermath caused by the destructive power of the flame, but now standing before them was their hope and salvation from the demon that had plagued their lands.

Thalom was granted a massive army that brought together soldiers from each kingdom, massing in the thousands. The people rejoiced as they set out to find the Demon Wielder and put a stop to his cruelty. Thalom led the army throughout the kingdoms, searching every town and village, checking every person's home, leaving no stone unturned as they searched. He gave the best description to his soldiers that he could provide. He hadn't seen Taroth in years, but it wouldn't matter. The most distinct feature Taroth possessed was the scars on his face, above and below his left eye.

Traveling into the north with his army, Thalom came upon a small farming village that could easily be eclipsed by the sheer size of his army. It was there, in the village, that Thalom came face-to-face with Taroth. Upon discovering him, Thalom questioned what his eyes had seen. He asked his men to stay back as he approached the man he suspected to be Taroth on foot. Thalom was within inches of Taroth for the first time in years, the first time since the murder of Thalom's parents.

Ron turned the page to see that the book abruptly ended; pages had been ripped from the book's binding. It didn't surprise him, as the book was centuries old, but he was so enthralled with the story he wanted to read the rest. He closed the book and put it to the side. Ron knew how the rest of the story played out. It culminated in the Battle of the Storming Mountains.

Picking up the next volume from the stack, he began to read. Halfway through the time-stained book, Ron came across a passage mentioning the Orbs of Ember and a word he did not recognize. The passage stated that the Orbs had been created by the champion, chosen by the Essenti, to open the forge gate if the need ever arose to banish those of the Falla Essen that dwelt in the shadows. Each Orb was crafted from the condensed flame of the champion, compacted, then rapidly cooled to form a perfect spherical structure. Three wielders of great power were required to activate each individual Orb, with no Orb being lit by the same wielder.

Ron didn't know what the Falla Essen was, but he thought there must have been a good reason if they were banished to the forge. The following pages detailed unrest amongst the other wielders after the champion's death as power struggles ensued. Claim over the Orbs of Ember gripped the wielders, leading to a war in which whoever controlled the Orbs could turn the tide in their favor.

Amid the countless dead and constant fighting, the Orbs were stolen from the wielders' possession by an unknown assailant during the night.

The war had ended, and the Orbs were lost to the world. After a time, they were forgotten, only talked of as an old legend. Eventually, they became thought of only as a myth, with some questioning if they'd ever truly existed.

Ron finished reading. Disappointment washed over him. He was hoping for any mention of how to destroy the Orbs. If it wasn't written, they might be impossible to destroy. If they were made with such raw unrivaled power as the champion possessed, why would he think he could destroy them? The only way to stop Lord Hadal was to steal the Orb, and somehow make it disappear.

He placed the book on the already-read pile, but it slipped off the edge, falling to the floor. The book lay open as he picked it up and saw an inscription he'd missed in his prior readings. Written at the tail end of the last page, Ron found what he was looking for. The inscription stated that once the Orbs had a steady glow with the power of the flame swirling inside, they would become active. However, if a constant flow of power continued to be released, the flame would overload the capacity of what the Orbs of Ember could contain, forcing them to shatter. This was the only way to destroy them; any other method would be useless.

Relieved that he'd found something of use, Ron looked up from the books on his desk as he heard a powerful wind blow past his window. Pulling the red curtains back, he gazed out at the howling wind, carrying the loose dust off the ground, forcing it every which way. Thick, heavy clouds rolled across the sky, blocking the sun. Ron closed his eyes and let the power of the flame run through his body to his senses. He could hear the low rumble in the dense clouds, the intensity of the wind continuing to grow with every gust that followed, and he could smell the rain in the air. He felt the coming storm.

* * *

Rain tapped on the windows of the lords' quarters as the guards waited patiently with the rested prisoners for Nathill's arrival. Finally, the double doors of the main hall were pushed open and Nathill walked through, shedding his soaked cloak and handing it to one of the guards.

"Are these prisoners ready?" he asked.

"Yes, sir, they have been cared for just as you requested." Nathill looked over each of the prisoners, examining their frightened faces; he couldn't help but feel a sense of sorrow for these men. They didn't know what would happen to them once Nathill brought them to Lord Hadal. He could see the worry and the fear in their eyes. Each man, while a prisoner of the First Born, was not necessarily a criminal. Most who found their way to the Ark of Redemption were people that had not submitted to the new lord, people who'd believed their freedom was more important than the rule of a madman, or who unknowingly had the gift of the Essenti.

Nathill led the prisoners up the right staircase, following the balcony straight back to the left until he came to a door in the middle. He walked through, knowing full well he was leading these men to a fate worse than death, but he held firm to the same rationale he used for years as a justification for his actions. Nathill believed that to stop a great evil, a great sacrifice had to be made. Every cruel act he'd carried out had led him closer to his ultimate goal. Now, with Ron's help, each and every sacrifice, every person who gave their life, would have meaning.

As the prisoners followed Nathill through a dim-lit bedroom, he opened another door on the right wall. He held it open for the men as they piled in, passing the guard in charge of keeping the room secure when not in use. Fire danced on the oil-soaked wicks of the lamps hanging on the walls, showing the room was empty, with no paintings and no furniture to speak of. All that was in the room was one table draped in a white cloth. In the center of the table, forming a line, were two glowing Orbs, one of blue fire and one of cloudy gray. A few scattered pieces of paper were placed off to the side.

Lord Hadal stood to the left of the table, watching the flame circulate inside the Orbs. He briefly acknowledged Nathill and the prisoners as he walked along the table, picking up the first glowing Orb. On the right of the table was a large, constructed metal triangle standing as tall as an average person. Each corner had a round opening that could fit one Orb, so Lord Hadal placed one filled with the flame in the bottom left corner. Next, he motioned for Nathill to place the second Orb in the bottom right corner, and once he did, Lord Hadal finally placed the opaque gray Orb at the top. The Orbs on the bottom erupted with a blue flame spreading across the center bar of the triangle, but the two bars leading to the last Orb did nothing.

"You may leave us," Lord Hadal said, waving his hand at Nathill.

The prisoners' eyes darted from each other to the flame of the Orbs to Lord Hadal. They waited for whatever was to come next.

"You four have been chosen to aid me in a task that, if successful, will not just elevate myself and the First Born. For whoever can activate the last Orb, your life will change considerably. No longer will you be imprisoned. You will have full, unrestrained freedom. You will be awarded a title regardless of your current status, and I will grant you any land in which you choose to live. All I require is for one of you to activate the last Orb." Lord Hadal pointed to the Orb at the top of the triangle. "Light it by flowing all the power you can into it, and I will grant you all I have promised. Once you begin, you cannot stop until the Orb is activated. If you quit at any time, your chances of freedom will be forfeit, and the next person in line will have their chance."

The look of hope in each man's eye brought a grim smile to Lord Hadal's face; they dreamed of being free, and he knew just how to exploit their desire. He'd learned that giving a man a chance for something he truly craved would bring forth more effort and determination.

Lord Hadal had not always offered such a special reward before this idea came to him. He'd tried the other, more traditional routes. Torture worked well for a time, but he found it drained the person's ability to focus their power entirely into the Orb. He used the fear of being tortured as well, as some responded just to the idea of insurmountable pain. But the processes had taken far too long for Lord Hadal's liking, and he would end up torturing them anyway. Now his best method was to do nothing but watch as the men did the work for him, all in the name of hope, which was perhaps his cruelest plan yet.

Rain battered the windows, thunder boomed, and lightning struck in the sky. Lord Hadal watched as the first man placed his hand upon the opaque Orb of Ember and began the flow of power through his body. The man's face strained as he forced the power out of his body; the Orb pulsated with a blue glow that came and went. Sweat began to bead down the man's cheek. He ground his teeth while his hand gripped tightly around the Orb. The pulsating slowed, showing a low glow starting to build in the Orb. Blue fire shot down the metal sides of the triangle, connecting to the Orbs below. Finally, in the center of the triangle frame, the air began to shimmer with heat.

"Yes, give it more power—you're almost there," Lord Hadal said, feeding the man's desire. The man swung his other hand on top of the Orb, flowing more power than he had. Agonizing screams burst from his mouth, but he did not stop. The offer of freedom was too good to pass up. The shimmer swelled within the triangle as the man continued to scream; he closed his eyes, pushing more power into the Orb. Smoke began to rise from his hand. His skin burned and split at a rapid rate, quickly overtaking his hands, his wrists, and then his arms.

At the same time, Lord Hadal reached for a piece of paper, rolling it up and quickly tying off each end. An ear-shattering crack echoed within the room. The other three men covered their ears as Lord Hadal stared at the forge gate before him. He could hardly hear the suffering cries of pain from the man still holding on to the Orb. Lord Hadal threw the rolled paper into the forge gate, and then suddenly the gate vanished, but the screaming remained.

The smell of burnt flesh, hair, and clothing rose within the smoke filling the room. Relentless screams persisted as the man holding the Orb was lost to the flame, lost to the curse of the Essenti. He was no longer in control. Power flowed freely from his body to the Orb, but soon the screams stopped. The man stood, his eyes rolled back in his head, his arms fell to his sides, and his scarred body collapsed to the ground. The other three men huddled together, looking at what just happened in panic.

"Looks like he wasn't strong enough. Hopefully, one of you is." Lord Hadal said casually as he walked to the door and tapped on it. The guard on the other side came in. "Take his body to the Ark before he wakes up."

"Yes, sir."

The guard dragged the scarred man from the room, shutting the door behind him. Standing by the metal triangle, Lord Hadal looked to the men. "Who's next?"

A thunderous boom shook the walls of the room; a forge gate appeared for a brief moment, just long enough for Lord Hadal to throw another rolled message in before it folded in on itself and disappeared. Another boom crashed in the distance, louder than any thunder heard by ordinary men and women.

That sounded close. Power surged from the second man attempting to gain his freedom, his will and power stronger than the last; his eyes widened as he saw the Orb under his hands glow a steady, bright blue, thinking he might be able to activate it. Lord Hadal waited patiently for another forge gate to appear. To his dismay, all he heard was another distant boom. The power put forth by this man was not enough to create stability. He watched the hands upon the Orb crack and smoke as scars raced down the man's arms. The destruction of this man's body was much faster.

The burning and scarring made it all the way to his chest and torso before he lost himself to the flame. The curse had taken over his body, the damage was done, and his screams became hoarse before they were silent. His scarred hands slipped from the Orb as he fell on the ground, convulsing violently with drool spilling from his mouth. Lord Hadal shook his head in disappointment, reaching down to grab the shaking arm of the man on the floor. He dragged him to the door, passing his limp body to the guard on the other side to be taken to the Ark.

Lord Hadal waited for the next participant to take their place when the door closed, but no one moved. In fear, they huddled together, pressing against the far wall, no longer wanting the guaranteed freedom promised by the lord. All they wanted was to walk out of this room alive, but after seeing what happened with the other two men, they were not sure it was possible. Sensing the hesitation, Lord Hadal called the flame to his hand.

"Either one of you willingly goes up there, or I will kill you where you stand. If you choose the first option, you may walk away with your life."

One man timidly walked to the Orb. Placing his hands on it, he closed his eyes and began the process.

The thunder was eclipsed by the shocking booms of the opening forge gates outside in the rain and darkness. With smoke rising and screams coming faster than from either man before him, the third prisoner let go of the Orb, holding his hands to his chest, weeping from the pain.

"I can't do it, my lord. I'm not strong enough to do as you wish. Please forgive me." The man sank to his knees, sobbing openly. Lord Hadal quelled his frustrations as he approached the crying prisoner, placing his hand on top of his head.

"It's okay. Not everyone is strong enough to handle such power. Such power is not meant for those who are too weak to see the true gift they possess. This power is not meant for people like you." The man looked up from the floor, beginning to speak, but Lord Hadal tightened his grasp on the top of his head, and with a quick twist of his wrist, snapped the man's neck. Without letting go of the lifeless body dangling from his hand, Lord Hadal hurled it across the room, sending it crashing into the door. He made his way to the last prisoner, who shrank against the wall.

The lord's cruelly twisted face was inches away from the prisoner before he stopped and slowly backed away. While the power of the flame flowed through his heightened senses, he thought he heard something. He listened intently, searching for sounds other than rain and thunder. All was quiet when he found the sound he was searching for. A bell was ringing. It was faint, but he recognized the sound. Lord Hadal rushed to the door, kicking aside the dead prisoner and swinging it open. Standing before him were dozens of guards, preparing to open the door themselves, worried expressions across all of their faces.

Chapter Twenty-Six

The Storm's Arrival

"**M**y lord, there's an attack happening in the outer encampment of Noic," the soldier in front said, trying to catch his breath.

"Why didn't you alert me sooner? How long has this been going on?" Anger was attached to each word Lord Hadal spoke.

"We were just alerted to the rising fires, my lord; as soon as we saw them, we sounded the alarm."

"Who's attacking us?" he demanded to know.

The guard looked afraid to answer. "We don't know, my lord—it's too dark to see."

Hadal was seething, ready to strike the guard for how little he knew about the attack, but Nathill came running around the corner.

"Lord Hadal, you're needed at the front gates immediately. I've received word from one of the messengers from Noic." Nathill wiped the sweat from his forehead.

"Do you know who's attacking?" Lord Hadal asked, wanting to know who would be foolish enough to try to attack the First Born in the cover of night.

"It's not a who. The messenger said creatures came through the forge—abominations, as he called them. He doesn't know how many came through, but Noic has been overrun."

A quick look of worry dispelled any anger Lord Hadal had left. "I will make for the gates as soon as I retrieve my weapon. Guards," he commanded. "Take the prisoner back to the Ark."

Before the guards could comply, Nathill spoke. "My lord, they're needed more at the front; I will take the prisoner and alert the guards in the Ark to reinforce the entrances."

"Fine, I don't care, just make sure once you're done to come and join me at the front."

Nathill gave a slight bow. "Yes, my lord."

The guards went to their duties while Hadal retrieved his sword; Nathill took the prisoner by the arm, walking quickly down the stairs and into the courtyard.

There, Nathill let the prisoner go. "I have no intention of taking you to the Ark. I have other things I need to attend to. I'm giving you one opportunity to take your freedom back—don't waste this chance. Find a way out. If you get captured again, you will be killed." Nathill turned away, wasting no more time with the prisoner as he headed for Ron's room in the east wing.

Alarm bells rang in the night, clashing with the ever-present thunder and rain vying for attention in the darkness. Nathill pounded his fist on the door, shouting his brother's name.

Pulling the door open, Ron stared at him. "What's going on? Why have the alarms sounded?"

"Ron, now is the time. You have to take the last Orb of Ember and escape. Something is attacking the outer encampments, and now it's coming toward Oroze. Lord Hadal is out of his quarters, and the guards are at the city's front gate. No one is guarding the room with the Orbs. You have to go now—I don't think you will have a better chance than this."

Ron acknowledged the urgency in Nathill's voice but asked, "Where is the room? I don't know where to go."

"I had a guard tell Conrad to meet you here. He will take you there, but be careful—if anyone sees you, they will not hesitate to attack."

Ron grabbed his blue jacket, throwing it over his shoulders as he stepped out onto the balcony. He turned to see Conrad coming down the hall. "What about you? What are you going to do?" he asked.

"I have to go meet Lord Hadal at the gates. I can buy you some time by bringing any guards I see with me, so you have a clear path."

Ron did not like the idea. "Come with me—we can escape together. You shouldn't have to stay here any longer."

Nathill shook his head. "I can't just yet. If Lord Hadal were to double back for some reason, I would need to stall him to give you more time. That's what matters, getting you and the Orb out of here. First, take the tunnels—that will be your best path out. Conrad will show you where the entrance is. You will have to fight your way through. Guards are stationed all along them. The best advice I can give you is if you feel like you are going downhill, that's most likely the way out."

Conrad joined Ron and Nathill outside his room and got caught up on what the plan was.

"I can't just leave you, Nathill, not again. Please come with us," Ron pleaded.

"We're running out of time. The best I can do is to try and meet you in the tunnels, but if I take too long, don't wait for me. I will do my best to meet you there, but I can't promise you. Now go!" Nathill shouted, giving his brother a light shove to get him moving.

Ron and Conrad ran down the stairs, across the courtyard, and into the lords' quarters. As they burst through the doors into the dimly lit hall, Conrad directed Ron toward the right staircase. Then a door opened on the far left of the room. Four guards emerged and rushed to join the rest of the soldiers at the city gates, but they stopped in their tracks once they saw Conrad and Ron heading for the stairs.

"You two, stop right there! What is the meaning of this? You have no business being in here." The guards walked over, pulling their swords from their scabbards.

"Go up the stairs, hurry," Ron yelled.

As Conrad ran up, he shouted back, "What about you?"

"We can't let them alert anyone else. I have to stop them here and now if we're to have any chance of getting out."

The lead guard shouted, "You're not going anywhere!" As he approached with a menacing scowl, Ron stepped forward, clearing his mind as the hum of the song filled his thoughts and the flame sprang forth, covering both hands.

Each guard paused, worried, as they did not expect to find a wielder wandering in the lords' quarters, but after the initial shock came to an end, they all charged at Ron. Ron pivoted to the right as the first sword swung past. Using the flame inside his body to amplify his speed, he felt the power surge through him into his muscles as he balled his fist. He struck the guard hard in the face, sending his body straight down. It broke the marble flooring, leaving a small crater; the man lay there motionless.

Yelling came from the other guards as they attacked all at once. Ron's speed was unmatched. He was able to watch each attack as they came, dodging and moving out of the way. The frustrated guards continued their onslaught, but one broke from the others in an attempt to catch Conrad.

Ron knew he had to help. Channeling more power into his movements, he evaded the next barrage of attacks, swiftly moving between the guards. He elbowed one in the back of the head, then ducked, avoiding the other guard's sword as it flew over. Ron rose, and as he did, he delivered a punch to the man's stomach, causing him to double over, heaving for air.

With his path now clear, Ron ran to the steps as the last guard ascended them. Ron pulled power into his hand, feeling the weight of the flame as it built. Then he cut the flow of power and hurled the ball of flame at the guard. It smashed into the guard's back, immediately setting him ablaze. He screamed and fell down the stairs, hitting each step, finally coming to a stop at the bottom with his limbs bent and broken.

Ron felt a tight knot turn in his stomach, and without thinking, he let his body take over. The power of the flame coursed through him, igniting his senses. He was right to listen, but he didn't realize what was happening soon enough. As he turned his body, the blade of a sword sliced his upper right shoulder, tearing the skin. Ron had saved Conrad, but he'd focused too little on the guards that had recovered from his blows. Pulling back, Ron rushed over to the body of the first guard he'd killed, retrieving the sword still clutched in his hand.

With both remaining guards now on their feet, they came at Ron. Steel clashed against steel, with Ron blocking each incoming attack, one after another. Then, feeling the flame course through his veins, he saw an opening to respond. Ron stepped back to avoid a downward slash, and before the guard could bring the weapon back up to defend himself, Ron brought his own sword down, splitting the man's head in half. The last guard swung at Ron's neck, hoping to take advantage of Ron's sword momentarily being stuck, but he let go and dropped to a knee, taking the dead guard's sword from the ground. He quickly eviscerated the last guard, almost severing him in two.

A wave of fatigue briefly came over Ron, and he took a deep breath as he stood looking at the blood and bodies on the cold marble floor. Then, with no time to dwell on what had just occurred, Ron shook off the tired feeling and ran up the stairs to catch up to Conrad, who was already waiting at the door.

"Your arm—you're bleeding."

"It's nothing; I'll take care of it later, after we get out of here. Now, where's the Orb?" Ron asked.

"Through here, follow me."

They passed through Lord Hadal's personal quarters. Conrad pushed open a door, leading Ron into the room containing the Orbs of Ember. "They're in here."

Conrad tripped over something on the floor just beyond the door. In the soft blue glow of the two activated Orbs, he looked down at what had softened his fall and found himself staring into the open eyes of a dead man. Conrad tried to push away in a panic, but fear had taken his feet from under him as he scurried away. Ron reached under his arms, pulling him off the dead body, making sure he was alright.

Once Conrad assured him he was fine, Ron looked at the Orbs. The two on the bottom glowed a steady blue, with the power of the flame swirling around. The one at the top of the metal triangle was gray, waiting to be activated.

Ron took the Orb from the top, holding it in the palm of his hand; it felt as if it were made of glass based on how smooth it was to the touch. It felt weightless but dense at the same time. Ron wondered how something could feel so fragile yet be near impossible to destroy. He placed the Orb on the ground, bringing the flame to his hand, relieved as the song hummed in his mind. It made the pain of calling the flame no longer a burden, so he focused on the Orb, held out his hand, and sent a stream of liquid blue fire into it.

He held steady, waiting for the glow to appear. Then he stopped the flow of power and stared at the glowing Orb as the flame drifted around inside it. No longer was the Orb opaque or gray. Ron took a deep breath, held his hand out, and continued to pour the flame into the Orb. Beads of sweat rolled down the side of his face; this was taking longer than he'd hoped. So Ron dropped the sword and brought the flame into his other hand, adding more power, waiting for the Orb to break.

Nothing happened. Ron cut off the flow of power; he didn't know what he was doing wrong. He did what the book said, but the Orb remained the same. Ron knew he couldn't put any more power into the Orb tonight, or else he might not have enough strength to fight his way out of the tunnels. He picked up the Orb and shoved it into the bottom inner pocket of his jacket, snapping the two buttons closed.

He nodded to Conrad, ready to head to the tunnels, but then suddenly turned back to the other two Orbs. Ron thought for a moment. Why take just one when it would be better to take them all? That way, he could hide the Orbs in different locations, making it all the more difficult for Lord Hadal to track them down again. He bent a knee and reached for one of the activated Orbs, but he could not move it when he tried to pick it up. It was the same with the other one.

He didn't understand how the first Orb could be weightless, but the other two wouldn't even budge. Ron let the flame flow through his body, then attempted to pick them up once more. He struggled just as much as the first time. He didn't understand why this was happening, but he knew he had to leave them. Trying to figure it out was wasting too much time.

"Damnit!" he said to himself before he turned and left the room with Conrad in tow. "Alright, Conrad, where's the entrance to the tunnels?" He was already following the man, but he knew Conrad would feel better telling him.

"Funny enough, they're right below us." At the bottom of the stairs, past the dead guards, they walked to the back of the hall. A door just as ordinary as any other within the lords' quarters stood before them. Ron opened the door to the dark tunnels leading into the mountain; he walked in and didn't hear any footsteps other than his own.

"Conrad, what are you doing? Let's go."

"I can't. If I go with you, the lord and all the First Born will know it was me that helped you, and they'll come after me. But if I stay, I can keep working here and live with some sort of peace," Conrad said quietly.

"You can't stay here, Conrad. what do you think will happen when all the soldiers and Lord Hadal return? They all know you've been the one to escort me everywhere; you will be the first person they suspect of helping me escape."

Conrad remained silent, thinking over Ron's words.

"Look, I can't promise life will be easy if you come with me, but at least you will have a life, a free one." Ron paused. "Please, Conrad, I can't leave my friends behind."

The reminder that he still had someone he could call a friend was what Conrad needed to push past his fear of leaving Oroze. Then Ron turned, facing the tunnel's entrance and calling the flame into his hand, lighting the way as he and Conrad began their journey into the darkness.

The smell of wet mold filled the corridors, reminding Ron of his time locked away in a cell. It was a scent he wouldn't mind forgetting if he were afforded the chance. The tunnels twisted and turned, with different pathways leading to other sections within the mountain. Some would lead right to the heart of the Ark of Redemption, a place Ron and Conrad wanted to avoid at all costs.

They used the light from the flame to navigate; it was much brighter than the candles. If Ron suspected any sound or movement ahead, he would quickly extinguish the flame in his hand and hold position, hoping to have the element of surprise once he attacked. Luckily, Ron and Conrad didn't come across any

First Born soldiers for some time, but Ron had no idea where he was going as everything in the tunnels looked the same. Minute later, it still didn't yet feel like they were walking downhill.

"Does anything feel familiar to you?" Ron asked Conrad, hoping he knew.

"No, I have never gone through the lord's entrance before. Even so, I only know one route, and that's to the cells and back."

"Well, we will just have to get lucky, I guess." Ron stopped walking as he came to the head of a four-way junction with better lighting than the entirety of the tunnel they'd started in.

"Which way do you think?" Conrad asked. Ron didn't know, but before he could reply, he heard movement. He placed his hand to Conrad's chest, pushing him back into the tunnel against a wall and dropping the flame from his hand at the same time. Ron gripped the sword tightly in his right hand as he heard footsteps and voices growing louder.

"You stay here—I'll take care of the soldiers. Do not move," Ron whispered, catching the agreeing nod from Conrad in the low light of the candles.

Three First Born soldiers came from the tunnels to the left, walking single file. Ron waited until the last soldier passed, knowing he would have to be quick and keep the noise to a minimum if he didn't want all the soldiers from the ark to hear the sounds of fighting. Ron stepped out silently into the light, trailing close behind the last soldier in line. He pushed the power of the flame through his body and began his assault.

With power and speed, he grabbed the last soldier, covering the man's mouth with his hand and slicing his throat. He set the soldier down gently, hoping to not alert the other two. Still, the black armor shifted, plates rubbing together, making just enough noise to catch the middle soldier's attention. Ron rushed forward and struck before the man's sword was pulled from its scabbard. Blood gushed from the soldier's now-broken nose, which Ron had bashed in with his hilt. The soldier fell to his knees, and without pause, Ron drove the blade down between his collarbone and neck.

Once Ron removed the sword, he saw the soldier leading the line, ready to fight to the death, but Ron had other plans. The soldier attacked while Ron defended against his strikes, stepping back over the bodies toward the four-way junction, giving the soldier the impression he was gaining the upper hand.

Then, stepping into the light with much more room to maneuver, Ron put his plan into action as the soldier swung hard from the left. Deflecting his attack, Ron spun around to the right, grabbing the soldier's wrist in one hand and tightening his grip on the sword with the other. Ron punched the soldier's elbow as he pulled with his left, snapping the bones clean in half. The man cried out in pain as his arm dangled at his side, but Ron covered his mouth and wrenched his good limb behind his back, applying pressure.

"Now you're going to tell me which tunnel leads to the mountain entrance. I'm going to point you in the direction, and all you have to do is shake your head yes or no. Do you understand?"

The soldier nodded.

"If you lie to me, your death will be long and painful." Ron brought the flame to his hand. The intimidation tactic seemed to work as the man nodded much faster.

Ron pointed the soldier to the left tunnel. He shook his head. Then he pointed him to the middle tunnel—another head shake. That only left the tunnel on the right, but Ron pointed him in that direction anyway. The soldier nodded, then shook his head.

"What does that mean?" Ron asked.

Conrad had seen the soldier give both answers as he emerged from the darkened tunnel. "It must not be as simple as going left, right, or straight from here. There must be other turns we will need to take." The soldier nodded and mumbled in agreement.

"So we'll take him with us. He will lead us to the entrance," Ron said, and the soldier continued to nod eagerly.

"But what if he doesn't? What if he takes us to where more First Born are? He could lead us right to the ark," Conrad argued.

The soldier frantically shook his head as he tried to speak.

"If I remove my hand and you yell, you will be dead before a sound gets out." The soldier agreed, and Ron removed his hand. The man breathed in deep, wincing as any movement of his arm sent waves of pain through him.

"You're the wielder from the banquet. Why are you here? Why are you killing your own men?"

The soldier's question caught Ron off guard.

"What do you mean, my own men?"

"There was a rumor spreading among the men that a new wielder was going to lead us when the time came to march on the other kingdoms."

Ron's thoughts raced. There was no possibility this rumor was about him. Lord Hadal would know better than to think he would be part of the First Born, let alone lead an army to attack another kingdom. Ron wondered who the other wielder could be.

"No, I may be a wielder, but that doesn't mean I want any part of Lord Hadal or the First Born."

"But why? Lord Hadal is trying to unify the kingdoms. He's trying to create a better life for all his followers. Why live in a fractured land when we can all live as one, together? The lord is doing this for the good of the people."

Ron couldn't believe the nonsense coming from the soldier's mouth.

"It's for the good of the people, huh?" he scoffed. "What about not having the freedom to choose how you want to live, or any freedom at all? Or the fact that hundreds of thousands of innocent people are going to die in his pursuit of peace? People should not be forced to submit to the will of a madman." He was trying his best not to shout and draw attention.

"You don't understand—" the soldier began, but Ron had enough.

"No, we're done talking. I refuse to listen to someone that believes this madness. Take us to the entrance." Ron kept pressure on the soldier's good arm while Conrad searched the bodies soldiers for anything they could use as a restraint. Finally, he loosened the buckle of a baldric from around a corpse's waist, stripped it of its scabbard, and bound the soldier's wrists behind his back. Ron held on to the armor plating at the back of the soldier's neck as they cautiously walked through the tunnels.

* * *

Lord Hadal ordered the archers to form a line along the top wall. Rows of soldiers braced the gates, waiting for the inevitable impact from the creatures shrieking in the distant darkness. First Born soldiers came and were directed to their posts by Lord Hadal. Rain clinked off the black armor as it reflected the fiery glow of the oil-soaked torches and lamps, giving light to the soldier's movements. Between the thunder booming in the sky and the flashes of lightning, high-pitched shrieks cried out, one after another.

Nathill finally made his way to the front gates. "I'm here, my lord. What orders do you have for me?"

Hadal finished directing the incoming soldiers before answering. "I want you to hold the line at the gates if whatever is out there breaks through. Whatever these creatures are, you and I may be the only ones strong enough to stop them. I don't know how these things come out of the forge; why is it happening now?" The lord brushed his wet hair back; he'd read all the books in his library and more during his youth, and he knew what lived in the forge, but he didn't understand why or how they could be coming through an unstable forge gate. Sending objects through the gate posed an imminent danger due to its lack of stability. If the gate were to close on an object that had not fully passed through, the object would be split in two.

"We will hold the gates, I'm sure—"

A First Born soldier rode in on a horse, interrupting Nathill. "My lord, there are soldiers, dead soldiers in the lords' quarters. We have been breached."

"That's not possible. There is no one who could—" Lord Hadal looked scared but brushed it off before turning to Nathill. "Where's Ron?" he asked.

"Last I saw, he was locked in his room in the east wing. Why? What's happening?" Nathill asked quickly.

"Did you see any guards posted by my personal quarters?" he asked the soldier on horseback, anger and panic taking over his voice.

"No, my lord, the door to your quarters was open when I arrived and found our murdered men."

Lord Hadal ran both hands through his dripping hair, his face twisted in a fury. "It's him. It has to be. He must have taken the Orb. Give me your horse now!"

The soldier jumped down, passing the reins to Lord Hadal as he mounted the horse.

"Lord Hadal, I'm coming with you," Nathill said.

"No, you're needed here in case those creatures break through."

"But I have an idea of where he might have gone, and if I'm right, I am the only one who knows how to navigate the tunnels without getting lost. So the quicker we find him, the quicker we can be back here."

Lord Hadal weighed his options. His men could be replaced, but finding Ron and his Orb was the highest priority. "Fine. Get on the horse, Captain," the lord shouted at a passing captain, calling him over.

"Yes, my lord," the man said, slightly bowing.

"I need you to send a handful of men to the tunnel entrance in my quarters at once. A dangerous prisoner has fled into the tunnels and must be flushed out. Go now." The captain bowed again and left.

Once Nathill was situated on the horse, Lord Hadal kicked its ribs, riding full speed back toward his quarters. At the base of the steps, they both dismounted, then quickly ran through the doors, past the dead bodies, up the stairs, and into Lord Hadal's quarters. The lord rushed to the open door on the right that held the Orbs. A blue glow filled the room. Nathill followed and saw Hadal standing next to the metal triangle looking at the two remaining Orbs.

The lord shouted, grabbed the table on his left, and heaved it across the room, smashing it into pieces. "That bastard, I'm going to kill him. Once I find him, I'm going to tear him apart."

Lord Hadal headed toward the tunnel entrance, grabbing Nathill's arm to keep pace; all patience was exhausted, and only rage was left. He looked down the hall through the open doors leading to the courtyard and saw what appeared to be no less than thirty soldiers racing to assist their lord. Hadal stormed into the tunnels, shoving Nathill in front of him. "You had better find him, or there will be hell to pay."

Nathill led the way at a run, with the lord right behind him.

* * *

Ron took more turns than he would have thought possible, wondering if anyone would be able to remember their way around such a randomly constructed labyrinth. Then, feeling less weight to his steps, Ron realized they'd found the downhill slope Nathill had told him about. "How much farther?" he asked the soldier.

"Not long—just have to clear a few more cross-sections that run across this passageway. After that, it's only a few hundred feet or so." As they pressed onward, a loud thud shook the ground beneath them.

"What was that?" Conrad asked.

Ron gripped his sword. "I don't know," he said, looking back to Conrad as worry seized him once more. A passageway came into view on the left, and slightly farther up was another passage to the right; they advanced with caution, wondering if anyone else had felt the ground shake. Ron walked in front of the soldier, peering around the left passage, checking to see if it was clear, which it was. As he went to check the right passage, he heard raised voices.

Ron walked back to grab the soldier's armor, but before he could get behind him, as they were standing side by side for a split second, the soldier rammed his head into Ron's temple. It disorientated him for a moment, just long enough for the soldier to push off the wall and slam his shoulder into Ron's chest, knocking him against the other wall.

The soldier took off running, shouting, "A prisoner is loose—he's here, he's here!" Steel echoed from the right passage before the other soldiers came into view as they offered aid to their fellow First Born, cutting his restraints and placing him behind them.

"Be careful. He's a wielder," the wounded soldier warned. The others smirked.

"I've never killed a wielder before. You wielders think you're better than us just because you have power—well, perhaps it's time we show you your rightful place."

The soldiers started in on Ron and Conrad, but then a loud shriek echoed through the entire tunnel system. Another cried out and left a ringing in Ron's ears, but over the ringing, he swore he heard something else. He let the flame flow to his senses and listened closely; he heard the sound of running footsteps, heavy breathing, and shouting as it grew closer. He also felt a knot build in his stomach, and knew something was coming.

The sounds of panic and terror filled the tunnel. Ron called the flame to his hand as he listened to the warning in his body, but he froze once he took in the sight that came barreling from around the corner. He thought his mind, along with the dark, was causing him to imagine things, things that couldn't be real.

Nora, Grant, and Shaw were running in his direction.

They saw the three First Born soldiers but paid little mind, shoving them out of the way, only to stop when Nora came face-to-face with Ron. There she was, standing right in front of him, a vision he had pictured in his head a thousand times since he was taken captive.

He stood speechless, but his eyes were soon pulled to the monstrosity that followed them. The feeling in his stomach faded as the threat now presented itself. The wet, thin, gray skin covering the abnormally long, deformed arms and legs shone in the dim candlelight. Its bulging eyes searched the people standing before it. Saliva slipped past the rows of razor-sharp teeth, falling to the floor. The creature let out a shriek and charged forward. Ron grabbed Nora's hand and pushed Conrad back toward the left passageway, ushering everyone in as he watched the creature swipe the wounded soldier, instantly cutting through the armor as if it were paper.

The force of the attack launched his body and the parts separated from it into the wall, making a bloody mess. The other two soldiers attacked, swinging wildly at the creature, with some strikes cutting the gray skin, but the monster was stronger and faster. Swinging its long arm, it caught one of the soldier's legs, taking it out from under him, then struck the next soldier, pinning him against the wall. The creature was inches from the soldier's face as it looked him up and down, almost as if it had sensed something familiar, something it recognized.

Fear filled the soldier's eyes as he tried to plead for his life, but it was no use. The creature opened its mouth wide and bite down on the soldier's head, crushing his skull with the pressure from its jaw. The lifeless body hung from its mouth and was then tossed away, discarded like trash.

The last soldier rose to his knees, watching the creature stalk closer with the blood of the First Born staining its teeth, and in a matter of seconds, his life too was over. Long, sharp claws burst through his midsection. Raising its elongated arm, the creature let the body slide off.

Ron left the safety of the tunnel and stood before the monster. It looked at him just as it had when it gazed at the soldier it pinned to the wall. Ron could feel it was looking for something; for a second, it seemed like the beast longed for something, something it was missing.

This wasn't the first time Ron had seen this monster. He remembered seeing it from afar in his dream. Now, with the creature standing before him, he started to question how many of his dreams might be real.

As quick as the moment came, it vanished. The creature moved closer, but Ron called the flame into his hand, letting it burn bright. The monster screeched, taking a step back almost as if it were experiencing fear, but then Ron saw what the look in its eyes really was. He knew what the creature was searching for.

Its eyes darted back and forth between Ron and the flame surrounding his hand.

"What are you?" he asked without breaking eye contact. The creature leaped forward, swinging its claws and throwing chunks of dirt forward, leaving large indentations in the tunnel walls. The flame flowed through Ron as he let it spread unchecked; he didn't know what to use against this creature, so he decided his best bet was to let his body and power do the thinking for him. Ron raised his sword, blocking the powerful claws that came down on him. He had to let the flame go from his hand just to be able to withstand the blow.

Ron's sword sliced through the air with such speed that any ordinary man would have fallen victim to it in seconds. However, this creature's ability to track each movement while effectively guarding itself was worrying. Swinging hard from the right, Ron intended to slice at the creature's midsection only for his sword to be stopped before reaching its target. A smirk glided across his face as he put more power behind the swing, forcing the creature to use both hands to stop the attack.

Ron used his free left hand, rapidly flowing power into it. Feeling the weight gather in his palm, he cut off the flow and threw a ball of flame into the creature's right side. Blue fire exploded, sending the creature backward, where it struck repeatedly against the tunnel walls until it came to a rolling stop. The dust settled in the flickering light of the few remaining candles as Ron brought the flame into his hand yet again to make sure the creature was dead.

Prepared to attack at the slightest movement, he inched closer. The creature lay still, with no breath escaping, its eyes open and unblinking,. Ron turned from the body, walking back to the passageway, and saw Nora step out. Her smile faded as she screamed Ron's name and pointed behind him.

"Turn around!"

Ron's stomach dropped as he looked to find the creature again standing upright. He frantically looked to the right side where the flame had exploded only to see a smoldering mark blackening the thin layer of gray skin. The monster lashed out as Ron tried to defend himself, but he was thrown off balance. The claws rammed into his sword and he stumbled back, leaving himself exposed.

Ron scooted back, but the claws attached to the ghastly long arm followed. The tips ripped open the flesh of his right shoulder and across his chest. Ron fell to a knee, holding his shoulder, taking deep breaths. His blood mixed with the dirt. He got to his feet and felt the pain radiate through his shoulder and chest. Not using his shoulder hindered his strength, so he took the sword in his other hand and formed a new plan of attack.

He figured if the creature's body couldn't be hurt on the outside by the flame, he would have to make an opening and force the flame inside. But, unfortunately, Ron didn't have the time he wanted to hatch an entire plan as the creature came running at him. He ducked beneath the claws and moved with his sword, not managing to get in a single attack of his own.

Then he saw his opening, a chance to end the fight and escape. Ron jumped back after blocking the long, arching claws and took a moment to picture his plan. A moment was all he needed. He ran straight at the creature. The long arms attempted to grab him, but Ron swung his sword to counter the attacks. He ducked below the next arm and continued his charge without losing momentum, sliding beneath the monster and slicing off its left foot.

As it stumbled, Ron turned, pushing his foot off the wall, and jumped on its back, wrapping his arm around its neck. The creature reared its head, screeching when Ron placed the sword's blade sideways in its mouth, holding it open. Then, bringing the flame to his right hand, he sent a stream of fire down its throat, melting the sword. The screeching ceased, and the creature's body wobbled lifelessly before falling to the ground, burning from the inside.

Nora, Grant, and Shaw ran to Ron once the monstrous body hit the floor. Ron rolled onto his back and opened his eyes, taking in each face of concern as he smiled up at them.

Once they helped him to his feet, Grant asked, "Are you alright?"

"I'm fine, but we have to go," he said, taking Nora's hand and guiding them toward the entrance of the tunnel.

"Wait, we can't go that way," Nora said, pulling back lightly.

"Why not?"

"The doors collapsed, and even if we could squeeze through the opening, more of those creatures are still out there."

Ron looked forward, then back, thinking of what to do. Time was running short, and he knew other soldiers must have heard the fighting. "Conrad, is there any other way out of here? I don't care if you know the way or not. I just need to know if there is one."

"There are other ways in and out, but I don't—"

"That's fine. We'll just have to try and find one." Ron held tightly to Nora's hand and led them down the passageway on the left.

Amid the twist and turns, Ron had everyone occasionally stop to let a passing patrol go by. He didn't want to risk another fight, completely drained from the last one. If it weren't for the adrenaline and fear coursing through his body, he would have been a complete wreck. Then, halting everyone again before crossing an intersecting passageway, Ron overheard the conversation among the passing soldiers.

"Did you hear Lord Hadal is in these tunnels, looking for that wielder?" the soldier said.

"I did. I can't imagine what he's going to do when he finds him. I heard the lord wanted to collapse the whole mountain all for one person."

"He must be angry."

The soldiers' conversation faded as they walked away, but Ron was worried. *If Hadal is in here, then what about Nathill? What if we can't get out, what if we—*

His thoughts were interrupted when Nora placed a hand on his cheek. Such a simple gesture from a loved one would have seemed like a distant memory only a few hours before. She gazed into Ron's eyes, and he felt his mind ease. The panic fell away as he returned to a more rational mind.

"Where do we go next?" she asked calmly.

"Let's go this way."

As they pressed on, a distant shriek echoed through the tunnels, and boots came running in their direction. They turned down an empty passageway and waited while Conrad extinguished the nearby candles. A large group of soldiers passed by, no doubt headed to the remote shrieks farther down in the tunnel, but the number of soldiers had Ron wondering where they were coming from.

After the last soldier rounded the corner, they hurried on their way. More sounds started to fill the tunnel, but they were not shrieks or armor banging from running soldiers. Ron had heard these screams before—when he was held in the Ark of Redemption. In his cell, the screams had been faint, muted even, giving Ron the impression they were a ways off from the Ark. He looked to Conrad, and his suspicions were confirmed; they were headed toward the holding cells of the scarred.

The screams overtook any other sound as they got closer, finally coming to a large opening in the tunnel where the sound was most prevalent. Thick steel poles placed an inch apart spread in a semicircle, taking up half of the large room. Hundreds of men and women had been placed together in a single large cell, scars ravaging their half-clothed bodies. Fingers protruded from the bars as everyone saw the people locked behind them. It didn't take long for the scarred to notice that other people had entered the room. Their eyes held a steady gaze while they screamed and banged on the bars, piling up behind one another.

"What are these people?" Nora asked.

"I'll explain everything later, but we need to keep moving." The initial shock from seeing the scarred took a moment to wear off, but soon they were on the move.

The farther they went, the more it felt as though they were going uphill, the opposite of what Nathill had told Ron, but he kept going. Finally, another passageway came into view. They waited for more soldiers to pass, only this time, it wasn't just soldiers. Ron recognized Nathill's voice.

His brother trailed behind the soldiers, giving Ron enough time for an idea. Once the soldiers passed, Ron called the flame into his hand, letting Nathill know he was in the passage.

"Ron, what are you doing here? You were supposed to be gone by now." The soldiers looked back at Nathill, but he just waved them on to continue, and they did as he commanded. As Nathill got closer, he saw Ron's bloodied shoulder and chest as well as the four other people standing behind him. "What in the world happened to you?"

"The creature from the forge—it found a way in, so I killed it. It was not an easy fight. If you see one, you need to know the flame doesn't affect the outside of its body."

Nathill looked confused. "What do you mean the flame doesn't—never mind, look, you need to get out of here now. Lord Hadal is not far behind me. He just sent my men and me to take care of whatever is making the noise."

"If you're going that way, then how will you escape with us?" Ron asked.

"I don't think I will be able to. It was never about me getting out anyway. You take that Orb and make sure it can never be found," Nathill said.

"I'll come back for you. I'll—"

Nathill stopped Ron. "No, you will do no such thing. If Lord Hadal gets what he wants, then all those years I spent keeping you safe will have been for nothing." Ron tried to speak, but Nathill wouldn't let him. "Take the first passage on your right just up there. Once you reach the first left, go past it and take the next one. Then take another right—there should be a way out at the end of the tunnel. I don't know if it was finished or not, but something should be there." Nathill placed his hand on Ron's good shoulder. "Don't worry about me. Just make sure you and your friends get out of here."

Nathill walked down the tunnel and disappeared around the corner. Ron balled his fist in frustration. It hurt to see his brother leave, but he didn't want Nathill's years under the First Born and Lord Hadal to be in vain, so he led the way, taking the first passage on the right.

It was slow going, but soon after they took the second left, another group of soldiers walked by. They in the dark passageways, waiting for men to pass, and Ron could smell the fresh air wafting into the tunnels, removing the scent of dirt and mold that took over the lower areas. Anticipation grew as the last soldier went by—their escape was closer than it had ever been.

Then Conrad placed his foot in a hole. He tripped and reached out for anything to break his fall. As he fell, he grabbed for one of the candles, knocking it from its fixture and spilling hot wax onto his face while the flame on the wick caught the cuff of his shirt on fire. Conrad yelled as the wax burned his cheeks and the ever-growing intensity of the fire scorched his arm. Grant and Shaw knelt to help Conrad, throwing loose dirt on his arm to smother the fire and placing hands over his mouth.

"Quiet, quiet. The fire's out," Shaw said, removing his hand. Ron listened in dread, hoping no one else heard the shouting. He stood still, flowing a small amount of power to his senses, and listened. He heard nothing for a few short minutes, but just as he was about to let his guard down, he saw a soldier peer around the corner of the passageway.

"They're here! Tell Lord Hadal now!"

They ran. All Ron could hope for now was to find the exit before the gap between them closed.

The smell of rain filled their nostrils; lightning flashed with each strike, illuminating the tunnel. The sound of the wind rushed over the open passage Ron was looking for. Suddenly he, and everyone following, came to a grinding halt before the exit of the tunnel. A large steel grate filled the exit, blocking their one chance of escape. Ron put his fingers through the grate, giving a sharp tug and feeling its stability.

He placed his forehead against the metal, looking down at the large river rushing swiftly at the base of the mountain. In the time they'd spent running, Ron had lost track of how much they'd continued to ascend. Now at the tunnel's end, they were hundreds of feet above the river. Ron told everyone to step back, and they reluctantly complied even as the First Born's footsteps came closer. Ron brought the flame to his hand and felt the weight build. Then he threw the ball of flame at the steel grate.

Dirt and metal burst outward, tumbling down the side of the mountain into the river below. Ron urged everyone to get behind him as the First Born began to pile into view. Then, he turned his palm up and lifted with the flame still in his hand, placing a wall of fire between them and the enemy.

"We're going to have to jump. Is everyone ready?" Ron looked to the others, who nodded in agreement even though were scared, just as he was. Ron turned back to the First Born, watching them as everyone inched closer to the ledge. Then he saw Lord Hadal step in front of his soldiers.

"Ron, I think you have something that belongs to me. Why don't you hand it over, and then we can discuss what's going to happen from here?" His voice was calm, but Ron knew that beneath it lurked the vile tongue of a madman.

"No, I'm going to destroy it." Ron locked eyes with Lord Hadal.

"Oh," he said inquisitively. "Might I ask how you're planning to do that?" Hadal stepped closer to the wall of flame.

"I found out how it can be done. All that matters is that you won't be able to have control over the forge."

The lord smirked at Ron. "How did you find out? Wait, let me guess, you read about it in a book from my library, didn't you."

Ron's stomach dropped. "How do you . . ."

"You didn't really think I would give you full access to my library if there was something of such significance as to how to destroy one of the Orbs of Ember. So let me ask you, have you already tried to destroy it?"

The look on Ron's face told Lord Hadal everything he needed to know. "I knew you would never willingly give your power to the Orb, so I had some of those books amended, and since you have activated the last one, I will let you in on a little secret. The Orbs cannot be destroyed." He laughed.

"You're lying. There has to be some way."

"I may lie about some things, but not about this. I think you know that."

Ron did. "Alright, so even if it can't be destroyed, all I have to do is make sure you never find it. You still lose." He returned the smirk, but Lord Hadal was one step ahead.

"You're right. I never planned on you taking the Orb and running. That was an error in my judgment." Hadal took another step. "So you could hide it from me, but what good will that do? There will be nowhere to hide once I have claimed the five kingdoms. Also, I don't know if you know this, but I only told one person about the Orbs of Ember and where I keep them. Would you like to venture a guess as to who that would be?"

Ron was speechless; he knew the lord was talking about Nathill. Hadal called the flame in one hand and drew his sword with the other. He spread the flame over the blade and effortlessly slashed away the wall of flame Ron had created. Ron raised another and another, but Lord Hadal kept striking them down as he walked closer.

"Give me the Orb and we can end his foolishness—it's that simple. Or, if you choose to make this difficult, I will give the father full permission to have his way with Nathill, and believe me, you have no idea what he is capable of. You only got to experience a taste of what he can do." Ron stepped as far back as he could without pushing anyone off the ledge, but he was out of the room. Lord Hadal continued, "Do you really want to leave your brother again? Think of how devastated he would be to know you abandoned him for a second time. What kind of brother would do that?"

Ron's body was tired. He felt the desire to pull more power, but he knew he might not come back if he did. Tears filled his eyes. "You're wrong. If it hadn't been for you, none of this would have happened. You've taken everything from me, but now I'm taking this from you." Ron placed his hand over the Orb in his jacket pocket.

Lord Hadal's face turned in anger. "Give me the Orb, or Nathill will be locked away in my quarters with the father until he draws his last breath."

Nora was first to jump, then Grant, Shaw, and finally Conrad. Ron pulled his power and threw a ball of flame at Lord Hadal before he jumped off the ledge as well. The lord swatted it away and ran to the opening, throwing balls of flame down, one after another. Ron made a flame shield that dissipated the second Lord Hadal's attack made contact, but he kept pulling more power. Flames soared down among them as Ron tried to create a wall. He saw the others were being targeted, but Ron was losing control and was not fast enough.

The last thing he heard before he hit the water was a scream, followed by a bright blue explosion.

Chapter Twenty-Seven

The Falla Essen

Ron walked through the narrowing roads of Regis as it burned. Bodies covered the streets, the stench of burnt flesh filled the air, and the faces of those he knew from childhood were plastered among the still-smoldering bodies. Crackling fires roared in the night; the smoke and ash stung his eyes as he continued along the familiar streets. To his left was the schoolhouse, the doors chained shut, but no screams came from there.

The only sound was the fire noisily thriving as it burned. Ron wandered aimlessly, staring at the destruction, burning buildings hollowed out with only the bare-bones framework remaining. Then he heard two screams break through the buzzing fire. He rushed toward them, not knowing what he might find as the wails continued to come.

He turned down streets and alleys, following the bloodcurdling screams until he finally reached the source. Flames roared behind him and tears streamed down his face as he looked at the bodies splayed on the ground. One was clad in dark armor and the other in plain clothes. He fell to his knees between the bloodied, lifeless forms of Grant and Nora.

Ron picked up a sword lying between them. Shaw was nowhere to be found. He held the sword in both hands, seeing the ornate emblem of a flame on the hilt, a deep blue stone set in base, and a blue ribbon hanging off the end. He knew this sword; this was the sword of a wielder.

Ron opened his eyes, looking around a dimly lit room. Brown shades hid the light, and oil lamps flickered among the subtle gusts of wind intermittently finding their way past the brown cloth partition set in the doorframe. Soft whispers came from the other side of the wall. Ron spotted Nora sleeping on a small cot under the window on the left side of the room. He moved, adjusting his position as something was poking him under the soft fabric of the cot. Then he saw the exposed hay sticking out of the seams.

He sat upright, wiping the sweat from his brow when he quickly reached for his shoulder, checking for his injury. To his surprise, he found himself without his shirt or bandages. Ron ran his fingers along the newly formed scars, covering the gashes from the creature's claws.

He panicked—he didn't have the Orb.

Ron whispered to Nora, trying to wake her up, "Nora, Nora, are you awake?" She rolled over, but he saw someone push aside the partition and enter the room out of the corner of his eye. An elderly woman in red robes and a brown shawl across her shoulders carried a cup with steam rising from the top.

She gave him a kind smile. "Awake already, are we?" she asked, handing Ron the cup. He looked at it reluctantly before taking it. "Oh, don't worry child, you have nothing to fear here. Now go ahead and drink the tea. It's nothing more than an herbal mixture that will help you regain your strength." Her smile held while watching Ron sip the tea. He was happy to find it carried a pleasant taste that lingered on his tongue.

"What's that flavor? It's delicious." He began to take bigger sips.

"It's just a hint of ground cloves to give it a little spice. This particular tea also helps with something very specific, but before I tell you what that is, you need to answer a question."

Ron lowered the cup, looking suspiciously at the woman. "What would that be?" he asked.

"Are you still having nightmares?" she asked, gauging his reaction.

"Why do you think I'm having nightmares?"

"Well, for starters, you move around constantly, and you shout as if you are being attacked. You're also sweating profusely, so there's that." Ron felt embarrassed; he hadn't considered how he might be reacting when he slept. "I also know you are a wielder," she said, sipping her tea. "So, are you still having nightmares?" she asked again out of politeness, not hiding the fact she already knew the answer; she only wanted to allow him to tell her himself.

"I still have nightmares. They started a few months ago. One night they came and never left. They always feel so real," he said.

Nora listened intently, having just woken up.

"Drink the rest of the tea, and I will bring you more throughout the day. This blend will allow you to sleep through the night free of nightmares." The lady smiled and took the now-empty cup from Ron's hands.

"Why are you helping me? I don't even know who you are or where I am."

"Well, I'm Bonnie, and now that we know one another, I think there's someone who has been waiting to see you." Bonnie looked over at Nora. "We can talk later. Do be gentle with him, dear—he still has to recover."

Nora nodded, waiting for Bonnie to leave. Once she did, they held each other in a deep embrace, an embrace they'd both thought they would never feel again.

Nora lay in the bed with Ron until the sun faded. They fell fast asleep in each other's arms, and it felt all too brief when she woke up next to him in the morning.

Kissing Nora on her forehead, he said, "Good morning."

She looked up into his eyes. "Good morning to you. How did you sleep?"

"Better than I have in a long time. Looks like Bonnie's tea worked." Ron laughed, but Nora watched the happiness fade from his eyes and fall into a vacant stare as he felt her fingers caress his chest, passing over the scars left from the spikes and claws.

Her tone turned somber. "I'm sorry we couldn't find you sooner. We never stopped looking, and the moment we found out, we—"

Ron interrupted, grabbing her hand from his chest and kissing it softly. He placed his cheek in her palm, feeling her loving touch. "It's okay. Despite all that happened, we are here now."

Nora helped Ron out of bed since he still felt the fatigue of drawing too much power. She helped him put on a red shirt Bonnie had left for him. They walked into the other room past the partition. Bonnie greeted them with a good morning and handed Ron a hot cup of tea. He drank it slowly as he, Nora, and Bonnie walked outside.

The sunlight stunned his eyes, but after they adjusted, Ron was amazed at what he saw. Water lapped the edges of the island in all directions. He had never seen such vast amounts before, let alone been surrounded to the degree that the only other landmass looked almost nonexistent on the horizon. Lush green grass peppered the land, with a rich, red-brown soil forming the walkways around the island. Gardens with plentiful fruits and vegetables were being tended to, reminding Ron of the countryside outside of Regis.

Families walked the grounds of the island, with children running in and out of their homes. The houses on the island looked to be constructed out of the same red material of the walkways, but Ron didn't know how they'd achieved such a vibrant color. Bonnie saw the wonder in Ron's eyes and explained. "These homes were made from the clay our people found beneath the ground on the island and hardened by the flame. The color comes from the richness of the minerals."

To the far east was a dock housing ships with sails and large nets meant for fishing when the opportune seasons arrived. The island was calm and peaceful, something Ron had forgotten about over the last month or two or however long he was held captive in Oroze.

Ron looked to Bonnie. "Where are we?"

"You're on the island of the Falla Essen," she replied. "The people who live here are the descendants of the last remaining wielders who vowed to follow the ways of the Essenti from a time long ago. We have lived here in peace for generations, separating ourselves from the concerns of others just as our ancestors did." Ron couldn't believe there had been wielders here all this time. He brought his hand to his right shoulder.

"So you're the ones that healed me. How many wielders are on this island?" he asked.

"On the island, there are roughly two to three hundred people, but not all are wielders. Those who can wield make up about half of our people, while less than half of those wielders can produce the flame. Over generations, our parents, just as theirs, have passed down the knowledge, including skills of wielding, but some do not possess the power necessary to wield the flame."

Ron was astounded. So many wielders all in one place—it didn't seem real.

"I'm sure that number seems small to you, but . . ." Bonnie said, but Ron interjected.

"Small? No, I'm shocked there're so many of you."

"I'm afraid I don't follow." Bonnie's eyebrow rose.

"Where I come from, there are only three wielders capable of producing the flame. As for people who can wield the power, I am not sure."

Bonnie was the one to be surprised now. "Only three?" she asked.

"Yes—myself, my brother, and a self-proclaimed lord who seeks to control the Alumma Biyar kingdoms," Ron said.

"What happened to all the others?" she asked, but then waved her hand, dismissing her own question. "Never mind, we can discuss that later, along with other things."

It would take time to discuss everything Ron wanted to talk about with Bonnie and her people, but the time was not now. Walking along the reddened road, Ron heard his name called by a familiar voice. Grant and Shaw cut across the grass, making their way to him, and Grant soon hugged him as a long-lost brother would.

Shaw gave Ron a hug as well, tearing up lightly as he told him how glad he was to see him.

Ron was overjoyed to see that his friends were all here and safe. "Where's Conrad? I'm sure he would like to meet all of you." A grave look gripped their faces. "Where is he?"

Nora took Ron's arm. "I don't know how to tell you this, so I'll just say it. Conrad is dead."

Ron didn't believe it; he couldn't. Conrad had escaped just as they had. He should have been here with them.

"No, that's not possible. He was with us, he . . ." Ron searched his memory, but the last thing he could remember was falling into the water.

Bonnie took her leave, telling Ron to come find her when he was ready. Then she gave him directions to find Conrad.

Soon, he stood next to a freshly covered grave where the Falla Essen ancestors were buried, with Nora, Grant, and Shaw beside him. It was their sacred burial ground, but the Falla Essen believed no person should be left without a proper burial. Ron collapsed to his knees before Conrad's grave.

"What happened?" he asked as his eyes became blurry.

"After we jumped, Hadal sent flames down after us. You tried to stop them, but one broke through and hit Conrad," Nora said softly. Ron's memory was slowly coming back. He remembered pulling more power to make the flame shield. Then he remembered, just before he hit the water, someone screaming as the flames exploded.

"It's my fault. He died because of me." Tears ran freely down Ron's face.

"No, it's not your fault." Nora bent down.

"Yes, it is. I convinced him to come with me. He wanted to stay, but I asked him anyway. I told him it would be better than staying in Oroze, and now he's dead. He believed me. He trusted me. I was the only friend he had, and I failed him. He would still be alive right now if I just listened to him and let him stay. I should've listened. I should've—"

Nora placed her hand on Ron's cheek. "Why don't you tell us about him?"

No one said a word as Ron told Conrad's story and how they ultimately became friends in a place filled with death and hopelessness. When he finished, Nora just held him as he wept for his fallen friend.

They walked to the east docks, sitting at the edge, looking out at the endless sea while Ron told them of his time in Oroze. He told them about the torture he'd suffered at the hands of the father, the manipulation of Hadal, whom he refused to call a lord, and the people who died either by his hand or indirectly by his actions. Lastly, he told them about his brother, and how Nathill was the masked wielder who had pursued them from the beginning. He told them all the details, the attack on his home, and how Nathill had been keeping him safe from a distance as he tried to give Ron a normal life.

"So in the tunnels, what was Hadal talking about when he said to give him an Orb?" Grant asked.

"There are three Orbs of Ember that, when activated by three wielders, will grant complete access to a fully stabilized forge gate. We all saw what came out of the forge. Who knows what else is in there? If he has full control, then he could unleash those creatures at will, destroying the five kingdoms in the process. So I took one of the Orbs, but I didn't mean to activate it."

Ron shook his head. "He knew I would try to find a way to destroy it. That's why he gave me access to his library. I should have known better. Now I don't know how much of what I read was real or a lie, but I know I'll have to go back and get Nathill out of Oroze," he said with determination.

"Go back? You just barely got out. How do you plan on getting back in?" Grant asked.

"I don't know. There are a lot of things I need to think about. That just happens to be one of them," Ron said, staring into the water. "How did you guys end up in the tunnels anyway?"

Shaw, Nora, and Grant took turns telling Ron about the people they met in Meno and the First Born's plans to wipe them out. They told him of Malen and meeting King Ahven, and then Nora jabbed Grant in the side. "So, are you going to tell him about her?" she asked with a short laugh.

Grant's face flushed. "Of course. He always told me about his feeling for you, so it seems fair that I tell him."

Nora gave Ron a sideling look. "Oh, did he now? What else has he told you?"

"Nothing, so Grant, who are you talking about?" Ron quickly asked, changing the subject as Nora laughed and scooted closer.

"Well, when we were in Noic trying to find out where the First Born took you, and we blew our cover, Nora . . ."

Shaw broke in, "What do you mean, 'we'? You were the one who insisted on gathering information while trying some ale. Didn't quite work out for you, did it?" He said it mostly in jest.

"Definitely sounds like something you would do, Grant." Ron laughed.

"As I was saying, after *we* were discovered, Nora brought a woman with us. Her name is Abby, and she's the one that told us about the ark. If it weren't for her, I don't think we would all be here right now." The mood drifted into somber territory for a moment, then Grant said, "She also has a son, Yulis—he's a good kid."

"Sounds to me like she might be someone special," Ron said.

"She is. I don't think I've felt this way about someone before. Something about her is different than the women back home. I'm not sure what it is, but it's something I really enjoy about her." Grant had more to say, but he wanted to keep it to himself for now.

"So you guys always talk like this when I'm not around?" Nora asked.

"We do. I mean, what do you think we talk about?" Grant asked.

"I have some ideas about what it is you might also talk about," she said knowingly.

"Oh, believe me, they talk about both. I can promise you that," Shaw said.

Of course, no one expected Shaw to chime in at that moment, and they broke into laughter. It was a moment sorely missed, a moment they would never want to forget since they were finally reunited.

Chapter Twenty-Eight

Wielders of Power

I t was getting late, and Ron remembered that Bonnie wanted to talk with him, so the four of them walked back to her home. Once they entered the main common room, they saw the light from the lamps reflecting off the red walls and Bonnie sitting on the floor in a circle surrounded by other island members. "Please have a seat. I have already taken the liberty of giving your names to the others, so please sit." She pointed to the four empty pillows on the left side of the room; once they sat down, the circle was complete. "I have gathered the eldest wielders of the Falla Essen. There's much we need to discuss, especially the specifics of what you carried in your jacket onto the island. First, we will start with Elder Joseph."

Elder Joseph called the flame to his hand. "Flame of the Essenti, by your gift we prosper." He let the flame go and asked, "How many wielders remain? Bonnie mentioned you said only three with the gift of the flame. What about the others? Besides you four?"

"Wait a minute, what do you mean us four?" Ron asked, only to disregard his own question as he looked to Nora, Grant, and Shaw. "You can wield? All of you?"

Nora spoke first. "I'm not sure entirely. But you know how I can usually tell you when something doesn't feel right, or for instance, when I would train in the Arena I always—this might sound strange, but I was always one step ahead of what the other person was doing, almost like I let my body react for me."

"I had no idea," Ron said, feeling he should have known based on what he'd already learned, but it had never crossed his mind. "Elder Joseph, I don't know how many can use the power. I don't even think most people know they can. Wielders are more of a myth than anything—I only found out a month or so ago. As Bonnie mentioned, there are not many wielders left. After the War of the Wielders, the victor, Ermon, tried to track down all the remaining wielders, and when he did, he slaughtered them, bringing an end to those possessing the gift. Even I don't know all the specifics, but many, many years after that war, the last two remaining wielders fought one another. Then wielders just vanished. I went my whole life without knowing about them, as have many other people. Like I said, they were mostly myths."

Joseph looked to each of them. "How much do you know about the power bestowed by the Essenti?"

"Very little," said Nora, and Grant nodded his head in agreement.

But Shaw remained silent. Joseph's gaze stayed on him for a moment before he continued, "For those of you who are unaware, the power of the flame, the gift of the Essenti, is in all of us. Every living person has this gift. Now, that's not to say every person can wield the flame of the Essenti, but the gift can manifest itself differently in each of you. For instance, Nora, from what you just said, your gift allows you to channel your power through instinct. That's why you feel the drop in your stomach or the shocking pulse through your spine. Your gift is trying to tell you to listen," Elder Joseph explained.

"I never knew—that's incredible. How can I learn to listen to it?" she asked.

"It comes with time and practice, but while you all are here, we will each take some time to teach you how to properly use your gifts. I will be teaching you, Nora, as I am well versed in the instinctual arts." Joseph bowed his head and looked to the elder on his right.

Elder Ida called the flame to her hand and recited the chant, letting it go once she finished. "I am Elder Ida. Do you know the significance of what you carry?" she asked Ron.

"I do. It's the last Orb of Ember."

"How did you come to have such a relic in your possession?" she asked, studying his face.

"I took it from the Lord of the First Born. He's one of the wielders capable of using the flame. He already activated two Orbs, so I took this one," Ron explained.

"But this one is activated. How did that come to be?" Her gaze was piercing, but Ron held firm.

"I was lied to. Hadal, the Lord of the First Born, made me believe there was a way to destroy it," Ron said, feeling the shame of his mistake with the eyes of the elders watching him.

"What do you plan to do with this Orb?" Ida asked, her gaze remaining the same.

"I don't know. Hadal has my brother, and if I don't return the Orb to him, he will torture him. But if I give it to him, he will have power over the forge. I already lost my brother once, and I can't do it again. So I don't know what to do. I can't give the Orb to Hadal, but I have to do something."

Nora saw his vacant stare return.

"Honesty, even if it's painful. I find your answers to be true, and I will discuss matters of importance with the other elders," Ida said. Her gaze then shifted to Grant, who began to fidget with his fingers. "Grant, tell me, what have you experienced with your gift?" Her gaze focused on his eyes.

"What I can tell is that in the last few battles we have encountered, I will be in one place one moment, and then the next, I'm in another. I look to where I want to go, and I move there, but it doesn't feel like I moved at all. After everything ends, my legs feel weak, almost to the point where I can't walk on my own."

"When you're in these battles, what's going through your mind?" she asked.

"Staying alive mostly, and anger. I mean at the First Born, anger at the lives they've taken." Grant didn't like her constant stare.

"So you're channeling your gift through your anger to enhance your body's speed. Interesting." She held her gaze a moment longer, looking for something, something she'd known once, hoping she wouldn't see it again. "I will teach you how to channel your gift through a different outlet, a safer outlet."

Grant didn't know what she meant, but he nodded. "Thank you."

The next elder called the flame, chanting. "Elder Quintin is my name, but please call me Quin. Ron, are you able to tell me what these nightmares are to you or what they represent?" he asked.

"No, not at all. They seem random. Each one is like a memory, a normal memory, but then the flame destroys everything, and I can't stop it, so I wake up." Ron stared in thought, and Quin looked to Bonnie and shrugged his shoulders. "But one was different."

Quin looked back to him. "Different? Different how?"

"One nightmare wasn't a memory. I dreamt I was somewhere I've never been before. I've heard my name called in my dreams before as well, but this time, in this place, it was different. I heard the voice—I felt the heat, the wind, and the dirt. I saw things, and before I woke up, I saw a face in the dust screaming my name." The elders in the circle were silent, their faces pale against the light red glow.

Quin cleared his throat before speaking. "Do you know where you were?"

Ron stared blankly at his hands. "Yes, I was in the forge."

Silence fell over the elders; each looked to the others with the same expression of confusion and worry. Finally, Bonnie broke the silent tension. "What did you see in the forge?"

"At first, there was nothing, just wind and dust. It was hot. Then I saw the sun but no clouds. It looked like a sunset just frozen in place. Then there was a city beneath the ground; it stretched miles wide, and who knows how far below. I remember it only had one entrance leading down, but I couldn't get to it. The next thing I knew, I saw hundreds of creatures running toward me, some we'd seen before. I tried to run, but then the face appeared in the dust, shouting my name. The wind hit me. It almost felt like something pushed me; I fell from the ledge and woke up."

Quin rubbed his chin. "I see. That is very troubling to hear, very troubling indeed."

"How are these nightmares even possible?" Ron asked, looking to the old man as he gathered his thoughts for a moment.

"Some of what I'm about to tell you is still not fully understood, but based on what I know to be true, I can at least give you an assumption. There are two schools of thought regarding this matter. The first, which is no speculation on my part, is that one of the wielders you have mentioned before is actively trying to make you afraid of your own power. Make you fear the destruction that can come from it, make you afraid to use it."

"How can that happen? I've read multiple manuscripts from centuries ago, and they didn't mention anything like this," Ron said.

"And neither would they. You see, the Orbs of Ember are more than just for opening the forge; their power knows no boundaries. Once the power of the flame is inside an Orb, the power is duplicated. The only way for the Orbs to lose the flame is time. Time away from a wielder, away from any source of power."

"So, how are the Orbs connected to my nightmares?" Ron asked.

"Since the flame can replicate itself," Quin explained, "its power never fades. If used properly, the power from the Orb can amplify the wielder's gift, letting them accomplish what we would deem impossible. However, the only way for this wielder to do such a thing is to be taught. Someone must have taught this method to whoever is doing this to you. The flame is also partly to blame as well. It acts as a connection or a bridge, if you will, allowing this connection to be formed."

Ron ran his fingers through his hair. "If Hadal can get into my head, how can I stop him?" The more he heard, the more it seemed like the lord always had the upper hand.

"Since this Hadal can influence your dreams, the only defense is the flame. It's a double-edged sword. The flame connects you, but it can also protect you if you're able to realize he's in your dream." Nora put a reassuring hand on Ron's back while he tried to understand everything Quin said. "As for the other nightmare, the best I can do is to speculate on how you came to be in the forge, seeing as how such a rarity has only been witnessed once or twice, and not by anyone living here today, but our ancestors."

"What do you think it could be?" Ron asked.

"My best guess would be that someone is trying to contact you, someone within the forge. How this is possible, I do not know. It would require an unimaginable amount of power, not seen for centuries over, to form a connection between worlds." Ron didn't know what to say or what questions to even begin to ask; he'd thought he finally understood his power but now felt he was only scratching the surface.

Elder Quin looked to Shaw next, asking what gift his power bestowed upon him, but Shaw gave an unexpected answer. "I used my power to understand the world, the people I met, and the places I went, but I have given up using my gift. I severed all ties, cutting it off completely. Even if I tried to use it now, I'm afraid I have forgotten how."

The elders couldn't comprehend such a notion. "Why would you do such a thing?" Quin asked.

Nora knew why, and looked at Shaw as he took a deep breath, preparing to relive the pain of loss. "I used my gift with my wife Thea and my daughter Allurin to understand and explore the world. I would teach Allurin all I knew. Thea and I were so proud to watch her grow and learn. After they both died, I had no need for this power. Without them, there was no more world to explore, nothing left to understand. Whatever power I had became a reminder of what I could never get back. Without them, my gift is useless."

Quin looked to Shaw. "I am sorry for your loss."

The old man wiped his eyes in the quiet room.

Bonnie lifted herself off her pillow after a moment. "It's getting late, and if we are to begin teaching you how to use your gifts, we all could use some sleep."

The other elders began to rise, but Ron stayed seated. "Aren't you forgetting something?"

Bonnie wrinkled her brow. "What do you mean?" she asked.

"Why have you not told them about the curse? If you're going to train them, why would you not tell them about the curse of the Essenti? I have seen what happens, what this power can do to a person if someone indulges in the seduction of the flame. Do you know what can happen?" Ron asked.

Bonnie stood tall and put her hands behind her back, imposing her status as an elder while she answered Ron. "Yes, we know of the curse, but throughout the history of the Falla Essen, we teach each young wielder to control their power. We do not put fear into our pupils. We teach them to use the flame as the gift it is—to enrich their lives and the lives of the ones on the island."

Ron shook his head. "So you teach them to be ignorant?"

Anger flashed across Bonnie's face.

Nora turned to Ron. "What are you doing? Why would you say that?"

Bonnie raised her hand. "It's alright, Nora." She turned back to him. "We teach them to look at the positive aspects of the gift given by the Essenti. Why would you call that ignorant?"

"Because you can't just teach one side of a coin. What happens when someone decides to turn the coin over and see that the other side is completely different? What if they think that side is better or don't know how to protect themselves from what the unknown side offers? You expect to teach Nora and Grant how to use their power, but what do you think will happen when we return to the Alumma Biyar kingdoms? We will have to fight—we won't be afforded the same comforts you enjoy by staying on the island. What you teach them or what you won't teach could end up getting them killed, or worse.

"If they don't understand the limits of their power and continue drawing the flame during a battle, then what? Perhaps they should know that the flame wants you to pull more power, that at one point you will crave it, and after that, there is no going back. Then you become one of them, one of the scarred. Madness would rule their minds with no logic or reason, only the desire for the power of the flame. Their body would become a scarred mutated shell, and the person they once were would be gone. I don't know about you, but I would like to avoid that fate."

No one said anything after that, and the meeting ended.

* * *

The next morning, when Ron and Nora pushed the partition to the side, a group of elders stood in the common room, chatting among themselves. "Ah, you're up. Nora, if you could come with me, please. I would like to talk before we begin your lessons. We could also grab a quick bite to eat," Joseph said.

"Okay, but where's Grant?" she asked.

"He's already with Elder Ida. He was eager to start first thing this morning."

"Alright, lead the way," she said.

Joseph walked out the door with Nora. Ron began to follow, but Bonnie grabbed his arm. "If you could stay, the other elders and I would like to talk about last night."

Ron watched Nora walk away before turning to the elders, a small amount of his anger carrying over from the night before. "What do you want to talk about?"

"Early this morning, the elders and I discussed what you said about teaching both sides of the Essenti's power. We all agreed that you brought up a good point, and we, as humbling as it is, must admit our faults. It's not that we didn't want to teach what can happen if the curse of the flame presents itself. The fact is, we are afraid to teach it. We are afraid to teach the young wielders that such vileness could corrupt the beauty of our gift." As humbling as it was to admit the elders were wrong, the way Bonnie carried herself did not show any vulnerability. Instead, she showed the strength she possessed as an elder by learning to grow and judge the situation by looking at both sides.

Ron saw her strength and felt ashamed of his outburst, as he only understood one side. "I'm sorry, Bonnie, to all of you. I shouldn't have behaved the way I did. Ever since I learned about the flame, all I've known is how to fight and avoid the curse. I guess we learned to use this power in completely different ways."

"There's no need to apologize. We discussed it and have decided to teach you as well. Our teachings will focus on opening yourself to the power, learning to embrace it without violence. We will help you understand that the flame of the Essenti is more than just fighting but a way of life, a way of peace."

Ron smiled. "I would like that."

Bonnie, along with Quin and Elders Mariam and Gregory, took Ron to the temple of the elders, a building to the far south of the island made with the same style of wooden frame and hardened red clay. The temple was made to be indistinguishable from other buildings on the island so it would not stand out to anyone who happened to come across the Falla Essen.

The second he set foot in the temple, Ron understood why the elders wanted that way. The temple held centuries of knowledge brought over from the ancestors of the Falla Essen. Ancient tomes written in strange languages occupied many of the desks and bookshelves in the open room. Artifacts of unknown use hung on the walls, and pieces of battle armor were individually placed on waist-high pillars, showcasing what Falla Essen ancestors would wear during times of war.

Still, none of these were the reason Ron was brought to the temple. Elders Mariam and Gregory walked to the center desk in the room, channeling the flame through their bodies, and lifted the desk. The desk's legs touching a section of the floor were raised as one piece, revealing a staircase below the ground.

They descended, instructing Ron to bring the flame to his hand, lighting the way as no candles or lamps were fixed to the dirt walls. Once at the bottom of the stairs, Ron walked into the darkened room, passing thick wooden support beams bearing the weight of the ceiling. The blue glow of the flame illuminated the red clay surrounding him, and he saw markings etched into the walls.

"What is all this?" he asked, tracing the markings.

"This is the language of the Essenti, written by our ancestors. It speaks of the promise given by the people after the Essenti gifted us the flame. To remain faithful in our devotion was all that was required of us, but as you know, it did not end up that way," Mariam said.

"Why did you bring me here?" Ron wanted to know what good it could do to bring him to a dark room underground. It seemed to serve no purpose.

"Our ancestors said this room holds a power of its own. But, unfortunately, we have not successfully figured out what sort of power it holds since we are centuries removed from the capabilities they once had. We think you might have a better chance at finding this room's purpose," Gregory said, moving to the center of the room, where an item was covered on the floor. He removed the cover, and the swirling glow of blue light filled the room.

Ron walked toward the Orb. "How did you get this in here? When I tried to move the other Orbs of Ember, it was impossible, even with the power of the flame."

Mariam explained, "As you know, the only way to move an activated Orb is by the wielder's own hand, but that doesn't mean we can't move you. When one of our fishermen found you and your friends floating in from the river, he saw what you carried, so after we healed your wounds, we carried you down here, knowing it to be the safest place for the Orb until we found out who you were."

"Clever—move the person to move the Orb. So what is it exactly you want me to do down here?" he asked again, still unsure.

"Since the Orb can amplify the power of the flame, the first thing we thought you should try would be to call the flame in each hand and hold the Orb. Then, let the power flow through you just as life flows through you. Find the embrace of the gift, not the need, or the fear, or even the curse. Just let the power flow and see what happens." Mariam made it sound so simple, as if sitting down with the Orb would just trigger some sort of response.

Ron was skeptical, but he trusted the elders enough to give the process a try. "Okay, I'll see what I can do," he said, sitting down in the center of the floor while the elders left him to his task. He brought the flame to his other hand and picked up the Orb, cradling it between the two. The separate flames melded into one, encompassing his hands and the Orb. Ron closed his eyes and listened to the hum of the song sung by Erin and Diana as he let the power drift through his body.

Nothing happened at first. He only felt the calm within the temple, the peace in the stillness of time he found himself in. The power moved like a gentle river stream, and he felt it. He felt the life in his body, the beating in his heart, and most importantly, the want for nothing. In the calm, he sensed something; he began to feel the connection to his power, to the flame of the Essenti. It felt strange to him. As much as it felt like a part of him, something about it seemed foreign, like it didn't fully belong to him. He explored the feeling but stopped as a voice called out his name.

"Ron."

He shook his head, thinking it was just part of a memory. He continued to search his power, going deeper into the vast well of the unknown. The more he searched, the more uncomfortable and disconcerted he became, but why? Why did his power feel this way? He had used it for some time now in more than one capacity, yet something set off a warning within him. Then the voice came again.

"Ron, you need to listen. Stop what you're doing—you are not ready."

Ron knew this was no memory. Never had anything other than his name been said before, so why was it possible now? Ron wanted answers, and even though a small portion of fear had found its way into him, he didn't want to lose this chance.

"Who are you? What am I not ready for?" he asked, then waited in silence. He didn't know how long he sat there, but after a time, the voice returned.

"You know who I am, and you may seek me out when the time is right, but you must not push further into the flame. It will break you," the voice warned.

"How can I seek out a voice? Why would the flame break me?"

Each pause grew longer.

"You are not strong enough. There is much you have yet to learn. Heed such a warning, or see your world fall to ruin like others before it."

"Others before it? What are you talking about?" Ron asked.

"You must stop the one who seeks the bridge between worlds, stop them at all costs for the sake of the living. When you start to understand, seek me out." The voice did not return but instead left Ron to decipher the meaning of what it said. Ron opened his eyes as he set down the Orb, letting the flame go from his hands. His body was tired, his stomach growled, sweat stained his shirt, and a terrible thirst gripped him.

He went up the stairs and saw Bonnie anxiously waiting for him. As she saw him, she rushed over. "What happened down there? Are you alright? You've been down there for a long time." She looked him over.

"Yes, of course I'm okay. How long was I down there? It couldn't have been longer than a few hours." Ron didn't understand why she was so worried.

"Ron, you have been down there for three days."

"Three days? It didn't feel that long. How could so much time have passed?" Ron asked, running his fingers through his hair, feeling the sweat and grease that had accumulated.

Bonnie placed her hand between his shoulders, pushing his toward the door. "I'm not sure, but let's clean you up and get you something to eat. Then you must tell us what happened."

Once he was clean, Ron sat down and ate more fish, rice, and bread than he ever had before. He also found the rice ale delicious, not having known ale could be made in such ways. After taking the last sip, he told the elders what the voice had said, and they seemed just as confused as he was, but Ron explained the part he knew.

"The voice didn't know his name, but it was talking about Hadal. Somehow they know Hadal wants to control the forge, and they want me to stop him."

"How do you plan on stopping him?" Bonnie asked.

"I don't know, but I'll need to go back to Oroze if I'm going to have any chance of stopping Hadal from—" Just then, Ron realized what the voice's words meant. Everything became clear, and he knew what he had to do to stop Lord Hadal.

* * *

Shaw wandered around the island, taking in the exquisite beauty and peaceful calm as he listened to the sea, the squawking of the seagulls perched on the ship's masts, the chopping of wood being prepared for the cold nights that were soon to be sweeping across the island. For two weeks, Shaw walked, enjoying the clarity in his mind. He found solace on the island while mingling with people, teaching the children new games to play, and every now and again checking to see how Nora and Grant were progressing while they learned with the elders. Shaw knew Nora was a natural, almost like himself in a way. She learned fast, picking up the intricate details of her lessons. The first day, he walked over to see how she was doing, and it looked like was struggling to channel her power.

Shaw overheard one of their conversations when Elder Joseph asked her if she'd ever used her power when there was no threat to be found. Nora said she hadn't. That gave Joseph a starting point to work with; he knew she felt safe on the island. But he needed to make her think otherwise for her to channel her power. Sparring proved to be little help; she was much better in combat with a weapon. So as Shaw watched, he saw Joseph blindfold Nora, taking away her greatest advantage until she learned to focus her power. They continued this method until she took off the blindfold when she'd had enough of getting hit blindly.

"This isn't working. I don't feel anything. What am I doing wrong?" she huffed.

"You're trying too hard. You're not letting it come naturally. Think about it. What is the one difference between trying to use your power now as opposed to using it before you came here?"

Nora knew the answer but didn't see how it related to what they were doing. "I was being watched or attacked or running for my life. None of which is happening now."

Joseph saw she was frustrated, but he smiled anyway. "No, Nora, before you came here, you didn't even know you possessed the power of the Essenti. Your power came to you naturally, but now that you are here and know about it, you are trying to force the power to work for you, not with you. That is the difference." After Nora understood what Joseph meant, Shaw saw her flourish during each lesson.

When Shaw would stop to watch how Grant was doing, things were different. From the day Ida began teaching the young man, he could call upon his power almost instantly, much quicker than she'd expected. So she instructed Grant to find peace or calm in his mind to access his gift. Once he did, she had him use his power in short bursts, nothing prolonged, as he still needed to let his body adjust to the rush of power.

Grant and Ida would use their speed not just for fighting but also to build stamina, as he heard Ida explain to Grant. She told him that using the power to accelerate the body could put a strain on it—a strain that could cause permanent damage to his muscles, joints, or ligaments if they were not allowed to recover. Grant understood, as each time he used his power, he felt exhausted afterward.

As their lessons were ending, Ida asked him, "What have you been thinking about to access your power so quickly?"

"I'm thinking about who's waiting for me when I get back after all this is over," he said, but Ida watched his eyes, and she saw something she just couldn't put her finger on.

"I'm sure they will be happy to see you."

"Not as happy as I will be." Grant smiled as they parted ways, but he knew that wasn't what he was thinking about when he called upon his power; what he'd told Ida was a lie.

During Shaw's walks, he noticed he never saw Ron during the day, only when he would leave the temple of the elders to go see Nora. At one point, Shaw didn't see him for several days.

* * *

Besides the times Ron would see Grant or Shaw, he spent most of his time with Nora, sneaking off to secluded areas around the island just to be alone with her. They would talk for hours as they walked or lay on the grass, waiting for the stars to come out just as they used to do in Greyland. Then, finding a soft patch of grass hidden behind a hedge of lofty bushes overlooking the water, they made small talk, mostly just enjoying each other's company. Neither wanted to ruin such beautiful evenings with the concerns they knew they needed to discuss.

Finally, one night, Ron decided it was time to tell Nora what he was planning. While they stared up at the brightening stars, Ron said, "I have to go back to Oroze."

She let out a heavy sigh. "I know. I wish we didn't have to. I just got you back." Nora rolled on her side and threw an arm over Ron, placing her head on his shoulder. "Why can't things just stay like this?"

Ron desperately wanted that, but he'd known they couldn't, not since he realized what he had to do. The cost was unbearable, but he could think of no other way.

In his silence, Nora asked, "Ron, what's wrong?"

"I can't ask you to come with me. If something were to go wrong, I would never be able to forgive myself. This is something I need to do on my own. I can't lose anyone else like I lost Conrad. I can't afford to make that mistake again. Everyone would be safe if I went on my own."

Nora sat up. "You know that won't happen. After everything Grant, Shaw, and I went through, you should know better than to think we won't come with you."

Ron sat up. "Not this time."

He stared into the distance, and anger followed in her words. "Why not? What makes this time so different? I know it hurts that you lost Conrad, but we would have a better chance of stopping Hadal if we went together."

Ron sat quietly, not wanting to answer because he knew it would upset Nora. But she reached over, turning his head toward hers. "Why do you think you need to do this by yourself?"

Pain held his voice. "Because I might not come back okay. If that happens, I want to know all of you are safe and away from Hadal. If I succeed at stopping him and don't come back, someone will have to continue fighting against him and the First Born."

Her voice caught in her throat. "Why wouldn't you come back?"

He wanted to tell her, he really did, but he kept it to himself.

"I can't say." Ron never wanted to hurt Nora, but keeping this from her was doing just that. He knew she didn't understand why he wouldn't tell her, but she didn't argue. She did, however, give him a choice.

"Since you think there's a chance you won't come back, you need to decide. Either you tell me what you're planning, or we all go with you." Ron did not like either of those options, but he couldn't tell her. If he did, she would try to stop him from going through with his plan, and if anyone could convince him not to, it was her. At the same time, he didn't want to have everyone cross paths with Hadal.

"If I agree, and you, Grant, and Shaw come with me, you have to promise me that when I tell you to run, you will do it, no questions asked," Ron said, leaving no room for negotiation.

"I promise. The others will too," she said, pressing her forehead to his and running her fingers through his hair. "Hopefully, if we are there, we can all leave together."

"I hope so too." Ron's words were empty, but he had to say them, not just for her to hold on to hope but for him as well. "I love you, Nora. I always have. I'm sorry it took so long for me to tell you."

"I've waited so long to hear you say that," she said, kissing him deeply. "I love you too, more than you know."

He kissed her passionately, pressing firmly against her body as their lips parted. Nora moved closer, wrapping her legs around his waist as she sat in his lap, his strong yet gentle hands caressing her sides, moving up and down while she held him tight. The warmth of their bodies pressed together made them forget about the cool wind passing over the island. Ron's hands slipped under her shirt, touching her lower back; she moaned gently at the tender pressure of his hands as they traveled to her shoulders.

"Make love to me," she said, feeling the intensity rapidly build.

"Are you sure?"

"Yes, more than anything." When she stopped kissing him, she pushed against his shoulders, sitting up straight, and slowly removed her shirt, revealing her beautiful light brown body as the glow of the moon cast down upon her.

Ron looked at the radiant beauty of the woman before him, thinking himself to be the luckiest man in the world. She pulled him close as he kissed her neck, moving down slowly with each subsequent kiss. He gently pressed his lips to her body, kissing the top of her breasts while Nora ran her hand over the back of Ron's neck, holding him close as she indulged in the feeling of his touch, the pleasure mounting within her.

The fulfilling satisfaction of being with the man she loved finally arrived. She had been waiting for this exact moment, a perfect moment when they could genuinely be together. Ron held Nora as he rolled her onto her back. He kissed his way back up to her soft, delicate lips while she took off his shirt, feeling the muscles in his back tense and tighten as she ran her fingernails down his back, passing over the scars she'd never felt before. She rolled back over and sat up, looking at his chest, softly touching the round scars left behind by the father's creative works. She bent down, kissing each scar. "I'm sorry I wasn't there."

He reached out, brushing her cheek.

"You're here now. That's more than I could ever ask for." He pulled her in, kissing her as their love and desire became an uncontrollable force, and Ron and Nora joined as one together under the stars.

* * *

The following afternoon, while Nora, Grant, and Shaw socialized with their friends on the island, Ron went to see Bonnie. She greeted him with a smile after opening the door. "Good afternoon, Ron. I wasn't expecting to see you so soon—I thought you would still be in the temple."

"That's kind of why I'm here. I need to talk to you."

"Well, alright, come on in. I was just making some tea; would you like some?" she asked, walking back toward the pot hanging above her fireplace.

"That would be great." He closed the door behind him.

"Please, have a seat."

The common room was rearranged with the furniture Ron had seen when he woke up after coming to the island; a large, wooded table with a set of four chairs occupied a space below the right-side window, which looked out over the sea. During Ron's lessons, the room had been cleared out to make space for the elders assisting him. In the course of three weeks, Ron had spent time learning to use the flame of the Essenti for everyday purposes. When he wasn't in the temple or with Nora, Shaw, and Grant, he was with the elders in Bonnie's home.

To his surprise, the elders told him that to maintain a stronger connection with his power, he had to learn to channel it at all times. At first, he thought they were crazy. Who in their right mind would run the risk of using so much power? Ron could only use his power for a few hours at most. Bonnie explained that he would have to control the slow release of power throughout the day, heightening his senses, strengthening his muscles, and resisting the urge to move at an accelerated rate.

She told him that that was where the true gift lay—not in the power to fight, conquer, or destroy, but in the ability to see the world as it was meant to be seen.

To witness what had been created with such splendor and grace, to have peace and serenity while the flame flowed within. Ron finally felt what she was talking about as he let the flame course through him slowly every day over the last three weeks to the point where doing so felt normal.

Bonnie came around the corner with two cups of tea. "Here you go." She handed Ron a cup and took the seat opposite of him. "So, what is it you would like to talk about?" she asked while blowing on the rising steam. Ron took a sip of the clove-scented tea, the tea he knew he would miss. Since he'd started drinking it, the nightmares had disappeared, giving him his most peaceful nights of sleep in recent memory.

He savored the flavor, taking one more sip. "I just wanted to say thank you for everything you and the other elders have done for us, from taking us in to teaching us how to further understand our power. But I was wondering if I could ask one more thing of you?"

Bonnie lifted a brow. "Why does it sound like you're saying goodbye?"

"Because I am. We were hoping to leave tomorrow, and I was wondering if you could help us get to the mainland?"

Bonnie set her tea down with a sigh. "I will help you, but I wish you wouldn't leave. I understand you want to save your brother and stop Hadal, but you could also be putting yourself and the ones you care about at risk. What if you stayed and let someone else do the fighting? That way, the Orb will be safe, and so will you." Her concern was understandable, but the people in the Alumma Biyar kingdoms would suffer if he did nothing.

"If I let someone else try to stop Hadal, they will lose. As for the Orb, I'm also taking that with me. It's the only way to stop him from controlling the forge. If he can conquer the kingdoms, then nowhere will be safe, not even this place. He will find you eventually, but if I can stop his plan, I can at least give the people and the other kingdoms a chance to win the war that's coming."

Bonnie saw he wasn't going to change his mind, but she still had questions. "Why would you take the Orb so close to him? How do you plan on—" She stopped, realizing what Ron had already figured out. "So that's your plan then?" she asked sadly.

"Yes, there's no other way," Ron replied.

"What about Nora, Grant, and Shaw? Do they know?"

"No, Nora is getting the others ready to come with me, but I can't tell them. If anything goes wrong and the First Born get ahold of them, I'll lose the only chance I have."

"Alright, I'll talk to Marcus at the docks, but before you leave, come by the temple. There's something I want to give you."

Ron sipped the last of his tea, and Bonnie walked him to the door. "Thank you, Bonnie, really, for everything."

She hugged him. "Just be careful." Ron smiled as she let go.

He found Nora, Grant, and Shaw helping one of the farmers harvest their stocks of corn before the winter months arrived. They were laughing and telling funny stories of times they'd had in Greyland. He saw how happy they all looked at that moment, so he didn't say anything, just watched and listened as he helped gather the ears of corn.

Once they finished walking around the island, talking among themselves, Grant asked, "So we're really going back, huh?"

"Yes, but you don't have to. It would be perfectly fine if you stayed here. I wouldn't blame you if you did," Ron said.

"Nora said you would say that. Don't you remember when we wouldn't let you leave without us?"

"I remember."

"Then you should know we started this with you, and we will see it through. After what we have seen the First Born do to innocent people, there is no way we can stop now. If the First Born intend on starting a war, then someone needs to fight—might as well be us." Ron couldn't believe the way Grant sounded. Not that he said anything wrong, but Ron expected him to say something funny or make light of the situation. Looking at his friend, Ron saw that he wore a more hardened face, one he hadn't seen before.

"You're right, Grant." Ron wondered if Grant now having someone to go back to had made him adopt a more serious demeanor, or if it was due to the horrible things he had to see. Ron wasn't sure what it was, but it seemed fitting.

"After all this is over, I think I will come back," Shaw said. Everyone was surprised. "Don't give me those looks. This place gives me peace, clarity, a sense of ease. I think this is where I need to be."

Nora put her hand on his back. "I think that's a great idea." They talked until it got dark, then headed back to Bonnie's house for the last night. Nora gave Shaw the hay-stuffed cot by the wall. She slept with Ron on the more oversized cot. Grant didn't mind sleeping with a few blankets on the floor. Ron held Nora as he played with her hair between his fingers, wishing such a simple embrace could last a lifetime.

The following day, they ensured that all their belongings were packed, which wasn't much since they only carried their weapons and the clothes on their backs. Then they walked to the temple of the elders to retrieve the Orb of Ember and talk with Bonnie. Inside the temple, Nora, Grant, and Shaw were in awe of the artifacts and books. Ron helped Bonnie lift the desk in the center of the room. Then he went down the stairs, lighting his hand aflame as he entered the room, picked up the Orb, and headed back upstairs.

"I still wish you wouldn't go, but I know nothing I say will change your mind. In any case, I want you to have these." Bonnie turned around, picking up an item behind her, and handed it to Ron. "These are the clothes our ancestors would wear into battle. I had some of them hemmed to fit your particular size, so they should fit just right."

Ron looked at the clothes in his hands. "Bonnie, I don't know what to say. This is incredible." She beamed with pride. Seeing a wielder holding the colors of the Falla Essen reminded her of her ancestors. Ron first held out the brown pants. They looked like the ones he wore back home, except these pants didn't have holes in the knees. Next, he held up the shirt; it had a color reminiscent of the red-brown clay found on the island. Lastly was a dark cloak, it hung along his back by his knees, and the front pinned to a circular metal brooch on the left side, leaving the cloak to cover the top half of his torso.

"There is one more thing," she said, holding something behind her back that she had picked up while Ron looked over the clothes. "This is a rare piece of armor—treat it well." She took it out from behind her back, holding it up for

Ron to see. He was speechless at what lay before him: an armor made of hardened leather but that afforded mobility to the wearer, with three black straps connecting the front and back on both sides. The leather curved to protect the left shoulder and a quarter of the upper arm.

The armor itself was neither red nor brown but a mixture of both, forming a dark maroon that stood out from the pants and shirt. Ron focused on the middle of the armor and saw a faint symbol fixed into the leather. It was a flame.

Bonnie handed it to Ron to inspect. He felt something was different about the armor once he touched it. "This armor was made centuries ago, but never used, as the Falla Essen left the lands in search of peace. It was created when wielders knew how to use the flame to strengthen their creations. To fight other wielders, the Falla Essen created an armor that could withstand another's flame—that is what this will do. It is not indestructible, but it will protect you against another wielder."

"I've heard stories about the weapons of wielders, but to actually hold something created by the flame . . . How could I ever thank you?" He knew there was nothing he could do to repay her for what she had given him.

"Just make sure the choice you make is the right one. That is all I ask. Oh, and be careful with that symbol. We don't know who remembers what it means."

Ron nodded silently. Bonnie left the temple and headed to the docks, letting him change into his new clothes. They fit remarkably well. Ron had no idea how she could have gotten the size right, but at this point, it didn't matter; he was more than happy to take off the clothes given to him by Hadal. Ron pinned on a brooch to cover the wielders symbol and put the Orb in the cloak's inner pocket.

Soon, everyone made their way toward the docks.

Ron saw the ship's mast as they got closer; it was not large by any means, but to Ron, it was the biggest ship he had ever seen. It was even big enough to carry a smaller boat on the side. Bonnie was there, talking to a young bald man no older than Ron's age. She introduced them.

"Everyone, this is Marcus. He will be taking you to shore and then to Baddon."

Marcus greeted them with a bow. "It will not take long to get to shore, a day or two at most depending on if the wind decides to grant us her speed. Bonnie has told me about your situation. First, we will head to Baddon, where I will introduce you to a friend of mine who does trading between Altara and Oroze.

"Once we meet him, he should have no problem taking you to Oroze discreetly. He and I have done some less-than-reputable business before, so this will not be anything new to him. I will say, however, that once you are inside Oroze, you will be on your own. Let me know when you are ready, and we will set sail." Marcus bowed and left to make the final preparations with his crew before they got onboard.

"Thank you, Bonnie. I hope we will see you again," Nora said, giving the woman a hug.

"So do I, child, so do I."

Ron, Grant, and Shaw said their goodbyes and boarded the ship while Marcus untied the dock lines, and his crew rowed forward with their oars. After rounding the island, the crew pulled in the oars, dropped the mainsail, and caught the westward wind.

Chapter Twenty-Nine

Perspective

S haw watched the wake come and go from the back of the ship. Ron stood behind Nora, holding her in his arms, trading sweet kisses as they talked. On the other hand, Grant was hanging his head over the side of the ship, heaving whatever was left in his stomach. None of them had been on a ship before except for Shaw, who had taken boats, ships, and smaller water vessels back and forth on many occasions during his travels. Nora and Ron got along on the ship just fine, but Grant vowed never to travel this way again—he couldn't understand why someone would want to rock up and down. It didn't make sense.

For Grant, the two days spent on the ship were never-ending torture, so when the shore came into view, he was ecstatic at the sight, knowing he was finally going to get off this cursed ship. Marcus was familiar with what the sea could do to the inexperienced, so as a precaution, he kept a store of herbs and spices belowdecks just for such occasions.

He clapped Grant on the back. "It takes some time to get your sea leg. By the looks of it, this must be the first ship you have ever stepped foot on."

Grant hung his head wearily, leaning forward over the side. "I wonder what gave that away." He wanted to say more, but his stomach turned once again.

"Here, take these—they should help ease your stomach. Go lie down. It will help to not look at the waves rocking the ship." Marcus extended his hand.

"What's this?" Grant asked.

"It's peppermint and ginger."

"How am I supposed to eat it, just chew it all at once?" Grant asked, looking at the peppermint leaves and raw ginger in his hand.

"Roll the peppermint leaf and put it in your cheek. You should start to feel better. As for the ginger, you should take small bits; it can be quite overpowering all at once. Now go lie down."

Grant did as Marcus advised and headed below. Down there, he saw multiple hammocks strung between wooden posts for each crew member. Marcus had already set up hammocks for everyone when they first boarded, so Grant went straight to his hammock, crawled in, and nibbled on the ginger.

It wasn't long until they reached the shore. Each crewman went about their duties, bringing in the mainsail and storing the oars in their proper places. Finally, the crew slowed the ship to a halt and dropped anchor. Marcus had made the venture before and knew how close he could take his ship to shore. The crew lowered the smaller boat steadily down into the water, then threw a rope ladder over the side.

Nora, Ron, Grant, Shaw, and Marcus climbed down into the boat. Marcus took up the oars, rowing the rest to shore while the crew stayed behind to look after the ship. He took to the south shore as he did most times to follow the river leading to Baddon without navigating the mountain ranges on the north side. Grant was the first volunteer to help pull the small boat onto shore, as he couldn't wait to feel the solid ground beneath his feet. Marcus and Grant pulled the boat far enough from the water that the high tide wouldn't sweep it away.

"Alright, from here on, we'll have to walk along the river. It won't be long until we reach a small town. I have a friend there who runs the stables, so we can rent some horses. After I leave you in Baddon, I will take the horses back. Ron, can you grab that pack over there?" Marcus pointed to the pack toward the back of the small boat. He'd tossed it down the ladder before they left for the shore.

When Bonnie told Marcus how many people needed to go to Baddon, he'd packed enough food and water for the journey. Ron handed him the pack, and Marcus opened it, handing out four water skins.

As they followed the river upstream, they listened to the soothing cascade of water into the sea, taking their minds off the growing heat of the day. Occasionally, Ron or Shaw would splash water on their face, keeping cool since there was little shade to be found. The sporadic trees along the river were only a minor reprieve from the heat.

"Is there anything farther south? I can't believe people would choose to live in this heat," Grant asked Marcus, wiping the sweat from his brow.

"I haven't been that far south myself, but the Kingdom of Altara lies that way, and even farther south, from what I hear, lies a fallen kingdom from one of the first wars."

"How do the people of Altara survive in this heat?" Grant asked.

"Altara, just like Oroze, trades exclusively with Baddon. You see, since Baddon's kingdom was built on both sides of the river, they supply water, fresh fruits, vegetables, weapons, and armor to the other kingdoms. So without Baddon, Altara would suffer greatly, as would Oroze to a degree."

Grant stayed silent. He didn't know why, but something about what Marcus said sounded familiar; he just couldn't place it.

"What's the name of the ruined kingdom?" Ron asked.

"I don't know—never cared enough to ask. Nothing can survive that far south. They say it's all desert after Altara." Not much concerned Marcus if it wasn't about the island or the Falla Essen, but he'd picked up tidbits of information about Baddon over the years.

Shingled rooftops peaked as they came to the top of a small mound. "Here we are, the town of Barrdin," Marcus said. "Come, I'll introduce you to my friend, and then we will get some horses."

As soon as Marcus began walking, Ron grabbed him by the shoulder. "Quick, get down." He pulled Marcus to the ground and everyone lay flat, peering over the mound.

"Ron, what is it?" Nora asked, her eyes searching intently.

"I thought I saw something there. Look." Ron pointed to First Born soldiers walking around the corner of a house, carrying a banner.

"What are they doing here?" Nora asked, wondering why they were so far from Oroze.

"I don't know, but whatever it is can't be good," Ron answered. He scanned the other homes and the area by the river until he caught a glimpse of more soldiers passing by the watermill as the current turned the wheel.

"How many do you think are over there?" Shaw asked aloud, wishing he had arrows in his quiver.

"It's a small town, so if they have as many men as Meno did when we passed through, then I would assume twenty, twenty-five soldiers at least," Nora said, hoping there were not actually that many.

"Wait," Grant said. "I think I know what they're doing here."

"What?" Nora asked.

"Remember when we first met Alas, and he said Baddon used to send food and supplies to the people of Meno when they were forced out?"

"I remember."

"I think the First Born's going to try and take control of Baddon. Think about it—if they control the bordering towns, they can move men without anyone batting an eye. Who's to say they won't attack Baddon once all their men are in place?" Grant continued putting the pieces of his thoughts together.

"That would take a lot of time and a lot of men. Marcus, how big is Baddon?" Shaw asked.

"It's a big city. The streets are cramped with peddlers, beggars, guards—all sorts of people live there. Shaw's right. It would require a lot of men to take the city."

Nora looked to Grant. "What are you thinking?"

"I think that's only half their plan. If they can take Baddon, they will do what they did in Meno to Altara. Wouldn't that be the easiest way to conquer both kingdoms at the same time? You said it yourself, Marcus, that Baddon trades with Oroze and Altara, so if the First Born control Baddon I think they will sever their trade lines and wait for the people of Altara to surrender. That way, the First Born won't suffer any casualties, and Altara will be too weak to defend itself. We need to clear out Barrdin, give these people a chance, and hopefully, they can tell the others what's happening."

Each thought turning in Grant's mind brought him back to what the First Born did to the people of Meno. He remembered the bodies lying in the mud, stripped naked, broken, with missing limbs all piled on each other. He felt the anger build within him, and let it course through his veins. He longed for the feeling, he wanted it, just like he wanted to kill the soldiers as he watched them from the mound.

"Grant's right. If that's their plan, we need to help these people. We can't let Hadal take the other kingdoms. Once we get into Barrdin, we need at least one soldier alive. I'll make him talk," Ron said. He was steadfast in this decision, and even though he didn't have a sword, he was more than capable of fighting, especially with Nora, Grant, and Shaw at his side.

"What should I do?" Marcus asked.

Ron looked at him. "You're going to stay here. You will be out of harm's way, and we won't have to worry about you once the fighting starts, so just stay here. We will get you when it's over."

Marcus nodded, knowing he would be a distraction if he went with them. He couldn't produce the flame, and he'd never had an interest in learning to fight on the island; he found his enjoyment in sailing on his ship.

"So, what's the plan?" Shaw asked.

"We wait until the coast is clear, then we make for the first house. They don't know who we are, so we can use that to our advant—"

Marcus interrupted. "They might not know who you are, but your weapons will give you away. Barrdin does not have many fighters. Perhaps a few guards from Baddon, but that's all. They breed horses."

No one felt comfortable going into Barrdin without their weapons since they didn't know how many First Born were there. "We will have to risk it. We can take out as many as we can quietly, but once we're seen, we will have to fight," Grant said, watching the First Born make their rounds, trying to find a pattern in their patrol.

"Alright, we'll split up. Shaw, you stay with me. Grant, you go with Ron. Let's hope there aren't too many of them," Nora said.

Marcus stayed behind the mound as Shaw and Nora took a left while Ron and Grant went right once the soldiers were out of sight. Nora pulled her staff from the latch on her back as she and Shaw reached the first house. The homes were spread a good ten to fifteen feet apart, giving them ample room to maneuver between. However, they stopped short at the corner of a house when they heard a First Born patrol coming their way. "I'll distract them while you go around back and attack them from there," Shaw whispered.

"But you don't have a weapon."

"Don't worry, I know what I'm doing. Now go."

Nora hurried around the house while Shaw stood up, smoothing his clothes as he stepped around the corner. "Ah, just who I was looking for!" he shouted to the patrolling soldiers.

"What do you want, old man?"

"I was hoping you could tell me if you have seen my son around here. He said he was going to be back in a jiff, but he's been gone an hour now." Despite Shaw's age, he was rather youthful, but he was more than capable of acting older than he was.

"All able-bodied men should be working. Are you telling me he's not doing as the First Born have instructed him to do?" The soldiers stepped closer to Shaw. "You know the punishment for defying the rules, so you better pray you find him before we do."

Shaw saw Nora coming up from behind. "You're absolutely right. If you found him before me, then you would most certainly be dead."

"What did you say?"

Then Nora's staff burst through a soldier's midsection. His hands grabbed the blood-covered metal before he fell to the ground. The other soldier turned in horror, giving Shaw an opening to reach for the man's sword, unsheathing it and slicing his neck open with a quick flash of the blade.

Nora wiped off her staff. "So you were playing up the old man bit, huh?"

"Yes, it works every time," he said.

"I'm sure it does."

"It worked on you before you left Greyland, didn't it?" he said with a grin.

Nora shook her head. "That's fair." She let out a small laugh as they made their way through the houses.

Ron and Grant cautiously approached a patrol of two First Born soldiers from behind. Grant had one blade drawn, and Ron let the power of the flame feed into his muscles. With a quick burst, the pair were right behind the soldiers, giving them no time to react as Ron wrapped his arms around one soldier's neck, snapping it with a loud pop. He set the soldier down gently to avoid any sound while Grant covered the other one's mouth and drove the blade into his neck. The soldier struggled as blood bubbled and the air left his body. Grant eased him to the ground, hiding the smile on his face before looking to Ron. "Well, that's two down. How many more?"

Ron and Grant heard shouting and saw Nora and Shaw come running around the corner. "They didn't see us, but they know we are here. They found the bodies of the first two we got," Nora said, catching her breath,

"Okay, we'll stick together. Did you see how many there are?" Ron asked.

"I would say about a dozen, maybe more."

The clanging of boots and armor grew louder. "Let's find somewhere with more room—I don't want to get surrounded." Ron reached down, taking a sword from the dead soldier. They ran through the homes, noticing the people inside closing wooden shutters and bolting their doors. Next, they ran into the town square, where people were working under the watchful eyes of a handful of soldiers. Once the crowd realized what was happening, they began to panic; they ran for their homes, pushing others out of the way, doing whatever they could to escape the impending violence.

Steel collided on steel. Ron's first thought was to kill these soldiers before the others arrived. He didn't want to end surrounded and under attack from sides. Nora and Shaw dispatched the attacking soldiers with ease; it was easy to tell that the training of the First Born was less than adequate, but their lack of skill didn't matter. They made up for it with their numbers.

Ron killed the soldier in front of him as he sidestepped a strong thrust only to slash the soldier's back, splitting it open in a single stroke. Then he looked to Grant and saw the true speed at which he moved; even with Ron's power flowing

PERSPECTIVE 477

through him constantly, he was barely able to see his friend's movements. Ron saw a body fall, blood spurting out of multiple open wounds before he could even find where Grant was. There must have been five or six different wounds, but he didn't see Grant attack, not even once.

The call to arms from the First Born sounded behind them. Men poured out from around the houses, coming into the open square. Grant stepped forward, ready to continue fighting, and Ron put a hand on his shoulder.

"Not yet," Ron said. A brief flash of anger crossed Grant's eyes, but Ron dismissed it as he focused on the First Born gathering. They rushed forward, charging with blades drawn.

Ron stood still, calling the flame to his hands, and in the next moment unleashed a devastating blast of fire, engulfing the soldiers in a raging inferno of swirling flame. Soldiers dropped to their knees, crying in agony as the flame consumed them; their voices cracked and faded to silence. More than fifteen of the First Born were burning as life left their bodies.

The remaining soldiers, shocked by what they saw, turned to run, hoping to save themselves from the fate of the others, but Ron was too fast. Before they had a chance to run, Ron raised a wall of flame behind them, blocking any chance of escape. For them, the choice was presented: cross the flame and burn or stand and fight to the death. The last four soldiers turned back around, dropping their weapons as they got to their knees before the wielder as he approached.

Ron let the wall of flame burn behind them. "Who among you will tell me the purpose of your presence here?" he asked. The soldiers remained tight-lipped in solidarity. "I won't ask again. If none of you choose to answer, you will suffer a fate much worse than that of your fallen comrades. A much slower fate." Ron intensified the flame, growing it larger in his hand. "For the ones that tell me what I need to know, I will let you go." Grant looked at Ron as if he had lost his mind, but Ron subtly shook his head.

The First Born soldier on the far left cleared his throat and spoke up, earning deadly glares from his companions. "We were sent out as a detachment from a larger unit. Our orders were to secure the borders, that's it." His lip quivered.

And Ron saw this was not a soldier; this was hardly even a grown man. If Ron had to guess, he was probably no older than eighteen.

Grant's attention went to the boy. "Secure the borders? How many people did you kill when you secured these borders, huh? Was it ten, fifteen, twenty? How many?" His rage was starting to show, thinly veiled by his calm exterior.

"I don't know. I just did as commanded. New recruits are not supposed to question orders; each of us has seen what happens to those who question the officers. Questioning orders or an officer is looked upon as if we are challenging Lord Hadal himself." The young soldier looked frightened when Grant stepped in front of him, bending down to eye level.

"How many have you killed?" The calm in his voice terrified the boy.

"I've lost count of how many."

"You don't even know how many you killed, and yet you sit here frightened like a child about to cry because you are now on the other side?" Grant shook his head and walked away, letting Ron get back to questioning the soldiers.

"Anyone else have anything to say? I'm a man of my word, which might mean little to you, but if you choose to speak, I will let you live." Ron was giving them one chance, which was one more than Grant would have. If Grant had it his way, they would all be dead and tossed in the river.

The residents of Barrdin began to open their windows and doors now that the commotion had settled to see what was happening. They gathered all around the square in awe and fear of the wall of flame burning bright behind the four soldiers, waiting anxiously to see what would happen to them. Next to the young boy was a First Born soldier who was further along in years, though still not too much older than Ron. Finally, he seemed to come to reason and broke his silence.

"The lord wants Baddon, but currently, it's too heavily fortified to take, and he is unwilling to leave Oroze unguarded to come deal with the city himself. That's why we are here, to get men around and then inside the city."

"Shut your mouth, traitor!" growled the soldier on the far right. "If we get out of here, we will have your head on a pike."

Grant moved swiftly, crouching down in front of the two soldiers on the right. "You won't be getting out of here." Grant's blades stabbed each man below the sternum, piercing their hearts.

Ron, Nora, and Shaw looked confused and concerned as Grant wiped the blood from his daggers and returned to his position. "We would've had to kill those two regardless. They already made up their minds—they were never going to talk."

After witnessing Grant's speed and lethal resolve, the crowd of people looked just as frightened as the last two First Born soldiers. "You said if we talked, you would let us go. Please don't kill us," the young boy pleaded.

Grant's gaze turned to him. "Don't kill you? Did any of the people you murdered ask you the same thing? How many . . ." Grant took a step toward him, but Ron's arm caught him across his chest.

"You need to cool off. I'll deal with the rest of this," Ron said, meeting his friend's intense glare. Ron had never seen such a look in his eyes before. He wondered how Grant could carry such unbridled rage. "Go calm down. Find Marcus, and bring him here. That should give you enough time to clear your head."

Grant turned away, huffing as he left. Ron locked eyes with Shaw; he nodded in understanding that he would accompany Grant to get Marcus. Then, letting out a deep breath, Ron dropped the wall of flame.

Nora came to his side. "What are we going to do with them? We can't let them go and run the risk of them telling the other First Born. What do you have in mind?"

"I plan to stay true to my word. After that, whatever happens to them is not my concern." The emotionless stare returned to Ron's eyes, the same gaze Nora had seen when they were gathered with the elders in Bonnie's home. Only this time, she saw a sadness hidden behind them. She reasoned Ron would, in fact, let them go, fulfilling his word, but she knew the fate that awaited the young boy. Ron rested his forehead against Nora's before heading back in front of the two soldiers.

"I won't kill you. As I said, I'm a man of my word—you are both free to go." The soldiers let out a sigh as Ron turned from them and addressed the crowd. "These two are now in your hands. Find whatever justice you deem necessary for the crimes they have committed against you."

Ron knew he'd just sentenced the young boy and soldier to death; regardless of the guilt he felt for such a young life to be ended, he rationalized that everyone had choices to make, and had to live or die with the repercussions. Nora wrapped her arm around Ron as they walked away from the crowd. Yelling and shouting erupted from the mob as they closed in on the two soldiers. Pleading cries for mercy quickly turned to screams of pain as the mob beat the soldiers to death in the name of justice.

* * *

Shaw walked behind Grant as he grumbled to himself with his hands in his pockets. The screams of the soldiers echoed from the square, loud enough for Grant to hear; he eased the tension in his shoulders and relaxed, knowing the First Born had gotten what they deserved.

"Is everything alright, Grant?" Shaw asked calmly.

"Of course, why would you ask?"

"You seemed more on edge than usual. Given the circumstance, it's completely warranted, but if I'm being honest, this is not the first time you have done this."

It was only a matter of time before someone noticed. Grant was just glad it was Shaw instead of Nora or Ron. He could talk to them about anything, but when he spoke to Shaw, it made him feel as though the man wasn't trying to find an acceptable reason, something to make his behavior warranted.

"I know, and you're right. I just—I just don't understand why it's so hard for people to do the right thing, and I get so angry they can't realize it even when the right thing is staring them in the face." Grant shook his head. "It just doesn't make sense."

Shaw thought for a moment. "Have you thought that perhaps the concept of right and wrong presented to the person was not in the correct manner?"

Grant wrinkled his brow. "What do you mean?"

"Maybe they think they know what is right, when in fact it's not. For example, someone could be taught how to tie a knot one way their whole life, knowing it to be the only way to tie it. Then, one day, they're shown a different way they have never encountered before. It might seem strange or foreign even, so much so they might consider it to be the 'wrong' way. When it comes to a difference of ideals, things tend to get a lot more complicated. It becomes about more than just right and wrong. It starts to involve beliefs, ego, and the lack of them wanting to change. Still, if presented with reason, logic, facts, and the ability to listen, the gap between the differentiating ideals begins to narrow, unless—" Shaw said.

"Unless what?" Grant asked.

"Unless someone has convinced themselves beyond a shadow of a doubt that their actions are justified. To believe with such absolution that they are making the right choice, nothing can change their mind. I'm afraid that is what we are dealing with when it comes to Lord Hadal and the First Born."

"Can't we just remove the choice altogether? If we did that in Meno, all those people would be alive, not rotting away," Grant reasoned.

Shaw sighed. "That's true, they would be alive, but if we did that, we would be no better than the First Born. People need to choose a life for themselves, even if it means they end up dying because of it. It sounds awful to say such a thing, but all we can do is give them a different perspective and hope it was enough." Shaw continued walking up the hill beside Grant, calling for Marcus to come down.

Ron and Nora were sitting on an old wooden bench pushed up along the outside of a house when they saw Marcus leading Grant and Shaw.

"I saw the flames from the hilltop. I hope you all are alright," Marcus said, greeting Ron.

"We're fine," Ron said.

"Can't say the same for the First Born," Grant added.

Ron gave him a sidelong look before addressing Marcus. "Where are the stables? Do you think we will have enough light to make it to Baddon?"

"The stables are just a little south of here, but if you wanted to make it to Baddon before nightfall, I don't think it's possible today. I think it would be best to stay the night and leave early in the morning."

Ron liked the idea of getting some rest, but he didn't think they could afford to rent a room. "We don't have enough money for a room. How do you suppose we pay for it?"

Marcus scratched his head. He hadn't planned on staying at an inn; he would have been more than halfway to Baddon by now if he were traveling by himself. A voice came from behind them.

"You needn't worry about paying for a room, and nor should you." A group approached, led by a short older man, who used a carved walking stick. His voice surprised them, as no one expected such a deep tone from the short man. "The lot of you will not have to pay, not even a copper coin. Those soldiers have been here for weeks, eating all our food, trashing the rooms of my inn, and helping themselves to whatever they fancied." The man extended a hand, and Ron did the same. "The name's Sutter, and if you give me a few hours, I can have some rooms cleaned up and ready for you."

"Thank you. We definitely appreciate it, but are you sure there's nothing we could offer for the room?" Ron asked.

"You all have done more than enough by getting rid of those despicable animals. A room for the night and a hot meal is the least we could do for you." The men and women behind Sutter nodded their heads.

The people of Barrdin went about disposing of the bodies, after searching each for anything salvageable. Most found only a few coins, but they would strip the dead soldiers of their blackened armor, the chain mail that lay beneath, and their weapons before tossing the corpses into the river. Each item went to the blacksmith to be melted down and appropriated for better use, such as horseshoes, stirrups, and pummels. Barrdin smiths had a reputation for making some of the finest saddles to be sold in the markets of Baddon, with most fetching a high price. Now, with all the extra metal, the smiths could continue making saddles to be proud of instead of being forced to craft quick, low-quality versions for the First Born.

As it was getting dark, the townsfolk lit fires, played music, and danced in celebration. Men and women would occasionally stop Ron, Nora, Grant, and Shaw to give their thanks, offering a toast to their freedom for those who restored it. The quartet tried to make it to the inn as quickly as possible, but the more they attempted to dodge the crowds, the more conspicuous they seemed. They finally made it inside after partaking in several more toasts and rounds of gratitude.

Finally, they sat down, sliding into a position of comfort in the chairs around a table. The exhaustion of the day set in, and the soothing glow of the fire roared from across the room. A warm and calming effect fell over them and the other guests.

Minstrels played an upbeat tune as the other patrons sang and cheered. Grant had a big smile on his face as he sipped the ale in his mug. Ron watched the people rejoice, and it reminded him of Greyland. The smile on Grant's face put one on his own, and Nora's and Shaw's too. The aroma of the food drifted throughout the inn, escaping from behind the kitchen doors. They felt as if they hadn't eaten in weeks.

The moist and tender chicken was placed caringly on a bed of perfectly fluffed mashed potatoes smothered in thick gravy, with roasted carrots, peppers, and onion mixed together on the side of the plate, waiting to be dipped. If the fire hadn't made them tired, the food most definitely did. Grant was soon leaning back in his chair with his eyes half closed, Shaw had his arms folded across his chest with his head down, and Ron and Nora sat side by side, leaning on one another, listening to the music. Ron woke Shaw and Grant once Sutter came to the table and gave him the keys to three rooms upstairs.

They went up, and Shaw said, "Goodnight."

Grant mumbled under his breath, still half asleep, and disappeared into his room. Nora walked in and used one of the lit candles to light a few more; Ron sat on the edge of the bed, removing his cloak, armor, and boots. "Nora?" he said.

"What is it?" Nora asked, sitting next to him on the edge of the bed.

"I'm worried about Grant. He didn't seem like himself today. There was something about him that seemed off." Ron's eyes couldn't hide his worry.

"I think some of the things we've seen are starting to get to him, Nora said. "Unfortunately, this isn't the first time it has happened. At first, I thought it was just a reaction, but each time we confront the First Born, he seems to be getting worse. Ever since the death of Alas and the people being massacred in Meno, he has been getting angrier and more violent. I know we are fighting the First Born, but I can't help but feel like he enjoys killing these people." She wished she had something better to say.

Ron turned toward her and took her hands in his. "Can you promise me something?" he asked.

"Of course."

"Promise me that you will look after Grant when this is over. He's like a brother to me, and if anyone can make sure he's okay, it's you." Once Ron said the words, the reality of his choice settled in.

"Why are you saying that? You're making it sound like we will never see you again. It almost sounds like you're trying to say goodbye."

Ron turned his face away, but she put a loving hand on his cheek, turning him back toward her. The palm of her hand was wet, and when she looked at him, she felt her own tears as she saw his falling down.

The lingering shadows from the candlelight danced and flickered through the night, waxing and waning from Ron's constant pacing. Nora was adamant about not asking what he was planning to do to stop Lord Hadal, but something told her she needed to know. She knew what her power felt like when a threat was close or when her instincts were attempting to tell her something, but the feeling she had at this moment was different. She felt it in the pit of her stomach, an ache that struck each time she would look to Ron while he paced.

The way he'd asked her to make a promise and avoided answering her questions left her uncertain about why he was saying such things. During the quiet moments when they weren't making small talk or reminiscing about Greyland, Nora would try to assess what the feeling in her stomach meant. It was a feeling she'd buried down deep a long time ago, one she'd felt only once before in her life. Remembering what it was, she stopped talking mid-sentence.

She'd felt it the day she got the news her parents had disappeared. The day she realized her parents would never be coming home. The feeling of loss took over. She had experienced something like it when Ron was first taken by the First Born, but it wasn't the same as when she found out about her parents. With her parents, there was a certainty to what she felt, but with Ron, she could still hope. She also got swept up in trying to find him, and helping the people of Meno, talking to King Ahven and escaping the creatures from the forge. She hadn't had time to sit and figure out what her power was trying to tell her, but now she knew. She was going to lose him. She didn't know how, and she didn't know when, but she knew.

"Don't do it," she said. "We don't have to go to Oroze. We can find another way to save your brother and stop Hadal. It doesn't have to be this way." Her eyes found his as he bent to a knee, taking her hands.

"I wish that were true, I really do, but I don't think there's another way." His voice was calm.

"But why? Why isn't there another way? I don't understand. You said not telling me was to protect me, but all it's doing is breaking my heart." Her eyes were wet with tears.

Ron had thought he could avoid hurting her if he shouldered this burden by himself, but he'd managed to do the opposite. He'd managed to do the one thing he never wanted to do, so he leaned forward and kissed her forehead. "I'm sorry. I thought it would be better this way. I was wrong."

"I'm here with you in all things. No matter how hard it may be, I'll always be here, but you need to be able to tell me what's going to happen if we're to get through this together."

Ron kissed her tender lips and pulled away. "I love you, Nora, I always will, but . . ."

She placed her hands on the sides of his head, running her fingers through his hair, "And I love you, so just tell me."

"Okay."

They talked through the night as he explained his plan. At first, she hated what he was thinking. She tried giving other possibilities of what he could do, but they all led to the same conclusion. No matter how they went around the subject, nothing changed.

Finally, they lay down together. Nora listened to Ron's heartbeat, knowing he hurt just as much as she did. After talking, they understood what they must do and the role they each had to play, even if every fiber of their being told them not to. Ron held Nora tightly, hoping that one day he would be able to do so again.

"This won't be the end. We will figure something out. No matter what, I'll come back to you." He ran his figures through her smooth, silky hair.

"I hope so." She reached up, kissing him as if it would be the last time. "I love you, Ron."

"I love you too." Time seemed to slow down for the rest of the night as Ron and Nora surrendered themselves to each other completely, as every ounce of intimacy and passion wove through their bodies.

Chapter Thirty

At Any Cost

With the horses saddled, everyone was ready to reach Baddon. Marcus explained that the ride would only take a day or two, so they had to decide whether they wanted to make camp or ride through the night. The people of Barrdin were kind enough to fill their saddlebags with food and water as a last token of appreciation before they left. Marcus then led the way, waving to the people as they departed. Once again, they followed the river heading west; they rode quickly to cover more ground while they had the sun's light.

Shortly before they left Barrdin, they'd been told that night was the most dangerous time to travel, not just because of the First Born but also because of the unusual sounds. It had been almost a month since the creatures had come through the forge gate, and no one knew how many had come through, but with them not having been seen since, it was safe to guess they had not crossed the river yet. Even so, there was no telling what lurked in the dark on any given night.

The horses panted loudly as the sun rose on the second day. They'd ridden hard through the night, bringing everyone before the grand kingdom of Baddon. Not far in the distance, they saw the massive kingdom straddling the river. High spires of stonework rose above the walls, watchtowers stood by each gated entrance, and long walls stretched in four directions.

Entrances in the north and south connected the roads leading to Oroze and Altara. Caravans of wagons and single horsemen looked like tiny dots as they traveled the road, some only visible as clouds of moving dust.

The east and west corridors ended in walls on top of the river, leaving no entrance to either side, only a small opening for the water to move through the kingdom.

After joining the procession of travelers, merchants, dignitaries, guards, and other various people, they blended into the crowd. No one batted an eye as they entered the sprawling kingdom of Baddon. For once, it seemed no one cared who they were or why they had come to the kingdom. The surrounding people were too busy dealing with their own lives to be concerned about the lives of strangers.

After dismounting their horses and bringing them to a feeding trough, they patted each horse to let them know they'd done well and deserved rest. The streets moved fast, with people bumping and brushing against one another, too much in a rush to be bothered with using simple pleasantries. Shops were built from stone, with colorful tapestries hanging over the front of each, providing shade from the sun and an identifiable marking for different shops.

Marcus moved through the crowd with ease, as he had done so many times before. He knew the ins and outs of the kingdom, making it somewhat easy for the others to follow him through the crowded streets, only slowing down here and there when they got cut off by large groups.

The center of Baddon was much different than the shopping corridors; once they were in the open, they saw where the large spires began. Each spire was interconnected by a stone walkway almost twenty feet in the air. Following the walkway around each spire, Ron, Nora, Grant and Shaw saw that it led to where the king and queen must reside, overlooking the people of their kingdom. Multiple beautiful bridges spanned the river, with ornate wooden side rails built into the smooth stone, connecting the north and south. Water rapidly swept through Baddon, flowing under the constructed roads and bridges.

"Where is this friend of yours?" Ron asked.

Marcus pointed to the eastern and western sections of the kingdom. "He will be in the east residential district. Hopefully he's home. He tends to converse with people between both districts, trying to find the best bargains for his necessary provisions. But, in the event he's not, we can just wait around here."

Benches lay next to the bridges for people to sit on and gaze at the serene beauty of the flowing water, the bright green trees, and the shrubbery dotted with budding blue, red, and yellow flowers that gave color to an otherwise sun-bleached courtyard.

Ron, Nora, Grant, and Shaw followed Marcus down the courtyard into the east residential district; homes were stacked on top of one another, the likes of which they had never seen. Multistory buildings were not uncommon, but the height and number of rooms were staggering.

Stretching along each side of the road were six to seven floors of living quarters. People stepped onto their front balconies, looking over the stone sidings, watching the other residents. Some hung clothing to dry over the ledge. An older man scraped the innards of his pipe, letting the burnt contents drift down and away on the breeze. Some people stayed to the shadows provided by the stairs leading to the other floors, eyeing those looking to have more value than others, only to slink away once they spotted a passing guard.

"How could anyone find someone here?" Grant said under his breath, expecting no answer.

Almost at the end of the corridor, Marcus turned sharply to the right and headed to the second floor. Stopping before an aged door that looked as though a strong breeze could topple it, he knocked. The door pulled back sharply but only opened a few inches, enough for a man's hazel eye to emerge from the crack. "State your business or leave my sight. First and last warning," a gravelly tone uttered from behind the door.

"It's Marcus—I've got a job for ya." The hazel eye examined Marcus's face before shutting the door. Then locks and latches slid and clicked open. It must have been at least four or five different bolts. "In this line of work, he feels the need to protect himself. Sometimes, situations can get rather unpleasant," Marcus said, responding to everyone's looks of bewilderment. Finally, the man opened the door. He stood in the frame at roughly five-foot-ten; scruff and dirt accumulated around his face and shaggy brown hair.

"Marcus, I almost forgot your face. How long has it been now? Two months, perhaps three?" he said, extending his arm.

Marcus met the arm with his own. "Oh, I'd say about a two and a half by now. It's good to see you, Walt."

"Likewise, my friend. Now what is this you say about a job?" Walt's eyes darted between Ron, Nora, Grant, and Shaw, trying to get a sense of who they were.

"I think we should discuss that inside, if you don't mind?" Marcus asked.

"Oh, it's one of those jobs, then, is it?" Walt asked.

"I'm afraid so."

"Well, then come inside, and we can discuss the finer details." Walt motioned for them to enter. Once they did, they saw the home was no bigger than a room with one nook built for the bed. The light filtered in through a time-stained window. "Please find a seat. I can't offer you much, as you can see by my living arrangements, but we here in Baddon, despite what the marketplace is like, do show some hospitality." Walt sat down on the edge of his bed.

"Thank you," Ron said.

"So, Marcus, what does this job entail? I'm assuming it has something to do with these four. Otherwise, they would have no business inside my home."

"Yes, they require safe and discreet passage into Oroze. I have enough to pay their way, and more once the job is completed," Marcus said.

Walt eyed them suspiciously. "And what business would these four have in Oroze to need my assistance?"

Marcus began talking, but Ron cut in. "The less you know, the better it will be. Like Marcus said, all we need is to get into Oroze. After that, your job is done. We heard you know how to get us in without being seen. So now that you know what the job is and what we can pay, the only question left is, will you help us?"

"Oh, you cut right to the chase, don't you, boy?" Walt asked, meeting Ron's eyes. "Well, what you heard is true. I can indeed get you into Oroze, and if this is as simple as you say it is, and at this price"—Walt eyed the coin purse in Marcus's hand—"then yes, I will take you. But know this: if these are the terms we agree upon, then I hold no responsibility for what happens to you and yours once we have arrived."

"Those are fair terms. Once we get inside Oroze and the coast is clear, we will go our separate ways, simple as that," Ron said.

"Simple as that then, ah? Well all right, we have ourselves an arrangement. When do you suppose you want to get to Oroze?" Walt asked.

"The sooner, the better—and preferably at night," Ron said.

"I'll tell you what. Give me an hour or so to get my wagon and horses set, and we can leave today. It's about a four- to five-day ride by wagon, and that's without getting stopped by those First Born for inspection, so let's hope we don't run into them. I would suggest you take whatever provisions you need before we leave—oh, and do bring something to keep you warm; the back of the wagon can get mighty cold at night." Walt stood up and made for the door. "And Marcus, I expect the first half of payment before we leave."

"Don't you worry, Walt—you know I have it. Once I take them to get their supplies, I'll help you with your wagon."

"Alright then." Walt walked through the door, followed by the rest. Once the saddlebags were detached from the horses and slung over Ron and Grant's shoulders, Marcus led them back to the courtyard, where he told them to wait while he helped Walt prepare the wagon.

"Do you think we can fully trust this guy? He seems a little strange," Grant asked openly.

"I guess we can. I don't think Bonnie would send us with Marcus if she knew he couldn't be trusted," Ron answered. "What do you think, Nora?"

"He might be strange, but I'm not getting any sort of feeling about him. If we can trust Marcus, I think we can trust Walt to a degree."

"I've met people like Walt during my travels," Shaw added, "and what seems to be a reoccurring trend with them is that as long as they get the coin they're promised, they will commit to the job they have taken. The coin is a powerful motivator to the right person."

"I hope you're right," Ron said.

Walt brought his wagon around with Marcus sitting next to him, laughing as they came to a stop. Walt moved to the back of the wagon and gestured for the others to come around. "So here is where you will stay for the duration of our time together." Walt lifted up the false bottom to his wagon, exposing a space big enough to fit three people as long as they lay flat. "Now, this won't be the most comfortable ride you've ever had, but you will be able to rest and perhaps sleep until we go through the hills. After the hills, it will be smooth sailing."

"How are we all to fit in there?" asked Nora. "It doesn't look big enough."

"Well, one of you can ride upfront with me—preferably you." Walt pointed to Shaw. "No one would think twice about an old man riding with me, no offense."

"None taken," Shaw replied. He didn't like being called old, but he also knew he was probably the most indistinguishable one out of the group.

"Alright, are we all set and ready to go?" Walt asked.

"I guess so," Ron said, turning to Marcus and extending an arm. "Thank you for helping us. I know you didn't have to, but I'm glad you did."

"You're welcome. I would do it again if I could."

The others said goodbye and climbed into the wagon—first Nora, then Ron, and lastly Grant. Once under the false bottom, they heard objects being placed on top. "Don't you worry, Walt and Marcus are putting the items he trades on top. He said it will keep him from getting inspected if he has a full load," Shaw said before he climbed into the front of the wagon. Within moments, they were moving, on their way to Oroze.

The road ahead was long, bumpy, cold, dusty, and for the most part uncomfortable. Sleep came in waves, especially during the first day as the roads were smooth and everyone was tired from riding through the night to reach Baddon, but the days that followed were pure misery. Yet as much as Ron, Nora, and Grant didn't like staying in the wagon's false bottom, they knew it was the best alternative.

Sometime later, they heard Walt yell that they would reach Oroze in less than a day, so everyone should rest as much as possible. Ron stayed awake as the unease of being back in Oroze crept up on him. He remembered the time he'd spent with the father, Hadal, and Nathill. He heard distant chattering the closer they got, and he decided to let Nora and Grant sleep just a little longer before they had to wake up and worry about being caught or killed.

They arrived at the gate not long after the sun went down. Ron heard the First Born guards ask what was in the wagon, but seeing as Walt had come and gone from Oroze so many times, he talked to the guards in his usual manner, offering to show them his wares by personally unloading everything he carried. No guard wanted to stand around and waste that much time, so they allowed Walt and his wagon to pass. After a few left and right turns, almost as though the wagon was going in circles, it came to a stop.

Ron had a sinking feeling in his stomach, but then he heard two loud thuds. Walt walked around to the back of the wagon, quietly taking out his supplies so as to not draw any unwanted attention. As the last item came off, he asked, "Are you all okay in there?"

"We are," Ron whispered, though his feeling of unease grew stronger. Walt then turned the latch and opened the false bottom of the wagon.

Ron sat up and saw that Walt wasn't alone. Before he had the chance to react, he felt the heavy hilt of a First Born soldier's sword bash against his head. In a haze of confusion, Ron saw blurred shapes descend on the wagon. Muffled sounds reverberated in his ears before darkness caved in around him, and he succumbed to the nothingness.

* * *

The throbbing pain radiated through Ron's head as he felt the dried blood pooling on his skin. He blinked slowly, making sure he wasn't dreaming. His vision was still blurry with the sound of his surroundings slowly coming back; he heard the soft groans of voices he recognized. He shook his head, trying to clear it as quickly as possible.

Then he heard Nora. The cold ground pressed against his temple as he lifted his pounding head from the floor. His hands were bound behind his back, making it more difficult to sit upright. Once his vision returned, he saw that he was back in Lord Hadal's quarters, kneeling before the large metal triangle housing the other two Orbs of Ember. Looking to his left, he saw Nora, Grant, and Shaw on their knees, each covered in varying degrees of blood, no doubt from trying to fight back before being overwhelmed by First Born soldiers.

"Nora, are you all right? Grant? Shaw? How are you guys holding up?" Ron asked as he saw no one else in the room.

"I'm fine, we're fine, but what are we going to do? The plan has fallen apart," Nora said.

"What happened exactly? How did we get here?"

"It was Walt and Marcus. How else would the First Born know we were in his wagon? I can't believe we trusted them; I can't believe we were so foolish yet again. I swear, if I get out of here, I'll kill them both," Grant said, seething in anger.

"How can you be so sure Marcus was part of this? He's part of the Falla Essen. It doesn't make sense," Ron said.

"Marcus was the only one who knew who we are. Do you think it's just a coincidence that Walt would want to turn us over to the First Born? To him, we're just random people."

Ron knew Grant was right, but he didn't know why Marcus would betray them so easily.

"Ron, what should we do?" Nora asked again, but before he could answer, the door behind them opened. Lord Hadal emerged with the father right on his heels, wearing his signature sinister grin that Ron had seen so many times before in the Ark. Then guards came in, carrying a beaten and bloodied body. Lord Hadal ordered the guards to place the body by the metal triangle; once they relinquished their hold, it fell to its knees and slumped over.

The father grabbed the back of the figure's cloak, wrenching upright and removing the hood. Ron's anger burst forth at the state in which he saw Nathill. Blood stained his face, dried from weeks of abuse. His eyes were swollen, lips cracked and bleeding as a hoarse breath heaved in and out. Ron met the father's eyes. "I'll kill you. I swear it."

The father smiled. "I don't think you're in the position to be making those kinds of threats, now are you?" His laugh filled the room.

Lord Hadal dismissed the guards, but not before bringing the quartet to their feet while removing their restraints. Ron looked at the lord. He knew what he was doing. Lord Hadal had done the same thing to Ron—gave him a false sense of freedom, letting him think he had more choice than he did. Ron saw Grant's hands brush along the sides of his daggers, checking to see if they were still there. Nora knew she had her staff as she felt the weight on her back. Shaw had his bow, but his quiver was empty.

Ron held his hand out cautiously. "Don't try anything. This is what he does. He will be expecting you to make a move—don't give it to him."

Lord Hadal smiled at Ron. "Now why would you go and say that? I figured we could all just talk and solve this problem that you created."

"I've created? You're the one that wants to start a war and bring the forge to this world. I didn't start anything. I'm just someone who wants to stop a madman."

The smile faded. "A madman, you say. Perhaps you don't know everything about the situation. How about I enlighten you?"

"You think anything you have to say will make a difference?" Ron said.

"Oh, I do, I very much do. For starters, I already know what Nathill has told you. I wish he hadn't, and as much as it pained me to hurt him, it was necessary. Now, what you might not know is that Nathill here was a perfect soldier for some time, but I fear his allegiance began to slip the moment we started looking for you. I thought his connection with you would have been far removed since we destroyed Regis, but that was the flaw in my plan.

"I didn't expect him to get soft. Over the years, he excelled at what needed to be done, but I didn't think his loyalties would have shifted so fast when it came to you. It still baffles me that he would throw away everything we worked so hard for. I was so close to achieving the dream we once shared, almost a decade in the making, and he gave it up for you. Once I understood I couldn't trust him as I had, I fed him information only he was privy to.

"I didn't want to hurt him, but if I make an exception for him, how would that make me look? You should know better than anyone that actions have consequences, and Nathill's transgressions were the worst of all; he betrayed me in a way that I swore I would never suffer again."

"I'm sure trying to do the right thing is the worst when it comes to you," Ron said. "How could wanting to stop you from bringing the forge to our world be such a betrayal?"

Lord Hadal's face twisted in anger. "You think that's what this is about? The ambitions of a young man, naïve in his beliefs, for something so simple as a merging of the two worlds? No, once I have you open the forge, I will begin to build my empire. I will take the five kingdoms and have an army of wielders loyal to my rule. Each kingdom will be led by the strongest wielder, and this world will be ruled by the rightful leaders. I will have the final say over who or what is deemed worthy of life and power. I will decide before any is just cast aside and branded as you see before you." Lord Hadal slowed down, taking a breath. He was starting to lose his composure.

"That doesn't make sense. Why is it so important for you to have such a claim to other people's choices and lives? You're the reason the people of Regis didn't have a choice. They did nothing to you, and yet you still killed them all. So why does this matter so much?" Ron shouted, angry and confused.

"The people of Regis had a choice. More than one, actually," Lord Hadal said calmly. "I was the one that didn't have a choice."

"What are you saying? Are you from Regis?" Ron asked, not knowing what to think.

"More than you know. More than Nathill knows." Lord Hadal paused, composing himself before he began. "Do you have fond memories of them? Do you remember what it was like to be comforted, to be held as a child, to be loved?" he asked.

"By who, my parents?" Ron asked as Lord Hadal's stare met and held his own.

"No, Ron. By our parents."

Nathill's head slowly turned as Ron shook in disbelief. "What? No, we're not—there's no way." Ron couldn't form thoughts clearly in his head. The others looked just as shocked and speechless as he felt.

"This power was already a part of me, but our loving father saw it as a curse; he marked me as a monster, a failure, a useless child. I didn't know father followed the beliefs of Ermon, the wielder from the first war, and how would I have? I was a child. I conjured my first flame in front of him. I felt so proud. Perhaps I thought I was doing something that would prove to Father I was special. But instead, I showed him, and that was my first mistake.

"He took me into the woods, miles away from home. He told me we were going to go camping, but instead, he branded me with a hot iron heated from the flames of our campfire. He branded me just as Taroth's mother branded him, and then he just left me. He left me out there to die, scared, cold, and alone. I was five years old. I was a child, a child damn it! His firstborn!

"I was near death when I was found by a group of wielders hidden from the world. Wielders who never strayed from their beliefs that the rule of the strongest wielder will assume the mantel of a champion amongst all others, the Rassen Domani. I was raised in the ruins of Thalom's palace. It was all but destroyed after the Battle of the Storming Mountains. There I learned the histories, the true histories. I learned the language of the Essenti, but as I said, merging the two worlds was a young man's dream."

Ron refused to believe it. "No, Father would never do something like that, and neither would Mother. They were good people—you're lying!"

"You don't believe me? Then ask Nathill. Granted, he only found out now just as you have, but after spending so much time with me, he will know it to be true." The smile returned to Lord Hadal's face as Nathill only nodded his head. "Now, since you took the Orb from me, and with us being family and all—"

Ron interrupted, "We will never be family. Someone like you will never have a family." Hate radiated from his eyes.

Lord Hadal continued, "You seem to have betrayed me just as Nathill did, so we will settle the dispute right now." Lord Hadal turned to the father. "What do you think a fitting punishment would be for betraying a family member?"

The father scanned the room. "Well, my Lord, if I may be so bold, I don't think torture would work. And it may show a lack of originality."

"Go on," Lord Hadal said.

"I think since he took such a precious item from you, you should take one of the same value from him," the father said.

Lord Hadal paced back and forth. "Sounds fair."

The next moments went by in the blink of an eye as a bright blue flame shot across the room, striking the wall behind them. Looking around in panic, Shaw collapsed on the floor, holding his chest just below his heart. "He won't last long, so if you have anything to say, I would say it now." Lord Hadal smirked.

Nora, Ron, and Grant all rushed to Shaw's side. The old man was gasping for air. "Shaw, Shaw, hold on, it'll be alright, it will be alright," Nora said frantically, trying to calm herself as much as him.

"Shaw, what can we do? Tell us, what can we do?" Grant was just as panicked, hoping the man would tell him what to do, but he only looked at each of them, seeing the pain in their eyes, even Ron's, as he understood Ron wasn't able to heal him.

"There's nothing you can do," Shaw said, reaching into his cloak's inside pocket, pulling out the lady's thimble flower encased in hardened tree sap. He held it out for Nora along with his bracelet.

"Shaw, what are you doing?" she asked.

"I want you to have these. I won't be needing them anymore; I'm finally going to be with my family. I want you to take these with you as a reminder for when times get hard. Never give up hope."

Nora took them, holding them close as tears ran down. "I won't, Shaw, I promise."

"Grant, remember what we talked about back in Barrdin? Use what you learned, and you will be alright." Shaw patted his hand. Grant was unable to speak through the sorrow. "Ron, I'm glad I got to watch you become the man you are today. Even if I didn't have a hand in raising you, I'm proud of who you became. I'm just glad I got to be there when you needed me."

"I'm sorry, Shaw," Ron said.

"Don't be. I lived a good life. Just make sure you can do the same." Shaw looked away. "I feel cold. Tired. I think I'll just close . . ."

Shaw breathed his final breath, and a heavy sadness fell over Ron, Nora, and Grant.

Then Hadal spoke.

"Now that we have that settled, would you do as your older brother asks and put the last Orb in its rightful place? I would hate to see another one of you suffer the same fate."

Rage seared through each as they stood, turning to face the lord. Ron pulled the Orb from his cloak pocket, walked to the metal triangle, and placed it at the top. A shimmer appeared, and the forge gate opened.

Lord Hadal walked to Ron as he stood in front of the gate. "Beautiful, isn't it? With this, we can achieve anything. We could be unstoppable." He placed his hand on Ron's shoulder, but Ron quickly rejected it.

"No."

Lord Hadal saw the look in his eye and grabbed him by the back of his cloak, throwing him against the far wall away from the forge gate. "What do you know? You hold an ideal of what is considered right or wrong, and yet you fail to recognize that with this power, the kingdoms will finally be united under one banner for the good of the people!"

Nora and Grant helped Ron to his feet as they watched the forge gate glow. Before long, a leg started to come through. A person with dark gray rags draped over their body and covering their face walked through the gate, greeting Lord Hadal. Three more people dressed in the same attire soon joined them.

"Now a choice is before you, brother. I will give you one last chance before I begin my rule, not under the Alumma Biyar kingdoms but in the unity of all the lands. The realm of the Rassen Domani has been born. So choose wisely, brother, for each choice will bear a consequence that you will be held responsible for.

"First, you may join me and have any kingdom you want. The only caveat is that you submit your will and follow my rule with absolution. How does that sound? To live free with the ones you love, not having to worry about the conflicts of war, starvation, disease, or any of the concerns that plague these lands now? And this choice will not only affect you, but it will also allow

your friends, especially him over there, to check on the ones they care about."
Lord Hadal pointed to Grant. "I hear there has been some trouble in Malen,
something about all the people you rescued from Meno being taken prisoner
on account of someone being murdered. From what I understand, if they don't
find the killer, they will start executions."

Grant looked to Lord Hadal. "You don't know what you're talking about.
How would you know anything about the people of Meno?"

"I don't know, perhaps I have some of my loyal subjects embedded there,
sending messages detailing their situation, or maybe I had my own people go to
Malen, or maybe I'm lying. Regardless, if you all join me, you can go and see for
yourselves. I'm sure that woman and her child would be glad to see you again,"
Lord Hadal said.

Grant's voice wavered. "How do you . . ." The smile the lord gave Grant
conveyed the truth of his words.

"Second, I can kill you and all of your friends here and now, making you regret
your decision as I kill them first while you watch, only to slowly and painfully
torture you until you beg to join them in death. I will then resume my intentions
anyway.

"Third and lastly, you can go through the forge and attempt to save Nathill."
Lord Hadal grabbed Nathill and threw him into the orange glow of the gate.
Ron was in disbelief. Nothing was going according to plan; he could not speak as
anger and pain held him. "You might want to decide quickly. From what I hear,
the other end shifts every couple of minutes, opening up in different locations.
I mean, I don't know why you would save him anyway, with him being so close
to death, but the choice is yours. Now make it."

Ron stood silent, giving the impression he was fighting with the choices
before him. Lord Hadal became impatient and called the flame to his hands.
"What will it be? Answer me now, or I'll kill everyone and remove the choice
completely!"

"I'll go," Ron said. A genuine look of surprise crossed Lord Hadal's face. "I'll
go," he said again, turning to Nora and placing his forehead to hers. "Remember, when I say run, you take Grant and you run."

"I understand. Promise you will find a way to come back to me," she said through the tears.

"I will, I promise. I love you, Nora."

"I love you too."

Ron turned to Grant. "I need you to listen and follow Nora. Everything will be okay if you do."

Grant didn't understand. "Ron, no, you can't just leave. We need you here. You can't just leave us," he pleaded.

"There is no other way," Ron said. "Just listen to Nora."

"Ron, you can't do this. Please, don't go through with it."

Ron heard the anger and pain in his friend's voice, but still, after one last glance at Grant and Nora, he turned away.

He walked toward the forge gate, stopping a few feet before it. Closing his eyes, he listened to the song hum in his head, and in one violent burst of power, he shouted, "Run!" He drew more power at that moment than ever before, filling his hands with the weight of the flame, sending a ball of fire toward the wall behind Nora and Grant. It exploded outward.

With the other hand, Ron sent the flame toward Lord Hadal and the wielders from the forge. Hadal quickly brought up a flame shield, protecting himself and the others. Ron ran toward the forge gate, hoping beyond all hope that Nora and Grant would make it out.

Amid the chaos, rubble, and dust, the lord realized what Ron was doing, and dropped the shield just as Ron had hoped he would. As soon as the shield fell, Ron sent another ball of flame to the ceiling. It exploded, bringing down thousands of pounds of stone on top of Lord Hadal and the wielders. The lord was caught off guard and swiftly brought up another shield, but one wielder from the forge was crushed beneath the weight as the rest of the falling stone melted away.

Ron ran, pulling the power of the flame into his body, hoping he would be fast enough. Lord Hadal and the other wielders watched from behind the flame shield as he jumped through the forge gate. Before passing fully through, Ron grabbed the last Orb of Ember, taking it into the forge and sealing the gates forever.

End

About Author

Matt Trevizo, a captivating author and high-spirited active-duty firefighter for the United States Air Force, has led a life filled with adventure and inspiration. With numerous deployments under his belt, he has traversed the globe, exploring diverse countries and cultures, all the while nurturing an insatiable passion for writing and storytelling.

His journey as a writer began when a sudden spark of creativity ignited within him, and the vivid worlds, intriguing characters, and compelling themes inhabiting his imagination demanded to be brought to life. What began as a humble hobby to combat the clutches of boredom has now flourished into a dynamic career path with limitless potential.

When not crafting enthralling tales or fearlessly battling blazes, Matt indulges in an array of hobbies. He cherishes time spent with close friends and family, delves into thought-provoking books, immerses himself in narrative-rich video games, and stays fit through regular exercise. Currently, Matt calls the vibrant city of Las Vegas home, where he resides with his loving wife and two spirited sons.

Made in the USA
Columbia, SC
17 June 2024

36812260R00305